GENESIS

Book 1 of The Evolutioneers Series

Anna Alexander

AnnaAlexander.net
Newsletter
http://eepurl.com/Q0tsz

Genesis

People suck, at least according to reclusive inventor Max Madden—except for his friend and mentor, Anthony. But now Anthony is dead after uncovering evidence that an avaricious financier caused the current economic crisis and is out for world domination, a man Max knows has the money, resources, and charm to succeed—his own father. Now Max is out for vengeance and he doesn't need a distraction like Crystal Evans tagging along.

The provocative psychic may have soft lips, curves like a Ferrari, and a scent like vanilla sugar, but she also has a thirst for redemption that will never be quenched. Max can't help but admire her tenacity, and when she leads him to others who also have superhuman powers, he agrees to lead this team of crime-fighting supers if they all agree that he will be the one to take his father down.

But fate and circumstance has a way of bitch-slapping a man to awareness, and emotional hungers Max once detested have become what he now craves. When Crystal becomes the key to Madden Sr.'s downfall, Max must choose: Can he send the woman he's come to love on the mission, a mission during which she has seen her death in a vision, or have his revenge?

Dedication

Para mi familia. Siempre.

And to all of the girls who poured over their weekly comics, cried when Gwen died, sat by Diana's side in her invisible jet, and swooned over the love Remi had for Rogue.

This one is for you.

Find Anna Online

Website

annaalexander.net

Facebook

facebook.com/pages/Anna-Alexander/282170065189471

Twitter

twitter.com/AnnaWriter

Newsletter

http://eepurl.com/Q0tsz

CHAPTER ONE

"I REALLY NEED to see you, Max. Now."

The fear in Anthony's voice shot right into Max's ear and sent a shiver down his spine.

Max squinted at the speaker that Anthony's voice was coming through over the phone line. "What's going on?"

"I—I have to talk to you and I can't do it over the phone. Please."

Max held his breath, his brow furrowing while he considered Anthony's words. Urgency filled the pause and seemed to pulsate like an electric current against his cheek as he puzzled out why Anthony DeMateo, the most self-sufficient, even-keeled man Max had ever known, sounded as if the snap of a twig would send him into hysterics.

He rubbed his hand against his jean-clad thigh and eyed the security monitors that displayed the storm raging outside. There was little that would draw Max out of his mountain home even on a good day. Anthony was one of those exceptions.

A wave of guilt for not keeping in better contact with his mentor dried out his throat. Whenever Max was in need, Anthony had been there. Well, except for that one occasion. But even then he had stayed by his side until Max was ready to stand on his own. Besides, it wasn't as if making the effort for a friend would kill him.

"Yeah. Okay. I'm leaving now."

"Thanks, Max," Anthony replied with a palpable sigh of relief. "See you soon."

Max turned back to his virtual reality game and grinned when he saw the number of open dialogue boxes flashing on the jumbo LED television that served as his monitor.

"Yo man, where are you, M3?"

"Where are you?"

"We're waiting on you."

"Sorry, guys," Max said after he engaged his headset. "Reality is calling. Have fun storming the castle without me."

"Man, that's lame. We need you to get past those Arasai."

"You'll be fine. We'll do it again another day."

As he held his fingers over the keys to terminate the game, he paused, suddenly reluctant to disconnect from the one place he felt at home. On more than one occasion, Anthony had voiced his concern about Max's life of complete solitude, even though he was never entirely cut off from society. When he wasn't dealing with his software buyers, he was in contact with hundreds of people a day playing online video games.

Yeah, yeah. Max was not blind to the irony of his choice of escapism. And just as in real life, gamers sought out his avatar for his power and abilities. The only difference was in the gaming world they were upfront with what they wanted from him, instead of playing coy games of false flattery while they plotted how to exploit his intelligence.

What would the people in both of his worlds demand if they had any idea of what he was really capable of? A general distaste for the world at large warred with his amusement over that mental image. His blood, his life, his soul?

Didn't matter anyway. Never again would he allow another to take what was his. Never.

In the quiet of his home built deep in the side of a mountain, he closed his eyes and the silence began to weigh on him as if he were lying on an inflatable raft that kept expanding around him, bulging in giant bubbles until it hugged him in a suffocating grip. No one would even know Max Madden was no more as he withered away in his man-made cocoon.

He sucked in a sharp breath and tried to shake the oppressive loneliness from his mind. His life was shaped by *his* choices, the way *he* wanted, and it suited him just fine. These occasional…misgivings were probably signs of cabin fever. A change of scenery would take care of the cobwebs right quick. Yeah, all he needed was some fresh air.

He logged out of the game and raised both hands in the air. The familiar sizzling sensation gathered in his chest and radiated down his arms to his fingers. Waving his hands as if he were conducting an orchestra, he gestured at the keyboard and watched it levitate. As it traveled across the room and slid gently onto the shelf, the television turned off and the cabinet doors closed with a flick of his fingers.

With a small smile of satisfaction, he got to his feet and rubbed his hands together before searching for his coat and keys. It had taken him years of moving objects to and fro before the use of his telekinetic powers stopped leaving him fatigued and battered. Carving out his mountain home had almost killed him. But just like with any set of muscles, the more he used his powers, the stronger he became. If only he had more use for them than tidying up his place.

On his way out the door, he set the elaborate security

system that monitored his property. Although his lair had yet to be found, it wasn't for lack of people trying. When your net worth was in the billions of dollars, everyone wanted a piece of you.

Max slid behind the wheel of his black Ferrari 488 GTB—affectionately nicknamed the Beast—and squinted into the dark rainy night as the two-inch-thick galvanized garage door disappeared into the rock face.

The scents of exhaust and wet earth filled the tight, posh interior of his car as he pressed down on the accelerator. The thick tires caught on the cement with a squeal, leaving hot rubber on its surface before the car took off in a plume of smoke.

The Beast was a phantom in the night, hugging the slick curves of the mountain highway like spandex on a stripper. The growl of the monster V8 echoed in the downpour, clearing its way of both animal and machine. Vibrations shot through his body, making him giddy with the rush of handling such a powerful machine. It was almost as good as sex. Almost.

God, he loved this car.

In less time than was legally allowed, Max arrived at the gate surrounding five acres of forest and lawn that sat at the base of Cougar Mountain. Before he touched the button on the call box, the gate swung open, allowing him entrance. He pulled the Beast to a stop in the circular driveway, then cut the engine.

The rain continued to hammer down as if Mother Nature was seriously pissed off at the world and decided to engage in a cleanse. Max grimaced at the deluge. He'd be soaked in seconds in his leather coat. The duster wasn't practical for this type of weather, but it suited him.

Fortunately, it wasn't as if he needed to impress anyone with his appearance.

He stepped out of the car in quick movements to minimize the amount of water splashing into the Ferrari's black leather interior, then jogged up the front steps of the log cabin–style house. As with the gate, the door opened before he lifted his hand to knock.

Anthony stood at the door with a highball glass full of ice in his hand. Behind him, the house was dark. "Come in, come in." He gestured with his free hand and scanned the front yard with fear in his eyes before shutting the door behind them. "Thanks for coming, Max."

"How did you know I was at the gate?" Max asked, pushing the wet fall of his hair out of his eyes.

Anthony shot him an 'are you kidding' expression and gestured at the door. "The entire county can hear that monster of an engine. Were you followed?"

"No," Max drew out slowly. He blinked rapidly as his vision struggled to focus in the dark entryway. Unease coiled in his gut as he took a good look at his friend in what little light streamed in from the windows.

Even in his late forties, Anthony had retained that youthful, healthy appearance that came with being an avid outdoorsman. But tonight he looked exhausted. His blond hair stuck out as if he had been repeatedly running his hands through the strands. The top button of his shirt was open, his tie loose around his neck, the cotton rumpled. Anthony was always immaculately dressed, even if he were out on the soccer field or in the woods on a hike. Never anything less than tidy. Something was wrong.

"You got here fast. I thought you were home in that mysterious cave of yours." Anthony's dry chuckle cracked.

He led the way past the large, open living room and down the hall. "Can I get you a drink?"

"No, thanks." Max followed him into his study and frowned as he took in the odd setup in the office. A linen handkerchief covered the Tiffany lap on the desk, muting the light, and the blinds and curtains on the massive window were drawn shut, the sides held together with binder clips. "Anthony, what's up?"

Anthony swallowed hard and took a seat behind his desk. He traced a distracted line on the smooth mahogany surface with the tip of his well-manicured finger. "I don't know, Max. I don't know." He made another pass through his hair with his shaking hands. "Have you spoken to your father lately?"

Max stilled as he fought the surge of violence that roared through his blood at the mention of that rat bastard.

Matthew Maxwell Madden II. A man whose name was as big as his ego and ambition. Max's father and Anthony's boss.

Max preferred to forget that the man who had supplied DNA to him even existed, but Anthony always held out hope that they would reconcile. Family is forever and all that sentimental shit. Pigs would write code before that ever happened.

"You know we haven't," he replied in a low tone.

Anthony nodded, his eyes downcast. "I was hoping that one day you two would be able to put the past behind you. Maybe if…" He turned the open laptop on the desk around to face Max. "I guess it won't matter now anyway. I was hoping I was wrong, but I don't think so. You know how the economy is still tanking? Government bailouts aren't helping. Domestic markets are as unstable as ever. Hell, the world is on the brink of nuclear war." He shook his head. "Madden Financial stands to lose big."

Anthony sat on the board of Madden Financial, a conglomerate of financial institutions owned by Max's father. When it came to business, Anthony stood by Madden 100 percent. But the way Madden had treated Max and his mother, as though they were his personal property as opposed to human beings, had caused more than one heated argument between the two men.

It had been ten years since Max had broken ties with his father. If Anthony was worried enough to get him involved in Madden business, it had to be bad.

Frowning, Max crossed his arms. "How much damage are we talking?"

His mentor's Adam's apple bobbed twice. "A billion. Give or take a hundred grand."

"Ha-ha. Funny."

"Ha-ha. Not funny." Anthony's blue-eyed stare was as impenetrable as stone. "I'm serious, Max."

"Th-that's impossible," Max exclaimed as his knees buckled and he fell hard onto a chair. "A company isn't set to lose that much money without there being talk somewhere on the internet."

"That's just it. There hasn't been talk because we're doing better than we should be." He swallowed again. "Much, much better. Look at this." He clicked open several files on the desktop and arranged the spreadsheets side by side for comparison. "I've been monitoring the situation, and for some reason, money that Madden Financial should have lost isn't gone, so I dug deeper and found this. Something seemed off with these ten investors here." Anthony pointed to the middle spreadsheet.

"Off how?"

"On the surface there is no connection. This company makes handguns, this one here is a pharmaceutical company, and this one here develops automobile engines. They're not publicly traded, nor are they sole proprietorships. They are owned by conglomerations, yet I can't find a board member or contact information anywhere in our files or online. It's almost as if they're run by ghosts. I asked your father, but he said that he's working with the owners and their investors personally. Look, when hundreds of millions of dollars are on the line I need more than a 'Trust me,' so I—" He rubbed the back of his neck. "I broke into your father's office."

"How the hell did you manage that?"

Distaste tightened Anthony's lips. "I used that hidden entrance to his office from the hallway that leads into the parking garage. I waited until he was...occupied elsewhere in the building to go through his things. His computer was still logged on."

Max didn't need an explanation of what had kept Madden "occupied." Anthony's expression said it all. It was a well-known fact that the only thing Madden loved more than money was women. His political power and wealth made him the ultimate babe magnet. A pretty young thing in a tight skirt and a down-to-there sweater was like waving the green flag at Daytona. Madden made no excuses for the behavior he claimed was compelled by his colossal sex drive, and his exploits had become the stuff of legend in his social circle.

"Anyway," Anthony continued, well aware of the damage Madden's sex life had had on Max's mother. "It took me a few attempts, but I found emails, and those emails led to documents I found hidden in his office. Matthew is the sole owner of all these companies. Not Madden Financial, but Matthew personally."

"So you're saying that my father is using Madden Financial as his own personal piggy bank to develop other companies?"

"Not just that, he's using those companies to hedge his investments against each other. So when one defaults, the others collect on the original investment, plus the base points, all at the expense of the bank's shareholders. And there's more."

Max dropped his head in his hands and rubbed his eyes. Of course there was.

"Funds from these companies are being deposited into off-shore accounts tied directly to Matthew. I found statements that show there's more sitting in those accounts than what he's earning as the head of Madden Financial and these companies combined. Lots more."

"How much?"

Anthony swallowed again and looked away. "Billions."

Max couldn't have heard that correctly. "Billions? As in plural?"

"Almost one hundred billion total."

"That's impossible. Someone would have had to notice at some point. You can't have that much money changing hands without the FDIC, SEC, and IRS catching wind of it."

"I know. That's why he stole it."

"What?" His father was cold, calculating, and manipulative, but master bank thief? No way. "How?"

"Come on, Max." Anthony barked and jumped to his feet. "You know how. With computers. You broke into every US satellite system with nothing but a PC and dial-up when you were thirteen."

"Hey." Max held up his hand. "They asked me to check their firewall. It was perfectly legal."

Anthony grunted. "He's been doing this for years, and the other financial institutions have been covering it up. Did you honestly believe that many mortgage lenders and banks had practically every loan they issued default at the same time? If you were Fannie Mae or Merrill Lynch, what would you say? That you had thousands of homeowners default on their loans or you had *ninety billion* dollars stolen from you? It was all stolen, but they covered up. Think of the world-wide hysteria that would cause. There would be a run on every bank in the world."

"Why would Madden—hell, anyone—*need* that much money? You couldn't spend that in several lifetimes. And he sure as hell wouldn't leave it to me if he died."

Anthony didn't say anything, just slid several sheets of paper across the desk.

Max looked at a series of emails and charts, his light-ning-quick brain processing the words on the page as disbelief grew into a mushroom cloud of epic proportions.

Madden Sr. had gone on a purchasing spree of obscene amounts of weapons, chemicals, and large pieces of land in locations all over the world. Missives arranging those transactions were written in Russian, Spanish, Korean, and Arabic.

That rioting ball of what-the-fuck sparked again in Max's gut. "Are you telling me that my father is planning a terrorist attack?"

"No. Total world domination."

A full minute ticked by before Max let out a huge belly laugh and melted in his seat. Intense relief drained into his frantically beating heart, leaving him dizzy.

"Man, you really had me going." He slapped the papers across his thigh. "My father bilking people out of millions of dollars I totally believe, but 'total world domination'?" he repeated in a spooky the-end-is-near voice. "That's funny. I almost bought it. Almost." He sighed and wiped the tears from his eyes, getting to his feet. "Now, where's your Scotch?"

"Max." Anthony latched onto his wrist with a bruising grip. "I'm not joking. Exaggerating, maybe, but he's working on something huge, like military coup huge. Matthew is building an army. Look at what's happening in Portugal, in Greece. Brazil! Jesus, man, who backed 65 percent of the eleven billion dollars in loans they took out to fund the Olympics? And who's going to foreclose on them?"

"Madden," Max mumbled.

"Greece and Brazil were just the test runs. Look at how divided our country is now. The West Coast states are threatening to secede, for Christ's sake. When the United States collapses, there will be chaos and desperation the likes of which we have never seen. He is setting himself up in the ultimate position of power. I've seen him go off to closed-door meetings with leaders of third-world countries. He claims it's to negotiate the conditions to help them rebuild their economies, but I know that's a lie. He's providing them with money, weapons, and drugs in return for their loyalty. I wouldn't be surprised if he *is* dealing with terrorist organizations. Max, I—I don't know what—" he broke off and tugged at his hair again.

The reality of the situation sank into Max like a bad sunburn. His father, the man who for years tried to fleece every ounce of brain power Max produced, who used his wife's family connections in the government to further his own financial agenda, who walked upon the earth as if it were created just for his pleasure, was setting himself up to take over the world.

Max stood before Anthony, and for the first time lacked a smart comeback or ready answer. Staring at his friend, he now understood why the man looked as if he had stuck his finger in the light socket after a night of heavy drinking. Actually, that Scotch was sounding pretty good right then.

"What do you plan on doing?" Max asked, the softness of his voice at odds with the enormity of the situation. "Who else have you told this to?"

Anthony shook his head. "No one. I didn't want to risk endangering anyone else. And you're the only one I trust not to betray me."

"Have you contacted the authorities?"

"I can't. Do you think they can protect me from *that*?" Anthony looked at him, his eyes shiny with helplessness. "Max, I've been marked for death."

"What?"

"I think your father knows I've been collecting evidence. He's been shutting me out of discussions about the company all week. Today was the first day I spoke with him and he asked me about my plans for the weekend, about whether I would be home or not. He said it was in case I would be up for a round of golf." He tittered with borderline insanity. "Can you believe that? Golf? He has to be sending a hit out after me."

Max's heart sank. If he believed only a morsel of what Anthony was saying, then he knew that Madden would do whatever it took to stop the evidence against him from getting out.

Max leaned over, bracing his hot hands on the cold desk. "Then what the fuck are we doing here? You have money. Why are you not on the first flight out of here?"

"I needed to talk to you first."

"No, no. Skip town and then call me. That's what phones are for."

"I'm sorry." Anthony tossed his hands up in defense. "I didn't know what to do. I've never been marked for death before. I'm a little out of my element here." He removed the flash drive from his laptop and held it out. "Take this. If anything happens to me, you have to get the word out. You have to stop him. How many different governments and agencies have sent men after you to convince you to work for them? And you've outsmarted every one. If anyone can stop Madden, it's you."

Max placed the drive in his coat pocket. "Look, Anthony, I can protect—" The shrill ring of Anthony's cell phone cut him off.

Anthony stared at the display, his eyes widened in horror. "Oh God, already?"

"What is it?"

He held a finger up to his lips and whispered, "I set the security alarm so if anyone crossed the barriers around the property it would ring to my phone. Someone's approaching the house."

Max aimed his palm in the direction of the office door across the room. It shut with a bang, the lock clicking into place. The wet bar slid smoothly in front of the door as he waved his other hand in the direction of the lamp, turning it off and plunging them into darkness. "I'm not going to let you die."

Anthony stared at him in shock as the swirling glow of

the laptop's screen saver painted his face to look like a Salvador Dali painting. His mouth opened and shut twice before he wheezed, "How—"

The ping of breaking glass made them both drop to the ground as bullets shredded the windows and heavy curtains.

Max rolled across the floor. With his back flat to the wall, he inched up the plaster to peek through the tattered rain-soaked curtain and out the broken window. A shadow ghosted sideways across the lawn. He glanced at Anthony, who lay sprawled on the ground, his hands covering his head.

"Are you hit?" Max whispered.

Anthony cautiously lifted his head. "No. You?"

Max shook his head. "I saw one outside. Can your security system detect how many there might be?"

"No. You were still working on that program when you installed the system."

Max grunted and leaned against the wall. His brain fired, racing to form a plan. Plans were good, plans kept you alive.

He considered the layout of the house and where the Ferrari was parked near the garage. If they could get to the Beast, they could outrun anything. His breath let out in a low growl. Oh, if those assholes touched his car...

Max reached out and grabbed Anthony by the back of the collar and heaved. "Stay close to me."

They crawled along the floor to the door. When they got there, Max slid the wet bar over and strained to hear through to the other side. When nothing but silence met his ears, he eased the door open.

A barrage of bullets ricocheted above his head, showering him with bits of splintered wood.

"Holy shit," he exclaimed. White spots danced in his vision as a second spike in his adrenaline burst through his system.

Focus, focus. Pretend it's just a video game and get the fuck out of there.

He sucked in a breath, then another as the tingling began again in his hands. He peered through the slim opening. In the shadows, two figures dressed in black huddled near the front entrance. The smoking AK-47s in their hands glinted in what little light came in through the windows.

From his position, Max spotted the heavy, buttery leather couches in the living room. With a flick of his wrist, he sent the furniture soaring across the room toward the assailants. The crash of broken wood and smashed plaster drowned out their howls screams of surprise and pain.

"Now, now!" Max shouted, bursting out into the hallway with Anthony. Racing toward the kitchen, Max kept Anthony in front of him as he watched out for more gunmen who might have followed.

The kitchen had two escape routes: to the patio or to the garage. Without knowing how many others were out there, Max figured both could be covered. Which to choose? Enclosed space or out in the open?

The moment his feet hit the tile of the kitchen, the patio door in front of them shattered. He pushed Anthony to the floor behind the island then raised both hands. Using the deck chairs outside as missiles, he hurled the furniture toward the direction of the attack just as a grenade sailed through the doorway to land at his feet.

He shouted in surprise as his reflexes took over and he kicked the grenade back out the door as if he were lobbing the winning goal in the World Cup.

Seconds later the explosion rocked the log house as a choked yell ripped through the dark. The stench of burnt flesh confirmed that another gunman was taken care of.

More shouts, in Russian and Italian, came from the front of the house.

"Who the hell did they send after you?" he asked Anthony.

Anthony struggled to his feet, his eyes bulging. "What the fuck, Max? How are you doing that?"

"Not now."

On their left, the door to the garage flew open, followed by another volley of bullets. Anthony grunted and fell into Max. Blood seeped through his shirtsleeve.

"Anthony!" Max locked his knees to prevent them from collapsing.

Juggling Anthony's taller frame, he frantically looked around the kitchen for a weapon and spotted the knives sticking out of the wood block across the way. The moment the gunman cleared the door, Max launched every knife in the man's direction, embedding one deep into his torso. A giant butcher blade nearly decapitated him as it lodged into the wall.

God damn. Well… that was way nastier than it looked like in the movies.

Oh no.

Bile rose in his throat and his abdominal muscles clenched, threatening to unload the contents of his stomach as the stench of blood filled his nostrils.

It had been years since he had been witness to so much blood. Years since the acrid metallic scent had flooded his senses and robbed him of thought.

"Come on," he choked as he tamped down the nightmarish memories. Hefting Anthony under the arms, he dragged him to the garage.

Heavy footsteps pounded down the hall after them as Anthony's shoe caught on the top step, tumbling both of them down the short flight of stairs. Max landed flat on his back, his head smacking on the concrete. Stars flashed in his eyes, blinding him for a moment.

The patter of rain on asphalt drew his attention. The garage door was up, but the rain and blackness made visibility shit. In the dark, he could barely make out the sleek outline of his Ferrari near the bushes. He dug into his pocket for his keys and pushed the start button on the fob. The engine roared to life and ignited a spark of hope. The loud pounding of his heart drowned out the din of rain as he waited to see if the car had been rigged with explosives. When his baby remained in one piece, he whispered a prayer of thanks.

He reached out a hand and willed the car closer. Anthony was in no condition for a dash across the driveway.

"Come on, come on, come on," he grunted.

The three-and-a-half-ton machine barely moved an inch. Max slumped on the ground, exhausted, his lungs burning with exertion. Damn, that thing was heavy.

Anthony struggled to his knees with a groan, his back to the door of the house.

Goddammit, didn't the man have any instincts for self-preservation? Max hauled the bleeding man behind Anthony's shiny blue BMW as more shots were fired from the kitchen.

Max flung everything within range at the door with what was left of his powers: tools, shovels, bags of fertilizer.

"Come on, Anthony. We just need to make it to my car."

"Okay," he panted, wincing.

"Follow me. Shit," Max muttered as his knees started to buckle, but he forced the starch back in his legs. "On three. One, two, three."

They popped up and sprinted for the Ferrari in a macabre version of three-legged race, Max supporting Anthony around the waist.

Rain soaked Max's hair and his soggy bangs flopped into his eyes, further obscuring his vision. Next to him, Anthony yelped and went down, hitting the asphalt hard. Max turned to see a cable around Anthony's ankles stretch taut as he was pulled back into the inky black of the garage as the articulated door began to close. The metal came down between them as Max dove for Anthony's outstretched hands.

"No, no, no, no, no!" Cement scraped the skin off his knuckles as Max tried to jam his fingers under the door. Shit, it was locked. He scrambled back to use his powers to lift the steel. Metal grated on metal, screeching like a banshee.

Never had he been tasked to use his powers to such an extreme. With his energy depleted, his powers were shot. His head ached and his limbs felt as substantial as a deflated balloon, but he kept going. He had to keep going.

He was not going to lose another one. Not again. Never again.

Suddenly, it was as if all his senses fired at once as the rest of the world seemed to fall silent. A ringing filled in his ears while his vision sharpened, and it was though a million needles pricked his skin. A second later, the world tore asunder as an explosion rocked the earth.

Anthony's house rent in two, the mushroom cloud of debris and flames briefly turning night into day. The concussive wave sent Max flying through the air. Instinct kicked in, but the last of his powers barely cushioned his fall into the rose bushes near the driveway. The thorny limbs tangled in his clothes and hair as he struggled to stand.

His stomach twisted as he watched ash and rain fall from the sky. Orange and white flames consumed every piece of wood and fabric like a gluttonous monster.

Nothing but the sound of the rain and the crackle of the fire met his ears. No screams, no cries for help. No sound of life.

Anthony was dead. His friend gone.

With a bellow of rage, he flung his arms out wide. All around him the foliage flattened as if it were all smashed to the ground by an avalanche of boulders as his screams were swallowed by the roar of the fire.

The light of the yellow and orange flames danced across the slick leather of his coat as if they were celebrating the creation of a new breed of devil. A demon forged with a hunger for revenge only one man could satisfy.

The sins of the father demanded restitution. And the son would see it done. No cost was too great. No sacrifice too big. The death of his friend would not go unavenged.

CHAPTER TWO

"HERE YOU GO, Max." Noel Dietrich, lawyer extraordinaire of the rich and powerful, pushed a thick accordion file across the tabletop. "Everything that belonged to Anthony is now yours."

"Great," Max replied in a whisper. He rested his hand on the dark red file. The crimson color was fitting, since the contents held the life's blood of Anthony DeMateo.

Was this really happening? Was he actually sitting in the middle of your average, run-of-the-mill coffee house, holding all that remained of the man who had given him his first video game? Who had sent him care packages when he started college at the tender age of twelve, and stood by his side as they lowered his mother's casket into the ground? Three inches of paper and a couple of metal brads. That was all that was left.

Around them the murmurs of conversation and the roar of an espresso machine faded as the realization that he was truly alone in the world seeped into his bones. The horrors of the week before ran on a constant loop, robbing him of sleep and leaving him numb. Carnage. There had been so much carnage, the memory alone forced forcing him to take a deep breath to still the rioting that had yet to subside in his gut.

Did he regret the actions he took in the effort to save his and Anthony's hides? No. He just wished he could have been more effective. One, in saving's Anthony's life, and two, being able to find at least one of the assailants to interrogate. On both counts he failed.

With the house engulfed in flames, it had been impossible to search for any survivors. And even Max knew that to wait around for the fire department would only place him in trouble. The fact that the fire was only a ten-second blip on the evening news and a three-paragraph story buried on the third page of the newspaper hinted that there wasn't going to be a deeper investigation beyond the theory that it had been a gas leak that had caused the explosion. And now that almost a week had gone by without any further development, Max was certain of it.

It didn't take much of a stretch for Max to reason why there was so little being reported on the grisly death of one of Madden Financial's executives. From what Max had read in Anthony's notes, Madden had his fingers in so many pots, it was a wonder how he managed his busy scandal sheet–fodder social life.

God, what a mess.

And now he was not only responsible for stopping his father, he was also in charge of Anthony's estate. At least the decision Max had made about how he was going to manage that task had been an easy one to make, and fitting for the man he had loved as a father.

He slid the file back toward Dietrich as his eyes stung with tears. "Give it away," he said, his voice catching.

Dietrich paused, a cup of espresso hovering at his lips. "Excuse me?"

Max pulled a sheaf of papers from his inside jacket pocket and laid it on the table between them. The leather of his coat bore the battle scars from that hellish night but gave him fortitude of what had to be done. "Sell it all and divide the proceeds between these charities."

The older man let loose with raucous laughter that turned into a hearty chuckle before dying a slow death as Max continued to stare at him with unwavering determination. "Are you shitting me?" the man shouted.

"Excuse me?" gasped one of the mothers at a nearby table, one of whom covered her toddler's ears with her hands. "Watch your language."

"Shut it, lady," Dietrich snapped with a raised hand. "This is important. Give it away?" he repeated, but in a lower voice. "Are you serious? Do you have any idea how much money we're talking about?"

"I have enough money."

"There is no such thing as enough money." Dietrich drew a deep breath and smoothed a hand down his tie. He shot a scowl at the mothers who continued to watch them with disapproving frowns. "I know you're joking. You and Anthony were tight. I know you want something of his to remember him by."

Max raised an unamused brow. Oh, Anthony had left him plenty to be remembered by.

"Jesus, you're serious, aren't you?" Dietrich shook his head. "It's hard to believe you're Matthew Madden's kid."

"I'll take that as a compliment."

"Look, Max, I know that Anthony's death is a shock and you're grieving, but I can't help but feel some...moral obligation to beseech you to think about what you're asking me to do."

Think? *Think?* As if his brain had been able to shut down for one millisecond since he had watched his best friend go up in a fireball.

Over the years Max had dreamt of various ways to end his father's life. One of his favorite fantasies involved shoving hundred-dollar bills down the bastard's throat until his eyes bulged and he lost control of his bowels. But never once had he thought about going through with it.

Until now.

Now the urge to kill made his fingers twitch and his muscles tense to track down his father. Max liked to think that he was a badass and would be able to kill without remorse, but did he have it in him to be a cold-blooded murderer? It was one thing to kill in self-defense and another to hunt a man down and stare him right in the eyes as the life drained from their body.

Max stifled a shudder as he recalled the screams of the men he killed with his powers. He could have sworn he still carried the stench of gunpowder and blood in his nose. It was an odor he thought he would never have to relive again, and it brought back horrors he spent years trying to run away from.

And if he did find the fortitude to kill his father, then what? Say he was able to plot the perfect murder and get away scot-free, what happened next?

No wonder Anthony felt Max was the only one to stop Madden's plan. The intel on the flash drive Anthony had given him suggested that Madden's reach ran far and deep with law enforcement, politicians, and military personnel all on his payroll. As it was, the general populace already treated Madden as its financial savior, despite his rather salacious social life.

However, one did not accumulate that much power without help. His father had to have a committee or some kind of executive team helping him. And if Max did find the guts to kill his father, it stood to reason that there was another who was able to take over Madden's cause. A person didn't invest the amount of years it must have taken to amass that much firepower to have the movement die with its leader.

So while Max's personal vendetta might be satisfied, his father's work would continue. Perhaps making him a martyr for the cause. Sons of bitches. And Anthony would have died for nothing.

No. No matter how much Max wanted to charge into his father's office and smash and destroy, for once he needed to be more like Madden Sr. Patient, methodical. Especially since Max hadn't voluntarily spoken to the man since the death of his mother ten long years prior. If he suddenly turned up and started asking questions, Madden would know something was up. Besides, who knew how many of Anthony's attackers had survived the explosion and reported Max's involvement? So far, he hadn't seen any suspicious activity on his property or evidence of anyone trying to break through his firewall, but circumstances could change in a nanosecond.

Patient and methodical. Play Madden like a game of Jenga and topple the entire infrastructure with the removal of one vital piece at the right time without any detection. That was the plan.

The sheer size of the impending mission engulfed Max in a powerful grip that tightened around his chest. Not even the soothing ambiance of the coffee shop's cream-colored walls and the aroma of warm cinnamon rolls could temper the edge of nervous energy that made his skin itch.

His gaze drifted to the women in the corner enjoying their lattes while their toddlers drank from sippy cups full of chocolate milk.

One of the mothers reached out to idly sift her fingers through her daughter's curls while she continued her conversation. The little girl sighed and leaned against her mother's side, both blissfully secure in the knowledge that all was right in their world.

Drink it up, kiddies, he thought with grim realization. *I'm the only thing standing between you and a totalitarian existence.*

He turned away as his throat grew tight and achy. Even with the decision made to go after his father, emotions he had buried under thick layers of fuck-all bubbled through the cracks of his control. He reached up and grabbed a fistful of his hair, desperate to ease the pressure off his brain. Protecting innocents, like these children, was Anthony's last wish. It didn't matter how Max felt about the world and his place in it. Anthony died because he dared to care. Max could do no less than to honor the only request his friend had ever asked of him.

The sound of husky female laughter went right to his ears and skittered down his spine like a low-level electrocution.

For the first time in a week he felt something…pleasant. Almost familiar. For so long he had felt nothing but pain and anger. The unexpected balmy heat of awareness seemed to thaw the layer of ice that encased his battered heart. The sensual notes formed a tether around his head and dragged his gaze to the woman who had paused in the doorway between the kitchen and the customers.

Long hair snaked down her back in waves of red and brown. The tie of the apron around her waist rested above the full flare of her backside, enticingly encased in denim.

His attention fully captured, he waited with bated breath for her to turn around, hoping that her front looked as good as her behind.

When she finally turned his way, his breath sucked in with a hiss as every muscle in his body grew tight. Even in his depressed state, he couldn't help to notice her beauty.

Beautiful, hell. Mouthwatering, that's what she was.

Holy shit. What am I doing?

He wrenched his attention away from the magnetic valley of her cleavage and their gazes met, his world shifting on its axis.

Her eye color changed from green to brown as they widened in surprise and she stumbled. After another halting step, she straightened and a bland smile settled on her features.

That brief flare of recognition triggered his internal alarm system. His vision sharpened as the hairs on his arms stood on end like receptors reading the air.

"Ah," Dietrich drawled out with a knowing chuckle. "Now you see why I hold most of my meetings here instead of my office across the street."

Max turned back to Dietrich in time to see him smooth the thinning hair off his forehead. "Who is she?"

"The vision I jack off to in the shower. Crystal, honey," he called out and held up his cup. "Can you get me another Americano? Hot and strong, just like I like it."

Her eye color flashed back to green, and she eyed Max with a long considering gaze before nodding. "Certainly, Mr. Dietrich."

Max turned away from the delightful way her back arched as she reached for a bag of beans from the shelf above her head. He pulled on his bangs again and took a deep breath. He was overstressed. That's what it was. Eyes do not change color, not like that.

Wait. What the fuck had he been thinking about?

Avenge his friend, save the world. Right. Important stuff.

"Here you go. One Americano." Crystal placed a ceramic cup and saucer in front of Dietrich.

"Thank you, sweetie." He ran his fingertip down her bare arm. The sight of the man's yellowish nail on her perfect skin had Max biting back a growl of warning. "When are you going to leave this no-end job and come work for me? I can offer you a better position that's more suited to your talents."

She pursed her lips and blew a short, high-pitched whistle that brought Dietrich's gaze from her breasts to her face. "As I keep telling you, I'm happy here."

"I don't believe you."

"It's not my job to convince you." She set a chocolate chip muffin on a plate before Max. "For you, sir."

Max blinked in bewilderment at the pastry. "I didn't order this."

A secret smile curled the corner of her lip. "I saw the way you looked at my muffins and thought you might like a taste."

Dietrich choked on his coffee as a series of inarticulate sounds stuttered from Max's lips. "I-I didn't—"

"When you first came in." She gestured at the display case. "I have never seen a man look at a chocolate chip muffin the way you did. Nor have I seen one look so sad when the last one was bought before you had your chance to try it. This one's fresh from the oven."

Flames of heat raced across his cheeks and singed the

tips of his ears. "Oh, well. Thank you."

She smiled a little lopsided smile that brought out the dimple in one cheek and moved on to wait on another customer.

He stared at the muffin and waited for the hidden agenda to burst out of the golden-brown top with both barrels blazing. In his lifetime, people didn't do nice things for him out of the goodness of their heart. A muffin was never just a muffin. Angles, slants, and schemes always accompanied the tiniest of gestures, and the sweeter the act, the greater amount of flesh the bearer demanded of him.

"Max, let me float an idea past you."

Case in point.

"I can understand if you don't want to deal with the responsibilities that come with maintaining property. Let me sell the assets, but instead of donating the proceeds to charity—" here Dietrich barely kept the sneer out of his voice—"why don't you let me make a few well-chosen investments for you. I know of a startup tech firm that is ready to revolutionize the satellite industry, beyond what you've already been able to accomplish, of course, but with your name and money attached, they can literally launch into another orbit."

Max pointed to the papers before them. "Sell everything and donate the money to those charities."

"What are you trying to prove, Max? Besides Gates and Carnegie, you are from one of the most philanthropic families in the world. Leave the do-gooding to your grandmother, and let's make some serious money."

"Give. The money. Away," Max snarled. "Or I find another attorney to make it happen. How much are you charging an hour again?"

"Okay, okay." Dietrich held up his hands. "How about this. We donate *some* of the money, if that's what you really want, and we invest the rest. Anthony would want you to."

Max tuned out the litany of excuses Dietrich launched into why a faceless corporation was more deserving than a women's shelter and narrowed his gaze onto the cup in Dietrich's hand. The dark liquid began to bubble and hiss with each passing second, until the ceramic cracked, bursting into tiny shards. Dietrich jumped with a shout as hot coffee splashed into his lap.

"Ooo, Noel, what a shame." Max handed over a wad of paper napkins. "I hope that doesn't stain."

Dietrich dabbed at the wet dark blue silk. White flecks of paper lint added a snowflake pattern to the mess. "Damnedest thing. I better get back to the office and clean up before my next appointment."

"Yes, you better." Max held up the folder and list. "I want a progress report on the sale and on the distribution of funds once a week until everything is gone."

"Max—"

"Follow my wishes to the letter, Noel." His voice dropped an octave. His low, badass voice used when he wanted to impose his will was the only thing that he was grateful to have in common with his father. "I may not be a money-hungry asshole like my father, but I'm still a Madden, and I get what I want. If I don't hear from you in one week, I will find out what you've been doing. In every facet of your life."

Dietrich paled with the implied threat, for he was well aware of Max's ability to retrieve any piece of information, no matter how deeply buried. He reached for the file. "Sure. Once a week."

Max tightened his grip, drilling Dietrich with his icy gaze before letting go of the folder. With a lingering glance over his shoulder, Dietrich beat a quick path out of the café.

Crystal appeared with a rag in hand and began to wipe down the table and chair. "That was a very impressive display."

"Sorry about the mess."

"Noel Dietrich is a lecherous ass and had it coming. But if I had your powers, I would have levitated the fork and stabbed his puffy hands a few times."

"Powers?" Her laughing eyes came into sharp focus as the rest of the room blurred and the blood rushed in his ears. "Nah, it was just a freak accident."

She rested her hand on her hip. "Right. You don't have to hide with me, Max. I know all about your special abilities."

He felt sweat gather over his lip as he muttered, "I have no idea what you're talking about."

"Sure you do." She lifted her hand and waved her fingers across the air as if they were floating.

What. The. Fuck?

The chimes on the door jingled as a man entered the shop. He wore a rumpled gray suit with the knot of his tie pulled down a few inches. When his gaze landed on Crystal, he paused and settled his hands on his hips. The movement pulled back the bottom of his jacket, revealing the police badge attached to his belt.

"Detective Sanchez," Crystal greeted the newcomer before Max had the chance to grow nervous about the arrival of a police officer on the premises. "I wasn't expecting you until later this afternoon."

For some reason the officer didn't care for her pleasant

welcome, because his brows lowered and his nostrils flared. He pointed his finger at her then at the beaded curtain hanging in the doorway at the back of the shop.

"It's time for a chat, Evans," he said in a gruff voice. "Now."

Crystal's sunny smile faltered and her lashes fluttered. "Sure. Uh, if you need anything, Max, just call for another server and they'll help you out."

Max stared after her as she went through the bead-curtained doorway. His heart beat so fast he could feel the pressure in his ears.

Okay. He was officially intrigued. Getting a visit by the police *and* hinting that she knew about his powers?

There was no way she could know. The only other person who knew anything about his telekinetic ability was Anthony, and he learned about them just before he died.

Who the hell was this woman?

CHAPTER THREE

HE WAS HERE.

And by "he" Crystal didn't mean Detective Sanchez.

For the last month, images of a man with wavy black hair and eyes so blue they glowed with an inner fire that could light the darkest night had played in her mind and tormented her with smoldering heat, anticipation, and no clue whatsoever as to why he was haunting her dreams.

In her visions he stood tall and proud, with an oh-so-sexy black leather duster swirling around his legs as objects danced in the air to the movements of his broad out-stretched hands. When she'd awakened, she was left with a residual arousal and an excitement that convinced her he was going to change her world.

No matter how hard she tried, she could never get over the glitch in her power to learn more about what part he played in her future. Yes, she saw glimpses, but only the next step. The vision played again and again until it came true or the outcome was diverted and the vision changed.

Knowing this mysterious man was going to come into her life didn't do her any good unless she knew the why. Based on her visions, she hoped Max's arrival was the catalyst she needed to grow her powers. Of course, it could also mean that a cute guy who could move objects with his mind was going to come, order coffee, and leave. Sometimes it was a toss-up as to which she wanted it to be.

Now he was here and she was about to find out.

She tempered her smile as she remembered the expression when she called him by name. Was it that big of a surprise that she knew who he was? His father was the head of a ginormous bank, a local celebrity who was frequently in the news for one reason or another. On occasion the estranged son would be mentioned, at times accompanied by a photo of the man himself. It hadn't taken much online digging to discover the identity of her dream man.

"I'm not here for a reading, Miss Evans," Detective Sanchez interrupted her musings as she escorted him to the room where she read tarot cards for paying customers.

Oooo. Now it was "Miss Evans," was it? Apparently, the detective was determined to keep his tough-cop persona. Too bad she didn't have a vision about this visit to prepare her for what he was about to say.

The nook she used to read tarot cards was tiny, but large enough for the table, two chairs and the small chest of drawers that held her supplies. Three wall sconces shaped like medieval torches hung on the wall, shedding an intimate light that was excellent for creating atmosphere. The space was warm and cozy and allowed her clients to relax.

But Detective Sanchez wasn't relaxed. Annoyed was more like it. His lips were pinched so tightly together, they disappeared into his face, and when he sighed, he shifted his weight as if he were a parent about to lay down the law to a child.

"I know you're not here for a reading, Detective. Remember? I know lots of things," she said with a knowing giggle. Yes. Best to keep him guessing as to what exactly she did know. "You're here to tell me I was right, wasn't I? About the postman. I was right. Again."

He sighed and rubbed the back of his neck. "I am here to officially tell you to stop interfering in police business."

Uh-huh. So he said. "I was right."

"Yes," he bit out. "You were right. But you still have to stop."

"Why? I told you that mailman was selling heroin along his route. I gave you information about which houses were his clients. You just confirmed I was right. You're welcome."

"That's not the point."

"Putting bad guys away is not the point? That's your job."

"Exactly," he said. "That's *my* job. Your job is to serve coffee."

"Ouch." She drew back and placed her hand on her chest. "That's low, Detective."

"It's the truth. Look, Crystal, you can't keep sticking your nose where it doesn't belong. Two nights ago my captain recognized you at the scene of that shooting on Dearborn. What were you doing there?"

"Not killing people."

He raised a dark brow. Clearly, he wasn't amused.

"I had a vision, obviously. Like the other times. I saw the shooting before it happened." Her throat closed with frustration at being helpless to stop the tragedy. "I saw the shooter walk down the street and stop in front of that crowd gathered outside the bar and start shooting. He was angry. He wanted revenge. The woman he shot was a former girlfriend, right? The crowd was dressed in blue and green, so I knew it was a game night. I went to the bar to try to stop him, warn her. But I didn't know what time he would be there. By the time I arrived..."

Chaos had erupted. Shots had been fired. People were screaming and running away from the scene. Police sirens wailed as patrol cars flew past her as she ran down the street toward the madness. A barricade was erected as she got closer, and past the officers she saw the bodies on the ground. More people she failed to save because her powers were too weak.

"If I'd just been a few minutes earlier—"

"Crystal. Stop." For the first time the cop expression left Detective Sanchez's face and the same compassion he had shown her the first time they met years before softened his features. "If you only knew how many times I've said those exact words myself. Look, honey, I know losing your family was hard on you. But you running into dangerous situations because you claim to have a vision is not going to bring them back. And if you're not careful, you may end up beside them."

Ha. Like that would ever happen. She had been nineteen when her parents had died, and she hadn't the money for a proper burial. She had barely been able to scrape together what she could for cremation and scattered her mother's ashes on the wind over the falls. Her father's she told the crematorium to do with what they wished. However, she figured he wasn't speaking literally.

"I'm not claiming anything. Everything I've ever told you has come true. You just need to follow the leads I've given you."

"That's just it, Crystal. There is a little thing called probable cause. I can't launch an investigation based on your hunches. The only reason I was able to look into the postal worker was because one of the homes along the route that you indicated housed a pedophile who was violating their parole by living too close to a school."

"And what about that Amber Alert a few months ago? I told you where to find the car."

"Lucky guess. Crystal, people are innocent until proven guilty."

But in her visions, they were always guilty. Once, just once, she would have liked to stop the crime before it was committed. Or have the vision change because something or someone made a positive impact on the person and the crime was averted.

That someone could be her, if she was just given the proper chance.

"I can't ignore the visions," she said as tears burned her eyes. "If I can save one person, it will all be worth it."

"If you don't stop, then you'll have to face the consequences." He held his hands palms out. "I've said my piece. I can't protect you anymore, Crystal. If I hear about you being involved in a crime scene again, I'll arrest you personally." The corners of his mouth turned down and sadness filled his dark eyes. "Don't make me arrest you. I like you, kid. And you won't do well in jail. You're too sweet."

"You have made your opinion known, Detective. I thank you for the warning." She held out her hand. "Can we at least part as friends?"

"I figured you'd say something to that affect," he grumbled but took her offered hand.

At the first touch, Crystal activated her second power. Not only was she able to see glimpses of the future, but direct contact with another person allowed her to scan the memories of their past.

With stops and starts of blurred imagery, she watched

the past events of Detective Sanchez play out. He lived a life of monotonous routine with brief bouts of intrigue. He enjoyed his work, treated his coworkers as family, and loved nothing more than catching the bad guy.

But he was lonely. Through his eyes, Crystal saw the toll his job had taken on his marriage. Witnessed his wife demanding more of his time and the disappointment in his son's eyes when he failed to follow through on another promise. Since his divorce and his ex-wife's remarriage, he had thrown himself into his work, seeking solace in the very thing that led to his marriage's downfall all while wearing a smile and cracking a joke when at times he felt like doing anything but.

A sad, solitary existence indeed. However, she saw one bright spot, if the detective was brave enough to go for it.

"Who is the blonde woman?" she asked, tightening her hold on his hand when he tried to pull away.

"What?" he asked.

"The blonde woman. I see her standing with your son and another boy. And soccer balls."

Sanchez gasped and pulled away. This time, she released his hand.

"You *do* know of whom I'm talking about," Crystal exclaimed with a delighted clap of her hands. She closed her eyes to focus on the image. "Why do you never talk to her? Whenever I see her, she smiles and tosses her hair. She even asked you where you stop for coffee. Dude, she's interested. And you'd have had a lot better evening last Friday going on a date than you did reheating Thai food and bingeing episodes of *The Walking Dead*."

"Tiffany?" He rubbed his palm against his chest as if he had heartburn. "She, uh… What does she have to do with anything?"

"You like her. And she gives me a good vibe. The next time she smiles at you, ask her out. It'll do you some good."

"I-I couldn't. She's my son's friend's mom. I just... It could be..."

"The start of something spectacular."

"Spectacular disaster, you mean." He shook his head and grimaced before turning and heading for the door. Under his breath she heard him mumble, "The world keeps getting weirder and weirder."

True. So true. She smoothed her palms down her hair as she blew out a breath, but the butterflies in her stomach would not stop fluttering.

The world was getting weirder. And if her hunch was correct, tall, dark, and brooding waiting for her out in the hallway was going to bring about an apocalyptic event not just in her life, but the entire world as they knew it.

CHAPTER FOUR

I T DIDN'T TAKE a psychic to know Max would be waiting for her outside of her little office.

Sure enough, there he was, leaning against the wall alongside the door with his arms folded and a scowl pinching his features.

Detective Sanchez and Max exchanged curious glances as the policeman passed on his way out of the cafe. Then Max turned that brilliant blue gaze on her and her heart slammed to a stop.

Max in the flesh was way more potent than he was in her dreams. He was a beautiful man, much too pretty than any man had a right to be, but the square cut of his jaw kept him from appearing too feminine.

She laughed to herself. There was no way anyone would mistake him for a woman, not with those large shoulders that stretched the leather coat at the seams. Although he was tall and lean, his strength was palpable, and she knew from her visions that he welded it with power and authority. Energy surrounded him like electricity. It was a warm hum that buzzed and sent goose bumps racing across her skin. The sensation was entirely too pleasant, encouraging her to brush up against him and feel it seep into her bones.

Between the fringe of his long black bangs, his piercing eyes were filled with silent questions. The blue matched the radiant glow that surrounded him like an aura and made his skin appear ethereal.

That effervescent light, more than his sudden appearance, was what shocked Crystal more than anything. Max literally glowed as if he were plugged into a light socket. The only other person she saw with a glow like that was herself when she looked in a mirror. They had to be connected. But how?

"You're a clairvoyant? A real one," Max added, getting right to the point.

She replied with a sharp nod.

"Is that how you know about…me?"

Crystal nodded again and swept a glance around the coffee shop. In the middle of the cozy Victorian décor, Max, in his black leather, looked like an S&M fantasy run amok. Whatever they were to discuss needed to remain private.

"Hey, Hailey." Crystal waved to the other waitress on duty. "I have a last-minute appointment. I'll be awhile yet."

"Okay," Hailey replied as if she hadn't a care, then behind Max's back waved her hand like a fan while mouthing, "Oh my God. You go, girl."

Crystal rolled her eyes. "Come with me," she told Max before walking back through the beaded curtain. When she turned again, she collided with his chest and jumped startled. "Whoa."

Usually her cozy reading room was a place of peace and comfort, but with Max and his dominating aura overwhelming the tiny space, she was reminded of the power he wielded.

Golden light bathed his skin in and effervescent glow that did nothing to soften his stern appearance as he looked around, taking note of every nook and cranny. So attuned was she to him that she swore she could sense him rating the level of danger she presented, almost as if it tickled her bare arms like the bristles on a wire brush.

"I guess we should start with a proper introduction." She held out her hand, hoping her palm wasn't sweaty. "I'm Crystal Evans."

"Max Madden. But you knew that," he replied in a voice that was smooth and fiery, like her favorite whiskey.

His palm was hot against hers, hard and strong. It was a capable hand that held many talents.

A perverse part of her brain wondered just what magical abilities of the sexy kind he might possess. She wasn't blind, the man was hot. And there was that vibration still ringing inside her, buzzing along her blood stream from her fingers to her nipples and everywhere in between. Since it was still undetermined if this man was friend or foe, she'd do best to keep her wits about her.

"Are you all right?" she could hear him ask through the sexual haze clouding her mind.

"Yeah," she breathed out in as firm a voice as she could manage before diving into his memories.

Holy crap. The power of his mind astounded her. There was so much activity, so much knowledge, she couldn't process the images fast enough. Flying objects, computers, large buildings and classrooms, always changing. A woman, dark like him, beautiful and haunted. Alive one minute, dead the next by her own hand. A man, someone close, shot in the back. A ball of flame lit up a rainy night sky.

Crystal broke the link and drew a shaky breath. So much sadness, so much isolation in his life. Was this why they were destined to meet? Was she supposed to help him somehow?

She choked back a snort of disbelief. Right. As if he was

going to allow her to grill him about the images she saw. And it wouldn't do her any good to make him think she was a stalker. At least not yet. Depending on the next few minutes, it might be in her best interest to have him believe she was batshit crazy, but for now she needed him to be willing to talk.

"What exactly do you know about me and how?" he asked.

"Well..." She considered just how much she should reveal. "Besides the obvious information that's on the internet, I know you're telekinetic. A real telekinetic. You see, for the last month, I've been having dreams about you. Saw you manipulate your environment at will. I also knew our paths would cross. I just don't know why." Yet.

"Why not?" He frowned and crossed his arms.

"My power is limited. I can only see the next step. It isn't until the vision comes to fruition, or something happens to change it, that I see the outcome." She gestured to the stack of cards on the table. "That's where the tarot cards come in. I use them to get a direction on what I'm seeing."

The furrows between his brows deepened. "That man earlier—I heard you. You knew details about his past. Not his future. How did you do that?"

Crystal sucked in a breath. Well. He was an observant one, wasn't he? With excellent hearing, too.

"I...had a vision he was coming and read the cards this morning for more information about his visit," she lied, not ready to spill all her secrets.

Tha-thunk, tha-thunk, tha-thunk. The longer he stared her down, the harder her heart pounded. Her eyeballs grew dry and itchy as she held his gaze. Unable to hold completely still, she swallowed against the tightness in her throat.

His sharp gaze caught the fluttering movement. He shook his head as his eyes narrowed. "No. You knew specifics about his day. Things that happened in the *past*. Psychics foretell the future. How did you know?"

She concentrated on keeping her breathing even and hoped the sweat she felt on her forehead didn't show. "What makes you an expert on psychics? I'm the first one you've ever met."

"A-ha," he barked and pointed his finger at her nose. "That's something specific about *my past*. What are you hiding?" He took a step closer, then another, backing her up until her butt hit the tiny table behind her, rocking it on its legs.

"Hey!" She shoved against his chest. "Stop crowding me."

The scent of leather and the outdoors filled her head and muddled her thinking. She didn't believe he would physically harm her, but he definitely wouldn't be happy if he found out she knew the darkest moments in his life.

"Stop lying to me," he demanded. "How did you know?"

"Back off." She punctuated the command by shoving again against the solid wall of his chest. The fact that her efforts to move him were completely ineffectual was more annoying than frightening.

"The truth, Crystal," he said with a hard glint in his eyes. The firm set of his jaw told her that he wasn't going to budge.

She glared at him, realizing that this was a no-win situation. "Step back three paces or I'm not saying another word."

He squinted at her and his nostrils flared in annoyance.

His lashes were so thick they looked like coal as they shaded the blazing blue of his irises. He issued a silent sigh before he took one step backward.

She pointed at him. "Keep going."

His nostrils flared again, but he stepped back until he was across the room. He was still too close for comfort, but the tiny space only allowed for so much maneuverability.

She licked her lips. "With skin to skin contact, I can see a person's past."

Those long lashes batted once, then twice. "You can see someone's past?"

She nodded.

"So when you shook my hand…" he trailed off. His breathing quickened. "What did you see?" When she didn't answer immediately, he got right back in her face. His lips pulled over his teeth as he snarled, "What did you see?"

She lifted her chin. "Enough."

"How much?" he growled.

"All of it."

"All of it?" He began to sway. "No. That's impossible."

"Says the man who can move objects with his mind," she reminded him. "And I'm sorry for your loss."

"No. No." He shook his head, but when she held his gaze, he snarled and turned away.

As he tried to back and forth in the alcove, his lips rolled and pinched as if he wanted to say a thousand things but he didn't know where to start. His hands alternated between tightening into fists and repeatedly brushing his hair out of his eyes.

"How dare you!" he grunted. "Do you understand any- thing of what you claim to know? About what I've been through? How dare you read my mind?"

"I didn't read your mind. Like, I don't know what you were thinking as events happened, and if I touched you now, I still won't know what you're thinking at the time. I only see what happens like it was a movie."

"That's semantics. You still had no right."

"I understand why you would feel that way," she said. "It might seem intrusive."

His eyes bulged. "Are you kidding me?"

"Can you look at it from my perspective, please? I've been having visions of encountering a man with unheard-of telekinetic powers that would turn my world upside down. You cannot stand there and tell me that you wouldn't use every ability you have to keep the advantage for your own safety."

He grunted and backed away as his lips drew into a thin line. Ha. She was right and he knew it.

"Look, Max," she began and held her hand out in a silent plea for trust. "I believe there is a reason we met. Maybe we were drawn together because we both have powers. Maybe there are others like us."

"Others?" He stared at her in genuine surprise.

"Yes, others." The corner of her lip ticked up. "What, are you such a special snowflake that you thought you were the only one?"

"Well…yeah." He shrugged.

"Why would you think that?"

"It wasn't like I heard of anyone else with powers. I thought… I mean…"

For some reason the defensiveness in his tone and the uncertainty on his face amused her. From what she had seen, Max had never been wrong, and the chance to open his mind to different possibilities gave her the courage to press her case. If she was ever going to get out of this nowhere existence and make a difference in the world, she had to make him listen.

"Think about it. Once upon a time people used to be covered with hair and they were four feet tall. It's evolution. The world is becoming increasingly unstable, and nature will do all she can to adapt to the environment. Maybe that's where we come in."

The leather of his coat creaked as he crossed his arms. "So humans evolve and gain powers. For what purpose?"

Like he had to ask. "To save the world."

He snorted. "That's very Pollyanna of you."

"What else do you think our powers are good for, working in sideshows? I have been given my power for a purpose. You have been given your power for a purpose. I knew we would meet, and now you're here. Why? Of all people to be granted such a gift, why you? It was destined. Just as you came to this specific shop. Destiny. You are here because—I think I'm supposed to help you."

A cool mask settled on his sharp features. "With what?"

"To stop your father."

"Nope," he barked like a shot from a gun. "No, no, hell no. You will not get involved with Madden. This is my fight. My mission. No one else's." He slashed his hand definitively in the air.

Argh. Now she was the one ready to pull her hair out. "I get it. You're a big bad alpha male. You are also making it personal. D'oh—" She pinched the bridge of her nose.

Stay calm. Don't argue. Keep it logical. Max is a logic kind of guy.

"Max, what you're facing is way too big of a task for any one man to take on alone, even with your powers. I can help you."

This was her moment. She felt it in her bones. This was her chance to use her powers for more than reading tarot cards for the lovelorn. When her mother was murdered, Crystal promised she would do whatever she could to prevent others from facing the same fate. If the police wouldn't allow her to help, perhaps assisting Max on his quest was what she was meant to do with her gifts.

"No," he said as if that was the final word and she would bow to his wishes.

For a smart man, he had a lot to learn.

She started to argue further then sucked in a breath as a vision hit her hard enough to buckle her knees.

Damn it. This one was big.

If she focused as the sensation began, she could slip into a vision as if she were sliding into a warm pool of water, but usually they hit her so hard her conventional sight and hearing were overwhelmed, leaving her vulnerable to anyone and anything.

Never had so much information been thrown at her at once. And never had any part of it not make lick of sense. What in the hell did cotton candy, penguins, and a Ferrari have in common?

While her mind raced to process the images, Max calling her name was a faint refrain in the background. Slowly, she became aware of a reassuring pressure on her back and a touch at her elbow that was keeping her from collapsing to the floor.

"Crystal? Crystal. What's wrong?"

"Who do you know in Portland?" she asked when she regained feeling in her lips.

"What? No one I can think of." He backed away when

she finally straightened, worry still etched on his brow. "What did you see?"

"I saw us in Portland. We're driving down the freeway in your car. Nice wheels, by the way," she added with a shaky grin. "But we are together and we're at the— Portland."

Yeah. There was no way she was going to tell him exactly where she saw them ending up. He'd laugh in her face and disappear without another word.

"That doesn't make any sense." He fixed a wary gaze on her and she could see the wheels in his head turn as he sorted through every possibility to find a connection. "I don't remember a source or contact of my father's in Oregon. Of course, that doesn't mean there couldn't be one. Did I miss something?" he muttered, more to himself than at her.

"See, you do need me," she said.

He snorted again. "*If* I believe you. Maybe I'll check out this lead in Portland, but you are not getting involved." He turned his back to her, and the tails of his duster slapped her in the legs with a whoosh.

She around him and blocked him before he got to the doorway. "I am going with you. There is a reason I have this power, and if I'm stuck with it, then I want to do something useful. And besides…" She placed her hands on her hips and stood as tall as her five foot nothing height allowed. "You know you need me."

"Do I?" he asked as his eyes flashed in amusement.

"I'm the real deal, and you're curious about what's in Portland. You won't be able to stop thinking about what it is. Every time you hit a dead end, you'll wonder if I had the key all along. You have to take me. I'm the only one who knows what we're looking for."

"Why don't you tell me what you saw, and I'll decide if it's worth my time."

"I'm with you the entire time. I saw that."

"Tell me," he repeated, his teeth clenched.

She flashed him her sweetest smile and batted her lashes. She so had him right where she wanted.

His lips pressed together in an expression of aggravation she was rapidly becoming used to, and for some perverse reason delighted in causing.

However, her time to gloat was cut short when he held up his hand. Before she knew it, she was lifted into the air and pressed against the wall. Invisible bonds held her immobile as she struggled against—nothing.

Max stepped closer until his chest brushed her breasts and his cool blue gaze met hers. He did that twitchy-lip thing again as if he were trying to start a sentence but was too frustrated to formulate a response. Every second that passed, his frustration reverberated through her as if it were a piece of thick metal struck with a mallet.

Okay. Perhaps she wasn't entirely safe in his presence. On the other hand, this testosterone-laden display was right dead sexy. Seriously, Max was an incredibly compelling man. The places where their bodies touched tingled with awareness, and everywhere else was jealous of the contact.

Good thing she was trapped against the wall. If she had the ability to move, she'd probably do something stupid like wrap her legs around him and gyrate as if she were a stripper trying to make rent.

She concentrated on calming her inner hussy and kept her gaze locked with his. He was behaving like an animal, and it was important to establish her refusal to kowtow. Not now, not ever.

He leaned back ever so slightly with a small sigh.

Yes! He blinked first.

His voice was deliciously husky as he rasped, "What do you know about taking down bad guys?"

"I'm not completely helpless. I've learned how to fight and how to use a gun."

He didn't look convinced. "These are not common hoodlums I'm after. These men are clever, conniving, and ruthless. You may end up staring death in the face. Can you handle that?"

"Been there. Done that."

He froze, waiting for her to deliver the punchline. Unfortunately, there wasn't one.

Max let out a sigh, but didn't back away. "You have tonight to tie up all of your loose ends. I don't know how long this will take." Somehow, he managed to lean in closer until they were nose to nose. She fought the urge to roll her eyes in pleasure at the press of his body. "I cannot be responsible for your safety. You come with me, I will expect you to keep yourself alive. You got that?"

She couldn't hold back the brief grin his warning provoked. "I'm not afraid."

His answering smile was tinged with darkness and 100 percent pure male ego. "When going up against my father, sweetheart, you should be."

CHAPTER FIVE

"ARE ALL OF the loose ends cleaned up?" Matthew Madden asked as he eyed his second in command and settled deeper into his soft red leather office chair.

Through the open window, the breeze rustled the leaves of the trees and a fountain gurgled merrily in the courtyard of his palatial estate. It was a gorgeous summer day in the Pacific Northwest, made especially brilliant with talk of death on the agenda.

His second in command laid a thin file on the desk. "Anthony DeMateo is no more."

Madden opened the folder and a smile stretched wide across his lips as he sifted through the photos. Such mayhem. Such destruction. All evidence blown sky-high in a spectacular display.

"Torching the house and making it look like a gas leak, well done. Your idea?"

The Second froze for a moment, his eyes widened as if the question had caught him by surprise. The hardwood chair squeaked as he shifted in his seat.

"Yes, sir," he replied slowly, so slowly that Madden wondered if the mission did not go as smoothly as it appeared.

"And the witnesses?" He pulled a solid gold lighter from his inside jacket pocket and lit the corner of the folder. The burning evidence was placed in the wastebasket beside the desk to smolder in silence.

"All those involved have been permanently dispatched."

"Good." Madden sighed and let the warmth of satisfaction seep into his bones. "Good. That was an excellent idea, having our allies use their best men, then taking them out and blaming DeMateo for their deaths. Weaken them from the inside. Brilliant."

"Thank you." He nodded, his pale blue eyes glittering under the praise.

"Any word on my son?" Contempt and yearning colored his tone.

His son Max had always had a fondness for DeMateo. The news of Anthony's death should drive him to make a rare public appearance. The two had been close, so close that Madden had often wondered what DeMateo's true motives were toward the boy. Anthony had never married, though he never lacked for female companionship.

Bile rose in Madden's throat at the idea that there might have been a sexual relationship between his colleague and his son. Perhaps DeMateo's demise was a necessity for more reasons than he had originally planned.

Still, Max would take this news hard, but life was full of unfortunate circumstances and sacrifices.

"Max was listed as the executor of the will. Our men spotted him with the lawyer this morning," The Second informed him. "Apparently, Max didn't want any part of the estate and instructed Dietrich to give it all away."

"You're joking."

The Second shook his head.

"Jesus Christ." Madden steepled his long fingers together and placed them under his nose. Where the hell had he gone wrong with his son?

"Will there be anything else?"

"No." Madden gestured to the door with an elegant, manicured hand. "Take a few days off. Lie low in case any of our friends start asking questions about their men. I'll send for you when I need you."

The Second stood and fastened the middle button on his suit jacket before bowing in respect. His footsteps clicked across the cold marble floor as he exited through the doorway hidden by a tall redwood bookcase.

Madden waited until the room fell completely silent before reaching under the desk and running his fingers through the tresses of the maid kneeling between his spread legs. She flashed her eyes up at him adoringly and smiled around his thick cock as she slurped him between her pouty lips.

He took off the noise-canceling headphones she wore and placed them on his desk. "You are very good at that, my dear. You almost had me coming in front of my man."

She preened under his attention and sucked harder.

He grabbed a fistful of her bleached blonde hair and pulled her up as he got to his feet. Turning her around, he pushed her over his desk, hiking her tight black skirt up to her hips. The sight of her thong dissecting the plump cheeks of her ass made his dick twitch.

With one hand, he sheathed his cock in latex while he kicked her feet farther apart. One stroke sent him in deep.

The scent of sex filled his nostrils as he closed his eyes to savor the tight clasp for a brief moment before shuttling back and forth in her heat.

Power and sex. His two favorite things, and in his office he was blanketed in his own nirvana. Drugs and alcohol left you weak and not of your own mind. Sex was the one thing he could manipulate at his will. He controlled his body's response. He determined his partner's pleasure. He was the master of carnal hungers, and in that he ruled.

The nameless maid cried out and writhed under him, distracting him from his thoughts. He slapped a hand over her mouth to stifle the noise and drove his hips harder.

For a moment he allowed himself to imagine that he was with another. A woman with dark eyes and hair as black as night, with a body so delectable that men ached to possess her.

Daria had been one of the most beautiful creatures ever created, yet inside she had been as cold and dry and unsatisfying as a martini made with cheap vodka. Physical contact was something she had been taught to endure, not revel in. In fact, he had been shocked he managed to knock her up at all, for they had had sex so infrequently.

His late wife had never understood his drive, his ambition to dominate in everything he set his mind to. Intelligence was not an attribute she possessed and she had had no compulsion to take an interest in anything he did, not that he asked that of her. However, some recognition of the accomplishments he had achieved would have been appreciated.

Now Max, on the other hand, was all he could have wanted in a son, save for the unwavering drive to walk his own course in life.

Together—ah, together they would have made an unbeatable team. His plan to rule the free world would have been completed by now, but the boy possessed a weakness of doing what he viewed was right. He used that magnificent mind to hide on his mountain. Shielding others from the destruction his ideas and theories could manifest.

If Madden had his son's intelligence...

His balls tightened with a surge of adrenaline at the mere idea of having all that knowledge.

Yet he wasn't without his own merits. He stood poised on the brink of success. Capitol Hill was eating out of his hand, desperate for him to pull them out of the quicksand he'd covertly led them into. Military leaders around the globe were waiting for his command to pledge allegiance to him. It was the perfect game of chess, and checkmate was in his sights.

The world would be his.

The promise of ultimate supremacy burst through every vein and exploded out the end of his cock. He clenched his teeth to hold back his moan as he jetted inside the woman.

As his heartbeat returned to normal, he reached down and squeezed his sac, ensuring that he was fully drained. He had a busy day planned and it wouldn't do to get distracted by a hard-on.

He plucked a white cotton handkerchief from the side drawer of his desk and used it to remove the condom before placing it in the trash to join its brothers. He allowed a small sigh to escape his lips before walking to the full bathroom that was attached to his office.

"Mr. Madden?"

With his hand on the gold doorknob, he turned back toward the slut on his desk. "Your services are no longer required. You may go."

"But don't I get to come?" she whined.

His gaze traveled over her, slow as a glacier and just as icy. He passed over her swollen lips, down to the heaving breasts spilling out of the stretchy top, then on to the black silk triangle covering her well-used pussy.

"Leave. Now."

He turned on his heel and shut the door behind him with a loud click.

CHAPTER SIX

MAX SNUCK A glance at his passenger and wondered when he'd lost control of the situation.

Who was he kidding? He knew the catalyst of his demise was the moment he first saw Crystal and the blood rushed from his big head to his little one. Even dressed in a simple hoodie with jeans, she was as stunning as any of the beautiful models his father used to bring home.

Crystal was a manipulative, fearless, pain in the ass who refused to be swayed. For some reason, instead of being annoyed, she impressed the hell out of him. Not even his psychotic, badass voice that he used to intimidate his online gaming foes seemed to cause so much as a twitch of unease in her. She demanded to be heard and didn't let up until she got her way. If she wasn't careful, sooner or later her attitude was going to land her in deep shit with no way out.

Well, if she insisted on tagging along, her safety was in her own hands. He wasn't her keeper and he had a death to avenge. He'd take whatever information she discovered. But if she fell behind, she'd stay behind.

"So," she said with a sigh. "Are we going to leave, or are you just going to stare at the dash all day? You do have a lot of dials and switches there, so I understand if you can't figure out how to make it start."

He leveled his most ferocious glare at her, to which she responded with a grin that brought out the dimple in her cheek.

He snapped his teeth together and did his damnedest to ignore the alluring swirl of cinnamon heat that coiled in his belly. So that was how this was going to play out between them. He was either going to end up throttling her or seducing her.

Good times ahead.

The engine caught with a growl with a flick of his finger. The vibration shimmied along the metal frame and acted like a defibrillator that jolted his soul, reminding him that he was alive and kicking. He toggled a paddle on the steering column and let the engine rev under his foot.

Crystal watched him with an expectant glow on her cheeks. The light in her topaz-colored eyes danced as she experienced the build-up of energy with him.

It wasn't lost on either of them that at any second he was going to let his foot off the pedal. In the span of a heartbeat they were going to begin a journey that could change their lives forever. Tighter and tighter, the tension grew like a band across their chests just waiting to snap.

Vroom. Vroom, vrooooom.

The brakes released. Tires squealed as the Beast rocketed down the road, throwing them back in their seats with the g-force.

Crystal tossed her head back and laughed. The melodic notes skipped down his neck to tickle his spine as her fingers tightened on the arm rests with a white-knuckled grip.

Max's lips twitched at the pure joy in her laughter. Hey, a man did love to show off his car.

Sure. He was still pissed she knew all about his past. Those were his own personal demons, and if he wanted to share them with anyone, that was his prerogative.

On the other hand, the fact that she knew so much about him was kind of liberating. He didn't have to hide who or what he was. He wouldn't have to play nicey-nice and apologize for his behavior, because she already knew the kind of man she was traveling with. If she willingly put herself in his company, then she best be prepared to handle what he dished out. And oh, he could dish out the cold shoulder with the best of them. If only…

If only she weren't so damn appealing.

Sleep the night before had been nonexistent as he recalled the softness of her curves when he had had her pressed against the wall. His expensive mattress was just too firm and far too empty in comparison. And those lips of hers. He bet she tasted as sweet as the cinnamon rolls she served in her shop. Yeah, sweet and sinful.

In the darkness of his room, he imagined Crystal sliding her kiss-swollen lips over his heated skin. The mental pictures had driven him to the point where he had to take himself in hand to release the pent-up desire she invoked. To see her again with a lust-addled mind would have been begging for trouble. Not only would they have never left the parking garage, he'd probably have ended up in handcuffs facing assault charges.

No, he liked to think he was more in control of his urges than some sex-crazed beast, but facing her with a clear head better suited his needs, which meant allowing his fantasies to take flight during the night and coming so hard the walls of his mountain home shook.

Unfortunately, that plan backfired. While his desires had been temporarily sated, he was left feeling empty and starving for the real thing.

He didn't like that feeling. Wanting. Wanting led to needing, and needing led to being used.

When he was a child that lesson had been drilled into his psyche as he busted his ass trying to please others, desperate and hungry to live up to the Madden name. A near-impossible task, truth be told. As he grew older, the need for acceptance had turned into *Fuck off, who needs you anyway*. And when his telekinetic powers came in—screw it, it was time to shut out the world for good. He was a loner, always had been, always would be. It was who he was, and how he functioned best.

Crystal wasn't like the other women Max had known who could be swayed with a charming smile or an expensive bit of something shiny. She was charmingly tenacious when she wanted her way, and that made her dangerous to his resolve.

This little road trip was going to remain strictly business, even if he had to strap his erection down with duct tape. They were going to find out what was in Portland, then he'd drop little Miss Hot Lips off at the airport to make her own way back to her cushy life of snickerdoodles and frothy milk. That's all this would be. Business.

"I see you have a healthy respect for the speed limit." She nodded at the speedometer that hovered at ninety miles per hour while they blazed down the freeway.

"If a car or a cop gets in my way, I move them."

"Move them?"

He let the wicked curl of his smile answer for him.

"Handy little talent there." She laughed again and relaxed in her seat.

Now that she was effectively trapped in the car, the time had come for some answers. "Tell me about your powers.

Did you always have them?"

Her instant silence he expected, but he was not going to let her off easy. He'd pull over and wait her out if she refused to talk. She owed him some information in return for digging into his past.

Several long minutes passed before she took a deep breath. "When I was a kid, I was very intuitive. Like, this horrible sense of dread would come over me and I would just know in my gut when something was wrong. Or I'd know what the weather was going to be like, better than the guys on TV, and dress accordingly, or I'd know which route had the better traffic. I just *knew* things. But I didn't need to be psychic to know when my dad would drink. It was all of the time, which led to him being unemployed a lot, and he would take out his anger on my mom."

She picked at her fingernails as she spoke, her body hunched over as if to protect herself from reliving the past.

"After high school, I went to the University of Washington on scholarship. One day, in the middle of class, this feeling of anxiety came over me that was so terrible, I ran out of class and raced home. My dad was beating my mom. She had finally decided to leave him and he didn't take too kindly to the news.

"I had barely made it through the front door when I saw him break her neck. Killed her. As her body fell to the ground, I felt it. A surge. It was like a million fireballs racing up my body, from my stomach to my brain. It hurt so bad that I thought I had been burned. I was dizzy and he just stood there and he kept yelling at me, blaming me for killing her. You see, I was the one who had convinced her to leave, and he kept screaming that he would make me pay for that."

She took another deep breath.

"That was when I had my first real vision. I saw him beating my sister Tina, who was twelve at the time, and strangling her in front of me as my punishment. It was so vivid, so clear. I lived it, even though it hadn't happened yet." She paused for another breath and licked her lips. "Then he rushed at me for real. I grabbed a knife from the butcher block on the counter. He ran right into it. Nailed him right in his sternum." Her hand floated up to rub the center of her chest in an absentminded gesture.

"Then I had another vision where I was stabbing him over and over. Blood flying everywhere. I wanted so badly to do it. Let out the nineteen years of hell he put my family through." She chuckled with derision and shook her head. "I was so close to losing it, I had actually ripped the blade out of his chest and laughed when he screamed. I had the knife in my hand, ready to plunge it back in, when something inside of me woke up. And I realized that to take such pleasure in his death would make me just as bad as him. So I put the knife down and the vision changed, and I saw myself and Tina at a women's shelter. By then all of the screaming had drawn the attention of the neighbors and someone called the police."

"What happened to him?" Max asked. Anger on her behalf roughened his voice.

"He died," she replied, killing the plans he was already formulating for revenge if the asshole had managed to survive. "Charges weren't brought against me. Self-defense and all that. But." Her breath hitched. "I lost my sister. Once we made it to the shelter, she was taken and put into a foster home. Child services thought it best for her not to have any contact with me while the investigation was going on. By the time I was cleared, she had disappeared into the system."

"They wouldn't tell you anything? Just separated you like that?" He snapped his fingers.

"Yep. Just like that."

"And you haven't seen or heard from her since?"

"Nope. I had no idea what city they might have taken her to. I searched school websites for years like some sort of stalker, hoping to see a picture of a team or activity that she might have been a part of. I was never able to find her." Her smile trembled at the corners as she turned toward him. "We're not so different, huh?"

Max tightened his grip on the steering wheel and said nothing. He knew what she was getting at.

Mile after mile passed as memories of the night his mother died whirled in his mind. It was as if the scenery they flew by were blurred images of his past and not the endless chain of small towns along I-5.

He was old enough now to realize his mother had suffered from a depression she hid with gin and painkillers. The perfect image had come with a price. And when it came to ambition, the politician's daughter was so far out of her wealthy and charismatic husband's league there hadn't been a way in hell she could've kept up with his demands.

To the outside world Daria Cassini Madden hadn't a care beyond fashion or status, but Max knew different. Behind the brittleness of her smiles and the trembling of her alcohol-medicated body he saw her longing to be considered as more than a pretty face with excellent connections, no matter how blasé she had acted toward his father. She never gained the knowledge or gathered the courage to break out of the mold she had been born into. So she had drifted on a platinum cloud of privilege and ignorance with only a few glimmers of sunshine and affection she reserved for her only child on the rare occasion she was sober.

When the elder Madden had stopped hiding his affairs and had begun to bring his mistresses home, the carefully constructed shell around Daria finally crumbled.

Ten minutes. Ten minutes was all the time an eighteen-year-old Max had needed to gather the last of his remaining things from his parents' home and move away for good from their constant arguing and his father's continued insistence that Max work for him. As long as he was under his parents' roof, the chance to have a life considered anything close to normal was as much of a pipedream as the US no longer being dependent on foreign oil.

What if he had gotten there sooner? What if he hadn't made such a production out of moving out? Honestly, he didn't think either of his parents had noticed his absence. And even now he doubted if they ever had.

It was either fate or misfortune that had the entire Madden family under the same roof at the same time that fateful night. As he had approached the second-floor landing, he had heard the sounds echoing down the marble hallway. A man grunting in a steady rhythm. The sporadic slap of leather followed by a woman's passionate screams.

Max knew the woman was not his mother. It had been months since his parents had stopped sleeping in the same room and his mother moved to a suite closest to the stairs. Her bedroom door had been wide open. Every light in the room blazed brightly, leaving her in a spotlight, center stage.

She sat at her dressing table, or rather her body was resting on the ornately cushioned stool. Her dark hair fell in disarray around her shoulders and her skin had been scrubbed free from all makeup. Without the heavy contouring, the blank expression on her face made the hopelessness of her appearance even more frightening. The mask of Daria Madden was no more, destroyed, leaving a hollow shell. The haughty, pretentious, magnificent woman he had known but still loved was no more.

By the time Max realized what was happening, it was too late. She had lifted the gun that had been resting in her lap out of his sight, and pointed it at her temple, pulling the trigger in less than a heartbeat.

As the sound of the gunfire echoed, electricity traveled along his spine and out the tips of his fingers in a powerful current. As he ran to her, he flung out his hands, suspending her limp form in the air until he got close enough to wrap his arms around her. Blood soaked through his clothes as he rocked her back and forth, all the while screaming to the heavens.

Why had she given up? Why hadn't he been enough to live for? The injustice of it all, the waste that she had allowed her life to become, had churned in his gut like acid, burning his insides until it boiled over with a scream of rage.

A shockwave had rippled out from him, shattering every window in the house. Mirrors exploded, the walls buckled as the floor undulated like the surf in a storm.

His powers were born.

Max swallowed hard as he blinked the road before him into focus.

Crystal had seen all of that in his memories. Seen his mother take her own life.

Just how did her powers work? Had she watched the atrocity as if it were a movie, or had she witnessed the horror through his eyes? Could she feel what he felt? Could she breathe under the crushing weight of utter helplessness that he was too late? That he was lacking?

Maybe she didn't have to. He flicked a glance in her direction as he remembered that she too saw her mother die.

She was right. They had more in common than he thought.

"Does your sister have any powers?" he asked, bringing the subject back to her and away, far far away from him and his past.

"No. At least that I know of. When I try to read her future, or see where she might be, all I see is her becoming a teacher." A grin stole across her lips. "For her sake I hope she doesn't develop any. Especially the power to see the future."

"Why not? Seeing the future must be pretty sweet."

"You would think so," she drawled in a way that suggested it was anything but. "Free will is a fickle bitch."

"How so?"

"Do you think the butterfly effect only affects those who can time travel? And don't give me that look," she admonished when he snorted. "Time travel isn't that far-fetched, considering what we can do. But the theory holds as true for the future as it does with the past. One change. One tiny, little, insignificant change in any person's life can alter a vision. Then there are the times when you work your ass off to influence a different course and the result is the same. Or what if you do find a way to alter the future and something worse happens as a result? Say you see your child is playing soccer, and they're injured during a game and become paralyzed. So to stop that, you take them out of soccer and enroll them in guitar lessons. Then one day they're walking to their lesson and are hit by a car and killed. What if, what if, *what if*?" She threw her hands up then sighed, leaning her head back. "It's the what-ifs that will keep you up at night. Trust me. It's a whole lot easier to go through life without knowing what's going to happen next."

"I guess so," he murmured, even though he wouldn't mind having a little foresight himself. Then again, he hadn't walked in her shoes.

They fell into a companionable silence for the rest of the journey and made excellent time as the Beast ate up the pavement like a strip of asphalt taffy. Crystal was an excellent passenger. She kept their pit stops short and asked before touching the dials on the car, as if he'd let her. When he refused to change the channel to the Broadway satellite radio station, her pout was kinda cute, not that he noticed.

They rolled into Portland just before noon, and the thrum of anticipation heightened all his senses. The sun seemed to burn brighter, turning the leaves neon green against the dark gray skyscrapers. The taste of expectation coated his tongue as smooth and sweet as chocolate. In the closed confines of the Ferrari, Crystal's cinnamon scent heated his blood, threatening his concentration. One more reason why he had to dump her luscious ass the moment he had the chance.

"Where to?" he asked.

"Take that exit," she directed. "Then the one after that. Turn here and park over there."

Max pulled into a slot and turned off the car. The sudden quiet was deafening after the growl of the engine during the long trip. As his hearing returned to normal, he looked around, not understanding why exactly they were at that specific location.

Before them passed a small version of a 1950s silver passenger train. The riders in the open compartments smiled happily as they trundled by. Once the train passed, he saw through the chain link fence and trees to the other side and spotted…was that a giraffe?

"Is this a joke?" He frowned.

"We're here," she sang.

"Crystal, this is the zoo."

"I know. Wow, you are as smart as they say."

That dimpled smile of hers was really starting to piss him off.

CHAPTER SEVEN

"WHAT THE HELL are we doing at the zoo, Crystal?" Max asked her through gritted teeth.

"In my vision I saw the two of us inside the Portland Zoo," she answered and quickly opened the passenger door, not needing her psychic powers to know Max was likely to blow a gasket.

What she didn't anticipate was him waving his hand and nearly decapitating her as the door slammed shut and locked, trapping her into place.

"Hey, stop that."

His nostrils flared. "Is this some sick joke? Why would an investigation on my father, the banker, lead us to a zoo?"

"I don't know. That's why we needed to follow the lead to find out."

"Why didn't you tell me?"

Seriously? She snorted and rolled her eyes. "Because I'm not stupid. One, you wouldn't have believed me. And two, you wouldn't have wanted to go."

His nostrils flared again, and a muscle in his jaw ticked in tandem as he sucked in a breath in that way she was beginning to learn meant he was five seconds away from throwing a temper tantrum. "Do you think this is a game? Madden is attempting to take over the fucking world, and you drag me to a zoo?" he shouted with such force that she actually felt her hair blow back.

Well, he could piss and moan all he wanted, but she believed in what she saw. The vision hadn't changed, which meant that one way or another, Max was going with her.

She lifted her chin with what she hoped looked like supreme confidence. "I saw what I saw."

"What do we find here?"

I don't know, she almost admitted with frustration both at Max and at her limited ability. "We just need to go inside."

And pray to God that another vision came to her fast.

She flashed a confident grin. "Look, no one is twisting your arm to go inside. You are more than welcome to wait in the car. I'll go in and look around, and catch up with you later to tell you what I find. Now, come on." She jiggled the door handle. "Let me out of the car, Cole," she said in her best Nicole Kidman impersonation.

The dance of his nostrils continued. Inhale, two three four, exhale, two three four.

Hmm, apparently he was not a *Days of Thunder* fan.

Just when she thought the blood vessel in his forehead was about to burst, the locks clicked open with a firecracker pop.

She stepped out into the sunshine and shut the door behind her before he could change his mind. When she turned around, he was right there, blocking her path. Impatience tightened his sharp features and seemed to add inches to his already formidable height.

He walked her back until the hot metal of the car's exterior burned through the clothes on her back just as hotly as his hard body warmed her front. She tried to hold her breath, but the tantalizing scent of man and his leather coat filled her nose.

That damn vibration was there too, electrifying her nerve endings and enticing her to press closer and crawl up his body like a lumberjack topping a tree, begging him to consume her. Her eyes threatened to cross as she imagined the pleasure. An extremely unhelpful reaction at that particular moment.

It helped that he was still pissed at her, reminding her why she had to ignore these inappropriate urges. From his memories she had learned that Max was used to people exploiting him, used to being cast aside when not needed. He didn't do emotional. He didn't play well with others. It was him versus the world and she believed he truly preferred it that way. Which was exactly why she needed to keep their potential working relationship in perspective.

It would be way too tempting to fall into the promise of those lips. Convince herself that she could be the one to "save" him, and forget why he was the man he was. Forget that as soon as she outlived her usefulness, he would most likely get back in his sexy Ferrari and disappear down the highway, leaving nothing but tire smoke and heartache in his wake.

She had to remain focused on the mission, even if it killed her.

"You have one hour, sweetheart," he bit out and leaned closer, forcing her to tilt her chin higher to retain eye contact. "After that, if you don't find what we're looking for, I will leave your ass behind. If you see something, *anything*, to do with my father, you tell me immediately and follow my lead. I do all of the talking. You understand?"

"Got it." *You arrogant, mouthwatering, son of a bitch.* "Now get out of my face," she snarled back in an act of self-preservation and pushed against his chest. It was either that or close that scant inch between them and kiss him.

Too late, she realized as a self-satisfied smirk curled his lips, she flinched first.

He pressed closer until neither light nor air separated them from breast to groin. "What? Am I invading your personal space? Getting a little too close for comfort?"

His hot breath caressed her cheeks and she locked her knees to keep from melting at his feet like some damn virgin getting felt up by her first crush.

"Is this too intimate for you?" he asked with a wicked gleam in his blue-blue eyes. "You know, we've already been intimate once, when you read my mind."

"I did not read your mind," she muttered without moving her lips.

He shrugged. "You still pried. I think you owe me. One intimacy for another."

"Don't even think—"

Oh, but he did.

His lips closed on hers, not hard and dominant like she expected, but gentle, coaxing, and oh so seductive. If he had groped and fallen on her like a slobbering pervert, her response would have been a swift and immediate knee to his groin. But this gentle conquering was an assault on her senses that made her gasp in surprise.

He pressed his advantage, his tongue stealing inside her mouth to taste and tangle with hers. Chocolate and coffee. Her weakness. And Max was on the verge of becoming another on the list. Strong hands gripped her hips. His long fingers dug into her flanks as he pressed even closer. Lord have mercy. She whimpered and sank into his hold as sweat broke out on her forehead.

His touch was electric. It short-circuited every rational

thought, fried all the arguments she made, all of the reasons why she should keep as emotionally distant from this man as possible, and blasted them to smithereens.

"Hey! There are children present," an indignant mother shouted at them as she passed with her two toddlers in tow.

Max lifted his head with a swift intake of breath. For several long seconds they stared into each other's eyes. The black of his pupils expanded and shrank as he panted. Thank goodness she wasn't the only one affected by that kiss.

The tip of his tongue swiped his bottom lip before his mouth twitched in a surprised grin. "You taste like snickerdoodles."

Crystal blinked as if she were waking up from a deep sleep. With horror she realized her leg was hitched over his hip and she was shamelessly grinding against the weighty bulge in his jeans.

She straightened to her full height, which still brought her only as high as his shoulders, and quickly ducked under his arm. The deep breath she took did little to clear her head, but she would not let him know just how out of control he made her.

"Well." She pulled the sides of her hoodie together. A trickle of sweat oozed along her hairline, but there was no way she was removing any layers of armor to cool off. "Now that we've gotten that out of the way, do you think we can get back to business?"

She didn't wait for him to answer before spinning on the heel of her boot and heading for the main entrance. All the while she prayed her knees wouldn't buckle and pitch her face first onto the concrete.

It was a hard battle to keep her posture relaxed and easy.

She knew Max's brain moved at the speed of light. If she touched her tingling lips like she wanted, or clenched her fist to suppress the urge, he'd spot the move in a nanosecond and seize the opportunity to exploit her reaction. She couldn't allow him to hold any more power over her and call all of the shots.

Dammit, why did he have to be such a great kisser? If he had been lippy or slobbery, she could have brushed it off, no problem. But no, it was perfect, just like the rest of him.

He's not perfect, she reminded herself. He has commitment issues, a huge ego, and a serious Batman complex. He was far from perfect.

Yeah, just keep telling yourself that, sweetie. Nothing will come of the two of you.

An image flashed through her mind, brilliant in its detail. Teal satin sheets, naked limbs entwined. Max above her with his head thrown back as his hips thrust between her splayed thighs. Under him, she arched her back, her eyes closed tight as she screamed his name.

And just as quickly, the vision cleared, leaving her gasping where she stood as if she broke the surface of the ocean after a steep dive.

Fuuuuuuck.

"Crystal? What's wrong?" Max laid a palm on her back. "Was it a vision?"

"Fine. I'm fine." She shook off his touch. "Just a little dizzy from sitting so long. Restless leg syndrome, or whatever. Right." She all but ran to the ticket booth and hoped he bought the charade. Of course, it would have been a better sell if she hadn't just ridden his leg as if it were a stripper pole.

She stepped under the awning of the ticket booth and

blinked against the spots in her eyes caused by the change in lighting. "Two adults, please," she told the girl behind the glass partition.

"That will be twenty-one dollars."

"Sweetie?" She batted her lashes at Max.

"Sure, darling," he drawled and pulled his wallet from his jacket pocket. He flipped it open and pulled out two crisp bills from the fat stack.

She tried not to choke and sputter at the wad of cash he carried on him. Jesus, how much had he been sitting on? Was he so wealthy he carried twenties around as if they were loose change?

Or was he so paranoid he only used cash so there wouldn't be a paper trail?

Sadly, it was probably the latter.

Did he always live on the run this way? Although she had seen events from his past, it wasn't the entire picture. His memories were only snippets, glimpses. She didn't know what he had felt, what he had thought. He could be perfectly happy being the lone wolf, although how anyone could be was beyond her. There had been so many times in her life that, if she had been on her own without her sister to fight for, she would have curled into a ball and given up.

Max accepted the tickets and turned toward her. Behind those baby blues she could see his brain working, measuring her, wondering how she fit into his world. As his assessing gaze drifted over her face, his tongue swept his lower lip as if remembering her taste, her texture.

Gah! There she was again, getting sucked into the intrigue that was Matthew Maxwell Madden III. She swallowed hard and marched ahead of him, determined not to go down that road.

"So, what are we looking for?" he asked, catching up and matching her stride. A predatory mask tightened his features as he looked around, scoping out the area. "Informants? A deal going down? Evidence stashed someplace inconspicuous to be picked up later?"

She rolled her eyes and sighed. "I'll tell you when I see it."

His hand brushed hers as they walked and she bit her tongue to keep from telling him to back away. No need to break his concentration now that it was no longer focused on her.

Their footsteps clipped along the sidewalk as they passed the restaurant area and mountain goat enclosure. The zoo was surprisingly empty for the middle of the day, but then again, who would want to be out in the unusually hot summer sun instead of a comfy air-conditioned house?

The trail forked near the otter exhibit. Bobbing on top of a cool pool of water, a half-dozen slick, furry creatures floated on their backs with their eyes closed in bliss. A rock archway was to the left on the path, and she followed her instincts and walked past the cove.

The delicious aroma of fried food teased her nose as they passed a food stand decorated in bags of pink and blue cotton candy. The few scones she had eaten for breakfast had long since been absorbed into her body, and her stomach rumbled in a plea for a corn dog dipped in spicy mustard. She took one step toward the stand then veered back on course. Max would probably throw a conniption fit if she deviated from their task.

Children dressed in brightly colored shirts with the name of a local day camp emblazoned across the chest crowded around the penguin exhibit. All of their attention focused on a man standing in the center wearing a blue shirt with the zoo's logo. He held two small penguins in his large hands as he educated the children on the birds' environment. They laughed as he encouraged the birds to perform a few simple tricks, and their teachers swooned when he turned his brilliant smile on them.

He stood tall and broad, like Gulliver among the Lilliputians. His tan skin crinkled around his cornflower blue eyes, which sparkled as if he knew exactly what the female teachers were daydreaming about. Shaggy blond hair lent him an animalistic air that could give a woman ideas about hot sweaty sex up against a tree trunk. A scar ran up from under the collar of his shirt along his neck and more scars crisscrossed his forearms, but they only added to his dangerous appeal. The muscles in his biceps bulged, stretching the sleeve of his cotton polo shirt as he gestured around the exhibit. He was a glowing picture of health and male vitality.

Crystal gasped as she took a second and third look at the man. He wasn't just glowing.

He glowed.

CHAPTER EIGHT

"**M**AX, WHEN YOU look at me, do I glow?" Crystal asked, excitement quickening her breath.

He opened his mouth to answer then snapped it shut and frowned. "What?"

"When you look at me, can you see a blue glow around me, like an aura?"

He blinked once. "Are you taking any narcotics or medications I should be aware of?"

She threw up a talk-to-the-hand gesture. "Never mind."

Max didn't see the halo?

Interesting.

Was this a new ability of hers? First herself, then Max, and now this stranger. People with freaky blue halos were not a common occurrence.

Seriously, there was something extremely intriguing about this zookeeper that went beyond his Malibu Ken good looks. A devious smile curled her lips. It would be remiss of her to not investigate further.

A round of clapping and cheers broke out when the man concluded his demonstration. When he dismissed the children, they scattered like Skittles hitting the floor of a movie theater. Their teachers chased after them as they rushed past Crystal and Max, corralling them as effectively as, well, a herd of children.

Crystal removed her hoodie and tied it around her

waist. Taking a second to straighten her shirt to present her cleavage at its best, she fluffed her hair before sauntering over and popping a hand on her hip, thrusting it out in an enticing fashion. Yes, she wasn't above using her feminine curves to her advantage.

"Your penguins are so cute," she called out to Mr. Hunk.

His assessing gaze caressed her from head to breast before he turned up the wattage on that killer smile. "If they knew just how popular they are, they'd demand more fish."

She smiled back at him. "Do they mind being out in this heat?"

"What are you doing?" Max whispered from behind her.

"These are Humboldt penguins," the man replied. "They're native to the Peruvian coast, so this is perfect weather for them." His nostrils flared as he looked between her and Max. "It's a nice afternoon for a midday date."

"Date?" She tossed a glossy lock of her hair over her shoulder. "No, we're just...friends." She leaned closer as if she were imparting a great secret. "He just got out of prison. I thought it would be best to slowly reintroduce him into society by bringing him to where there're animals, like he's used to."

"Are you fucking kidding me?" Max grumbled while the man tilted back his head and let out a hearty laugh.

The man—who bore some resemblance to a Nordic god, in her opinion—winked at her as if he recognized a fellow smart-ass. He nodded at Max's leather get-up. "So, what were you in prison for? BDSM scene gone wrong? Lost out for best costume at a *Matrix* convention and caused some trouble?"

Max scratched the side of his nose with his middle finger. "You two are hysterical," he replied in a deadpan voice that was as dry as the desert.

Actually, Crystal thought Max looked kind of badass, but seriously, the man should have left the duster in the car. She nudged him out of the way and murmured, "I'm working on something."

"I can see that," he replied with full sarcasm.

She sidled closer to her target. "So, what exactly do you do here? Do they actually call you a zookeeper?"

He settled his hands on his lean hips. "I'm the lead veterinarian. 'Zookeeper' is kind of outdated, plus most of our workers are volunteers." His eyes sparkled with mischief. "Hey, do you want to come inside? I've got something to show you."

"I just bet he does."

She ignored Max's rumble of discontent. "Don't I have to go through training or something?"

"Nah." He winked. "I won't tell if you won't."

"I'd love to." She jabbed her thumb in the direction of the simmering tower of man beside her. "But he has to come too."

He gave Max another scrutinizing once-over. "All right. Give me a minute to put these two away. I'll be right back." He scooped up the penguins and disappeared through the door.

She took two steps forward to follow before Max hauled her back with a firm grip. "What are you doing, Crystal? I did not let you drag me down here so you could flirt with a blond hulk."

She pulled free from his possessive grasp. "I'm investigating."

"Who is he? Was he in your vision?"

"Possibly. That's what I'm investigating. Look, your conversational skills suck, so just follow my lead and stop being—" she eyed his permanent scowl—"you." She pushed down on his stiff shoulders. "Relax a little."

The marked door opened and they were waved inside by her new friend. Concrete lined the walls and floor, which were stained with fluids she didn't want to think about. Disinfectant and animal dander tickled her nose, making her eyes water.

"I'm Crystal. This is Max." She held out her hand. One second, that's all she needed to find out this man's secret.

"Ripley." He slapped a pair of latex gloves in her open palm. He raised a blond brow at Max, who stood with arms crossed over his chest. He laughed at the lack of response and snapped on his own pair of gloves over his huge hands. "Follow me."

They passed several closed doors and a kitchen area that rivaled most restaurants. A volunteer tore the top off a plastic bag and poured thousands of wiggly mealworms into a cracked plastic container. Another volunteer used a large butcher knife to portion out a side of beef. The rhythmic thwack of the blade hacking through flesh squelched any appetite Crystal may have had.

She glanced inside an exam room and felt her heart stir at the sight of a cougar lying in the only occupied cage. It stared blankly around the bars, its head resting on his paws. Brown fur, once a sleek shiny maize color, appeared dull and gray in the low-watt institutional lighting.

"What's wrong with the cougar?" she asked.

Ripley shook his head. "I'm not certain yet. He's very old. I believe he's suffering from dementia."

"Really?" she squeaked. "That can happen to animals?"

"They're really not that different from you and me, gorgeous."

"Where are all the rest of the employees?" Max asked, his gaze combing every shadow.

"Isn't it amazing how many people suddenly fall ill and call in sick on such a lovely day?" Ripley smirked.

He led them through another door and into the back of the penguin habitat. It was a haven of rocks and cubbyholes, jetted Jacuzzis, and a wave pool that emulated their native land in Peru. Or at least tried to emulate. Cement slathered over chicken wire was still cement and could never replace the natural rocky shoreline of their origins.

Several of the penguins dove into the water like rockets, riding the waves on their slippery feathers. Krill and plankton floated on the surface like a convenient buffet.

"Why are those ones naked?" Max pointed at two birds that rested in the shade and brayed at each other like donkeys.

"They lose all their feathers when they molt. They're getting ready to mate." Ripley stepped over a few birds that refused to move from their path.

"That just looks like all kinds of wrong," Max muttered.

Crystal bit her lip to keep from giggling. Whether he liked it or not, Max was intrigued with their surroundings.

Ripley stopped at an alcove and slid open the top of a wooden box. "Look here."

Two baby chicks sat side by side and immediately began to bawl for attention the moment Ripley moved closer. Black eyes peered out from their little brownish-gray faces as their heads swiveled around.

"Oh, they're so cute," she cooed. "And you're making

me do baby talk, and I hate it when other people do that. Max, look at them." She glanced over her shoulder and saw him watching her with a little half smile on his lips.

"They're precious," he remarked, just as dry as ever.

She stuck out her tongue and turned back to watch Ripley examine the chicks.

"These little guys hatched about three weeks ago," he said. "See how this one is much smaller? For some reason the parents decided that he's not worthy and stopped feeding him. Usually they only do that when there is a lack of food and they choose the strongest to survive. Since that isn't the case here, then the issue is personal."

"That's awful," she gasped.

He nodded. "That's why *we* are going to take care of him." With fingers far gentler than his size implied he was capable of, he lifted the bird. "Hold out your hands."

She cupped her palms and her breath caught when the warm bundle of fluff settled in her hold.

Ripley stood. "Let's take him into one of the exam rooms."

"How do you know it's a he?" Max held the door open for them.

"I don't, not yet anyway. I'm just sexist and call all of them 'he.'"

Max laughed out loud at that.

Ripley led them to an open room down a quiet hall.

"Set him down there, Crystal." Ripley nodded at the exam table and closed the door behind them.

One wall was lined with cages of various sizes, while the opposite wall contained glassed-in locked cabinets and shelves filled with medical supplies. Papers, heat lamps, and wires hung from every available surface. The concrete floor had a drain in the center that she guessed was used to hose the room down if need be. Charming.

She shivered in the air-conditioned space, then trembled again when a low growl erupted from under the table, sending a streak of alarm down her neck.

"What the hell?" Ripley frowned and bent low to look. "How did you get out?"

The cougar from the other room lay low along the floor. His black eyes appeared dazed and confused as he watched them, his nostrils working as he separated their scents on the air. His mouth fell open when he saw the tiny bird in Crystal's hold and recognized the penguin-nugget as a tasty snack. His shoulder blades worked up and down before he leapt.

Everything happened so fast, Crystal barely had time to blink.

The cat sprang straight for her with claws unleashed and lips curled over its fangs. Sharp nails raked across her biceps just as a second cougar, this one with golden fur, crashed into it in mid-air, knocking the crazed feline away from her as she fell to the ground. A pile of shredded blue cotton and khaki was all that remained from where Ripley once stood.

Two balls of snarling fur tangled and thrashed, smashing into every piece of furniture. One cat latched onto the other's shoulder, digging in deep with its teeth. The bitten cat howled and fought harder for dominance. They rolled across the floor and into a shelf of supplies. Boxes and vials rained down, instantly destroyed in the battle.

Max flung out his hands and lifted both cats, their twisting bodies hovering in the air as he shoved them into separate cages and locked them in.

One of the large cats continued to hiss and charge the door, the metal rattling with the force. The other cat sat on its haunches and stared at them expectantly with bright blue eyes. As Crystal and Max stared at him in shock, he gave a short yowl and tilted his head to the side.

"Did what just happen just happen?" Max asked.

"I think so."

"He's...?"

"I think so," she repeated in a whisper.

Max approached the cage and slowly reached out his hand. The cougar continued to stare up at him, and if possible, appeared to be tapping his paw with impatience. Max unlocked the cage and the cougar sprang out, morphing mid-leap into Ripley, who knelt beside Crystal. Worry was etched on his brow and the firm line of his lips even as blood poured from his shoulder.

"Crystal, are you okay?" He eyed the slashes on her arm then reached for a box of gauze from a shelf above them.

She bit her lip to hold back the hysterical laughter bubbling up her throat. The man just turned into cougar and back again and was now standing before her in all his divine and glorious nakedness covered in bite marks and scratches, and he was worried about her?

"I'll be all right. You look worse." She hissed when he poured antiseptic over the slashes. "Oww," she whimpered as quietly as possible, trying not to look like a wimp.

"Sorry. God, I'm sorry about this. I've told people a thousand times to make sure the cages are locked. Max, shut and lock that door in case anyone heard and might be coming."

"On it."

"You shapeshifted," she whispered in awe, still not

believing what she saw. "You shifted. Why did you shift?"

He raised a brow, as if surprised at why she would ask such a question. "You were in danger."

"No." She shook her head. "You don't shift in front of anyone. Why did you do it in front of us?"

He looked back and forth between her and Max. "You two smell different. Not like…people."

"Not like *people*?" Max asked. "What the hell does that mean?"

"I think I understand," she said with a laugh and leaned her head back against the wall. "You glow. Blue. Just like me and Max."

"I glow?" The big golden man chuckled while he continued to wrap more gauze around her biceps and taping it to her skin.

"Just a little. Like a halo."

"Well, let me be the first to tell you, I'm no angel."

The two shared a laugh that was interrupted by Max clearing his throat. "Your shoulder is bleeding pretty badly, and maybe you want to throw some clothes on." He was going to have a permanent crease in his brow from all the frowning he did.

Ripley stood to his full height. Sunlight streamed in from a tiny window and bathed his golden body, highlighting the fine hairs that covered the slab of muscles on his chest and thighs. Crystal swallowed hard as his cock hung, long and heavy, just above her head. Damn, the man was built.

He looked down at her with an amused smile, not bothered in the slightest by her open admiration. "That arm is going to need stitches."

"It looks like you will, too." Max said tightly, displeasure branded in his scowl, and shoved a towel at Ripley.

"I'll be fine, but let me take you to a people doctor. I have a friend who can get us in right away." He blotted off the blood then pulled a change of clothes from a cabinet and dressed quickly.

Crystal got to her feet on shaky knees. "What about him?"

"Who?" both men asked.

"Him." She held out her hands to show them the little penguin, asleep in her palms.

CHAPTER NINE

MAX EASED UP on the gas pedal before he drove up Ripley's ass. Couldn't he make that piece of shit Chevy go any faster? He risked a glance at Crystal, who sat quietly in the passenger seat. All the blush in her cheeks was gone, making her appear far paler than he liked.

"How's the arm?" he asked.

"Stings like hell." She shrugged, her forehead puckered as she examined the bandage. "Don't worry. I won't get blood on the upholstery."

"That's not important," he mumbled and concentrated on relaxing the death grip he had on the steering wheel. A long, slow breath eased out from between his lips, but his blood continued to race.

When that large cat had jumped at Crystal, his heart had damn near exploded right then and there. For that half a second he thought he might lose her, and it was an outcome he couldn't bear. In the last twenty-four hours she had become important to him in a way no one had done before. It was a coin toss as to which was more frightening: the fact he was growing attached to her or the possibility of her loss.

The feelings he was developing for her were growing beyond sexual desire, although that kiss he stole about knocked him on his ass. Even now the cinnamon cookie taste of the inside of her mouth lingered on his tongue. She was smart, wicked smart, and funny. She didn't complain and wasn't afraid of jumping in with both feet. Throw in the body of Venus and lips made for sin, and you had a very attractive combination.

He shook his head, banishing thoughts of what shouldn't be. Her safety and well-being came first. He'd best remember that.

He nodded at the truck they followed. "Is Ripley the reason we came down here?"

"I think so. We'll find out more at dinner."

"Dinner?"

She rolled her head in his direction as if she were intoxicated. The crash of adrenaline was taking its toll, and her eye color shifted from topaz to brown. He noticed they turned brown when she was excited. Like when he kissed her. "Yep. We have dinner together. Nice house, very colorful. We're having Thai food, which is fantastic, because I'm starving," she moaned.

His lips quirked as his stomach rumbled in agreement. "I haven't been taking proper care of you, have I?"

"I didn't ask you to. Don't worry, I'm a big girl. I watch out for myself."

He opened his mouth to reply then snapped it shut. She didn't need to know that he actually enjoyed looking out for her. Hell, that was a fact he didn't need to know either.

"What did you find out about Ripley when you read his memories?"

"I didn't."

"What?" His voice rose with his surprise. "Why not?"

"First off, I was wearing latex gloves. Second, I was a little distracted by a two-hundred-pound cougar lunging at my throat."

"Still, aren't you curious about him?"

"Sure."

Sure...but... When a minute passed without her saying another word, he realized that was all to her answer. "Wait a minute, you read me the first chance you got. Why not him?"

"Ripley's different. I'm not af—" She broke off, her cheeks flushing as she looked away. "Seeing him shift pretty much answered all of my questions about why we're here."

She wasn't what? Affected? Afraid? Why would she be afraid of him and not Ripley? For Pete's sake, the man changed before their eyes into a beast with sharp claws and drippy fangs.

That kiss. Must be. It all came back to that kiss.

Well, good, he sniffed. He didn't want to be the only one affected by the chemistry between them.

"Finally," he muttered when Ripley's truck pulled into the parking lot of an urgent-care facility.

Before Crystal opened the door, Max was hustling to help her out of the car, tucking her under his arm as he escorted her inside. He tried to fool himself into thinking that it was only to make sure she didn't stumble from shock and not because he needed the physical contact to convince him she was really all right.

Ripley held the door open for them then strode right up to the front desk. Blood had seeped through his shirt and formed a horrific Rorschach pattern on his back. In spite of how shitty the wound must have felt, his charming smile didn't waver as he leaned over the desk.

"If it isn't the fair Alisia," he greeted the nurse standing next to the receptionist. "Doc Kelly is expecting us."

She brushed the lock of blonde hair escaping her ponytail behind her ear and adjusted the files in her arm. "I heard. She's finishing with a patient but told me to take you back."

"Excellent." He turned toward them. "This way."

They waited by the door to the left of reception until the nurse opened it and ushered them in. She assessed Ripley's bloody shirt and Crystal's bandage with concern. "Does anyone need anything? Water?"

"No, thank you." Crystal shook her head.

Ripley cornered the cute nurse with his big body against the doorway of the exam room she escorted them to. "How about dinner on Friday?"

She sighed deep from her toes. "The answer is still no."

"Why? Why won't you go out with me?" he asked softly, and Max and Crystal shared a curious glance. Obviously the two had a history. Max just wished he didn't have to be front-row center to the awkward exchange.

She swallowed hard and lifted her chin to look him in the eye. A slight tremble shook her shoulders. "I don't date patients."

"Then I'll go to another doctor," Ripley replied.

"Be my guest, but it won't change my answer."

"Why not?"

She glanced pointedly as his shirt. "I make it a point not to get involved with men who manage to find ways to bleed profusely at least once a week." She took a deep breath. "Will that be all, Mr. Jorgensen?"

"Yes, Nurse Caldwell." The second he stepped back, she escaped down the hall.

Ripley struck the flesh of his palm against the doorjamb in soft taps as he watched her go with longing in his eyes. With a final sigh, he turned and bristled when he noticed his audience. "She can't live without me. She just doesn't know it yet."

Max raised a dismissive hand. "Hey, man, it's none of my business."

He nodded. "Right."

"What have you done to yourself now, Ripley?" The doctor sighed as she entered the room and closed the door behind her.

Raven black hair hung to her shoulders and was held off her face by a bright red ribbon. Under her blue scrubs her figure appeared fit and trim as she pushed back the sides of her white lab coat to place her hands on her hips. An amused frown pulled her brows down and the corner of her mouth up. Max guessed her age to be mid-thirties, except her green eyes held shadows of knowledge and experience that suggested she had seen more in her life than someone twice her age.

Crystal gasped and stared at the doctor in shock while Ripley answered the question.

"A cougar got loose from his cage and jumped us. You know how that goes. These are my new friends, Max and Crystal. This is Dr. Megan Kelly." He noticed the stunned expression on Crystal's face and smiled. "You see it, don't you?"

"She glows," Crystal whispered. "You have a blue halo, like Ripley, and me, and Max. You have a special power too."

Doc Kelly inhaled sharply, her panicked gaze darting over all of them before settling on Ripley. "What did you tell them?"

He laughed and shook his head, holding his hands in the air. "Nothing. They found me. I thought you might like to meet them. I just wish we hadn't gotten injured in the process."

"Crap, I'm sorry." Doc pushed Ripley toward the gurney. "Heal first, talk second. Take off your shirt."

A buzz of excitement surrounded the good doctor and her gaze bounced back and forth from them to Ripley as if a million questions hovered on her smiling lips.

Max nudged Crystal. "Sweetheart, take a seat."

"What?" She blinked up at him in confusion.

"Sit down."

"Oh, right. Sorry." She stumbled to a chair. "I can't believe I've met not one but two more people with superpowers in just a couple of hours."

"You and me both," Max replied. And what did that all mean?

Ripley removed his shirt and Doc hissed at the sight of his wounds. "Jesus, Rip, you have got to stay away from the claws." She cleaned the slashes with gentle but firm strokes.

"That was from the teeth, not the claws. Crystal was holding a penguin the cat thought looked tasty. I shifted to fight it off, and Crystal got caught in the middle. I am really sorry about that," he apologized again.

"You shifted in front of them?" Doc gasped. "What made you trust them?"

Ripley smiled. "They smell like you. Different. Just like Crystal can see a halo. I guess we can spot others like us. Damn." He winced when Doc started to stitch him up. "What are you using the needle for?"

"To remind you to take better care of yourself. It's been a long day, and I'm tired." She tied off the thread and snipped it before working on the next section. Her gaze met Crystal's over his shoulder. "Your power is to sense other people with superpowers?"

"I guess so. You three are the only ones I've met. I'm actually clairvoyant. I had a vision that Max and I went to the zoo, only I wasn't sure why. It wasn't until I saw Ripley that I had a suspicion."

What? Max's focus whipped to Crystal. She made him believe their trip had something to do with his father and avenging Anthony. The little witch tricked him.

You could have left her behind if you had really wanted to, the voice in his head piped up.

Yeah, but still, she'd played him. A flash of heat ignited in his belly as he contemplated ways she could make up for her transgressions, and each one was naughtier than the next. If only he'd be around her long enough to play them out.

"Were you born a clairvoyant?" Doc asked, smoothing the last strip of tape into place on Ripley.

"No. I was nineteen when I started to have visions."

"And you have powers, too?" she asked Max.

He nodded. "Telekinesis."

"It was awesome," Ripley raved. "You should have seen it, Doc. He picked up the cougar and me and tossed us into the cages just using his mind. Although I would have preferred if it had just been the cat and not me."

"Yeah, I wasn't going to take a chance on picking the wrong animal."

"What are your abilities?" Crystal asked.

Doc smiled, anticipation lighting her eyes. "The only person I really get to practice on is Ripley, so this will be fun."

She lifted Crystal's injured arm and laid it along the counter next to her. Gingerly she peeled the tape back, exposing the open cuts.

"What did you clean this with?" she asked.

"Ripley put an anti-bacterial cream on back at the zoo."

"Good." Doc took a deep breath, then another, and then placed both hands over the wound.

Crystal held her breath and stared wide-eyed at Doc's hands on her arm. "It's getting warm."

Doc's shoulders relaxed and she let out a shuddering sigh as she stepped back. Three red lines were all that remained of the claw marks on Crystal's skin.

"Whoa," Crystal exclaimed.

"Holy shit," Max muttered. "That's incredible."

"Obviously I can't do that with all of my patients, but I try, in my own way, to lessen whatever ails them."

Crystal ran her finger along the faint scratches in amazement. "Can you heal anything?"

Doc tilted her head from side to side with a wary smile. "I've tried. When I look at a person, I can see exactly what injuries or ailments they have." She pointed at Max. "You need more vitamin K and D. Your bones will thank you." She stepped up to the sink and washed her hands while she continued. "I can heal small cuts, minor burns, and contusions with my hands, which I try to do as inconspicuously as possible. Anything more major becomes trickier. One, it's physically exhausting. I tried to heal a child with cancer once and blacked out. Was sick to my stomach for weeks. And even then, it didn't help that much. I guess the universe was telling me I can heal, but I can't play God." She dried her hands on a paper towel and tossed it into the bin before shoving her hands into the pockets of her lab coat. "But I do heal what I can. If I was given this power, I was supposed to use it for something. Right?"

"I believe that, too." Crystal smiled and looked over at Max with a narrowed gaze and a grin meant to needle him. "We are put here at this place and time for a reason."

A fact that still remained to be seen.

He folded his arms and leaned back against the wall. They found other people with powers. So what? He still had a death to avenge, a maniacal father to take down, and billions of dollars to return to fleeced Americans. His plate was full enough as it was, without adding a heaping spoonful of new people. Even those with superpowers.

"Look." Doc sat next to Ripley on the gurney. "I would like to talk, really talk, privately with both of you. I've being doing research in the hopes of finding out how we came to be."

Max pushed away from the wall. "We need to be getting back to Seattle."

"We'd love to," Crystal said at the same time.

"Crystal," he growled.

"Don't even start." She got up and stood toe to toe with him. "I told you we needed to come here for a reason. The least you can do is see this through. It's just dinner."

"Please," Doc implored. "Can't you see how important this is? Just dinner, that's all I ask."

"I know a great Thai place that has takeout," Ripley offered, pulling a clean scrub top over his head.

A nuclear reactor couldn't generate as much power as Crystal's smile did as she looked up at Max.

Shit. He closed his eyes and sighed. "All right."

Doc pulled a prescription pad from her pocket. "Let me give you directions to my house."

Crystal kept her dark chocolate gaze on Max and bit her lip in a vain attempt to hold back her smug smile. "Thanks.

By the way, I love the painting in your dining room. Renoir is one of my favorite artists."

Doc looked up in surprise. "How do you—" she gasped, then threw her head back and laughed.

CHAPTER TEN

"DOES ANYONE MIND if I have the baseball scores on in the background?" Ripley called out from the living room with the remote in hand.

"I don't mind," Crystal answered from where she stood in the open archway near the dining room and opened the last carton of pad Thai.

Max accepted the stack of plates from Doc Kelly and set them on the table. Doc's house was an explosion of color from the eggplant purple walls, to the yellow and pink pillows on the couches. She told them she preferred the rainbow effect because she was surrounded by so much white during the day. The floorplan was bright, vibrant, and open. Too open, in his opinion.

He eyed the massive floor-to-ceiling glass doors leading to the patio before closing the drapes tightly and selecting a chair where his back was to the wall. Since the night at Anthony's house, sliding glass doors and massive windows open to the visible world made him twitchy.

"This smells fantastic." Ripley sighed in appreciation and took a seat facing the television in the other room.

Max accepted the heaping plate Crystal handed him with a nod of thanks. "Ripley, when did you know you could shift?"

He wiped his mouth with a paper napkin before answering. "About four years ago. I was working with a group from Oregon State University who were studying the black bear population in the Cascades. Dusk had set in, and I was heading back to base camp. My boot caught on a root I didn't see and I went tumbling down a hill, right into the path of a mama bear and her cubs." A hint of a smile hovered on his lips. "Word of warning, don't use a bear cub as a landing pad. The momma bear and I stared at each other in shock for about half a second before she reared up and slashed me across the chest with her claws. Obviously, I expected to have it sting like hell, but the pain was different. It was like I had grabbed onto a live wire charged with fifty thousand volts. This horrible nauseating feeling swept over me, and all of my bones started to snap and pop. The next thing I knew, I was standing toe to toe, or rather paw to paw, with her. I had shapeshifted." His smile stretched wider. "Scared the shit out of both of us. The bears took off, and I collapsed in the dirt. When I woke up, morning had dawned, and I was lying naked in the forest."

Ripley gestured at Doc. "That's how I meet Doc here. She was part of the rescue team that was sent out after me when I hadn't return to camp. She was the one who treated my wounds. I could tell something was different about her right away. She smelled different, like electricity. Just like you two smell."

"Could you tell what had happened to him right away? That he was something different?" Max asked Doc. Despite the driving need to continue on his mission to take down his father, he couldn't help but be fascinated at the prospect of other supers. Now that he was committed to this little chat, his mind was eager to soak up every bit of information.

"I could tell his physiology was different, but I didn't know he could shapeshift. We danced around the possibility until it came down to an I'll-show-you-my-talent-if-you-show-me-yours showdown. After that, we learned to trust each other."

"So you can change into any animal?" Max asked.

"Any mammal," Ripley clarified with a pointed jab of his fork. "I can become a dolphin, but not a fish or bird."

"That's amazing." Crystal shook her head.

Max focused on Doc. "Then you've been able to heal for quite a while now if it's been four years since Ripley transitioned."

She nodded, pushing the noodles around on her plate. Her voice dropped to a husky murmur as she replied, "Almost seven years now. I was working the late shift in the ER. Some gangbangers were brought in after a drive-by at a party, and the rival gang burst in to finish the job. They opened fire, and I was hit in the shoulder. At first I thought I had been hit several times because I burned everywhere, but I realized later it must have been the change taking place. I passed out, and when I came to, my shoulder was healed. I knew I hadn't imagined being shot because of the hole in my shirt and the blood everywhere."

"That's odd." Crystal frowned down at her plate.

"What's odd?" Max asked.

"I didn't pass out. When I had my first vision, I had the same stomach-turning, electric sensation you two described, but I didn't pass out."

"Did *you* lose consciousness?" Doc asked Max.

"No. I was awake the entire time." Unfortunately. "But I did experience a similar sensation."

Doc nodded and folded her hands together on the tabletop. She was gearing up for something, Max could tell by the straight set of her shoulders, the glimmer in her eyes, and the way her lips pursed together as if she was forming a proposal he suspected he wasn't going to like.

"I have a theory. It's only a theory because the only people I've been able to do any research on is myself and Ripley." Yep. Here it was. "I've run tests on our blood, skin, hair, everything trying to find out how and why we have developed these abilities. What I've discovered is that Ripley and I have several compounds in our molecular makeup in common that we shouldn't, and I think the primary cause is our environment."

Intrigued, Max sat back, even though he knew where she was leading and knew he wasn't going to like it. "How so?"

"Look at the physiological makeup of the human body now and from twenty, thirty, a hundred years ago," she began, hands pressed flat on the table. "The appendix has grown smaller, people as a whole are fatter. We drink hormones in our milk, there're pesticides in our vegetables. The air we breathe and the water we drink has lord knows what exactly in it." Each time she made a point, she tapped the table with the tip of her finger. "Humans, as a species, are going to have to evolve in order to survive these assaults on our bodies."

She took a deep breath. "When I took the samples from Ripley and me and broke them down, I found three profound distinctions between ourselves and other random human samples I used as controls."

"Wait." Crystal raised her hand and leaned forward. "History major here. Science was not my strong suit. Go slow."

Doc smiled. "I borrowed blood and tissue samples from several average people at the hospital—"

"Borrowed or stole?" Max cut in.

Her spine went ramrod straight and a flush graced her cheeks. "I prefer the term 'pilfered.' If a test was ordered, I'd take two. One for the hospital, one for me."

Uh-huh. That's what he thought. Even the good doctor wasn't above using others for her own gain.

"Anyway, I cross-referenced those samples with Ripley's and mine. In both of ours, I found a large quantity of phenylpropanolamine. It's a decongestant used to treat asthma, but for a long time it was used as an ingredient in diet pills."

"I take it neither of you suffer from asthma or use diet pills," Max broke in, stroking his chin as his mind worked to catalog the information. "It doesn't make sense that it's in your bloodstream. It should have passed through your system within hours of ingesting it."

"Exactly." Doc nodded enthusiastically. "I also found large traces of epinephrine, which also should have long passed through our systems."

"Epinephrine?" Crystal frowned. "Isn't that a drug?"

"Yes, but it's also another name for adrenaline," Doc answered. "And I found feldspar."

Crystal's brows rose. "Like the mineral?"

"Yep. Feldspar, clinopynxene, and olivine. The research I dug up found these minerals are most prevalent in rock. More specifically—"

"Ash," Max interrupted, the pieces of the puzzle falling into place.

"What?" Crystal asked.

All eyes turned to him. "Ash. Volcanic ash. Those elements are found in basalt magma. And when was the most recent case of widespread contamination of basalt magma, or volcanic ash in this area?"

"Mount St. Helen's." Crystal gasped. "I remember for science class. The fallout from that spread over the entire Northwest."

Doc spread her hands out wide. "I believe our bodies have acted like an incubator for all of these molecules that have been changed by our environment. All four of us are from this area, all between the ages of twenty-five to forty. My mother took diet pills like they were candy. I took some myself in college."

"My mother did too," Ripley added.

"Mine too," Crystal chimed in. "I've even tried them."

Again, all eyes turned to Max. "My mother owned stock in Dexatrim. Seriously."

"You see." Doc nodded. "We've all been exposed to PPA, and volcanic ash, which conducts electricity. Crystal, what was the catalyst for your change?"

Crystal swallowed hard before answering in a soft voice. "I saw my father beat my mother to death."

Doc's breath caught, clearly not expecting such a tragic answer. "A traumatic event."

"Yes."

"And you, Max?" Doc asked.

If they thought he was going to open up and spill his heart in an *Oprah* show moment, they were sorely mistaken. He pushed his half-eaten dinner away, his appetite gone. "Similar to Crystal."

"Just as I suspected." Doc nodded and leaned back in her chair, her arms folded over her breasts as if she had solved the case. "We've all been exposed to chemicals and compounds that affect metabolism. We've all experienced a traumatic event. An event so catastrophic it caused a spike of adrenaline so great, it changed the molecular structure of our bodies."

"But why? And why do we have different powers from each other?" Max asked.

Doc frowned and propped her hand on her chin. "That, I'm not certain. Because I've only been able to test on Ripley and me, I assumed it was because the change emphasized a talent or knowledge we already possessed. Crystal, did you have psychic tendencies before your change?"

"A little. My intuition was usually spot-on. And when I played around with tarot cards, they almost always came true." She gasped and turned toward Max. "And Max is smart. Really, really, really smart. Is that why you're telekinetic? Because you're able to process knowledge so fast, you're able to move things with your mind?"

"That information would support my theory," Doc interjected. She was practically levitating off her chair in her excitement. "And why you two didn't lose consciousness. You experienced an emotional trauma while Ripley and I had a physical one."

Now that was an interesting theory. "Are you saying any spike of adrenaline will cause a manifestation of powers?"

"If that person has the same chemical cocktail as we do, and the spike is strong enough, I believe so," she answered.

"And will that power increase if the person experiences another trauma?"

"Potentially, yes. Ripley has had some run-ins with wildlife while shifted and is now able to control what he shifts into, instead of mimicking the animal he is around. And I noticed my ability to focus my healing energy increased after an injury. One time I had a gurney roll over my foot with a rather weighty individual on it. Broke a few toes. And there was another time I was almost in a car accident on the way to work. When my heart rate slowed, I felt the energy I use to heal had grown stronger."

Very interesting indeed.

Max hummed to himself and picked up his fork. Testing the weight in his palm, he then switched his grip so the tines were faced down as if he were holding an ice pick.

"Don't you dare," Crystal snapped and slapped at his arm. "Are you insane?"

"What?" he asked. "I'm just holding a fork."

"You're going to stab yourself to see if you can increase your powers."

"Did you just see that in a vision?" What happened to her falling into that trance-like thing she did when she saw into the future? Or had her run-in with that cougar increase her power?

She tilted her head. "As if I needed to. You broadcasted your intentions just as surely as if you spoke them out loud."

Well, that was disappointing. "Fine. So what if I was? What could be bad about increasing my powers?"

"Because it won't work, man," Ripley replied with a chuckle. He took a giant swig from his bottle of beer. "Believe me. I tried."

"What happened to you when you did?" Max asked.

"I got a bunch of scars for my efforts, that's what."

"I begged him to stop after his third attempt," Doc said. "Your pain receptors and body react differently when you anticipate the trauma. That's why some people are better able to withstand things like piercings and tattoos."

"So you're saying I could jump Ripley when he wasn't expecting, stab him, and his powers might grow?"

"In theory."

"No, no, no, stop," Crystal groused. "That's just psychotic."

"What? I can stab him, Doc could heal him? What could go wrong?"

"You could kill him, that's what. Oh my God." She ran her hand over her face. "Talk like that is just demented."

Doc put her hands out as if she were refereeing a boxing match. "No one is stabbing anybody. I'm not above taking a few tissue samples from unsuspecting people, but I draw the line at human test trials."

"Even if it gets you clearer results?" Max asked.

"Yes. I want to see how we came to be. Not create more of us."

More? Now there was an idea almost as frightening as his father's quest to take over the country. With an army of supers on his side, he'd be almost unstoppable.

Max's attention was diverted from the nightmarish idea of a Dr. Doom version of his father when Doc continued, "If I ran tests on you two, I know I would find similarities with Ripley and me. I can confirm how we came to be."

"What exactly do you want from us?" Did he really have to ask?

She blinked at him with all innocence. "Just a few bio samples. Blood, hair, skin...all bodily fluids."

Yeah, right. "Sorry, Doc, but I'm not jacking off into a cup. Even if it is for science."

"Max," Crystal admonished. "There could be more people out there like us, or about to become like us. This could be a major discovery."

"It already is. Her theory is sound and perfectly logical." He raised a brow. "Are you willing to stick your feet in the stirrups and be internally swabbed?"

A flush spread across her cheeks. "If need be."

He grunted and glanced back at Doc. "I understand what you are trying to do. Really. I'll give you some hair, maybe a fingernail, but no needles and no fluids." The last word came out twisted and bitter as if he had bit down on a bad snow pea.

Doc continued undeterred. "If I find a connection, will you agree to more testing?"

"Yes," Crystal answered for him.

"I *may* be willing to reconsider. And that is a big *may*." He leaned forward. "But whatever you discover, you cannot let your research become public knowledge. It's one thing to learn and understand how we came to be, and potentially life-threatening if the information gets into the wrong hands. There will be some twisted fuck out there who will take that knowledge and do something stupid, like create their own supers. And you can be damned sure that I will do whatever it takes to prevent that from happening." One nutcase playing God at a time was all he could handle.

"I understand." Doc raised her hand in a Girl Scout pledge. "I've told no one about my research except Ripley, and I keep it entirely under lock and key."

"No offense, Doc, but lock and key isn't going to cut it. You're going to need security and firewalls of epic proportions."

"You're exactly right." Crystal latched onto his sleeve, excitement quivering in her voice. "That's why we're going to be with you, Doc."

What that fuck did that mean?

"With you?" he echoed. "You mean us with her? Oh, no. I didn't say that. I said nothing even remotely close to that," he drawled out as a sinking sensation pulled his Thai food–

laden stomach to his knees.

"Don't you see, Max? This is why we're here. To find others like us. To band together and fight the bad guys. Like your father."

"Nope." He was out of his chair in a heartbeat. "Absolutely not. I am not dragging anyone else into that. That's my fight and my fight alone."

Crystal jumped up and chased him into the living room, but he mentally shut her out and concentrated on the scores scrawling across the screen. The Mariners lost again. No surprise there.

"Max, you cannot face your father alone. I know you have the element of surprise on your side, but this is too big for just you. You'll need help." She grasped his arm, refusing to be ignored.

"Don't go pledging others assistance without asking. And I'm not asking for help," he snapped over his shoulder.

Ripley joined them. "What is Matthew Madden up to?"

Max turned in surprise. "How do you know he's my father?"

He cocked his head to the side. "I might be part animal, but I do occasionally read the paper. Madden Financial is a major conglomerate, and how many people with the last name of Madden drive around in a Ferrari?"

Good guess. Which meant he was going to have to go deep undercover if a zoologist in Portland could make him out.

"It's none of your business," Max bit out.

"I beg to differ," the big man continued to press. "If you, his own son, is about to fight him in something, it must be big."

Max pinched his lips together. He was not going to go

down this road.

Unfortunately, Crystal was more than ready to embark on that journey. "Max has evidence that Madden stole the billions of dollars that was supposedly lost in the housing and mortgage bust."

"Motherfucker," Max shouted. "Crystal! What are you doing?"

"What?" She threw her hands up in the air. "They deserve to know what is really happening in our country, what could happen. Tell them. Let them decide if they want to join us."

Us? He dug both hands into his hair and pulled until his eyes watered. "Crystal, there is no *us*. Look, sweetheart, I know why you think you need to go with me, but it's not going to bring your mother back."

Her stricken expression told Max that a knife to the heart would have been less painful than his words. Blood rushed from her cheeks as her lips began to tremble. The fact that he was the one to put that look there made his hardened heart soften and reminded him of the bastard he usually was. Only this time, he wished he wasn't one.

"Ah hell, honey." He pulled her close and hugged her tight. "You want to help. I get that. It's very noble. But I can't put you at risk."

Under her cotton shirt, her body felt delicate. Memories of the night Anthony was killed, the remembered scent of gun oil and blood filled his senses. If Madden ever got his hands on her, Max couldn't begin to imagine the cruelties his father would subject her to.

While she was small in stature, there was no denying the strength of her character. She truly believed she could help him save the world, and part of him was afraid she would continue to try until the only thing that stopped her was death.

Just the thought of her in danger made him tighten his hold. "I don't want you hurt."

Her eyes turned green as she gazed up at him and whispered, "It's my choice. I deserve a chance. Like you."

Max closed his eyes with a quick prayer for patience, then spoke over Crystal's head to the others. "Madden is building an army, buying up land all over the world, and developing who knows what type of weapons. He plans to take over the country."

"Holy shit," Doc gasped then slapped a hand over her mouth. "Pardon my French."

Ripley's eyes narrowed. "Why haven't you gone to the authorities?"

"I had a friend who tried. He ended up dead. There's too much corruption to know where to begin," he answered bitterly.

"Max is trying to stop his father, only it's not as easy as walking up and slapping a pair of cuffs on the man. It's complicated and dangerous." Crystal rubbed his back in long, comforting strokes.

It was the first time she had voluntarily touched him since that first handshake. Through the layer of cloth and leather, her touch burned him, made him ache for her.

How long had it been since he spent so much time in the company of others? The day he had spent with Crystal was a hint of what could be if he were more social. Showed him what it was like to be with someone, to tease, to argue with, to laugh. Max never thought he would want someone that way, until her. Being all on his own was, well, lonely.

He shook his head. No, he couldn't place others in

danger, especially Crystal.

"If serious shit is going down, I want to be a part of it." Ripley folded his arms over his massive chest. "Madden has contacts, not just financial, but political as well. This isn't just some wealthy bigshot with delusions of grandeur. If anyone could pull off a major coup, it would be Madden. Crystal's right, you're going to need help."

"Yeah?" Max matched the hulk's pose. "And just what exactly are *your* plans to stop him?"

Crystal smiled with that damn dimple creasing her cheek and answered for Ripley. "We're going to find others like us and form our own army. We're going to train, and research, and find a way to stop Madden."

"And where do you propose we do all of that?"

"Your mountain."

"You own an entire mountain?" Ripley asked with a choking laugh.

"Most of one," Crystal replied. "He dug it out himself. It's private and we can outfit it with whatever we need. A gym, a lab for Doc, sleeping quarters. It's perfect."

"You need to stop reading my mind," Max growled.

"I don't read minds, just memories," she reminded him.

"Hold up. Jump back a second." Ripley held up a hand and pointed at Crystal. "Explain that."

She swallowed once then shrugged as if it was no big deal. "I can see a person's memories if I touch their skin."

"Seriously?"

"Yep."

He shuddered. "Remind me to wear a full body condom the next time I touch you."

The words *next*, *touch*, and *condom* went right into Max's ear and ate a hole in his belly. Just because he was fighting his attraction to her didn't mean he wanted other men to touch Crystal, platonically or sexually.

Crystal propped her hands on her hips and lifted her chin in a way that twisted him in knots. "Of course, Max, if you feel that strongly about being the Lone Ranger, I can't stop you. After all, I know just about everything you do, remember? The three of us can form our own group. We'll go after the organization, and you can go after your father. When we cross paths, it will be with a hearty wave and good wishes. How about that?" Her smile was as sweet as honey and just as sticky.

The manipulative little witch. She had him by the nuts, and he couldn't help but admire her for it.

Max bit the inside of his cheek and counted to three, not certain if he was going to blow up with anger or laugh his head off. But now more than ever he needed his head to overrule his heart. He was a smart man, and it would be remiss to dismiss the idea without serious consideration.

Could he open his sanctuary to other people? Complete strangers? Other supers?

He stroked his chin and contemplated Ripley and Doc. A shifter and a healer would be great allies.

But Crystal...

What would it be like to have her in his home, see her every day? She'd be hell on his self-control and test him in ways he'd never been pushed before, that was for certain. She was a puzzle he eagerly wanted to solve.

Anticipation spiked so hard, the spicy flavor coated his tongue and he wanted more. He was up for the challenge, but was she?

"You said it yourself, Crystal. It's not going to be easy. Someone will get hurt, maybe die. I meant what I said. I can't watch you endanger yourself," he said in a low tone, not caring that they had an audience.

"I can learn, I can train. You're going to need all the help you can get, Max."

"What about your job? What if you find your sister? She can't know about the rest of us. It will be too dangerous."

Ah-ha. A possibility she hadn't counted on, he judged, based by her intake of breath and the hint of doubt in her eyes. She looked over at Doc Kelly and Ripley, then down at the floor.

He had her. No way would she give up a chance to find her only family.

And then she lifted her lashes and a spark of determination turned the color of her eyes to a smoky umber. Diamonds appeared more malleable than the set of her jaw and the line of her lips right then as she replied, "Then so be it."

"Why?" How could she give up everything to put her lot in with him, a practical stranger? "Why do you care?"

"Because I—" She sucked in her lip, worrying the soft bit of flesh for a moment before turning those big eyes up at him. "Because this is my destiny. I'm supposed to do more than sling coffee and tell fortunes. I was given this power to save the world."

He couldn't resist pushing her. "Just like that? Just like that you'll give up the life you've built? You'll come live with me? Work by my side every day? And every night?" He let the implication rumble in his purr. She better be aware exactly what she was walking into, because he'd have enough going on to worry about keeping his attraction to her in check.

Crystal lifted her chin. Awareness, irritation, and desire

swirled in her eyes that turned brown. "I can do it."

He stepped in her personal space, daring her to back away. He held back his grin of satisfaction when she straightened to make herself seem taller. "I'll be watching you. Every day. Just know that it won't be because I fear for you." A statement that wasn't entirely true. "You're asking a lot of me. I'll be expecting a lot from you in return." He focused his gaze on those plump lips, remembering their taste from earlier that day. If she wanted to place herself in his path, who was he not to take what he wanted.

"I will be the consummate professional."

He did smile at that. And his grin grew when her eyes flashed and her nostrils flared as she realized how he took her statement.

"Hey, lovebirds." Ripley turned up the television. "Look at this." He rewound the DVR then pushed play.

Although the sports announcer was reading from a teleprompter, the excitement in his voice was tangible as he said, "There was excitement today at the NCAA track and field championships in Los Angeles, where everyone is talking about the amazing performance of WSU decathlete Chase Armitage." The scene changed from inside the sports studio to one of sunny skies and an emerald green infield.

Preparing for the shot put was a young man, tall, handsome, the textbook definition of healthy. Long dark hair curled around his ears and brushed muscular shoulders kissed golden by the sun. His farm-boy good looks reminded Max of Clark Kent in his early years.

The young man craned his neck to the left, then right, then worked his arms back and forth, pinching his shoulder blades together. In his hands, the sixteen-pound shot put looked as light as a tennis ball as he rolled it between his palms before settling it against his neck. Once, twice, thrice he spun, then launched the rock into the air with a soft grunt.

He turned and waved at the cheering crowd without looking at where it landed. His smile showed confidence that he tossed it farther than anyone.

"After the first day of competition, Armitage is leading the pack by an enormous margin," the announcer continued as more footage of the competition rolled. "The twenty-two-year-old senior from Centralia, Washington, has come out of nowhere and has shattered, no, obliterated every world record. Watch this replay of the hundred-meter dash."

Armitage took an early lead, leaving the others in his dust, but Max noticed that it appeared as if he pulled short before crossing the finish line.

"Wow." Doc whistled. "He made that look so easy."

"Yeah." Ripley wiggled his brows up and down. "Almost too easy?"

Crystal gasped and braced her hands against the couch. Max wrapped an arm around to steady her, waiting with hair-thin patience for her vision to recede and she returned to him. Damn, the first thing they were going to work on was her control. These spells left her too vulnerable and gave him a near heart attack each time.

Ah, fuck. She was so under his skin already. If he thought he could walk away from her now, the only person he was fooling was himself.

He held his breath until her shoulders relaxed and her vision refocused. "What did you see?"

She smiled. "We're going to LA"

CHAPTER ELEVEN

Three months later...

CRYSTAL TIGHTENED THE straps of her leather gloves and adjusted the fit of her fingers in the snug material as she waited for the search and rescue mission to begin. This was the fourth search their team had been on in the last month, and already they were gaining the reputation of being the best at safely and efficiently bringing the lost home.

October temperatures in the mountains averaged a cool forty-five degrees. Luck was on their side with the thermometer holding steady, and the sun shining bright and clear. If it were any warmer, the search for the missing hiker would be called off due to threats of avalanches in the higher elevations.

Not that a crush of falling snow could stop her team, she thought with pride.

"All right, people." A deep, booming voice broke over the din. Sheriff Lancaster clapped his hands to capture the attention of the volunteers gathered before him. "Our missing camper is Jeremy Monroe. Age twenty-two, dark hair and eyes. Deputy Davis is distributing a recent photo to you all now. Monroe was last seen leaving his campsite at about 22:30 yesterday evening. He was wearing khaki cargo pants, a red and blue striped long-sleeved T-shirt, and a black, down-filled REI jacket. This information will also be posted under the red tent in the parking lot at the park's entrance. I want all team leaders to meet me there in five minutes to receive area assignments."

He paused to take a breath. The lines around his mouth deepened as the professional, all-business expression on his handsome face melted. "On behalf of the department, the forest rangers, and the Monroe family, I thank you for coming out today and giving your time." His steel-gray gaze came to rest on Crystal and the rest of the team with her. "I have every confidence that with your efforts, this young man will be found and returned to his family. Thank you again."

Whispered conversations echoed off the snow-frosted trees as Lancaster and his men cut through the crowd.

"All right, pals and gals, I'll be back." Max set off for the tent, drawing the admiring attention of several women, and a few men, as he passed.

Who could blame them, Crystal lamented with both satisfaction and discontent. Max shouldered the mantle of leader with the same elegant grace as he did that black leather duster of his.

He moved with fluidity and purpose in a lethal combination of sex and power. His slicked-back ebony hair exposed the sharp angles of his cheeks and a jawline that begged to be coaxed into softening with gentle kisses. The dark wraparound sunglasses he wore only added to his mystique. Authority seeped from his every pore, demanding attention and respect. Assuming command was a position Max was born for, only he never believed it.

To her delighted surprise, and immense relief, Max had committed 100 percent into building them into a team of superheroes who could soon be able to take down his father's operatives.

Of course, it hadn't been all roses and sunshine. They had their growing pains, like every new partnership did, but Max led without being pushy or insulting, recognizing each person's talent and strengths, and deferring to their expertise if he didn't have the answer.

Crystal sighed and dug the toe of her boot into the dirt. The man was on her mind twenty-four/seven. If she wasn't in the same room as him, she was thinking of him. If she wasn't thinking of him, she was dreaming of him. Every night she woke with a moan in her throat and her hand between her thighs, trying to alleviate the ache he ignited.

Damn that vision that still haunted her. Naked, sweaty, entwined limbs as they rolled around on teal satin sheets. Who the hell owned teal satin sheets?

Once, she had snuck into his room just to check the bedding. The discovery of cream, four-hundred-thread count cotton under the thick black comforter had almost brought her to happy tears. If it had been anyone else, she would have found her illogical paranoia hysterical. It wasn't so funny when she was the one afflicted.

Her purpose of living on his mountain was to help mankind, not to fall into bed with a man whose past showed he used women as a relief valve to blow off steam. Oh yeah, she had seen more than enough memories of his previous relationships, if one could call a series of one-night stands relationships. Equally telling was witnessing how he had preferred it that way.

No way was she jeopardizing their work for a few nights of steamy kisses and mind-blowing sex. She had more self-respect than to get caught up in the promise of those magical hands.

At least she liked to think she did. The man was more tempting than the last square of a pan of double chocolate brownies.

"Oh my God," Chase groused, breaking into her maudlin thoughts. With his Native American heritage, his tan skin and sunglasses made him appear more ready for a day at the beach than one spent in the mountains. He huffed and thumped the back of his head against the back of their SUV. "What is taking so long? Why doesn't Max just tell them we can find this dude in ten minutes and get on with it?"

Chase had the ability to run, throw, jump, and lift more than any man on the planet. Unfortunately, he was also a product of the *now, now, now* generation and had the patience of a three-year-old.

"Watch it with the real names," Doc hissed. "These people don't know that we can. Remember?"

"Well, they should," he muttered. "They already look at us like we're freaks. Why can't we show 'em what we can really do?"

Doc sighed. "We're not ready. We don't want to expose ourselves too soon." She tugged her black knit cap over the tops over her ears. Crystal wore a matching one that fully covered her hair.

"These search and rescues are boring. I'm getting tired of going after people who are too stupid to take a cell phone with them before they head out into the woods. Look at Therian, he's asleep." He nodded at Ripley, who was dozing at their feet in the form of a German shepherd. "When can we go after the real bad guys? Like drug runners or Madden, even?"

Doc shared an indulgent smirk with Crystal. "We gotta

crawl before we can walk, sport."

"I can do way more than walk," he grumbled and flexed the muscles in his arms, straining the leather of his coat.

Crystal chuckled and scanned the crowd around them.

Chase was right about how they attracted curious stares whenever they went out as a unit. Although they were careful not to show their powers, she'd be shocked if people didn't suspect something was...different...about them.

Their colorful winter scarves didn't do much to soften the military cut of their liquid-armor-lined leather jackets and the lightweight, flame-resistant pants and black boots that protected their legs. Even though this was a simple search and rescue, this was also their chance to experiment with how best to protect themselves on future missions.

Completing the ensemble for them all were dark sun-glasses that Max had tricked out way better than anything available on the market. They were both camera and monitor yet appeared to be nothing more than an ordinary pair of overpriced designer sunglasses.

There was a soft pop from the earpiece Crystal wore before a woman's voice came across the line. "Is this the missing person?"

A photo of Jeremy Monroe appeared on the right lens of her glasses.

"Affirmative," she replied to Addison, the newest mem-ber of their team.

"Cool," she said over the click-click sound of fingers working away at a keyboard. "I'll see what information I can dig up. Check his social media feeds."

"Copy that."

Addison's talents were in technology. Max had discov-ered her just after they had moved in with him on his mountain and she had hacked into his gaming network. He reasoned her skills would be better used working for them than against them and had created a techno-geeks' paradise in his computer room.

Crystal resettled her sunglasses on her nose, anxious to get on with the search herself. "I'm going to question the girlfriend. See what really happened before Monroe took off at night by himself."

The others nodded, and she made her way through the crowd to where Monroe's family stood, huddled under a cluster of pine trees.

The information the mission commander had issued was that Monroe was on a camping trip with his girlfriend and a few friends from school. Supposedly he had gone to gather firewood and was reported missing when he didn't return.

Monroe's mother and father were talking with a deputy. Worry lined both of their faces, aging them in a way only fear for their child could do.

Off to the side stood a young woman. White blonde pigtails stuck out from under her pink knit cap. The red around her eyes matched the red of her nose as she struggled to hold back her tears. Her shoulders trembled under the comforting arm of the young man holding her. He was murmuring words of encouragement to her as Crystal approached them.

She gave them what she hoped was her most pleasant and unobtrusive smile. "Hi, I'm…Tabitha. You're Jeremy's girlfriend, correct?"

The blonde sniffed once and burrowed closer to the man as she nodded. "I'm Ashley. This is our friend Dan. He's dead, isn't he?" she burst out. "That's why the military is here, isn't it?"

"Military?" Crystal squeaked in surprise. "Where?"

"You." Dan gestured at her and toward the rest of the squad across the lot. "What are you guys, army or National Guard? Why would they call you out unless it was bad?"

Crystal laughed and rocked back on her heels. "Oh, no. We're not military. We're a private firm. We like to help out where we can."

"Really?" Ashley sagged with obvious relief. "You all look so professional. I thought—I mean—" She broke down into tears.

"I understand." Crystal placed her hand on the girl's arm in comfort. "I just wanted to let you know that we're going to do everything we can to find him and bring him back."

The girl nodded again, her breath shuddering with heaving sighs.

"Ashley, I'm sure you've been asked this already, but is Jeremy the type to wonder off on his own? Was he happy, agitated, inebriated?"

She paled under her cold-flushed cheeks and shot a nervous glance at Dan. "No, he was fine. We don't know where he could have gone, or why he disappeared."

Crystal smiled even as a weight of doubt pulled at her stomach. "Well, any information is helpful in a missing-persons case." She tugged her glove off and extended her hand. "Thank you for your time."

Ashley's mitten-covered hand grasped hers, meek and trembling.

She turned to Dan, who slid his bare palm against hers in a strong grip. "Thank you," he said.

Before he let go, Crystal scanned his memories of the

last twenty-four hours. Thank goodness the sunglasses hid the narrowing of her eyes, otherwise he might have suspected that she would have dropped him to the ground if she had the chance. Her smile faltered as she clenched her teeth.

The lying, cheating little SOBs. No wonder they were afraid for Monroe. A betrayed man alone on a mountain was usually not a rational one. They *should* be hanging their heads in shame and be sick with fear for what they had done.

A compassionate person would probably walk away and leave them to wallow in their guilt. But she abhorred cheating and couldn't resist twisting the screws a little. "You know, my team and I are going to do everything we can to find him, no matter what condition he's in."

"Condition?" Ashley's voice wobbled.

"Yes, condition. We don't know why he wandered off, so we have to consider the possibility that maybe Jeremy wanted to get lost. By finding him, we could end up angering him, or cause him to make poor choices. There is also his physical well-being to consider. He's been out in the freezing elements for hours with little protection, food, or water. He could have fallen down a ravine, been trapped under an avalanche, or worse. If we find him, the man who comes back will not be the same man you knew. You better prepare yourself for that." She paused to let her words sink in. "But like I said, our team always finds our man. Dead or alive. Have a good day."

With her cheeriest wave, she left them alone to simmer in their shame.

Ashley's renewed wailing turned several heads in their direction.

Okay. That might have been a little too evil. Karma might bite her in the ass later, but she couldn't help feeling a bit of satisfaction about pushing a distressed young woman to tears, but Crystal held little patience for those who believed their actions went without consequence. If Monroe had come to harm, it was all on the heads of those two.

Max met up with her on the way back to the others. "Did you know that you look like a cute little ladybug in those glasses?" he teased with his signature boyish grin. The one that made her want to smile back and curl under his arm and snuggle against his side for as long as...well, forever.

Oh, how she hated that smile. Fun, teasing Max was as just as difficult for her to resist as powerful, in-charge Max. Hell, the man was just plain irresistible, period. It was easier to hang on to her resolve to remain just colleagues when he spent hours in his workshop creating his inventions. When he emerged from his cave and tried to draw her into his world with his killer smile and requests to play video games, she felt like a shrew bitch when she turned him down.

Didn't he understand that anything other than a working relationship between the two of them was impossible? Friendship would lead to her wanting more from him, and that led to only one destination: heartbreak. Emotional distance was her only hope to maintain her professionalism where he was concerned.

"Did you get our coordinates?" she asked, all cool and no-nonsense.

The edges of his smile dimmed. "Yeah, I've got them."

"Good." She nodded once and kept marching.

"Hey, wait a second." He snatched her hand as she passed and pulled her close.

Physically she stiffened, while inside she melted like chocolate under a hot marshmallow. The heat between them grew as his hand came to rest on her waist, his fingers spread wide to caress her hip. She clenched her teeth to stop the shudder that threatened to give her attraction away.

"Later tonight, what say you and me grab my telescope and head to the clearing? There's supposed to be a spectacular meteor shower tonight." His voice dipped low to slip over her like warm honey.

Maybe she should have had a bigger breakfast, then maybe Max wouldn't sound so damn edible. "Is everyone else going?"

His lip curled in a snarl for half a second. "Nope, just you and me. We haven't had much of a chance to have any alone time."

She pushed against his chest, desperate for a millimeter of space. "That sounds like a date. Not a good idea."

His fingers tightened with possession, pulling her flush against his body. "Why not? I thought you wanted us to be friends. I know I do. There's a spark between us that I've been dying to investigate. Come on, come with me. Please," he whispered as his head lowered.

Their noses bumped gently before he brushed a line of soft kisses along her cheek. Crystal closed her eyes, fighting the need to agree even as her fingers gripped the leather of his coat as if she would never let go.

Her breath hitched as his memories of his morning traveled through the connection of his lips on her skin. She saw him in the car on the way to the site and getting dressed for the mission. And before that, standing in the shower. Steam billowed around him as he braced one hand against the tile wall and leaned his head back while stroking his cock. His features tightened before he groaned her name and released his cum into the hot spray. The mixture of relief, loneliness, and dissatisfaction on his face were emotions that she was all too familiar with.

Oh, God. Crystal jumped out of his arms with a strangled moan. Did he project his thought to her on purpose, or was it her own longing playing her, desperate for any intimacy between them?

In the end, though, she knew the truth. Lust and sex, that's all it was between them outside of a professional courtesy. A meaningful relationship was something neither of them wanted or needed at this stage of their training. In the hierarchy of global importance, hot sex was at the bottom of her list. Right?

"Stop. Please." The desire she couldn't hide, even to herself, roughened her voice. "Dating and work do not mix. This time is about finding Jeremy Monroe. We need to focus on that."

She stalked away before she said *Fuck you* to her convictions and ran back into his arms. The disappointment drawing his lips down matched the squeeze around her heart.

Being an adult about this was the right thing to do. Of course it was. Still, she was going to need a lot of therapy time with a gallon of mud pie ice cream the moment she returned home.

"It's about time," Chase exclaimed when he saw them. He tilted his head from side to side, popping the joints in his neck before swinging his arms back and forth to stretch his muscles. "Where to, boss man?"

Ripley jumped to his paws, eager to go as well. He shook his big body, knocking the dust from his fur. The glittering silver chain around his neck glinted in the sun. The snake-like design adjusted to whatever form Ripley took and contained a camera that connected back to headquarters so Addison could direct them when necessary.

"There are six teams heading out. We're heading north, north by northwest, not far from Madden's last-known location."

Her stomach jumped when Max mentioned the primary reason why they had agreed to assist on this case. It was the same reason for everything they did. Madden Senior.

Max's father was an elusive bastard. Whenever Max found an outlet to expose Madden for the traitor he was, it disappeared faster than the last pair of designer sandals at an end-of-summer sale.

Ripley had tried searching Madden's estate several times in a variety of different animal forms and always come up empty. His undercover work stopped when his rodent form was discovered and an exterminator was called in. The mark on his tight backside, from where a trap snapped on his tail, lasted for days, but it was falling ill to rat poison that was the last straw and he called an end to the dangerous searches.

Their focus changed to Madden's other installations when Addison discovered the businessman had secretly purchased portions of the Cascade Mountains. Satellite photos were inconclusive as to what was transpiring on the land, so this particular search and rescue mission was the perfect cover to go poke around. If Madden was nearby, he would have been notified that rescuers were combing the area, and wouldn't be surprised to see people wandering around his neck of the woods.

"This is reconnaissance only, right?" she asked. They were getting better as a team, but in no way were they ready to go head to head with the big man—yet. "Everyone is clear that this is not the time for any Rambo-Terminator type actions."

Max's reply was said in just a slow-enough tone to set off her internal alarms. "Right. We'll get a lay of the land and come back later with a more defined plan of attack." His smile was warm and reassuring. Not. "Does everyone have their earpiece in? Network, display a topographical map of the area on our screen."

"Uploading now," Addison replied.

Their custom earpiece was another of his inventions, designed specifically to pick up the sound of their voices from the vibration of their vocal chords through the inner ear. It eliminated the need for a microphone and funneled out background noise. The soft latex casing was flexible enough that Ripley could shift and it would remain in place, no matter what he morphed to and from.

"Did you find out anything else from the girlfriend?" Doc asked Crystal as she secured the straps on her backpack.

"Oh yeah. Either the sheriff was holding out on us, or the girlfriend was holding out on him. Monroe found her and his best friend having sex in the woods. A fight broke out, and he took off. That was the last they saw of him."

"Great," Doc huffed. "So instead of a missing camper, we now have an angry, distraught lover who may not be thinking rationally, wandering aimlessly in the woods."

"Exactly. I haven't gotten a vision of where he is, but I know where the fight occurred."

"Good thing I swiped this when no one was looking." Chase produced a gray T-shirt from his pack.

"What is that?" she asked.

"Monroe's shirt."

"Where did you get it?"

His smug grin revealed beautiful white teeth. "Being faster than lightning has its advantages. Swiped this from his bag when everyone was listening to the sheriff. Here, boy, get a whiff of this." He held the shirt down low for Ripley.

The German shepherd shot him a look that should have dropped him dead. Ripley hated being treated like a common pet in animal form, which Chase loved to exploit at every opportunity.

The kid had better watch it. Ripley was very good at retaliation. When they had first arrived on the mountain, Max originally designed Ripley's camera collar with a set of heart-shaped dog tags engraved with the name "Fifi." To add insult to injury was the electric shock device embedded in the chain that zapped him whenever he left his room.

In response, Ripley demonstrated how all of the monkey species flung their own poo. It was an Animal Planet lesson they could have all done without.

"Right." Max choked back his laughter and clapped his hands once. "Let's move out. Prism, take the lead."

Crystal nodded and settled her own backpack that carried water, some food, and thermal blankets on her shoulders.

Instead of leading them to the quadrant of forest they had been assigned to, she directed them straight to the campsite Monroe and his friends had been partying at earlier in the weekend.

The tents had long since been removed, and a few bits of trash littered the space. A black ring of soot was all that remained of the roaring, cheerful fire.

"This way." Crystal led them deeper into the woods,

retracing the route Dan had made to the rendezvous site he had arranged with Ashley earlier that day. A little secret nookie while the others were supposedly asleep. What an idiot he was to think they wouldn't get caught.

"The fight occurred right there." She gestured to a heavy cluster of trees. "There was a lot of yelling and shouting, then Monroe took off in that direction."

"What in the hell do you think you're doing?" A group of men emerged from the foliage, matching frowns were carved on their foreheads.

Marcus Boudreaux. Since Max and his group's first search and rescue mission, Boudreaux and his hunting buddies had been nothing but a pain in the ass. Something about the man gave Crystal the creeps, and that was without having to use her powers. Maybe it was his beady black eyes or the way he licked his lips whenever he glanced in her direction.

He was dressed as if he had stepped out of a LL Bean catalog and carried that air of thinking he was better than everyone else. Whenever he spotted them at the mission base, his lip curled as if he were smelling shit. The feeling was mutual.

Boudreaux set the tip of his teak walking stick with the ebony handle into the dirt near his shiny black boots. "This area was given to us to search. Quit poaching."

Max's dark brows arched over the top of his glasses. "I thought the goal was for the kid to be found, didn't matter by whom. We have a lead that brought us here."

"Tell me what the lead is. Lancaster gave us this area to search, not you."

"Like I care."

"Just who do you weirdos think you are, anyway?"

Boudreaux sneered like a child who realized he wasn't the coolest kid in school anymore. "Wearing those ninja outfits like a bunch of freaks. We're going to find this kid first and prove that you're nothing but a group of whack-jobs who got lucky a few times."

Crystal and her team froze. The forest stilled as if it sensed that a beast was being provoked. Even Ripley pulled his nose from the dirt to stare the pitiful man down.

"I don't consider a search where a man's life is at stake a game, Boudreaux," Max replied in a tone encased with ice. A slow smile curled one corner of his lips in a way that shot shivers down Crystal's spine. He was planning something. "But since you do, I'd like to propose a wager. First team that finds Monroe wins a thousand bucks."

"A grand?" Boudreaux sank back on his heels and shot assessing glances at his cohorts. "Make it two, and a date with the busty one." He nodded at Crystal.

Eww. "Right," she barked in laughter. "The busty one has taste, *and* a brain. I'm not a prize, asshole."

"Done."

"Hey!" She whirled on Max. "What the hell?"

He winked at her. "Don't worry, sweetheart. We can't lose." Ripley barked twice and took off into the forest. "See. We're already in the lead."

She saw Max's fingers twirl as he turned to follow.

A crack from above brought their attention up as a barrage of tree branches snapped from their trunks. With shouts of surprise, Boudreaux's men dove to the ground, scattering to escape the heavy, prickly pile that crashed to the ground in a cloud of pines needles. The impromptu blockade effectively blocked their path.

"I will so kill you," she muttered to Max's retreating

back.

His sly chuckle went straight into her earpiece and pooled into her center, warming her from within.

"Intrepid, keep pace with Therian," Max instructed, using Chase's code name.

"On it. You know, I kinda liked that ninja comment. How about I change my name to 'Ninja of Death'?"

"No," came the quick, definitive response from Crystal, Max, and Doc Kelly.

"Fine," the young decathlete sulked, then took off at a brisk jog, easily keeping pace with Ripley's long graceful strides.

The other three followed at a slower but still-rapid pace. Thick leafy ferns and twisting vine maple reached out to pull on their legs as they moved deeper into the forest and farther away from the trail.

The crisp mountain air burned Crystal's lungs and cleared her sinuses while the pungent aroma of vegetation and wet earth made the waffles she had for breakfast roll in her stomach. She was a city girl at heart, and all the nature she'd been exposed to recently was new and not altogether pleasant. At least she no longer flinched at every spider and bug that crossed her path.

"Network, bring up Therian's camera to our monitors," Max directed as they fell further behind the much faster pair.

"Image up now."

"Ooof." Crystal tripped over a root protruding from the ground and regained her footing. "Hey, can you move the image to the top left corner?"

"Oops, sorry, Prism."

The image of blurry forest floor zipped from the bottom

of the lens up and away from her view of the ground. "Thanks."

The shot from Ripley's camera showed a rapid stream of green and brown as he raced through the hemlocks. His paws were silent on the forest floor as Chase ran beside him just as soundlessly.

Half an hour passed as they climbed to higher ground, crossing the snow line. The temperature dropped, which worried Crystal. If it was this cold in the middle of the afternoon, how had Monroe fared during the black of night?

Chase's voice came across the line. "We're coming up on something."

In her glasses, Crystal saw Ripley slowing to a stop in a field of asters dotted with patches of snow. The sea of green and purple waved in the breeze and rolled to the edge of a steep drop. As Ripley leaned over the side, they saw down to the rocky bottom where a creek cut through the mountain. Brush, bramble, and piles of snow broke up the forbidding brown and white landscape that painted a stark contrast to the peaceful meadow of flowers. According to the map on the glasses, Chase and Ripley were a quarter mile ahead of them.

"To your left," Crystal said and picked up her pace. "I see a patch of red and blue off to the left."

"I see it, too," Chase said. "I'm heading down."

Max used his powers to flatten the foliage in front of them like a rolled-out carpet to speed their progress.

Crystal's legs ached as she ran toward the drop-off point, her pack bouncing wildly against her back.

"Hey. Hey, man. Monroe. Can you hear me?" Chase was picking his way down the rocks to the lump of clothing that didn't stir, careful not to scatter rocks onto the pile. He reached out and joggled the down-filled coat. After a few tries, he looked up at them with a grim shake of his head. "It's him. Oh man. This isn't good."

The image in their lens switched from Ripley's camera to the one from Chase's glasses. Monroe lay still, his leg twisted at a horrible angle at the knee. Blood crusted in his hair where his head rested against the rocks.

"Network, patch me to the sheriff," Max directed.

"Patching now," Addison replied.

"Lancaster," came the gruff reply over their earpieces a few seconds later.

"Sheriff, it's Garan. We've found your hiker. We are about a mile and a half northwest of the campsite, near the ravine. He's down and out near the bottom."

"How is he? Do you need an extraction?"

"I'm sending a team down to him. Stand by for more information."

"Will do. Out."

"Don't move him," Doc instructed. "Is he breathing?"

"No." Chase knelt and pulled off his gloves to lay his fingers alongside Monroe's neck. "No pulse either, and he's as cold as ice."

"Fuck," Max grunted and raced ahead to where Ripley barked and turned in circles, waiting their arrival.

Crystal skidded to a stop at the edge of the cliff, sending a shower of rocks skipping down the hillside. The steep drop appeared even more daunting in person. Doc immediately set off down the side, heedless of the danger. Her boots slid in the gravel, forcing her to reach out to grab at a group of vines to slow her fall.

"Doc, brace yourself," Max warned.

"For what? Ahh!" she squeaked as Max telekinetically

lifted her into the air and deposited her to where Chase and Ripley waited with the boy.

She looked up at him with her mouth wide open. "Thanks?"

Max nodded and crouched low to better observe the scene below.

Doc shook off the surprise of her brief flying excursion and knelt by the body. "Shit. Both the tibia and fibula of his right leg are broken." She pushed her glasses to perch on top of her head as she narrowed her eyes, sweeping her hand from the top of his head to his toes. "This isn't right. I thought he might have fallen down the cliff, but his injuries aren't consistent with a fall. His wrists and arms are fine, not even swollen, which means he didn't try to stop his fall. And look at his cheek. The bone is shattered, but this bruise is wide and has a definite shape. If he was injured in the fall, it wouldn't have such a crisp pattern."

"How did he die?" Max asked.

"Broken neck, but I don't think it was from a fall."

Max hummed low in his throat as he stroked his chin before turning to Crystal. "Prism, do you think you could still see his memories?"

"I don't know. Haven't been around a lot of people who've died. But I can try."

He shot her an encouraging smile. "I'm going to float you down. Ready?"

She braced herself and nodded, gasping as her feet left the ground. How was one supposed to hold their body while floating in the air? She bent her knees and tightened her core as if she were snowboarding. But since she had never boarded before, she felt as if she were a cartoon character, wildly waving her arms as she pitched forward and back.

"Relax, Prism," Max's soothing baritone cooed in her earpiece. "I won't let you fall." True to his word, he set her gently down on the sharp slope.

"Thanks," she said with a sigh and turned her attention to the task.

Tears blurred her vision as she dropped to her knees next to the lifeless body of Jeremy Monroe. No matter how the young man died, it was a crime that his life ended so abruptly.

The memory of the hope in his parents' eyes as she promised to find their son struck her like an iron fist, knocking the air from her lungs. If only they had been faster. If only her powers had warned her of the tragedy that was to be, the boy would still be alive.

Doc settled a hand on her shoulder and murmured, "We can still do right by him, sweetie. I believe in you."

Crystal jerked and met Doc's dark, knowing gaze. She was right. They hadn't been able to save him, but they could still right the wrong and bring closure to his family.

She swallowed her guilt and removed the glove off her left hand and lay her palm against Jeremy's dirty, blood-streaked forehead. Diving into his memories was as if she were swimming through dark molasses. Images faded the moment she touched upon them, swirling, shifting, never quite forming a solid shape until she came upon the last moments of his life.

"Anything?" Max called down to her.

She drew away with a curse and slid her glove back on. "Most of it was too murky to make out. Except his last memory. Two men, armed and dressed in black military gear. One of them swung and hit him across the face with the stock of his rifle. He blacked out after that."

Doc nodded. "Explains the damage to his cheek."

"What are two military guys doing out here?" Chase asked. "And why did they knock him out and dump him over a cliff?"

"Excellent questions, Intrepid," Max replied. "And we're going to find out."

"Maestro," Addison broke in. "The sheriff wants an update."

Max bit back an impatient curse. "Put him on."

"Garan, tell me something good."

His lips tightened before he answered, "I'm sorry, Sheriff. Monroe's dead. It appears he passed a while ago."

From her earpiece, the heavy rise and fall of Lancaster's breathing kept time with the beating of Crystal's heart. It grew deeper and slower, as if he were processing the information and dealing with it in a way so as not to draw attention from others who might have been nearby.

"All right," he finally responded in a low, hushed tone. "We'll get a chopper ready to go. They should be there in about twenty minutes. Can you hang tight till they arrive?"

"Twenty minutes? Yeah, we'll be here," Max answered.

"Good. Good." He signed off.

"Prism, where was Monroe when he was hit?"

Crystal blinked up at Max in confusion over the quick change in topics. "What?"

"Did you see where on the mountain Monroe was standing when he was hit?"

She pointed over their heads. "High up, in deeper snow." When Max disappeared from their sight she shouted, "Hey, what are you doing?"

"Going after the attackers," came the reply over her earpiece.

"What? Are you insane?" She grabbed hold of vines and branches and scrambled up the hill. "You can't just go charging around the mountain. You have no idea what you're looking for."

Max chuckled. "I might not, but Therian does. He's caught a scent."

"You motherfucker," she grunted as her boot slipped off a foothold and she dangled from the foliage.

"Hang on, girlie," was all the warning she received before Chase scooped her in his arms and charged up the hill.

Crystal let loose with a startled squeak and threw her arms around his neck in a chokehold.

"Gotta breathe, baby girl," he wheezed.

"Sorry." She barely loosened her grip. "We have to stop Maestro. He can't just go rushing into danger. You are not Rambo!" she shouted at where he disappeared into the tree line.

"You and I both know that ain't going to happen," Chase chuckled, not even breathing hard with the effort of carrying her and keeping up with the dimwits ahead.

"Hey, what about me?" Doc called out.

"Stay with Monroe and tell us when you see the chopper," Max instructed. "You heard the sheriff, we have twenty minutes."

A frustrated cry worked up Crystal's throat and burst from between clenched teeth. "Maestro, stop right now. You don't know who or what you're looking for. You don't even have a plan."

"Actually, sweetheart, I do." The smugness in his reply made her want to slap him silly. "We're on Madden property now. Monroe stumbled onto something he shouldn't have. The plan is to find out what or who that was."

"Great. That's a shitty plan," she muttered.

Ripley led them higher into deeper snow. It grated on her pride that Chase carried her as if she were a child, but she knew the boys wouldn't hesitate to leave her in a snow drift if she was on her own power. Did she want to nail the men who brutally ended Jeremy Monroe's life? Hell yeah, but not at the expense of her teammates' safety.

Without warning, Ripley pulled up short. He barked and ran back and forth in front of a fine wire fence, preventing them from going forward.

Crystal jumped out of Chase's arms before they came to a full stop. "Where are we?"

Trees and bushes, heavy with snow, surrounded them in typical forest fashion. Nothing signified that anything was out of the ordinary until she peered closer at the base of the fence and noticed the snow was darker in places where it had been tamped down in a line edging the fence. Foot-prints.

Max studied the fence as if it were a puzzle. "There's more than meets the eye here."

"Are we being watched?" Crystal scanned the trees overhead in search of cameras.

"Possibly." He held his palm out. "Let's get some mole-cules moving."

Before them, the air seemed to vibrate and grow thick. A wall appeared, shimmering as if it were made from a million fireflies. It stretched twenty feet high and ran in both directions as far as she could see.

Max chuckled and shook his head. "This is not your common electric fence, my friends. A normal fence pulses the energy, to give whatever latched onto it a chance to get away once they've realized their mistake. This is five thousand volts of constant electric current. Whoever is on the other side is not messing with the deterrents."

Chase rolled his head to the left and right. "I think I can make that."

He jogged back several yards and warmed up with a few deep squats.

Crystal stared at him, her eyes wide in disbelief. "Please tell me you are not planning on jumping over a wall of electricity."

With a wide grin, he set his feet then exploded into action. He leapt over the towering height as if he were Tigger, landing on the other side in a fine cloud of snow.

"Therian, watch over Prism." Max spread his hands out, palms down. He levitated off the ground, his boots barely clearing the top of the fence as he soared over to land next to Chase. He swayed for a moment on his feet then caught his bearing. "Stay hidden and let us know if anyone comes this way."

Without a look back, he turned and led Chase behind a series of boulders before disappearing through a fissure in the hillside.

Her throat closed in outrage, leaving her only able to emit a few grunts and peeps as if she were a choking bird as she stared with disbelief to where Max and Chase disappeared.

Was he fucking kidding? At the first good whiff of Madden, Max was off like a snot-nosed kid, thinking he could run with big boys. What about waiting until they were ready? What about working as a team? This was exactly the type of behavior she warned him about that was going to get him killed. They weren't ready for this kind of mission.

A wet nose nudged her hand and she turned on Ripley with a snarl. "Are you ditching me too?"

He barked once, then nudged her into a tight cluster of trees.

"What, are you my babysitter now?" He sat on her feet in response. "Thanks for nothing. Network, tell me—"

"Already on it, girlfriend. Jackass one is on your left, jackass two on the right."

Dual images of rock tunnels streamed in across the lenses of her glasses, leaving her dizzy.

"If either of you get hurt or maimed, I'm kicking your asses," she threatened.

Max's answering chuckle did nothing to ease her worry.

CHAPTER TWELVE

MAX DREW SMALL, shallow breaths, straining to hear every sound over his pounding heart as he followed Chase down the narrow tunnel deep into the side of the cliff. The infrared function on his glasses automatically came on the moment they stepped into the darkness.

"I'm going to race ahead and see what's shaking," Chase whispered before his green image blurred and stretched into a streak of lime-colored light that reminded Max of a tail of a comet.

The soft fall of Max's boots treading over the rocky terrain followed at a slower pace, much to his chagrin. But he made use of the delay by committing every twist and turn to memory with the intent of returning in the near future. With a pissed-off brunette waiting to cuss him out and the unknown lying ahead, who knew how much time he'd have to investigate.

Crystal's ire over being left on the safer side of the fence was unavoidable, and something he felt zero remorse over. Where he was going was far too dangerous for her skill set, and watching out for her would be a distraction of epic proportions.

Despite her determination to hold him at arm's length, her unfailing optimism and full lips drew him in like a tractor beam, making him hunger to experience that passion in other areas of their relationship. If he had his way, he'd sweep her away to a place where tragedy never touched her. And she'd fight him like a hellcat if he dared make the suggestion.

Goodness and right ruled her actions, and she truly believed she could make a difference in the world. But he saw how it crushed her that they had been too late to save the boy. By no means did he think her compassion made her weak, but she had to realize they weren't going to save everyone.

Crystal was a tough cookie, but if she didn't learn to distance her emotions from the mission, she was going to fall into a well of depression and guilt so deep she'd never crawl out of. To see that light in her spirit diminish whenever they came up short cut him to the quick.

But just because he was able to move on didn't mean he was immune to the horror they had stumbled upon. Disgust and rage twisted in his stomach over his father having a hand, although indirectly, in ending another life. Monroe was just a poor kid who had thought the worst thing in his life was a cheating girlfriend. And now he was another in a string of innocents Madden would destroy if he wasn't put down soon. Every day that man was allowed to do business was a day that Max failed.

Over the past month, to the world at large, Madden had presented himself as a model citizen and an angelic benefactor, courting Capitol Hill with plans to pull the economy out of the toilet. His "generous" offer to bail out several cities' infrastructures landed his pompous photo on the cover of major magazines around the world, calling him America's savior. Didn't those fools realize that Madden now had his finger in every energy-producing industry across the country? With the billions he stole from the same citizens he was helping, he was only a few strategic steps from controlling how the entire country functioned.

That was why this potential glimpse of Madden's operation was so important. A week prior, this stretch of mountain had come alive in a flurry of activity. Satellite photos showed movement too heavy to be an average group of hikers climbing the trails. But intel from the photos had been inconsistent, with blank spaces appearing in the images, probably from the interference of that wall of energy they passed.

Crystal could bitch at him all she wanted, but there was no way he was passing up this opportunity to investigate.

Chase's voice buzzed in Max's ear. "Hey, boss. Up ahead there's a fork in the tunnel. On the left, looks like barracks, enough for about twenty people. On the right is where it gets interesting. I'm in the shadows, just before the archway at the end."

As Max rounded a corner, a light glowed at the end of the tunnel. With each step, the scent of sweat and diesel exhaust grew stronger. He crept closer and nodded at Chase as he neared. With his hand hovering over the .45 at his side, he carefully peered around the doorway.

A ramp, carved from rock, curved around and down to an area that had been dug out to create a giant warehouse. Soaring high above, floodlights illuminated the area that covered a good fifty yards and was filled with men, crates, and forklifts.

About ten men were down below, all dressed like Max's own team in black winter gear. Bullet-resistant vests covered their torsos, and each had either a HK submachine gun or pistol strapped to their side. A helmet outfitted with a visor and headset obscured their faces. They worked with minimal communication as they catalogued and stacked crates and equipment.

A truck pulling a horse trailer entered from a tunnel opposite Max and Chase. Two men stepped out. The men might have been dressed as ranchers, but they moved like military, sweeping their gaze around the room while keeping motion to a minimum. One lowered the lift gate, exposing more crates inside.

A door near the ramp opened, and another man emerged. He wore a dark blue Helly Hansen coat and ski goggles. A knit cap covered his hair.

What was up with all the thermal wear? It wasn't that cold outside. How in the hell was he supposed to see people's faces if they were covered from head to nuts?

The newcomer motioned to one of the men who lifted out a crate and set it on the ground. A crowbar popped off the lid marked SADDLES with a loud crack as the man in blue knelt closer to inspect the contents.

"Network, zoom in," Max whispered.

The camera in his glasses narrowed in on the brand-new Heckler & Koch XM25 semi-automatic grenade launcher being pulled from its foam casing.

Max rocked back, his breath whooshing out in a gasp. These guys were armed for something the size of a genetically mutated oversized bear. Oh yeah, something huge was going to go down. The only questions now were where and when.

The man in blue nodded and motioned for the box to be added to the others.

Chase tapped Max on the arm and gestured to the un-known man. "Your father?" he mouthed.

Max shook his head. He didn't know who the man was,

but it definitely wasn't Madden. For one thing, Max's father would never cover his eyes. He used his stare as a weapon of intimidation.

So who was this man in charge? Someone from Madden Financial or an unknown from Madden's more illegal ventures?

Reaching into his inner coat pocket, Max pulled out several small disks that resembled a thick magnet. He levitated the tiny cameras and microphones off his gloved palm and sent them soaring through the air to attach to the rock walls and under the forklifts.

"Recording now," Addison announced once the devices were in place.

"*Monsieur.*" A soldier rushed in from the tunnel. His French accent was thick. "Radar is picking up an approaching helicopter."

Shit. Lancaster's ride.

"It probably has to do with that hiker 1032 killed. Monitor the progression and keep me informed," Mr. Blue barked out. His voice echoed oddly in Max's earpiece due to the cavernous space.

Max grabbed Chase by the sleeve and jerked him back into the tunnel to hightail their asses out of there. If those men went out into the forest, Crystal was in danger of being discovered.

And if she was discovered, Lord help them all if she came to any harm.

❖   ❖   ❖

"CRYSTAL, WE'RE COMING up on you hot and heavy," Max's voice crackled in her earpiece with a level of panic that made the air freeze in her lungs.

She poked her head around the tree trunk and saw Max and Chase running in her direction as if the hounds of hell were on their asses. After bearing witness through the video feed on their glasses as to what lay hidden in that mountain, she was more than ready to leave the area before one of those soldiers came along and did to her what they had done to Jeremy Monroe.

Max flew over the top of the electric fence as if he had been born to fly, and Chase hurdled the obstacle like the track star he was. He didn't even break stride as he picked her up and tossed her over his shoulder.

"Goddammit, Intrepid. I can run," she grunted as she bounced painfully into his shoulder.

"Another time, baby doll. We have a copter to catch."

She latched on to the back of his pants and hung on like a cat hanging from the curtains. Being carted around like a sack of potatoes was beyond embarrassing. How could she show her worth to the team if she wasn't even allowed to run on her own?

"It's about time damn time," Doc hollered when they appeared at the cliff's edge.

Crystal slapped Chase on his muscular butt until he dropped her on her feet. She wobbled to a stand and pointed a finger in his face. "No more snatching without permission."

His dimples winked at her. "I make no promises in times of desperation."

She curled her lip in a snarl then turned to look down the valley as the sound of a whirling helicopter blade reached her ears.

Just then, a horrifying *whumpf* came from above. She whipped her head around in time to see snow and ice charge down the mountain in a crashing wave headed straight for them.

"Prism. Prism," Max shouted, his hands hard on her shoulders as he shook her. "What is it?"

Future and present swirled in a kaleidoscope of crazy as she struggled to return from her vision. Biting cold hit the back of her throat as she sucked in a harsh breath that sent her into a coughing fit.

"Avalanche," she managed to wheeze and pointed above them.

"When?"

Thwap, thwap, thwap, thwap

She looked over her shoulder and saw a sleek black helicopter rocketing through the valley. A second later, the sound of a million shattering ice cubes drowned out the swish of the copter's blades.

"Now."

"Incoming!" Max shouted as he pushed her behind him.

He threw his hands into the air as if to catch the massive wave of snow and rock barreling down on them like a giant baseball. Under their feet the earth trembled with the force, trees toppled in the wake of snow like matchsticks in the crush of white. With each foot of ground consumed, the tighter Crystal's lungs constricted, until she nearly passed out from lack of air.

Max groaned, his body quaking as slowly, ever so slowly, the current of white split up the middle. An invisible umbrella curled over them as the snow rumbled past them on either side and down into the ravine.

She wrapped her arms around his middle as he began to sway, and locked her knees to keep them upright. Ripley leaned against her, supporting her behind her legs. Just a little more time was all they needed.

The cacophonous din in her ears continued long after the last of the snow settled. Not even the roar of the chopper registered in her brain.

Max turned in her arms and hugged her close. His chest rose and fell in rapid succession and he trembled in her embrace.

"Are you okay?" he rasped, caressing her back.

"Yeah." She swallowed hard. "You?"

"A little shaky. That was a lot of moving molecules." He chuckled weakly. "Thanks for the heads-up."

"I just wish it came sooner." The heat of his body tempted her to snuggle closer.

"At least it was a warning. Whoa." His knees buckled, but Chase was there to catch him from behind as he continued to cling tight to Crystal.

"Easy, boss. Man, that was awesome," Chase said, laughing with giddy delight.

"Are you guys okay up there?" Doc's voice buzzed in her earpiece.

"We're okay. How about you?" Crystal answered.

"All right, although I can officially say I never want to experience that again."

The radio on Max's belt clicked. His hand still held a fine tremor as he answered.

"Garan."

"Hey," Lancaster barked over the line. "Is everyone all right? I heard there was an avalanche in your location."

"We're good, Sheriff. It slid past us. Barely. Nerves are a little shaky, but we're fine. Looks like the medics are coming in now."

"Good. Get back to base and report in."

"Will do."

Now that the danger was averted, there was no need to continue to plaster herself to Max like a second skin. Although his arms around her did feel nice. Really nice. Too nice.

Yep, it was totally time to put some distance between them.

Apparently, he didn't feel the same, for his hold tightened as she tried to pull away. "Seriously, Max. I'm okay. I'm not going to fall. I'm more worried about you."

"I know." He tightened his arms and guided her away from the cliff's edge, his gaze remained on the helicopter hovering above Doc and the body.

They watched as a skiff and a medic lowered to the ground like an awkwardly shaped spider. Monroe was packaged and settled into position, then hoisted back into the chopper. After he was secured inside, the medic clipped himself to the line and was pulled up next. The pilot nodded at them from behind the windshield before he turned and lifted off. Bits of dirt and rock hit Crystal in the face from the wake of the jet wash.

Once the helicopter was out of sight, Chase raced down to scoop Doc up in his arms and zipped them up the side of the cliff.

She wobbled when he set her down. "I really would like more notice the next time someone sweeps me off my feet."

"I thought you older chicks dug being swept off their feet." When icy silence met his comment, he held up his hands. "What?"

Max shook his head. "Dude. No," he said, drawing out the word as Ripley barked in agreement and took off back toward base.

Doc hooked her arm through Crystal's. "Come on. Let's get back to where the real men are."

"Speak for yourself. I'm done with the entire male species." She matched Doc's long-legged strides the best she could and left the boys with a spectacular view of her swishing backside.

What a complete and utter fuckfest of a day. How were they going to take down a slick, evil mastermind like Madden if they couldn't get through one search and rescue mission without having issues?

Until the males in their group got it through their heads that this was not some complex war game, but real life-and-death situations, she was going to have to work that much harder to make them a success.

It was time to sharpen the nails, lace up the boots, and kick some ass.

CHAPTER THIRTEEN

T HE SECOND STOOD on a perch higher up the mountain-
side, watching through his binoculars as the four
figures disappeared into the forest. He swallowed against the
dryness in his throat and licked his parched lips while his
brain processed what he just witnessed his boss's son do.

Max Madden really did have telekinetic powers. He
wouldn't have believed it if he hadn't seen it for himself. The
night of DeMateo's death had been a flurry of bullets and
explosions that had left him unable to positively recollect
exactly how the events had unfolded. But what he had
attributed to a concussion and chaos had been real. Max
possessed the power to manipulate molecules.

And his father had absolutely no idea.

Hmmm. The Second stroked his chin. Withholding this
bit of information could go very well in his favor, or end in
horrible disaster.

A speculative grin curled his lips as he locked the
knowledge away in his mind. He didn't get to where he was
in the organization without taking a few risks.

With the decision made to keep this little nugget of
information to himself, the tension in his shoulders eased
and a swagger stole into his step as he strode back to the
warehouse.

The junior Madden being in this neck of the woods was
not a coincidence, and he'd be a fool not to suspect that the

brat was up to something. After having witnessed Max's powers, who knew what Junior would be able to do to their mountain stronghold. There were too many variables where the boy was concerned, starting with who were those people with him and how much of the operation had they seen.

Soldier 1032 approached him when he returned to his men. "Sir, the avalanche has blocked several of our exits."

The Second raised a finger to his lips, then to his ear, signaling silence, before turning an assessing eye to the men working around him.

These soldiers, all of who were smuggled into the country, had been plucked from hostile environments around the world. Stripped of their names and identities, they were mercenaries, pirates, warriors trained to use their bodies as weapons. But how would they fare against the mental powerhouse that was Max Madden? Would these men's ability to mindlessly follow orders and the poor strategic skills of Matthew Madden be the weakness that tumbled their grand scheme like a house of cards? Of that, The Second was positive. Fuck all. Apparently he did have to do everything.

With a sharp whistle, he held up his hand and gestured for the entire group to fall silent. In seconds, all work stopped as the men turned toward him with interest.

He sidestepped over to a set of small cases stacked to his right. Selecting one, he set it on top of a taller crate and popped open the lid. Nestled inside were three silver objects shaped like small traffic cones. He pulled one out and closed the case. Setting the timer on the bottom, he placed it in the center of the room. A faint beep sounded before a red laser flashed out of the tip, sending out a magnetic blast that shorted every object with an electrical component in the warehouse. Over the top? Yes. But it was best to err on the side of caution.

He raised his hand to quell the exclamations that burst from the men over losing their communications equipment.

"Gentlemen, our position has been compromised. Everything needs to be reloaded and sent to Delta section, including the barracks. Nothing is to be left behind. Replacement equipment will be issued once the new location has been secured. Move out. Now."

"Everything, *señor*?" 1032 asked.

His right eye twitched at being questioned. "Everything. 1096, 1097," he called for his demolition team. "The moment that the last man and piece of equipment is cleared, close off every point of entrance. Be mindful of how much explosive you use. The last thing we need is the university's seismology department rooting around here as well."

"But *señor*," 1032 interrupted. "*Señor* Madden instructed—"

The Second's fist shot out to connect to the subordinate's jaw with a wicked crack. He bit back a grunt and was thankful that the goggles hid his wince as his hand went numb and pain traveled up his arm. Maintaining authority was imperative at this stage of the game.

"Mr. Madden doesn't know all of the facts. I'm in charge of this operation. An operation that is now in jeopardy because you didn't follow the simple commandment of thou shall not dump the body in thine own backyard. If you have an issue with my leadership, I will deliver you to the immigration authorities myself, in a body bag. Any questions?"

1032 paled under his tan skin. "No, *señor*."

"You have two hours, gentlemen. Move it."

✧ ✧ ✧

IN OCTOBER, TWILIGHT arrived early in the Northwest, turning the sky a deep purple that matched the somber and dreary mood of base camp. The sullen faces of the few remaining volunteers, and the sobs from Jeremy Monroe's family, compounded the ache in Crystal's chest. Between the murdered victim, the avalanche, and the breakdown in the team, the day had been a disaster rivaling the Titanic.

"Oh, crap," Doc muttered next to her. "Here comes Boudreaux."

And the fun continued.

Boudreaux stalked across the gravel, his cronies forming a flock of fowl behind him. His brow was drawn in such a fierce scowl that his eyebrows formed a furry awning over his blazing eyes. His teeth were clenched so tight together, Crystal wouldn't have been surprised if they had ground down to nubs.

Behind her, Max stood strong and silent. An emotion-less mask had settled on his features, making it impossible to guess what he was thinking.

One thing she was certain of was if either man made a smart-ass remark about that stupid bet, she was going to kick them in the nuts. She had had it up to her knit cap with the Y chromosome set.

"I see you finally made it back." A smug smile tugged at Max's lip.

The older man leaned forward and sneered. "No one survives an avalanche without a scratch, and how did you find the body so fast? What's your game? There is some-thing unnatural about you. I don't know what, but I will find out."

"Great. In the meantime, I'll be having a beer."

Boudreaux took a step closer. "Why was it so important to you to find the kid first? Did you think that it would earn you favors from the punk's family or the police? Or were you afraid that your girl here would leave you once you failed?"

"That's it," Crystal snapped. How dare he trivialize the life and death of an innocent man? "You fucking asshole."

She leapt for the bastard with fingers curled into claws and red clouding her vision. What she would do to him once she made contact, she hadn't a clue and frankly didn't care. But she wanted the man to hurt on the outside as much as she did on the inside.

Max caught her around the waist and pulled her tight against his side. "It's okay, sweetheart," he whispered in her ear. His hand stroked down her back. "I know. As much as I'd love to see you rip him a new one, I don't want you to get your hands dirty on this piece of trash."

Max kept his arm securely around her and turned back to Boudreaux. "I can only guess that you would say such insensitive, asinine things because you have been fortunate enough not to have such a tragedy touch your own life. I know that if one of your children had been found in the bloody, crumpled condition we found that young man in, you wouldn't be so quick to be an ass. Although I doubt that."

Crystal blinked back the tears in her eyes and leaned against Max. So he had given some thought about all that was lost on that hillside. That didn't remove him from her shit list, but it did lessen her anger. Slightly.

Max held his hand out, palm up. "I believe money was discussed earlier. I can let it slide if it will put a crimp in your finances."

Boudreaux bit off his curse and reached for his back-pack. His solid gold pen shimmered in the rising moonlight as he opened his checkbook and began writing. "Who do I make it out to? I'm sure you have a real name, Garan."

"Just leave that part blank."

The other man ripped off the check and stretched out his hand. The paper vibrated in his outraged grip. "I'll be watching you."

"Thanks for the warning. I'll be sure to wear something nice."

"Motherfucker," Boudreaux muttered and turned on the toe of his expensive hiking boots and stomped away.

"What is up with that man?" Doc asked.

Crystal sighed. "Classic case of making himself feel better by belittling others. His ex-wife is harassing him for more alimony and his kids are a disappointment."

"Did you get all of that by reading him?"

"Hell no," she said with a snort. That would require touching him. "I overheard him on his cell phone during the last search and rescue."

Lancaster cut across the lot toward them and held out his hand to Max. "Garan, everyone. Are you sure you're all okay? The pilot said that avalanche looked like it was heading right for you."

"We're fine. It wasn't as bad as it appeared, although it was plenty close enough. I'm sorry we were too late to save Monroe."

"You tried your best, which is all I can ask." He re-moved his hat to rub his palm over his short blond hair and shook his head. "I don't know how you all do it, but I'm grateful for the work you've done. If only you could be so efficient with all of my missing-person cases," he joked.

"Actually," Max drawled, "I could have my team take a look, do a little consulting, if that's all right with you. We're very good at thinking outside the box." He handed Lancaster a jet-black business card he pulled from his jacket pocket. A phone number and the word SECURITY in big white letters was all of the information the card entailed.

Lancaster twirled the card around twice, the muscles in his jaw twitching as his eyes narrowed with contemplation. "I just may do that."

"Anytime. We'd like to help where we can."

The sheriff nodded and left, his gaze still focused on the card in his big hand.

"Excuse me."

Crystal turned to see Jeremy Monroe's mother standing a few feet away. Her blonde and gray curls shook with each shuddering breath as she struggled to rein in her tears.

"Thank you. Thank you for helping my boy."

"Oh, Mrs. Monroe." Crystal choked as her heart lodged in her throat. "Please, we didn't do anything. All we did was find him."

"I know. But at least now we know what happened to him and can give him a proper good-bye." She wiped her gloved hand at the wetness on her cheeks. "It was the waiting that was so terrible, and you all ended that. Thank you."

Words failed Crystal. At least aloud. Inside, she wanted to tell this woman that her son died for nothing. That he had been murdered and the ones responsible were alive and well, plotting the downfall of others.

Yeah. And what good would that knowledge do for Mrs. Monroe? Why compound the pain of a mother who could not avenge her child? That was Crystal's job, it was why she was created. Nothing was more important than helping those who couldn't help themselves.

"Mrs. Monroe." Crystal lifted her sunglasses to look the woman in the eye. "My mother was killed years ago and not a day goes by that I wonder if there wasn't some way I could have prevented it. The guilt of surviving is crushing, and there will be days when you can't see the light. When you doubt even the existence of light." She reached out and took Mrs. Monroe's wool-covered hand. "But you have to remember that there *is* a light. Jeremy was with friends and he was loved. That's all we can ask for in life."

The older woman's gray eyes filled with more tears but also understanding. She squeezed Crystal's hand, words she was unable to express caught behind her trembling lips.

Max held out Boudreaux's check. "Some of us started a collection. It's not much, but it should help out with some of your expenses."

Her mouth fell open on a silent gasp. "Is this for real?"

"Yes, ma'am. If you have any trouble, or need anything at all, contact Sheriff Lancaster. He'll know how to reach us."

She looked as if she'd argue, but then threw her arms around Max's shoulders and gripped him tight. "I can't thank you enough."

"Well, you're welcome." Max stood stock still, his arms hanging loose by his sides as he looked toward them for help. When none came, he raised his hands to pat her back with awkward taps. "Don't remember this as the day Jeremy died, but as a day that he had lived."

Mrs. Monroe nodded. "I don't care how weird people say you are. I think you're all angels." With a pat on Ripley's head, she stumbled to the car that was waiting for her.

Crystal sighed, her eyes drifting shut as the turmoil of the day wound down. Her legs trembled from a combination of physical exertion and crashing adrenaline. A hot bath topped her to-do list the moment she returned home. The image was so strong in her mind, she actually felt the heat rising from the water to slide up her back.

Nope. It wasn't a dream. The warmth came from Max, who wrapped his arms around her in a comforting hug.

He brushed a finger down her check and under her chin. "We'll do better the next time."

Right. Next time. If the afternoon taught her anything, it was that the world was just as dangerous as it was the day before. Maybe even more so.

Resolve straightened her spine and she gave him a curt nod. "Damn straight."

A touch of sin curled his lips into the sexiest smile. "After I go over the footage from the mission, how about you and I spend some quality time in a nice hot bath?"

"Oh my God," she groaned and shoved against his chest. Now he was invading her fantasies, too? "Absolutely not."

He tightened his hold as she tried to pull away. The laser-like bead of his troubled gaze burned her through his dark lenses. "Why do you fight me? I just want to be with you."

"Your impulsive actions put the team in jeopardy. You promised that we were in this together, and at the first opportunity you risked our safety and the mission."

"You're right."

"And another thing—Wait, what?" The head of steam she was gathering dissipated in confusion. "What did you say?"

He smiled with contrition and resumed stroking her cheek. "You're right. I risked the team. I risked you. I'm sorry."

"Oh."

Great, just great. How could she ream him out when he gazed at her with such sincerity? "Well, you should be sorry."

He moved his thumb to caress her lips. "Crystal, we needed those details on Madden's hideout. Every scrap of evidence we gather can be used to save millions of lives. I'm sorry that I leapt before I looked, but I don't regret doing it. I promise that I will be more careful in the future. Count on it."

Her lips tingled as he continued his soft touches. In her soul, a battle between her wants versus her needs waged for supremacy. She wanted to kiss away the frown from his lips and rediscover his taste, but she needed to remain aloof and professional. Giving in now would feel so good—now. Tomorrow, she might live to regret it.

"We should be getting back to headquarters." The rasp in her voice betrayed the cool unaffected tone she strove for.

His nostrils flared with exasperation. "What are you afraid of?"

"I'm not afraid of anything. We have work to do. Let's leave it at that."

This time when she pulled away, he let her go. "You are afraid. I don't know what of, but you know you can trust me."

"Can I? After today, I don't know."

CHAPTER FOURTEEN

"**N**ICE BLOCK, CRYSTAL. Do it again," Chase commanded, then swung his staff at her head.

She parried with her own stick. Wood clapped against wood, reverberating in waves into her palms. A quick feint to his head followed with a sweeping kick to his legs knocked them out from under him and sent him sprawling to the mat on his ass.

He blinked up at her from the ground with a gaze caught between impressed and surprise. "Whoa. Well done." He jumped back on his feet and shook his dark hair back into place. "Again."

Crystal nodded and wiped the sweat from her eyes with the back of her hand. Couldn't the little shit even pretend to look winded? She blew the lock of hair that escaped her ponytail out of her eye then braced her feet for his attack. "Bring it, pretty boy."

Well, she *had* asked for his help in building her fighting skills and increasing her stamina, after all. After the Monroe fiasco, she was even more determined to be able to pull her weight when they went out on their missions. If that meant having Chase kick her ass every day, so be it.

Those once-a-week kickboxing and self-defense classes she had taken over the years had laid the foundation, but after one lesson under Chase's tutelage, it was abundantly clear there was a lot she had to learn. It was the hardest she had ever worked, but the results were well worth it. She had lost twenty pounds since coming to the mountain, and toned her belly and the wiggle under her arms. She was growing faster, stronger, sharper.

"Man, Crystal. You're a fast learner," Chase praised when she took him down again with a roundhouse kick to his chest.

He took a sip of water then wiped his forehead with the bottom of his T-shirt, exposing his six-pack abs. Just because he had immeasurable strength and agility didn't mean he slacked off on honing the weapon that was his body to perfection.

Crystal squirted some water from a bottle on her face then wiped it dry with a hand towel.

"Come on, kid." She kicked at Chase's foot, anxious to lose herself in the fight. It was the only time her mind went completely blank, leaving behind thoughts of *him*. "One more round."

He threw his head back and laughed. "Damn, girl, you don't know when to quit. I like that in a woman."

"Less talking, more fighting." She twirled the staff from one hand to the other then rolled her shoulders, balancing her weight on the balls of her feet. She reached out with her third eye, searching the ether for an advantage.

After that cougar attacked her in Portland, she noticed her visions were coming faster and more frequently. Doc Kelly's connection that adrenaline caused by physical pain heightened their powers explained why Crystal's abilities had been so limited from the get-go.

Her ability to call upon the future was getting better, but was far from perfect. This workout session was about experimenting with that power. She might not be able to see exactly how the match would play out, but it was possible that she'd be able to pull a thread from time, anticipate his moves, and hopefully counter them.

No, she corrected. She *would* counter them.

With a quirk of his lips and a squint of his eyes, the battle began.

Chase swung first, aiming low to take out her tiring legs. The staffs clacked like blasts from a shotgun, echoing in the room as she blocked each swing.

From day one, her staff had become like another appendage to her. Guns could run out of ammo, and the recoil and loud pop was a dark reminder that she was preparing to take a life—a notion that disturbed her far too much. Knives required a person to get too close in order to wield them properly, although she did carry one in her waistband just in case.

But a staff, oh… Anything could be used as a staff: a baseball bat, a two-by-four, a dismembered limb.

Chase grunted when she connected a blow to his solar plexus, then spun away with a roundhouse kick that whipped the end of her ponytail.

"That stare you're developing is pretty menacing." He grunted and blocked a blow to his head that was more forceful than simple sparring. He was confident enough in his speed to keep that pretty face of his safe, and he told her never to pull her punches. "Cold. Emotionless. Very effective."

"Thank you," she murmured then ducked his swing.

A flicker winked in her vision, a flash of an image of him attempting to sweep her legs before using his speed to come up behind her.

A second later, Chase swung at her legs. She jumped

over his stick then immediately thrust her staff directly behind her. He doubled over and fell to the ground, holding his gut.

"Jesus, Crystal!" he grunted. "How did you do that?" He rolled on his back like a turtle flipped over on its shell.

"Vision. Saw you move before you actually did," she panted and held out her hand.

"That was awesome." He took her offer to help him to his feet. "Hurts like a mother, but that was totally cool."

For the first time that day, she grinned. It meant a lot for her to be able to keep up with the boys and earn her place on the squad. And Chase was more than likely to give a sarcastic quip than unwarranted praise. He truly was impressed. "I've had a good teacher. Just think how I'll do with more training."

"Lethal. Absolutely deadly. They won't see you coming." He walked to the cabinet and placed his staff on the shelf. "Same time tomorrow?"

"Yep."

"Excellent. I'm hitting the shower. See ya." He jogged out of the room.

Crystal sighed. Was there ever a time when she had been so youthful? Sometimes, it felt as if she had been born old.

Her back hurt, her muscles burned, even her joints ached. But it was all good. All of those aches and pains meant progress, improvement. Even if she was tempted to crawl the entire way to her room.

To ease some of the tension in her body, she bent over and stretched her back and legs, then reached up to the sky, releasing a groan that came from her toes.

"I'm seriously impressed with your skills."

Max stood in the doorway with his hands on his hips. A lock of hair hung in his eyes that her fingers were dying to push back.

He too had gained some muscle in the last few months. With Ripley in the house, the two of them competed over everything from who could stuff the most mini doughnuts in their mouth at once to who could bench the most weight without using their powers.

And now those muscles were displayed in all of their manly glory in a gray cotton T-shirt that stretched across his shoulders and bulging biceps. The ripple of his abs made a faint impression through the material tucked neatly into his black jeans.

Her throat tightened as her tongue swelled in her mouth, hungry for a taste of him. Talk about lethal, the man could make the most jaded prostitute pay *him* for the chance to bed him.

And with that thought, she threw up a mental wall between her head and the rest of her body.

"Chase is a good teacher." She hurried over to the weapons cabinet and closed up shop to make a hasty escape.

"I'd be happy to show you a few tricks," he offered and stepped closer. The spicy scent of his aftershave made her want to bury her nose in his neck and kiss his skin.

"That's okay. I know you're busy with…stuff." Lame. That was so lame.

"I'm never too busy for you." The liquid honey of his baritone slid past her mental barricade and awakened her nerve endings.

"Yeah, I'm, um… I gotta go."

"Wait." He latched onto her wrist as she tried to pass him then let go the moment she raised her brow at him.

"You're doing it again. Why do you deliberately avoid me?"

"I do not. I see you every day."

"For the few seconds it takes to run out of the room. I just want an answer, Crystal. A real answer. What have I done to make you shy away?"

"You're a busy man. I know you've had a lot on your mind." And by a lot, she meant his father.

Every day, they uncovered more of the web that Madden spun. And every day it became clearer that if they removed him with a clean shot to the head, someone else in his organization would continue his work. As much as it galled Max to allow his father to live, until they had a plan to treat the disease and not the symptom, Madden had to be allowed to continue to do business.

"Come on," he said. "You won't even spar with me. Why not?"

A strangled laugh caught in her throat. "I don't want to hurt you or mess up that handsome face."

He arched a black brow. "If you're going to make claims like that, you better be prepared to back them up, Evans." He lifted his hands and beckoned with his fingers. "Come on. Come get me."

"Don't be silly, Max." She turned her back to him and hastened toward the door.

"Have it your way," he warned. But then the thunderous beat of footsteps sounding like a professional left tackle taking a run at the quarterback pounded in her direction.

Newly sharpened reflexes kicked in, and she dropped to the ground and rolled. Max leapt over her and they both landed on their feet at the same time with hands ready in a fighting stance. Her heart pounded and electricity skipped over her skin as she debated whether to walk away or accept the challenge.

Max made the decision for her when he threw a left hook at her head, which pushed her from annoyed to really pissed off.

If he wanted a fight, so be it. He was going to get his ass handed to him on a silver platter.

She blocked his punch with her forearm and yanked a metal staff from her belt, extending the pole with a press of her thumb. In one smooth movement, she followed with a strike to his head and swung back, connecting with a blow to his left oblique.

He backed away with a grunt. Amusement and admiration sparkled in his eyes, turning them aqua blue. He rubbed his side and laughed. "You want to step it up? Okay. Let's see how you do against flying projectiles."

He waved his hands toward the wall and at the stack of clay disks he used for target practice sitting on the shelf. Two salad plate–sized disks hovered in the air then flew straight at her, one after another.

Smash. Smash. She batted them away with a crack of the staff, shattering the clay into bits. Clouds of dust were left in their wake, turning her blue shirt gray.

Another disk zoomed at her head and she ducked, tucking into a neat roll. When she popped back up to her feet, another disk slammed into her hand, smashing her fingers.

She dropped her staff to the floor with a clang as she bent over and bit her lip to hold back a cry. Pain radiated up the bones in her hand before numbness set in.

"Fuck, Crystal." Max rushed to her side. "I'm sorry, sweetheart. I didn't mean to hurt you." He placed a hand on her back and bent over her to better see the injury.

With her free hand, she reached around and grabbed his

wrist as she drove her shoulder into his stomach, knocking him on his back. Pouncing on top of him, she loomed over and pinned him with a knee placed at his groin. Snatching the switchblade from her hip, she pressed it to his throat as he stared up at her in shock.

"Sucka," she drawled and dug the blade a tiny bit deeper into his skin. Not much, but just enough to show she meant business.

His brows lowered with confusion. "I thought I hurt you."

"You did. It hurts like a motherfucker."

Beneath her, his body seemed to melt and become more supple. "Who are you? Who is this tough-talking warrior woman? Where is the soft, sweet, baking, psychic I first met?"

She let out a long breath but didn't relinquish her position at his throat. "That's just another side of me. Times are different now. I need to be different."

His gaze roamed her face, searching, looking for who knew what. "I liked you before. I like you now too, but you've grown...distant."

This time she did laugh. "You're calling *me* distant? That's rich."

"Haven't I tried, Crystal?" he asked, keeping his voice quiet and his breathing shallow so as not to get cut. "Didn't I let strangers into my home? Haven't I tried working with the team? I know things started out rough, but haven't I made an effort?"

Damn him for being right. She averted her gaze.

When it came to the others, he led with strength and conviction, but showed a willingness to listen to others.

But that was business. When it came to her physical

safety, she would put herself into his hands, no question. Letting him into her heart was another matter.

"You're a good leader." There. At least she would concede to that.

His eyes narrowed as he gritted out, "I don't want to be your leader."

An invisible force ripped the switchblade out of her hand and flung it across the room. She gasped in surprise, which was all the time he needed to grip her by the ponytail and bring her mouth to his.

His lips were both soft and firm as he took, and took, and took some more. His tongue tangled with hers, inviting her to play and infusing her very being with his essence.

How had she lived these last few months without his taste on her tongue morning and night? And how would she go on without it in the future?

Max moaned into her mouth and pulled her closer, his hand curving around her bottom. The hard length of his erection pressed the seam of her jeans against her core, liquefying her center. Without shame, she ground against him as his hand swept up her body to squeeze and fondle her breast, twisting her nipple through the heavy sports bra. She wanted, needed to be naked. Needed Max bare and between her legs, driving, thrusting hard.

Behind her closed eyelids she could see them. See the sweat pooling in the crease of his spine as he reared up, roaring his release as she screamed his name. Teal satin sheets.

But they weren't on teal satin sheets. They were on a rubber mat on the floor of the gym. This wasn't her vision. There was still time to stop the madness.

She tore away with a cry and struggled to her feet on

shaky legs. "Stop. We have to stop this."

For several seconds he lay there, struggling for breath. Then he heaved a huge sigh and wiped his hand over his face before sitting up with a grimace. "Why?"

"Why?" Her voice cracked with her frustration. "What do you want from me, Max?"

Both of his brows rose to his hairline. Reaching down, he adjusted the impressive bulge straining his zipper. "I think that's obvious."

"Be more specific."

"You want specifics?" His eyes widened and his nostrils flared. "All right. I want to strip those clothes off you. Take those puckered nipples into my mouth, and suck and tease you while my fingers thrust inside you, preparing you for my cock. How's that for specific?"

Damn. That sounded good. Really, *really*, good.

No, she blinked hard and locked her knees to keep her from dropping her to the ground and crawling to him. Focus.

"And then what?"

He smiled, looking as though he thought she was playing a game. He took another step closer and his eyelids lowered with hunger. His voice dropped to a purr. "And then I would fit my body between your thighs and drive my cock inside you deep and true. Over and over until you screamed."

She swallowed hard. "And then what?"

"And then I'd come. I'd come so hard, I'll probably pass out."

"And then what?"

He stopped and blinked at her in confusion. "Um, we'd take a nap then do it again?"

Figures. "And then what?"

"What do you mean? I don't get it."

"Exactly," she shouted and threw her good hand up in the air. "What happens after we spend the night fucking?" She used the cold, crude word to remind her what he was really talking about. Not making love—fucking. "Will your curiosity about us be sated? Do we go on like nothing happened? Am I your girlfriend? What if we break up? Am I then expected to sit back and watch you go off with other women and expect you to let me be with other men? What will that do to the team, our mission? What then, Max?"

"I don't know," he shouted back. "I just want you. I didn't think that far ahead."

"Of course you didn't. You were only thinking with your dick," she spat. Bitter tears burned the back of her throat. What did she expect? He was a man; he was never going to understand.

"Crystal," he began then sucked breath through his teeth. He pushed the hair off his face, his fingers tightening around his bangs. "What do *you* want from *me*?"

Everything.

Didn't he realize she was keeping her distance to the betterment of all of them? If they entered into a relationship that crashed and burned, which was practically a guarantee where Max was concerned, everything they'd been working so hard for would be ruined. The fate of the world was more important than their love life. Right?

Right.

"Just your professional courtesy." He was so close, yet so far away. "I'll work beside you. I'll live with you. But that's all."

"Crystal, wait," he called out as she ran past him and out

the door.

With tears streaming down her checks, she kept going, determined to never look back.

CHAPTER FIFTEEN

CRYSTAL STEPPED OUT of the shower and onto the fluffiest carpet imaginable. Her skin pebbled in the cool air as she briskly dried her skin with a thick cotton towel. The ends of the fabric snapped with her rough movement like flags in a storm. If only her self-disgust was so easy to remove.

She passed by the mirror, not even bothering to look at her reflection. She knew what she'd see. Bright sparkly eyes, flushed cheeks, swollen pouty lips. Basically the face of a woman who had been well and thoroughly kissed.

And dear God, she wanted to kiss him again.

She jerked a purple T-shirt decorated with dragonflies over her head. Denim clung to her still-damp legs as she awkwardly twisted and wriggled to pull her jeans on with her one good hand.

Damn the man.

"Why does he have to be so damn…male?" she grumbled aloud and reached for the pot of rouge on her dresser.

A touch of color disguised the heat in her cheeks. A bit of mascara and a smattering of lip gloss finished her primping. The fuss with her appearance was not to attract Max; she just didn't want to walk around looking like a slob. They were living in the same house, so of course she was going to run into him again. For some reason, she felt better able to hold on to her convictions when she wore a layer of makeup. It was weak armor, but armor nonetheless.

The sooner she showed Max she meant what she said, the sooner he should get it through that supposedly genius brain of his that it wasn't going to happen between them.

Which is what you want, right?

The tube of lip gloss slipped out of her hand with the thought.

No. She shook her head to clear away the doubt. Of course that was what she wanted. Even though it felt at times as if the urge to say "Fuck it all" and jump into his arms was locked in an epic battle with her determination to maintain her professionalism. If she wasn't careful, she was going to go out of her mind.

She tossed the gloss onto the dresser and took a step toward the door, and her convictions.

Soft lighting embedded into the rock floor guided her along the long hallway. Her fingertips brushed along the wall, using the rough texture of basalt and layers of volcanic rock as a balm for her ragged nerves. The sensation rippled out in waves of tranquility to the bundle of distress she carried in her heart.

The team had made a home in the fortress deep in the earth. It was cozy, impenetrable, and at times she swore the rock pulsed with energy. It was the perfect place to provide them with the security to hone their skills. In the few short months since the team had first assembled, their hard work was already paying off and the calls for assistance were coming in.

Two days after the discovery of Jeremy Monroe, they received the first call from Sheriff Lancaster concerning a newborn that had been abducted from a hospital. His deputies had hit a wall in their investigation, and the sheriff had wanted the baby found before the media got hold of the story. More accurately, the hospital's chief of staff wanted the baby found and was riding the sheriff to get the job done, post-haste.

Fortunately for the sheriff, it had taken all of five minutes for Crystal to use her unique "interrogation" skills on the staff and narrowed the suspects down to a nurse who had absconded with the baby. While she had sat chit-chatting with the suspect, the rest of the team had gone to the location Crystal pulled from the nurse's memories. Parents and baby had been reunited a short time later to many hugs and congratulations.

Despite their hush-hush involvement with the police, over the last week word had spread about their success at being able to find anyone, anywhere. Private citizens were seeking them out to help find their loved ones. A few cases they were considering, others they turned down. Money was never a factor in their decision. The work was for practice and to help those who genuinely needed assistance. Watching families become happily reunited convinced Crystal she had been right in choosing this path. This was what she was meant to do.

And she wasn't going to let Max screw it up with sex.

She restrained the frustrated growl climbing up her throat and stomped into the kitchen.

The light and cheery room seemed better suited in a multimillion-dollar home instead of where it lay beneath the bedrock. Max had expanded the kitchen once they all moved in, so it now boasted a multi-surface cooktop range and a ginormous refrigerator that held enough food to feed three ravenous men for a week. White cabinets and quartz countertops contrasted with the cobalt blue island and drawers and helped brighten the cave.

Sun and wind power generated the equipment on the mountain. The complex system of windmills and panels was an environmentalist's wet dream as it allowed them to live completely self-contained and off the grid.

"Hey," Doc Kelly greeted as Crystal entered. She and her assistant, Alisia, were busy putting away dishes.

As a trusted friend of Doc's, Alisia had been brought in to provide medical support and assist Doc with her research. After an extensive interrogation by Max, of course. The young nurse had taken the existence of superhumans with a nod of her head and an "Ah, that explains it."

It was that unflappable character trait and her self-proclaimed title of misfit who didn't mind being cut away from most of society that made her such a good fit for the team.

"Hey." Crystal nodded and reached for a wine glass. Using the utmost care, she gently set the glass down instead of slamming it onto the countertop like she wanted to.

Doc smiled knowingly. "What did he do?"

"Who?" She popped the stopper on her favorite bottle of Syrah. With her one good hand, the action was more difficult than necessary, which just made her curse Max even more.

"Max."

"Why would you think that?" Maybe another inch, she thought, and filled the glass to the rim.

"Because every time you two have a confrontation, you hit a bottle of wine." She nodded to Alisia. "Just like she hits the whiskey after speaking with Ripley."

"I do not," the blonde gasped, affronted.

Doc hummed and strolled to the other side of the kitchen and picked up a highball glass. The melting ice cubes tinkled with the jiggle.

"It was cheap whiskey and mostly soda," Alisia said in defense.

Crystal popped her head over the open refrigerator door, juggling an armful of fruit and cheese, closing the door with her shoulder. "Yeah, what is it with you and Ripley?"

Alisia shot back, "What's with you and Max?"

"Never mind." Crystal scowled and dumped the food on the island counter.

Doc snickered and shook her head. "I'm so glad I'm not either one of you." Her laughing gaze landed on Crystal's swollen hand and quickly turned to concern. "How did you break your fingers?"

"They're broken? Damn. No wonder it hurts so bad. I took a hit with a clay disk."

"Ouch. Bring it here." Doc held out her hands.

Crystal allowed Doc to take her hand between her palms. Warmth spread through her fingers, easing the ache.

"All fixed." Doc sighed and swayed a bit on her feet before dropping Crystal's hand. "Well, at least I can fix your broken bodies, just not your minds."

"There's nothing wrong with us, right, Alisia?"

"Right. Absolutely nothing." The young nurse snatched her glass with a tight smile and downed the dregs.

"That's healthy." Doc hopped up on the counter and leaned back on her hands to address Crystal. "I see how you look at Max. And I see how he looks at you. Sparks, baby girl, sparks. So what's the matter?"

"Seriously?" she snorted. "This is Matthew Maxwell Madden III. One of the smartest people on the planet, rich, and more beautiful than any man has a right to be. And every person in his life has used him in one way or another." She kept her gaze on the fruit she sliced as she repeated every argument she fought with herself over the last few months. "He doesn't trust anyone. You know that the only reason he tolerates us being here is because we'll help avenge Anthony's death. I don't want to be a fling because I'm handy. And Max has never had anything close to a serious relationship. The two of us as an item are doomed for failure."

"And you're sure about that."

She cocked her head and pursed her lips. "Don't need to be a psychic to see it."

Doc gestured to the smooth rock walls and the line of narrow windows that ran near the ceiling, letting in the last of the sun's rays into the room. "This doesn't appear to be the work of a man who is merely tolerating us. Crystal, look at where we are. Do you think any of us has a chance at a normal relationship if we're living here, doing this work? If you're positive that things with Max won't work out, why stay? Why torture yourself with what you can't have?"

"Kaitlyn Summerset," she answered instantly.

"The runaway we found last week?" Alisia asked.

Crystal nodded. "At first it looked like a typical runaway case, until I used my powers and saw that her uncle was abusing her. We saved that girl's life. Think of how many more people we can help. I don't want to ruin this opportunity because I couldn't keep my knees together."

Doc leaned forward and clasped her hands on her lap. "And what happens when Max gives up and finds solace in another woman's arms?"

The knife skidded off the top of the apple and scraped

against the cutting board. "Solace? That's a charming euphemism." Crystal tried to make it a joke when the thought absolutely sickened her and made her want to crawl into a hole. "I...uh—I can't stop him. I wouldn't stop him. I'd just have to remind myself that what we're doing is more important."

The disbelieving shake of Doc's head only confirmed she was being delusional. "Good luck with that."

She'd need it.

"Crystal!" Ripley's voice boomed down the hall.

"Crap." Alisia jumped and raced out of the room in the opposite direction.

Crystal frowned. "What *is* up with them?"

"Who knows." Doc sighed. "She refuses to talk about it, but I think it has to do with her past."

Out of respect for her friendship with Doc, Crystal had always refrained from reading Alisia's memories. Any demons the young woman fought appeared to be of the internal kind, and Crystal never saw a reason to use her powers to dig deeper. She liked the girl and hoped that Alisia would come to think of her as a friend as well.

Ripley's shaggy blond head appeared in the doorway. "Hey, there you are." He paused and inhaled deep. He frowned and turned to look down the hall in the direction Alisia had run off. His lips turned down at the corners for a second before he blinked and looked back at Crystal. "I need you."

"To do what?"

He swiped a cluster of grapes from her plate. "I need next week's lottery numbers."

"No. Besides, I was only able to do that once."

"Come on, please."

"No." She picked up her plate and wine and strode past him toward the great room.

He followed. "And that one time you only gave me four of the numbers. Not cool."

Yeah, she did. She held back a telling grin. "You still won some money."

"It wasn't enough. I need some work done to my truck and it's not like we're raking in the dough working these cases for free. I don't want to ask Max for money."

"So instead you are going to steal it from the state."

"I go to a legitimate store with legitimate money and buy a legitimate ticket that has not been tampered with. That's not stealing." One of her strawberries disappeared between his lips.

"Even if I could, I wouldn't."

"You're no fun," he grumbled.

"Yeah, Crystal," Max chimed in when she entered the great room. She had to tilt her chin way up to meet his icy gaze that narrowed in challenge. "You're no fun. Why is that?"

She took a moment to calm her racing heart. Oh, she wanted to give in to the desire. Craved to feel the flames, but that path only led to disaster. "I'm loads of fun." She lifted her plate. "Gouda?"

The muscles in his jaw flexed. "No, thank you."

She flashed him a tight smile and sat down in an over-stuffed chair clear across the room. "What's the score?" she asked Chase, who sat on the couch facing the large-screen TV.

"Mariners are losing. Enough said. A crappy end to a crappy season."

"They have to," Addison replied, her gaze fixed on the

tiny laptop in front of her as her fingers flew across the keys. "Owners want to sell. If the team does too well, the price ramps up higher than anyone wants to buy them for. If they lose too much, then the owners lose out. So the plan is to end the season with a nice and tidy slightly above-average win percentage."

Only the hum of the television broke the silence of the room as they all stared at the young woman. You'd think by now they'd be used to her relaying an obscure bit of information.

"And you know this how?" Chase ventured to ask.

"It was in private emails between the owners and management. If they agreed to let the team fail on occasion, they were guaranteed positions with the prospective new owners. They have a formula of which games they'll lose." She shook her head with a smirk, eyes still on her monitor. "Their network security is really outdated. You'd think they would be more careful with that kind of information."

"Addison," Crystal whispered. "You're not telling anyone which games to make bets on? Like Ripley?"

"I can hear you over here," he called from his seat across the room. "Exceptional hearing. Remember?"

"I wouldn't do that." Addison glanced up with a secret smile and pushed her wire-rimmed glasses up her pert nose. With her freshly scrubbed face and long, blonde braids, Addison looked like an innocent teenager but the girl was pushing thirty. Definitely not a woman to underestimate. "He knows that I wouldn't hesitate to mess with him. I could be giving him the answers, or not, then he'd run around in circles trying to decide which it was."

Crystal smiled back and nibbled on a water cracker.

The weight of Max's gaze from thirty feet away weighed

on her, dared her to look him in the eye and acknowledge the heat between them. Instead, she lifted her glass and took a healthy swallow of wine. The spicy fluid filled her mouth, a poor substitution for the salt of his skin and the heat of his mouth. Nothing erased the taste of him. She was beginning to think nothing would.

Tears of frustration threatened to spill as she realized that ignoring him was going to be next to impossible.

"Hey, guys. Look at this." Chase broke into her maudlin thoughts by turning up the volume on the television.

"Good evening." A male reporter stood under a bright light on a residential street corner. "This is breaking news. We have just gotten word that police have closed down 128th St. in the Coal Field neighborhood, where an earlier drug bust turned into a hostage situation." The reporter continued to talk over footage of a ranch house bathed in flashing red and blue lights. Behind the police and SWAT vehicles, a mob of locals had gathered and were shouting with their fists raised.

"The house was rumored to be a hub of heroin distribution and was targeted by law enforcement to be shut down. But when officers arrived on the scene this evening to enforce the warrant, they discovered small children were inside the home.

"According to sources, the accused, William Eggers, drew a gun when he spotted the police. He has shut himself inside and is threatening to open fire if they come any closer. It is also rumored that he has explosives in the house. Adding to the tense situation are neighbors who have gathered to protest the police presence. They believe that it is law enforcement who are endangering the children by not complying with Eggers's wishes."

Crystal's eyes flew open as her pupils widened like a lens of a camera.

In her vision, she saw what appeared to be a tall, thin man wearing a gray T-shirt with large sweat stains under his arms standing by the window and peering through the slit in the blinds. A pistol was gripped in one hand, a near-catatonic six-year-old boy in the other. Tied back to back in banged-up wooden dining chairs were two women, both gagged, with tears streaking their cheeks. A little girl of two sat on the floor under one of the women. Her faded pink shirt was stained in red Popsicle and matched the color of the rubber bands holding her pigtails high on her head.

Outside the dilapidated house, Max stood talking with Sheriff Lancaster with Chase by their side, preparing to rush the front door.

"No!" Crystal shouted and jumped to her feet, sending strawberries and bits of cheese flying. "No, no, no, no."

This time she was the recipient of the wide-eyed stare.

Max looked back and forth between her and the television before understanding suddenly glittered in his eyes. "What did you see?"

"No." She shook her head. Her mouth opened to protest again then snapped shut.

He was by her side in an instant. His hands were warm on her elbow as he pulled her closer. "Crystal, what did you see?" His tone was soft, but firm.

"We can't." Her voice trembled. "We're not ready. We haven't trained for anything like that."

Chase dropped his feet from where they had been propped up on the coffee table. "Do you see us there? I am so in."

"What did you see?" Max asked again. His blue eyes

danced as an anticipatory grin curled up one corner of his mouth.

Her heart lodged in her throat made it difficult to speak. "Two women tied back to back. A little girl sitting at their feet. Eggers using a young boy as a human shield. Outside the house, you're talking to Sheriff Lancaster."

"Yes." His smile widened as he pointed a finger at her, then the others, then back at her. "Now it begins." He turned to Ripley, excitement high in his voice. "Call in Doc and Alisia. Addison, hack into the police network and get all of the information of what exactly is going down." His hand tightened on her arm. "This is *the* test, right, sweetheart?"

As much as it curdled her stomach to admit it, he was right. This was what they'd been building toward. Putting themselves in harm's way so others wouldn't have to. It was another step in preparation of taking on Madden. If they succeeded, they were ready to go after the big man himself.

"What's going on?" Doc asked as she entered the room, Alisia close behind.

"Have you heard about the standoff in Coal Field?"

"Yeah. We just saw it on the news."

Max nodded at Crystal. "Crystal saw us there. Addison, what do you have?"

Her fingers blurred across the keyboard, her superhuman powers downloading, sorting, and arranging the information faster than any processor. A few keystrokes sent the images she collected to the television for everyone to see.

"William Eggers. Age twenty-six. Black male, six feet, one hundred-eighty pounds. At least according to his last driver's license. Out on parole three months now after doing four years for drug smuggling, dealing, and possession of illegal firearms. Warrant was issued for his arrest today after intel was received that he's dealing heroin from his home. The house belongs to his mother Roberta, age forty-five and one of the hostages. Also living there is his girlfriend Anita, age twenty-four."

As she spoke a mug shot of the young Hispanic woman and her statistics scrolled across the screen. "Served six months for prostitution a few years ago. They have one child together, Lucia, age two. A boy, Zach, is his child from a previous relationship. He's six."

The photos zipped off the screen and were replaced with blueprints of the house and an aerial map of the neighborhood. As Addison continued to speak, different graphics expanded into 3-D images.

"The two-story house is roughly twelve hundred square feet. Two bedroom, two bath. Entrances are here and here." She indicated with her cursor. "According to the chatter, police arrived at six p.m. with information that Eggers would be home alone with two other associates. Before police entered, they heard children crying inside. They called off the bust, but Eggers saw them and fired shots out the window.

"The standoff began then. It's not confirmed, but it's reported that he has C-4 on the premises, hence why the bomb squad is on the scene. Word spread throughout the neighborhood and brought out the crowds. It appears the biggest protesters are Eggers's brothers. They're the ones enciting the crowd and pushing for the police to leave. Of course, with explosives present, the bomb squad isn't going anywhere."

"Thank you, Addison." Max resumed his position front and center and clapped his hands together. "Right. This is how we'll do this. Two teams. Chase and Doc are in one Rover, with Ripley, Crystal, and me in the other. Alisia, stay here with Addison in the comm room to assist her. Guys, this is our moment. Now is the time we make our mark and let it be known that justice is going to be handled a little differently from now on. If we do this, it will send a message and maybe Madden will hear and it will rattle him into reacting. Now, Sheriff Lancaster is not going to take our assistance easily. We'll go in, make him see reason," he said with a smirk. "And end it quickly, with as little bloodshed as possible. Meet in the garage in fifteen minutes. Any questions?"

They all agreed as he looked each person in the eye. When his gaze met Crystal's, she nodded. Fight the good fight and save the day. Despite her nerves, she knew this moment had been on the horizon. Now that it had dawned, she'd be ready.

As soon as he dismissed them, she took off for her room.

"Crystal."

She should have known Max wasn't finished with her.

Turning to face him, she lifted her chin. Right now, he wasn't a man she cared for. He was her commander, and she would treat him as such. "Yes, sir?"

His footsteps slowed as he neared, his brows drawn with wariness and concern. "Don't call me 'sir,' Crystal. Will you be all right? You don't have to go if you're worried or afraid."

"I'm not afraid," she snapped then regained her composure. "You were right. This is what we've been working toward. What we are meant to do. The vision just surprised me, and I don't want you—anyone—to get hurt. Don't worry. I can do this."

His gaze softened as he nodded. He reached out with one finger and stroked the curl resting along her cheek. When he opened his mouth to speak, she pulled away.

"Twelve minutes, right? I'll be ready."

CHAPTER SIXTEEN

MAX TURNED THE key in the ignition of the Land Rover and in his peripheral vision caught sight of his Ferrari parked beside him. Man, how long had it been since he last drove that monster?

Once upon a time, his Ferrari had been his baby. His pride and joy. Cruising along the mountain pass or speeding down the streets of long-forgotten logging towns had been his release, his reason for going out into the world and clearing his mind. And now?

He didn't miss it one bit.

A wiry grin curled his lips as he adjusted his earpiece. "Audio up and ready?"

"Go ahead and commence with audio test," Addison replied from the comm room.

He nodded at Chase, who was waiting in the second Rover with Doc Kelly behind the driver's wheel. "Max, standing by," he began.

"You mean 'Maestro'?" Chase snickered into their earpieces. "The talent in command."

Max rolled his eyes. He wished that nickname hadn't stuck. It didn't sound near menacing enough. "Knock it off, Twilight."

"Doc standing by."

Chase replied, followed by Crystal, who sat in the backseat behind Max.

"Red leader, standing by," Ripley piped from the front passenger seat and shared a laughing glance with Max as the ladies responded with a groan that reverberated in their earpieces.

"Beta Team, ready to head out?" Max asked, still chuckling over Ripley's quip.

"Ready," Doc answered.

"Why do we have to be called 'Beta Team'?" Chase asked.

"Would you rather be 'Number Two'?" Max mocked as he pulled out of the cave and into the dark forest.

"I'd rather be 'Team Intrepid.' And why does Doc always get to drive?"

"Because she's older and has years of experience."

"Is that supposed to be a compliment?" she gasped.

"Of course," Ripley agreed with a laugh. "With age comes wisdom and all of that."

"Watch it, beast man. I control the access to your flea dip."

"I don't have fleas," he grumbled with an absentminded scratch behind his ear.

Max smiled at the banter. It reminded him of the smack talk he used to engage in while playing online games. However, it was ten times better to witness the snickering grins in person. Who would have guessed he'd prefer conversing with a group of real people over avatars?

Crystal had. She'd known from day one he was meant to do greater things than to hide out on his mountain, twirling rocks and sticks around with his mind. She saw in him what he refused to acknowledge: a man desperate to belong.

Years of being treated like a freak had contributed to his "fuck-you" attitude against the world. Now that he was working on being a part of something special with others who were also considered outsiders, he recognized the life of a loner was just that, damn lonely.

Plus, there was no denying that having these specific people beside him was definitely an advantage in the fight against his father, although he did find value in them beyond their powers. Their enthusiasm, their integrity, the willingness to just try made him proud to be included in their circle.

And what of the future?

There would come a day when Madden would be no more. What then? Could he walk away from his team? Return to the solitary existence he led before?

He glanced in the rearview mirror and observed Crystal sitting in the backseat with her face turned to the window. Her thick curls were knotted in a bun and tucked neatly under a knit cap. The black uniform made her pale skin appear translucent and gave her an air of vulnerability that hid the fierce warrior who had nicked him with a blade earlier that evening. Dark Jackie-Os covered her eyes, denying him access to what she might be thinking. Were they topaz in worry? Green with stress?

He tightened his grip on the steering wheel and returned his focus on the twisting trail to the freeway.

When it came to Crystal, there was no doubt in his mind, walking away was not an option.

It hadn't taken him long to figure out she was extraordinary. Her passion and ability to soak up knowledge like a flower absorbed the sun was both a turn-on and impressive as hell. This wasn't a game to her, it was a calling. And she pushed herself until exhaustion claimed her and there was nothing left to give. Crystal inspired him, inspired all of them, to never lose faith. At least until the Monroe incident.

Before that day, she looked at him as if he had all the answers. As if he were a savior. Now, there was doubt in her gaze. The loss of her faith was a blow he didn't expect to cut so deep.

She never tried to use him for his talent. And his money never impressed her. All Crystal had asked of him was his best, and he wanted to give that to her and then some. She made him want to be the leader she had believed him to be.

Their personal relationship, however, was about as passionate as potato soup.

With everyone else she was their sister, their friend, their confidante. She laughed and joked and engaged. With him she was cold, clinical, all business, and it frustrated him to no end. The few times she let her guard drop made him hungry for more. He wanted that warmth. He wanted her smile.

He wanted her.

Sweeping his tongue over his lower lip, he relived that scorching kiss and knew that his passion was not one-sided. He saw desire in her yearning expression, in the shaking of her hands, the scent of her skin. She ached too.

His parents' marriage had been perfection on paper and ended a nightmarish failure. It tainted love for him for what he thought would be forever. Until Crystal.

Somewhere between reconnaissance missions, strategy meetings, and plotting to kill his father, she became his light, his purpose. All the things he thought he never wanted, a family and a partner, she made him long for.

And if she stayed in the same room as him for longer than two seconds, he'd tell her that he wanted to give her more. He was ready for more.

Sure, his track record with women ran on the wham-bam-thank-you-ma'am side. A fact she probably knew about and saw first-hand in his memories, he acknowledged with a wince. But that was then. Crystal was his future.

All he had to do was convince her.

Ripley's low whistle snapped his attention back to the task at hand. "Damn. Looks like the entire town is out."

"Now would be a good time to shift," Max suggested.

The tinted windows shielded them from prying eyes as Ripley pulled off his shirt and handed it to Crystal, who folded it into a neat square and placed it on the seat beside her. The Velcro along the seams of his pants ripped as his bulky frame morphed into the large German shepherd.

He turned back in his seat to playfully lick her face. "Ugh, Ripley," she gagged. "I've told you before that's gross."

Max guided the Land Rover through the crush of people to the temporary police barricade. Upon their approach, officers pulled aside the sawhorses, allowing them entrance without checking to see who rode inside. The Rovers were outfitted specifically to blend in as law enforcement, and Max got a kick every time they were waved through without issue. As if the local authorities could afford these rigs. His vehicles contained gadgets and security measures the regular police didn't know existed. It was times like these that he enjoyed being a wealthy genius.

"Everyone stay back while I talk to Lancaster," Max instructed when they climbed out of the vehicles. "I'll see if I can appeal to his righteous nature. Network, turn up the volume a bit so you all can hear what he says."

"On it," she replied through the earpiece.

Sheriff Lancaster cut an imposing figure, being half a

head taller than the men surrounding him as he stood behind the barricade of a SWAT van. Despite the chilly night air, he was coatless and had his hands braced on his hips above his gun belt. The louder the crowd chanted, the tighter his lips pinched. The stress of the day deepened the lines around his mouth, aging him beyond his thirty-eight years.

He was a good man. Honest, fair, and willing to find solutions some would consider outrageous.

Max bit back a smile. They didn't get more outrageous than his squad.

Lancaster's gaze skittered over him once then back again in surprise. "Garan, what are you doing here? Who let you through?"

Garan. Maestro. The code names were a necessity to protect their identities, just as the slicked-back hair and wraparound glasses made it more difficult to recognize them. The fewer people who knew who they were, the better, because once word got out as to *what* they were, all types of hell were destined to rain down upon them. Especially if the night went as he planned.

Their disguises weren't much, he knew that, but it was better than the spandex one-piece and mask that Ripley had tried to push on them. Man, at times the beast man was a weird dude.

"Sheriff." Max nodded. "We heard what was going on and thought you might need our services."

"Did you now?" he drawled. His tired blue eyes narrowed as if he were trying to see through the dark lenses of Max's glasses. With a jerk of his head, he led Max away from his men. "I appreciate the offer, but this isn't a missing person or lost hiker. Civilians don't belong here."

Max lowered his shoulders and widened his stance. "I understand, Sheriff, and we are aware of the risks, but I believe we can be of some use to you. From what I've heard, you have a trigger-happy gunman who gets a little antsy when police start intruding on his territory. But you see, I am not the police." He nodded to the others. "With your permission, I can send my dog in to do surveillance. He's wired with some extraordinary equipment." He ignored Chase's snort of laughter in his ear. "And is highly trained, as you've seen. We might be able to gather the information you need to proceed, such as is Eggers packing C-4 in the couch cushions. I'm sure you want to finish this before this crowd becomes more vocal and dangerous."

"How did you know—" Lancaster's nostrils flared as he looked from Ripley to the crowd then back to Max as his upper lip curled. "Who told you?"

Max held out his hands and shrugged. "We all have our talents."

Lancaster took another look at the unruly crowd. The muscles in his throat worked as if he were swallowing bile. "Just the dog?"

Max's smile stretched as slow as warm taffy. "For now. Therian, come here, boy."

Ripley growled low in his throat before trotting to Max's side. The big man hated being treated like a pet, which was why Max did so at every opportunity. Especially when the shifter couldn't do anything about it except piss on his leg. "Monkey it up, my friend. See what you can find."

With a yip, Ripley tore off, becoming a gray streak in the night.

"Sheriff, Sheriff." A voice rose above the noise. "What's your strategy to having the hostages released? Who are those people in black? Hey, you, why are you wearing sunglasses at night?"

Max turned his head and spied a man leaning over the police barricade. He looked like a rumpled extra from the TV series *Mad Men* in his wrinkled charcoal suit and loosened necktie. In the crush of the crowd, his black pompadour didn't move a hair out of place. Max blew a stray lock of his own hair out of his eyes and wondered what hair product the man used.

"Carrigan," Lancaster growled. "Get back with the other newshounds."

"Why should I? This is where the real action is." He kept his digital camera held high. "Who are these people, Sheriff?"

"Network? Intel, please," Max murmured and shut off the man's camera with a thought. If any video of them was to be made public, he wanted it on his own terms.

"What the hell?" Carrigan looked at the camera and turned it back on with his thumb. Max turned it off again and popped the battery compartment open, sending the batteries tumbling to the ground.

The sheriff choked on his laughter as the man dropped to the concrete to rescue his batteries from under the feet of the protesters.

"Here you go, boss," Addison answered as Carrigan's driver's license photo appeared on Max's right lens. "Clancy Carrigan. AP reporter and blogger. Last piece he wrote was on the misappropriation of funds in law enforcement. Needless to say, he is not Lancaster's favorite person."

"You know, perhaps now would be a good time to limit the size of the viewing public."

"Already on it. Newsfeed coming down in three, two,

one."

A chorus of disappointment and frustration rose from the conglomerate of news vans the next block over.

"What is it now?" Lancaster shouted at one of his deputies.

"It appears that there's a problem with their equipment. They can't broadcast. A satellite must be down or something."

"Really?" A please smiled flirted with his lips. "Well, that's...that's their problem."

Max turned away from the sheriff and asked Network under his breath, "Is the face recognition software finding anyone else here of note?"

"Jeff and Kevin Eggers, the brothers, are a few yards north of you." A circle drawn on the inside lens of his glasses highlighted the two men. "Both have rap sheets that include drug dealing, burglary, and weapons charges."

"And they are the ones enticing the crowd?" He considered the situation. "Seems odd for ex-cons to be so concerned about the welfare of their sibling's children."

"That's an ugly stereotype, Maestro," Doc said and frowned at him from across the blacktop.

"Ugly but true."

Sure, he was cynical. Came with the territory when every time the government hired him to track down a hacker, he found confirmation that a person who walked on the wrong side of the law rarely looked out for anyone other than themselves. Hell, selfishness was not confined to criminals. He could count on one hand the people he knew who genuinely cared about the welfare of others. "What's going on with Therian?"

"He's around the back now."

"Show me."

Max's stomach rolled a bit as the image in his glasses changed to the view from the camera swinging from Ripley's neck as he crept up behind the house.

Not a branch snapped or a leaf rustled in Max's earpiece as Ripley padded to the lone elm tree that grew next to the house. A soft pop of bones preceded the shift to a chimpanzee. He swiftly scaled the branches and leapt for the house. With his rubbery fingertips, Ripley hung from the eaves as he tested the lock on the second-story window.

Bingo. It slid a few inches before it stuck in the tracks.

Another teeth-grating pop of bones echoed in Max's ear as Ripley shifted into the shape of a squirrel and eased through the narrow slit before transforming back into the chimp.

Holy shit. Max winced. That much shifting in a short span was going to be rough on the big man.

Ripley picked his way over the toy-strewn floor and eased down the stairs.

In the living room two women sat tied to chairs and a little girl played with a wooden puzzle on the floor, just as Crystal described. Eggers stood to the side of the window, peering through the edge of the blinds. Sweat bathed his brow as the muscles in his arms trembled from holding a boy who appeared to be about five or six years old in front of him while balancing the weight of the gun at the same time.

"Hurry up, man, just hurry up," he begged into the Bluetooth attached to his ear. "They're planning something, I know it. Just get it done."

Max would bet his left nut that Eggers wasn't talking to the hostage negotiator.

The cold dead look in the boy's eyes worried Max. It

was a look of hopelessness and betrayal. It was the death knell of a child's innocence wrought by the hand he most trusted. A feeling with which Max was all too familiar.

He was half tempted to tell Ripley to take Eggers out with a swift bite to the jugular, but it wasn't his call to ask Ripley to take a life in an act of vigilante justice.

The image in his glasses swung again as Ripley searched the rest of the house before he retraced his steps and left the same way he entered. Under the pitch dark of an elm tree, he took his human form.

"Not sure how much you were able to see, but the living room looks exactly as Prism described. The little girl appears oblivious to what's going on, but the boy is shell-shocked right now and reeks of piss and fear. Odd thing was I didn't find or smell explosives anywhere. Eggers is on a Bluetooth and he was talking to someone about hurrying up and getting something done. Network, did you catch any of that that?"

"Yep, Shadow is tracing the call now," she replied, referring to Alisia.

Max motioned to Lancaster. "Sheriff, who is Eggers talking to on his Bluetooth?"

"What?"

"My equipment is picking up phone calls to a number that is not associated to the police or the hostage negotiator you have in that van over there. Who is it?"

Lancaster's eyes bulged as his face reddened until his blond eyebrows stood out like pale caterpillars on his brow. Apparently, the sheriff wasn't as dialed in on the situation as he believed.

While Lancaster fired off terse questions at his deputies, Max glanced over at Crystal and frowned. Her lips were pressed into a thin white line and her arms hugged her middle, a reaction he suspected was caused by the footage of the children they had all seen in their dark glasses.

With Crystal, first and foremost was the safety of children. When anyone questioned her fervent determination as to why, she skirted the topic. But he more than anyone understood the scars someone could carry when terrorized by their parents' actions. If his superpower was mind reading, he'd bet his every dollar that she was reflecting on her childhood at that moment.

For some people, such wounds made them shut themselves off from society, but not Crystal. This compassion she gave to the world without pause stirred within him an empathy he didn't know he possessed. If Max was the brains of their group, Crystal was the heart.

She caught his gaze and offered him a weak smile. A heartbeat later she jerked with a gasp, her color fading as she fell back against the Rover.

"Cry—Prism?" he called out and dashed to her side, his stomach tied in knots. He rested his hands on her upper arms. "Prism. Sweetheart?" he whispered and curled his fingers, preparing to shake her awake when she jerked and filled her lungs with a huge breath.

"What. The. Fuck," she gasped and looked about in confusion.

Doc placed a hand on her back. "Sweetie, are you okay?"

"It doesn't make sense," she mumbled.

"Prism?" Max squeezed her arms.

Through the dark lenses of her glasses he could see her lashes flutter like hummingbird wings. "This isn't it. It's a decoy."

"What?"

"This. This whole thing is a setup."

CHAPTER SEVENTEEN

CRYSTAL'S HEARTBEAT SLOWED and her vision blurred in and out as she tried to gain her bearings. That was without a doubt the craziest vision she'd had yet, but since she'd never been wrong before, she knew the impossible was about to happen.

"What do you mean, a setup?" Max asked her.

"This. All of this isn't what it seems." She grabbed his hand. "Come on, we need to talk to the sheriff."

Chase and Doc followed on their heels as she raced across the concrete. Ripley sprinted from behind the house in his canine form and joined them in front of the bright headlights of the SWAT van.

"Sheriff," she called out as she neared. "Sheriff, wait. This is a diversion, a setup. There's more going on here than you know."

His bushy brows lowered. "What do you mean?"

"This is all a ruse. A way to gather as many first responders in one area as possible and away from the real crime taking place."

He blinked at her as if she were the one who needed to be locked up, but not in a jail cell. "And what crime is that?"

"Bank robbery. Two of them." She closed her eyes to recall more specifics of the locations. "The Bank of America downtown, and the Madden Bank on West 13th." At the mention of his father's bank, Max froze.

Lancaster heaved a long and heavy sigh and cocked his head. "And what makes you think that?"

She didn't hesitate in her response. "I saw it. I'm psychic."

"Right," he drawled out thick as molasses.

Seriously? After all she had done for him. Either he believed her or he didn't, but they didn't have time for this shit.

"Don't you see?" She turned to Max, knowing he'd understand. "Don't you think it's odd that a simple drug bust turned into a major standoff that required not only the SWAT team but the bomb squad on the same night as two bank robberies are set to take place? I don't know the logistics, but I feel they're connected. Maybe Eggers planted his family here on purpose."

She snapped her fingers. "Ah wait, I get it now. His brothers. That's why they're here, to create more confusion. So while all available units are here, two banks are being cleaned out. And with the way the world is now, the only story that will be in tomorrow's papers will be this story about the police persecuting a black family and causing a race riot."

"That is the stupidest thing I have ever heard," Lancaster exploded.

Max straightened, ready for action. "Are the robberies going on right now?"

"There was a clock on the wall that read twelve-thirty."

"It's almost midnight now. Network, what did you find out about Eggers's phone?"

"Damn, the girl beat me to the good stuff." Addison laughed with admiration. "Eggers is receiving and sending phone calls to three locations. The first is to a phone number to the satellite phone belonging to the police. The second is to a phone owned by Jeff Eggers. The third is to a prepaid cell, so I can't determine the owner, but the signal is coming from West 13th."

"That's where Madden Bank is," Doc pointed out.

"Who are you people talking to and what is going on?' Lancaster bit out. His chest heaved with the struggle to remain in control as his color began to rise again.

Max smiled. "A very good intelligence gatherer. Prism is correct. All of this was staged to bring as much law enforcement together in one location. Eggers is on the phone with someone at the Madden Bank location and to his brother Jeff. I'd bet Mr. Eggers would have some very interesting information if we questioned him."

"You expect me to just believe you in all of this?"

Max spread out his arms. "Have I ever steered you wrong? What would it hurt to ask him?"

The sheriff's lip curled in a snarl before his shoulders lowered. "No, you haven't." He pointed his long finger at them. "But that is the only reason I'll go along with this. Plus, it might be the only possibility to end this stalemate," he muttered, more to himself. "Davis. Bring the brothers over here."

"Deputy," Crystal called out. "Be nice. Their job is to cause chaos and get the crowd on their side. Tread lightly."

He nodded and disappeared around the van. A few minutes later Davis returned with a second deputy and the Eggers brothers, who looked ready to rumble. Both men walked with a strut and a glint in their eyes that warned others to keep their distance. It was very effective, Crystal thought as she shuffled back a step.

The taller of the two raked his gaze over Crystal and the

others and sneered. "Yo, man, Halloween was weeks ago."

"Gentlemen," Lancaster began.

"Excuse me, Sheriff," Max interrupted. "Prism has a talent at extracting information. Let her have the first shot at it." Curiosity narrowed Lancaster's eyes before he nodded. "Gentlemen, would you mind if this young lady touched your arm? In the most respectful and plutonic way, of course."

"You want a piece of this, sweet thang?" Jeff Eggers asked and ran his palms over his chest down to his beer belly.

"What part of 'respectful' didn't you understand?" the sheriff growled.

"I'll be all right, Sheriff," she said, mindful of Max's posture. He was a trap ready to spring, with his shoulders down and his arms hanging at his sides. If anyone made a move on her, she was certain they would find themselves flung across the street in less than a heartbeat. "May I?"

"For a pretty girl like you, sure." Jeff reached for her, but she dodged his hand and placed her fingertips on his forearm.

The outside world shrank away as she sorted through the images and sound bites in his mind. "The brothers were contacted by a man Jeff did time with in Walla Walla state prison. He goes by the name of Big Tim." She paused to roll her eyes. "He's short, Asian, about five-five, thin. Scar across his chin."

"What the fuck?" Jeff tried to pull away, but she tightened her fingers around his arm.

"The offer was to draw the police and SWAT team out with a phony hostage situation. Jeff was supposed to be the decoy but knew that his wife would kill him if he endangered his children. William offered up his family in return for half the money."

"Bitch, let go," Jeff demanded in a panicked voice that came from deep in his chest and pulled away. That was fine with her. She had seen enough.

"Big Tim was the one who gave the fake intel to the police to incite the warrant. In return for their efforts, these two received two hundred grand a piece." She rubbed her palm against her thigh. "Funny. I didn't see anything in regards to the bank robberies in his memories."

All the men around her looked at her as if she had flashed a blinding light in their eyes, except Max, who faced her with a smile at the corners of his mouth. "Well done."

"You're spewing nonsense, bitch. You can't prove any of that," Jeff spat at her in a trembling voice.

Her cat-ate-the-canary grin made him blink twice. "*I* might not be able to, but the copy you made of the instructions Big Tim mailed you tucked into the chest in the attic of your home can. It's under your grandfather's military dress suit and next to the large stash of your personal weed. Is that any way to show respect to a veteran?"

The man turned ashen as his brother whispered, "Holy shit."

Lancaster blinked long and slow, his stunned gaze focused on Crystal. "What did you just do? Read his mind?"

"No." She smiled. "Just his memories."

"Right." He rocked back on his heels.

"No. Really."

A shrill ring coming from Jeff Eggers's pocket made them all jump.

She exchanged a questioning glance with Max. Could

this be another call from William?

"Speak of the devil," Addison announced in their ear-pieces. "That call is coming from the house."

Max chuckled. "Sheriff, I have a hunch that's William right now."

Lancaster looked to his deputy. "Did you check them for weapons before bringing them over?"

"Yes, sir."

He gestured to Eggers. "Go on. Answer it. On speaker-phone."

"No." Jeff shook his head. "It can go to voicemail."

"Answer it. Or I will get a warrant and check the records in a matter of days."

"Or I can do this," Addison said. "Let's see if I have the coding right."

"Jeff? Jeff, man, are you there?" They all froze when William Eggers's voice came from his brother's pocket.

"I think that worked," Crystal whispered.

Addison snickered. "Oh, I am good. Let me try to turn up the volume."

"Brother, it's about to go down." Panic laced the brittle tone of William's voice. "I need you to make some more noise. Do ya hear me? It's going down."

"Dude, man," Kevin Eggers squawked and tackled his brother. "Turn it off. Turn it off!"

"Right." Max clapped his hands together as the police dealt with the feuding brothers. "I think we've heard enough. Wouldn't you say, Sheriff? How's this for a plan? Therian—"

"Now just a minute," Lancaster shouted, his hands raised. "I don't know what exactly is going on here, but this is still my investigation. I am not going to let a bunch of civilians run around all half-cocked like Dirty Harry."

Max turned to face Lancaster with his lips in a white line. She felt his impatience to find out what was happening at one of his father's banks, and it knotted her stomach as if it were her own. He wanted Madden so badly, she was surprised he hadn't run off at the mere mention of his father. The longer they stayed on the scene, the tighter Max was going to twist in the wind until he snapped like a string on a kite caught in a storm.

"I see your point, Sheriff," he said tightly. "But I ask that you indulge me. We're the best chance you have of ending this standoff quickly."

The exceedingly polite address seemed to have worked on the sheriff, until Lancaster drew his gun, his armed hand hanging loose at his side. "It's been a long day, and I'm still trying to wrap my head around the fact that the little missy here can read minds and see the future. I really don't want to arrest you, but you need to stand down now."

"No need for threats." Max waved his finger back and forth, levitating the gun out of the sheriff's hand and placing it back into the holster. "I'll make you a deal. If I don't end this peacefully in under a minute, you can shoot me."

Max turned to the rest of them, leaving Lancaster to gape at the re-holstered gun. "Therian, I want you to ease your way to the front door. I'll blow it open, and Intrepid will run inside to grab the kids. Take out Eggers however you need to, but alive would be preferable. Doc, Prism, get the Rovers ready. We're out of here as soon as the children are safe. Network, on my mark, take out cell service for at least two minutes. I don't want anyone doing a live feed. Speculation is better than proof where we're concerned. Ready, everyone?" Ripley barked as they all nodded.

"Places."

He caught Crystal's arm as she turned. "Prism, the kids will be all right. I promise." The conviction in his voice matched the intensity in his eyes.

She took a deep breath and let it out, slow and smooth. Protect the innocent. That was the most important thing. Even with the events of the evening speeding by fast enough to make her head spin, the fact that Max was still holding tight to that rule, despite the drive to find out more about Madden, calmed her nerves and snapped her focus into place.

Her lips tingled with the desire to plant a good-luck kiss on him, but she squeezed his hand instead. "I know. I have faith in you."

His lips twitched as he nodded and squeezed her hand back. "Get the car ready."

Once in the Rover, she cranked the heat to high even though her chills weren't caused by the cold. In her heart she knew the men would end this quickly and safely, but it would be a lot easier to watch if she already knew how this particular scenario ended.

Ripley's German shepherd crawled through the shadows along his belly up the porch stairs and settled to the right of the front door.

Lancaster directed his men to stand down. Uncertainty pinched his face as he watched Max and Chase go over the plan one more time.

The clouds parted to bathe them in pale moonlight. The silvery glow slid along the leather of their black coats, casting them as ethereal warriors before a battle.

As a unit, the masses all fell silent as if sensing that the standoff was about to come to a dramatic end.

The sudden quiet snagged the attention of William Eggers. "Stay back," he shouted through the cracked open window. "Anyone comes near and I'll blow us all up."

"On my count," Max said, his feet apart, his arms at ease.

Crystal's throat closed as her muscles tensed in anticipation.

"Three. Two. One."

Max's hand shot out at the same time Chase took off. The door blew open, coming completely off its hinges. Before the dust and debris settled, Chase streaked back outside with both children tucked under his arms.

Ferocious barking followed as Ripley lunged into the house for Eggers and sank his sharp fangs into the man's forearm, dragging him to his knees onto the porch.

Eggers howled and struggled, his gun falling to the wayside as the sickening crack of his arm breaking echoed into the night. Ripley dropped the broken limb and stood on Eggers's neck with his heavy paw.

Max turned to Lancaster with a bored sigh. "I believe it's safe to enter the house now."

The silence that followed stretched like a taut rubber band ready to snap.

Lancaster's mouth worked up and down before he could finally utter a choked wheeze. "Wha—?"

"Excuse me, Sheriff." Chase nodded at the children squirming in his hold. "Is there a social services agent around?"

"What?" He blinked rapidly then the man-in-charge hardness returned to his expression. "Oh. Yes. Right. Davis, get your men in there. Where's that social worker?"

People everywhere flew into action. Police and medics

rushed to Eggers while the crowd shouted in awe and disbelief at what they just witnessed. The door blowing open could have been explained with explosives, but Chase had those children in his arms faster than anyone could blink. Through the car window, Crystal heard the questions, puzzling out just who, or what, they were as camera crews and photographers struggled in the throng, equipment held high in an attempt to capture any frame of footage.

A matronly woman and another medic approached Chase and took the boy and girl into their arms. Crystal breathed a sigh of relief when the little boy clung to the woman as if she were a lifeline. They would be all right, physically at least. The mental trauma would take years to come to terms with, if ever, but technically they were safe.

She sent a quick prayer for the children to be placed in a safe environment where they could stay together. If the state couldn't provide for them, then she would take it upon herself to find a home for them. She still had friends in social services that she had made after her parents had died. With Max's money, she had the means to cut through some of the red tape.

Max turned away from the house and headed in her direction. "Let's move out."

"Just wait a goddamn minute," Lancaster shouted. "You're leaving? Just like that? Would you like to explain what just happened?"

Max pointed to his bare wrist. "Sorry, don't have time. I have two bank robberies to stop. You're welcome to join us."

He opened the back door of the SUV for Ripley before taking his own seat up front. "Beta Team, take the Bank of America. We've got Madden."

The sharpness in his tone drew Crystal's gaze to the tight set of his jaw. They all knew what he was thinking. What were they going to find at his father's bank?

CHAPTER EIGHTEEN

CRYSTAL KEPT HER eyes off the rearview mirror as Ripley resumed his naked human form in the backseat of the Rover. He took his discarded shirt and wiped the blood and sweat from his face. "Ugh. Water, please."

Max handed him a bottle, which he quickly opened and downed half of in a huge swallow. Rolling down the window, he stuck his head out to spit and rinsed again. "Man, that was nasty." He settled back in his seat with a shudder and reached for his pants. "He tasted like dirt and chemicals."

"You did real good, Ripley," Crystal said. "You too, Chase."

"Piece of cake," Chase replied through the headset from his seat in the car in front of them. At the stop sign, Doc turned left while Crystal went right.

"What about me?" Max asked in a low tone.

A chuckle escaped her before she could stop it. He might look like a strong, undefeatable he-man, but inside he was still that little boy desperate for approval.

"You were calm, controlled, and exceedingly polite." She shrugged. "Meh, good enough."

The squeal of the tires as she took the corner on two wheels drowned out his strangled laughter. When his warm palm settled on her thigh, it was her turn to stifle a choked cry as she tried to keep the Rover from veering into the curb.

"We would still be there sitting on our thumbs if you hadn't had that vision," he said. "And the way you read Jeff Eggers, truly amazing."

"Thank you," she managed to reply. Her heart beat faster with every caress of his thumb on her thigh.

"What exactly did you see in your vision?"

"I, um." She swallowed and focused on pulling her attention away from the massaging fingers on her inner thigh. "Three men were on the roof of Madden Bank. It was that building that also houses the physical therapy clinic and that sandwich shop that serves those shrimp po'boys. One of those men would text Jeff Eggers, then Jeff would start another round of ruckus to entice the crowd and keep the police distracted. The men scaled down the side and broke into a window of the physical therapy office. Then they crawled through the air vent that feeds into the bank. That vent dumped them into the office of the credit manager. That was where I saw the clock that read twelve-thirty."

"How did you know about the second bank?"

"I saw them, too. Another team of three. They're entering from underground."

"You've never been able to see so much before." Max's fingers tightened on her leg. "Why now?"

"I'm not sure." As soon as she said those words, her hand tingled and she remembered what had happened earlier in the day. "Oh, right. I think it might have to do with Doc's theory about adrenaline from pain expanding our powers."

"When were you hurt?" Ripley asked while strapping on his pants.

"Uh, um," she stuttered. Crap, he would have to ask

that. "Sorry, can't hear you. We're almost there."

"Crystal," Max pushed. "When were you hurt enough to change your powers?"

"It was nothing."

"Doc. Did you treat Crystal for any injury recently?" he asked, directing his voice toward his earpiece.

"Doc, don't—"

"Earlier tonight I healed two broken fingers," came the reply.

Max turned toward her, his expression stricken. "I broke your fingers when we sparred? Why didn't you say anything?"

"Holy shit," Ripley exclaimed. "You broke her fingers?"

"We're here," she sang, pulling the car to a skidding halt two blocks from the bank.

Before he could stop her, she jumped out onto the blacktop. They had enough going on at the moment than rehash what happened between them in the workout room. Especially when everyone was wired to listen in on every word.

Max rounded the front of the Rover, obviously not ready to let it go as easily. "Why didn't you tell me?"

"I didn't know my fingers were broken. Look, now is not the time to discuss this." She held up her once-injured hand and wiggled her fingers. "See, I'm fine. Now, what's the plan?"

He grunted once. Through the lenses of his sunglasses, his eyes promised the conversation was far from over.

"Network, separate team transmission. Good luck, you two," he said to Chase and Doc.

"No worries, boss. I see men in blue pulling up behind us now. Team Chase out."

Parked up ahead of them, a lone, nondescript gray van with missing plates snagged her attention. "Is that the getaway van?"

"Obvious much?" Ripley scoffed.

Max cocked his head to the side. "Just in case it is." All four tires hissed as they deflated at once.

Crystal looked around the empty street and wondered where the police were. Surely Lancaster had sent a unit or two after them. She blew warm air into her palms and rubbed them up and down her arms. The oppressive silence combined with the deep shadows and heavy fall mist creeped her out more than watching a horror flick.

"Where's the police?" she asked.

"I'm sure they'll be here shortly." Max shrugged, a smile hovering on his lips. "They might be delayed by the tree that fell across the road behind us unexpectedly."

"Maestro," she gasped while Ripley leaned his head back and laughed. "Why did you do that?"

"I'm getting first crack at what's going on inside."

"You don't know what that is. All we have to go on are the glimpses of my vision. This isn't like our other assignments. We can't go in without backup. We can't go in, period. This is police business."

"You're my backup, and you said there were three men in there. Are they armed?"

"Yes."

"Then I know there are three armed men inside." He spun around and strode to the back of the Rover. "If something is going down with Madden, I want to know about it first."

"This isn't a game, or a way to get back at your father. It could just be a coincidence that it's one of his banks."

"It's not a coincidence. The house was a diversion. Who's to say that one of these break-ins isn't also a diversion? There is a reason that these two specific banks are targeted, and I'm going to find out why."

Trepidation filled her as a firm resolve hardened his features. This was no longer Maestro, a man who helped the innocent and righted the wrongs of the world, but Max, a betrayed son thirsty for vengeance against his father. Could she trust him to remain focused on apprehending the criminals, or would his yearning to take down Madden put them all in danger?

"I take back what I said about you being calm and in control. This is just like on the mountain. I'm not going to let you face off against three thugs with guns because you have a hunch your father's involved. That's suicide."

He froze with his hand on the tailgate. His head pivoted to face her, his expression chilling her to the bone. "Are you questioning my ability to remain objective?" His low tone warned her to think before she answered.

"Well, I—" She swallowed hard then lifted her chin. "Yes. I am."

The muscles of his jaw flexed as he turned to loom over her. Through gritted teeth he snarled, "I am perfectly capable of remaining objective. I am in complete control. I will keep my promise. The only people you need to worry about are those three dumb shits in that bank who are about to get their asses handed to them. I am just fine."

"Color me relieved." Sarcasm dripped from her words. "You are not some berserker storming Mount Moracca for a golden spear, or some stupid shit like that."

His nostrils flared at her deliberate error. For all his strengths, Max's love for pop culture and movies amused her. "It's Norrath."

"Excuse me." Ripley extended his arm out between them. "Forgive me for interrupting this little lovers' spat, but there is a bank robbery in progress, and I'm freezing my ass off. Can we get on with a plan, please?"

Max pointed at her, which she understood to mean there was one more item to add to the list of things to be discussed later.

He turned back to the trunk of the Rover and lifted the floorboard that concealed a stash that included a laptop, a few tablets, an assortment of pistols and rifles, various sizes of blades, rope, and climbing gear.

Max picked up a tablet and booted it up, setting it on a holder to leave his hands free to strap various weapons to his belt. "Network, what security does this branch have?"

Addison sent a series of blueprints and schematics to the monitor. "It's fairly straightforward. Based on the building plans and security contracts on file with the city, the front door, windows, and teller area are secured with gates after closing. All forms of currency are locked in the main vault at the end of the day. There is one hallway to the vault and safety deposit box area, which are guarded by a laser field. If triggered, the alarm sounds and a signal is sent to the police and a private security firm, who are expected to respond to all alarms. Rolling metal doors will drop down at the end of each hallway, like on a ship, trapping whoever is there inside."

"Sounds pretty secure." Ripley frowned and scratched his bare chest. "How would you get around that?"

"Well," she said with a sigh. "First, I would brace the drop-down doors, so that they couldn't fall all of the way. Next, I would download a program into the security system that simulates the constant signal, even when the beams are broken."

"That's you. What about for those of us who can't talk to computers?"

"There's a program on the market that can patch or separate networks, so instead of a signal traveling from the beams to the alarm, you replace the beams with a computer and connect that to the alarm."

Ripley grunted. "Nifty program."

"Thanks." Max nodded. "I thought so when I created it."

Ripley gaped at him. "You designed a program to rob banks?"

"Of course not. I designed a program to patch networks and infrastructures to other systems in case of power outages or natural disasters. Robbing banks was not the intention."

"It must have been a possibility that crossed your mind."

"Not my problem. I was paid to design a program, not regulate it. Show me what's going on inside." Crystal coughed and shoved at his shoulder. "Please."

"The video feed has been tampered with. However, I have the footage from before the three men entered the building. I have to be honest, I'm quite impressed how they squeezed their bodies through that opening."

Addison uploaded the footage from the camera outside the credit manager's office. Three figures in blue shimmied out of an air vent in the ceiling. One immediately sat at the desk and opened a laptop. He typed furiously for fifteen seconds then suddenly he and his friends disappeared, leaving an image of a completely undisturbed office. If she squinted hard enough, Crystal was able to see a faint outline of their bodies as they moved around the room.

"A little blue-screen action. Interesting," Max murmured. "Thanks, Network. Monitor their movements and let them think that everything is on schedule." He placed the tablet in the trunk and secured another .45 into the holster under his jacket.

"Will do," she replied and signed off.

"Plan?" Ripley raised a brow.

"Keep it simple. We'll enter nice and quiet through the front door and say hello."

Crystal wasn't sold. "And if they greet us with weapons drawn?"

"Don't worry, I've got it covered." He cocked his head. "What did you think was going to happen when we got here?"

"That the police would go in and do their thing, and we would investigate once the criminals were apprehended." Duh.

He snorted. "Well, that was naïve. When there is anything having to do with Matthew Madden, I'm there first, and we don't leave until I'm satisfied that every molecule of information is squeezed from the source. If you don't like it, you can stay out here. Is that understood?"

"For now," she snarled through tight lips before pointing at him to indicate another item had been added to the discussion they would have later.

"Should I go in as a German shepherd?" Ripley asked.

Max flashed a wicked grin and chuckled. "Stay as you are. Wait until the last minute and choose something appropriately piss-pants producing."

"I love it."

Crystal stepped between them. "Boys. Stay focused. They are armed and not in the mood to be played with."

"We are focused. Let's go." Max locked up the Rover and led the way to the front entrance.

"Do you think a tiger would do it?"

"Absolutely."

"Boys."

The doors swung open under Max's power and the metal gate lifted, softer than a whisper. Of course, her heart was pounding so loudly, she couldn't hear anything anyway. It was as if she had just run a marathon, the way it thumped so hard and by the amount of sweat rolling down her back. What she wouldn't give to have a vision right at that moment. Or at least be relaxed enough that if a vision did hit, it wouldn't knock her on her ass. A tiny peek of the outcome would be so incredibly helpful.

Nothing looked amiss inside the dark lobby. Security lights were set on low and allowed just enough illumination to make out the service desk and teller areas.

Crystal tensed, ready for something, anything to jump out from behind the counter and go boo. It was a silly notion, but so was going after armed bank robbers.

Farther into the depths of the bank, the creak of a monkey wrench working on a bolt drifted to her ears.

She bit her lip to stop the nervous laughter that bubbled up inside her. It felt as if she was in her body, yet floating above the scene at the same time, observing the action with a detached eye.

The office that the would-be robbers used to enter the bank was located around the corner from the hallway that led to the vault. Two men, one short, one tall, stood at the end. Both were dressed in blue, including not only their clothes but their boots and the equipment that hung off their belts. Cave lamps strapped to their foreheads guided their movements. At their feet lay several candy bar–sized blocks, duct taped and connected with strips of wire. Above them stood a metal frame that resembled an erector set for a giant. The men worked quietly, efficiently, and were completely oblivious they were being watched.

"System is bypassed," a voice called from inside the office.

"Get ready. We're going to take a run at the vault now," the smaller of the two answered with an Asian accent.

The taller one picked up the bundles and crossed the glowing red lattice of lasers, triggering the rolling security door. It slammed into the arch, buckling the frame with an earsplitting metallic crunch. Even though Crystal knew the crash was coming, she still jumped with a startled squeal.

Ah, fuck. There went all of her street cred. Max was never going to let her live this down.

Four sets of eyes turned in her direction. "Sorry. That was louder than I expected."

The smaller man, whom she recognized as Big Tim, stared at them from under the light on his forehead. "Who the fuck are you?"

Max opened his arms. "Just curious bystanders. We saw a light on and wondered who was home."

"Cut the shit," Big Tim snapped. "Who are you?"

"Who we are is not important," Max replied. "Now, we can do this simply, and you pack up your things, and we question you nicely, or I let my friend here rip out your throat, and we throw your shit in the bags and question you not so nicely."

Big Tim smiled, his teeth flashing white in the semi-darkness. "Funny. You funny. How about I choose option three." He pointed to the blocks. "I push this button and blow us all to kingdom come."

"Right," Max snorted. "Because suicide would accomplish so much. Well, you can try that option, but I just took apart your detonators." The brightly colored plastic wires hit the floor with a soft pitter-patter. "Option two it is, then. If you will, my friend." He gestured at Ripley with an open palm.

"My pleasure." The brawny golden man rubbed his hands together with enthusiasm then hunched over.

Bones popped and cracked as Ripley's skin stretched. Orange and black fur erupted along his spine before an eight-hundred-pound Bengal tiger stood in his place. The head lamps caught the gleam of his sharp teeth as he let loose with a mighty roar, then leapt at the second bank robber.

Big Tim squeaked and fell back against the wall in terror, which Max took advantage of as he advanced on his own prey.

Suddenly, the hair on the back of Crystal's neck stood on end. Instinct and months of training made her muscles tense as she spun around. She leveled a kick, aiming straight and true, and caught the third man who was sneaking up behind her right in his groin. He fell into a heap with a nauseated groan.

Adrenaline raced through her bloodstream, sharpening her vision. Every sound echoed in her ears. The scent of manly sweat burned the inside of her nose and the spice of exhilaration coated the back of her tongue. Her boot fit nicely into the hollow of the man's neck as she pinned him to the ground. "Didn't you learn any manners? A simple hello would have been fine."

He wrapped his hand around her ankle and tugged, rolling out from under her as she landed on her knee.

"Ow!" she cried then sucked in a deep breath. She didn't want to distract Max from his fight with Big Tim, who had quickly realized that his plans were being shot to hell and woke from his shock with an upper cut to Max's midsection.

Crystal pushed the pain in her knee aside and jumped back to her feet, barely escaping the size twelve aimed at her head. She crouched low, waiting for his next move. Since he was a foot taller and a good thirty pounds heavier, she knew better than to exert all of her energy by immediately going on the offensive.

The man feinted left, then right, then threw a right hook followed by a roundhouse she blocked with her forearms. Each blow made her wince in pain. This was not training. This was not Chase pulling his punches and teaching her technique. This was a man determined to take her out any way he could.

Fear rose inside her, tightening her throat and accelerating her breathing. Instinct screamed at her to run, to find safety and hide under a thick blanket until danger passed.

Who did she think she was? She wasn't a superhuman fighting machine. She was Crystal Evans. Peace-loving, pudgy, cookie-baking psychic. She was going to go down and go down in a disastrous blaze of epic proportions.

Screams of agony echoed in the hall as Ripley's tiger tore the arm off the man holding the explosives. He tossed the bloody limb to the side as if it were a chew toy.

Near the vault, Max faced off against Big Tim. The diminutive man whipped his hands around, displaying a wealth of martial arts moves while Max watched, waiting for an opening. Suddenly, Tim stood straight and pulled a gun from his vest. The first shot he fired went wide as Max used his powers to rip the gun from Tim's hand with a gesture.

Max charged, his leather coat flapping behind him like bat wings. He wasted no time and lifted Big Tim by his shirtfront, hanging him from his tiny backpack on the large pull handle of the vault.

Fight! A voice inside her shouted. *These are your team-mates. Your friends. You cannot let them down. Prove yourself.*

A battle cry tore from her throat as she went on the offensive. Her fists and legs flew in punches and kicks, driving back her opponent. Her black Doc Marten boot landed solidly on his chest, knocking him into the wall.

He shook his head, then reached for the gun in his waistband. He immediately pulled the trigger twice in rapid succession.

"No!" Max shouted and leapt in front of her in the direct line of fire.

All the air in her lungs exploded in a burning gasp as Max barreled into her, knocking her flat on her back with him on top. Max's head hit the tile near her shoulder with a crack that made her stomach lurch as Ripley's roar rent the air and a blur of orange fur sailed over them.

"No, no," she cried and pushed against Max's heavy weight with tired arms. She shoved with a deep grunt and rolled him off of her. Panic swelled when his eyes remained closed. "Max—Maestro!" She pushed the lapels of his jacket aside, searching for bullet wounds.

Please no, please no, please no. Where's he hit? Where's he hit!

"Wake up. Please." A tear slid down her cheek and

landed on his lips.

He came awake with a gasp. His eyes flew open to stare at the ceiling in a daze. "Hey."

She laid a shaky hand along his cheek. "Where are you shot?"

His closed palm came up between them and he unfurled his fingers, revealing two bullets nestled in the center.

"Oh thank God," she sobbed and collapsed on top of him.

"I knew you cared about me."

She jerked up and slapped him in the face. "Don't scare me like that again. You... I—ooh!" She curled her fingers into his shirt and gave him a shake.

Torn between wanting to throw herself on him and kiss him senseless, or slapping him a few more times and weep with the fear that she almost lost him, she instead scrambled to her feet in a huff.

What she hadn't anticipated was the horror scene being played out behind her. She jumped and let out a blood-curdling scream that brought Max to her side in an instant.

Ripley as a tiger stood beside the body of the man who had tried to kill her. The man's empty eyes stared back as blood gushed from his torn throat and mixed with his blue face paint to form a sick purple puddle spreading on the tile floor.

When she met the tiger's blue eyes, he shifted back into human form as his gaze remained locked with hers. His sweaty chest heaved with exertion.

"He tried to kill you," Ripley said simply.

She snapped her mouth shut and nodded. If the roles were reversed, she'd do the same.

She hoped.

Man. This was bad. The last time she had been surrounded by so much blood was when her mother was killed. The sight and smell was something she had never wanted to experience again.

Memories of nightmares past churned in her belly and burned like acid up her throat. She would have lost her cookies all over the tile floor if it hadn't been for the voice that shouted from the darkness, "Freeze!"

They all started and turned toward the shout. Sheriff Lancaster and several local and county police officers stood next to him, their weapons drawn.

"Excellent timing, Sheriff." Max waved a hand at the chaos surrounding them. His skin went from pale to sickly green as he reached into his coat pocket and withdrew a handkerchief. "We were just about to start with the questioning."

"Uh-huh. Hands up, Garan."

"Yeah. Ah." His cheeks bellowed as he dry heaved. "I'm gonna need a moment here. Blood. Me. No."

"Maestro," Crystal gasped as he raced to a dark corner and promptly lost his stomach contents all over the marble floor. She moved to follow but was stopped by a deputy standing in her path.

Confusion swirled in the sheriff's gaze as he tried to process the scene before him. Crystal could only imagine what it looked like to an outsider. One man was dangling in the air, another writhed on the floor in agony missing an arm, and a third lay dead, torn apart in a puddle of blood. Lancaster did a double take when he spotted the naked, muscular man, quite alive, covered in sweat and blood.

"Who are you?"

"Therian." Ripley smiled. "Nice to finally say hello to

you, Sheriff."

Lancaster blinked once, then twice. "Therian? As in the dog?"

"On occasion."

"Yeah? Prove it."

Ripley sighed and fell to his hands and knees as his bones cracked and popped. The German shepherd barked twice in greeting.

The deputies let out squeaks and shouts of surprise that in no way sounded as if they came from the mouths of grown men, while the sheriff just stared and blinked.

A moment passed and Ripley shifted back into his human form.

"Whoa." He swayed on his feet. "All of this shifting is starting to catch up with me."

Gradually, Lancaster's lashes fluttered and he shook his head. "Okay. Um. Yeah. You're the dog. Right. Holy shit," he muttered, then turned back to his men. "All right, all right, shut up, all of you. I'm trying to process."

When he turned back to face them, he appeared to be his usual in-control self, but the hand he wiped down his face trembled. Did he even realize that was the hand he was holding his pistol in? "Okay. You're the dog. And you killed this man? Why?"

"He shot at Prism."

And in an instant, the sheriff's attention snapped to her, his eyes filled with concern. "Are you hit?"

"No," she answered. "Maestro was able to stop the bullets."

"He stopped the bullets?"

"I slowed their trajectory and caught them." Max held out his hand and showed him the dented lumps of metal.

"You caught them. Of course. I should have known." This time he rubbed both of his broad hands over his face and took a deep breath through his nose. Then another. And another. "All right. Someone get that man down and cuffed. Get a medic so that one doesn't bleed to death. That one can wait, he ain't going anywhere. You, put some clothes on. And you." He pointed at Max. "Explain. Maestro?"

Max wiped his mouth with his handkerchief and offered a shaky grin. "Where do I begin?"

CHAPTER NINETEEN

CRYSTAL HUGGED HER arms around her waist in a vain attempt to stop the shaking that rattled her teeth so badly her gums ached. A storm of activity ebbed and swelled around her as police and medics began to sort through the disorder of people and equipment while she swayed in the wind, numb.

Max stood to her right and between bouts of nausea relayed to the sheriff all the details of what they found when they had entered the bank. He stroked his chin as his gaze appeared to turn inward with thought. "There's something that isn't adding up. The explosives are too over the top, too cartoonish. There's a simpler way to break into the vault. And for what? Maybe a million in cash? A good chunk of which was promised to the Eggers brothers. There's more going on here."

"I'm inclined to agree." Lancaster braced his hands on his hips and cocked his head in her direction. "Prism, I don't suppose you can do that hocus-pocusy thing again so that we can get to the bottom of this quickly?"

"If it means we can go home faster, then absolutely." And by home she meant the bottle of wine that was calling her name. Crashing adrenaline made her entire being feel as sensitive as a frayed nerve. At any moment, she expected to crack like an egg and spill her emotions all over the floor.

Medics were strapping the man who had lost an arm to

Ripley's teeth onto a stretcher, preparing him for transport. She stepped to the head of the gurney and placed her hand on his forehead, diving through the images of his past.

"Big Tim hired this man for his expertise in explosives," she said. "But he was not privy to any more information beyond that they were robbing a bank."

She then turned toward the short man himself who sat on the floor in the corner. He smiled like a crocodile catching wind of his next meal as she approached and knelt by his side.

If it were possible, his smile showed even more teeth and bravado as he said, "Hey, pretty baby. If you're going to put your hands on me, let's make it good for both of us." He opened his knees further apart and bracketed his crotch with his cuffed hands.

She slapped her hand on his forehead, smacking his head into the drywall behind him. The time for niceties was long over. "His name is Victor Tseng. Talents include theft, larceny, and acrobatics." She flicked a glance at Max. "He also works for Madden, gathering information on his rivals."

"Madden?" Lancaster stopped her. "You mean Matthew Madden? *The* Matthew Madden whose bank we are currently standing in?"

She nodded, not ready to divulge more on that topic while Max appeared to have developed a noticeable vein throbbing at his temple. "It appears Victor here was approached by an associate of Madden's. They call him The Second." She paused to shake her head at Big Tim. "Seriously? You guys are as bad at code names as we are."

She wiped her palm on her thigh and backed away from the human rodent. "I can't see what this man looks like exactly, but he appears to be about Maestro's height, broad shoulders, fit. Wears a suit. But in Victor's memories, he's either standing in the shadows or facing away. The objective of this operation was to tap into the database of cashed checks, or more important, the signatures on the checks, along with the account holders' personal information."

Max nodded as he caught on. "Identity theft. Much more lucrative than larceny."

"This branch contains the mainframe for all Madden Bank customers. Which explains the big production going on with these explosives. Make everyone think they were after the cash, and the identity thefts would go unnoticed for months or years down the road."

"Why is the mainframe here and not at the main branch downtown or at some server farm out in the woods?" Lancaster asked.

"Too obvious," Max replied. "No one would think to look for the main frame in such an obscure location as this small branch, unless you already knew it was here." He turned to Lancaster with the corners of his mouth turned down. "What happened at the Bank of America?"

"Caught the guys as they came up through the floor. They were outfitted like these three."

"Why would Madden need to steal information on his own clients?" Max murmured.

"What?"

"Nothing, Sheriff." He shook his head and his frown deepened.

"I don't suppose there's any proof of these plans hiding anywhere?" Lancaster asked.

Crystal nodded. "They're stored at Victor's home in Vancouver, BC."

"Great." Lancaster swiped his hand down his face. "Now I'll have to get the Canadian government involved."

"Sheriff." Max slapped him on the back. "If you don't mind, we'd like to take off. I'm sure you can take it from here."

"Not so fast, buddy. What I want from you is an explanation as to how you can move things without touching them. And how can she read people's minds? And how the hell can that man turn into a dog?" With each question, his voice rose and the color in his cheeks deepened to a rich crimson. "I want answers."

"So would I." Max smiled without humor. "However, that's a story for another day."

✧　✧　✧

THE SECOND MAX turned the Rover into the garage, Crystal jumped out and made a beeline for her bedroom. She didn't give a rat's ass if she needed to be involved in any sort of debriefing with the other members of the team. Max and Ripley had been there too; they could go over the gory details again without her.

Her footsteps fell in a heavy, uneven pace on the smooth rock floor. Her skin felt too tight, her breathing labored as if she had run the entire way home. Ripping off her cap, she dug her fingers into her scalp, yet the pressure in her brain didn't ease. She peeled off her coat as she walked, but the band around her chest remained tight. Air. She needed air. And space.

She stopped in her room long enough to throw her coat on the bed and toss her boots in the corner. However much she longed to crawl into bed and put the wretched night out of mind, she knew rest would not be on the horizon. Max had kept a concerned eye on her every second since the police had appeared on the scene. For all she knew, he could appear at her door at any moment to check on her.

No. No. She was too raw to face him.

Racing out into the woods was not an option. In her current frame of mind, she'd probably fall into a hole or down a ravine. Not to mention the possibility of stumbling onto some form of wildlife.

She clawed at her shirt and turned in circles. *Who do I have to screw to have some space of my own on this mountain?*

"Wait. Oh yes," she whispered as inspiration struck, and she stumbled out into the hall and in the direction of the workout room.

Yes. Her soul rejoiced as the cavernous tomb of the empty gym cloaked her in absolute silence. The soft recessed lighting kept the darkest of shadows away and granted her tranquility.

Her lungs burned as she drew in huge mouthfuls of air. Slowly, ever so slowly, the tension in her back eased, weakening the wall of mental preservation she had thrown up the minute that man aimed a gun on her and pulled the trigger. In the quiet of the room where she had built up her physical strength, her emotional fortitude crumbled.

A cry burst past her lips, cracking through the silence like a leather whip. The second wail brought her to her knees. With each sob thereafter she pressed her forehead harder into the cold parquet floor as the reality of the evening's events carved its truth into her soul.

She almost lost him.

Behind her lids she could still see the smoke drifting from the barrel of the gun, like a spirit rising from the body of the life the bullet took. Regardless of how much distance she had placed between them, deep inside she counted on Max always being there, and that night she almost lost him.

A pair of strong, masculine arms wrapped around her and pulled her against a hard living body. The scent of sweat, blood, and Max's signature musk invaded her senses.

"Leave me alone," she choked out, not ready to face him. Not ready to face the truth.

"No."

"Please. I want to be alone."

"No. You don't." He turned her in his embrace.

Damn it. She hated when he was right.

She locked her arms around his neck and he returned her squeeze so tightly they fused together from chest to thigh.

"I thought I lost you," she whispered. Under her ear his heart beat a steady rhythm, soothing her with its cadence.

He pulled back enough to cup her face in his shaking hands. He brushed his thumb across her tear-streaked cheek. "I didn't think I would reach you in time. I was—I—" He pressed his lips together as he drew in a harsh breath through his nose.

When he tried to speak, a small mournful gasp was the only sound he made. His expression crumpled before he pressed his lips to hers. Her mouth parted under his demand, willing to give him anything he asked of her. His hands slid down her back and around her hips as his tongue glided along hers, searching, seeking the same affirmation that they were together.

"More," she whispered, digging her fingers into his shoulders. "More." This time she demanded with a cry. Surely she would expire if she didn't have him inside her in the next second.

Seams popped as they tore at each other's clothes. Her bra hit the floor a second before her back followed. The icy floor against her heated skin added to the shivers of want, making her tremble.

Max looked like an avenging angel as he hovered over her. Under the black fringe of his hair, the blue of his irises glowed like two lasers focused on her.

He traced his fingertips over her swollen lips, across her jaw, and down the column of her neck as he followed with soft kisses. "So beautiful," he whispered in reverence. A kiss fell on her collarbone then the curve of her breast. "Beautiful."

She arched into his touch as his hands molded and shaped her flesh. Pinpricks of energy zinged up her arms and settled into her breasts, making them feel heavy. He took a straining nipple into his mouth and sucked in strong deep pulls that left her gasping, aching.

Cold air hit the skin of her belly when the button on her pants unfastened and the wool skimmed down her thighs. Her giggle broke the cadence of their heavy breathing as she realized Max was undressing them both with his powers so he could continue to lavish her breasts with loving attention.

"That's a handy trick to use with the ladies," she teased, gasping.

Her laughter died at the solemn, ferocious light in his eyes. "This isn't like any other time, Crystal. Never."

His somber declaration settled in her soul as he captured her lips in a kiss meant to possess. A ravenous claiming of mind and body.

She reached out to stroke as much of his skin she could

reach as he drank from her mouth. The muscles in his shoulders and chest bunched and flexed under her caresses, reminding her of the strength he displayed in the bank as he had fought to reach her. The hand he had used to manipulate his powers in the bank glided down the satiny skin of her stomach and delved between her thighs. His finger stroked the slippery nub of her clitoris in tight circles.

He moaned against her lips. "Jesus, you're so wet." He speared two fingers deep inside. "So ready for me."

"Max." Her legs fell open, and her hips undulated, pleading for more. "I need you."

Where his fingers thrust and stretched, a fire ignited as the heat that always existed between them smoldered and caught flame. It tightened and eased. Soothed and ached. She was filled, yet empty. Frustration strangled her, preventing her from forming a coherent sentence.

With her nails, she scored his skin from navel to groin then along the underside of his rigid cock. The heavy length pulsed in her hands, alive and exhilarating. Up and over the plum-shaped head she stroked, delighting in his gasps and moans as she repeated the path.

"Next time." He broke away and pulled a foil packet from his trousers next to them. "I will spend hours learning every curve of your body. I promise."

She didn't care. All she wanted was him inside her, surrounding her, completing her.

Confusion disoriented her as he pulled her to her feet. A rubber balance ball rolled across the floor and stopped behind her knees. "Sit down and lie back," he instructed, smoky darkness and lust lowering his voice to a deep rumble. "Stretch out."

Arched over the ball, she presented the gift of her body.

A thrill of wickedness engulfed her knowing that simply looking at her caused his chest to heave, his body to tighten, and brought a pearl of cum to pool at the end of his cock. She licked her lips, eager to taste him.

"You're killing me, sweetheart." He covered his engorged shaft in latex. Kneeling between her thighs, he brushed both hands down her body from her shoulders, over her breasts, to her hips, where he grasped each thigh and parted them. "Gorgeous."

The tip of his cock slid along her slit until it nudged her opening. Her name fell like a prayer from his lips before he drove deep. Clutching her hips, he used the curve of the ball to rock her up and down his shaft.

"Damn, that's pretty," he grunted as he gazed in fascination at where his cock split her in two.

He filled her beyond capacity and still it wasn't enough. She wanted more. Needed more. "Harder, please," she panted.

The pace quickened, and still she hungered. The force of his thrusts would leave bruises, but she didn't care. The pain invigorated her, transformed her. An agony not to tear her down, but to build her back up into the woman who loved him with all of her heart. It pierced every shield and defense she had built between them and connected her to him, body to body. Soul to soul.

She curled around him, her hands seizing his shoulders as he breathed hotly on her neck.

"More," she moaned and whimpered as he struck sure and true. She teetered on the edge of a great abyss, waiting for the push into oblivion. Rebirth lay just beyond.

"I'm coming," he grunted. "Come with me."

His cock hardened to steel then twitched, pushing her

over the edge. Her back arched as she screamed, every muscle locking down. Her fingernails dug into his flesh, leaving crescent-shaped patterns in his skin.

Her body milked him, her convulsing muscles drawing out the pleasure. Tears spilled from the corner of her tightly closed eyes. Never before had she felt so complete, so wanted, so in tune with another.

Still, she wanted more.

Her heart slowed its racing and the sweat began to dry on her skin, but her tears continued.

The line she fought so hard not to cross was now nothing more than a smear of good intentions.

But she needed this. Needed to be in Max's arms.

Please, powers that be. Please let this not be a mistake. Please let this be the start of something wonderful and not the beginning of the end.

There was too much at stake.

CHAPTER TWENTY

MATTHEW MADDEN SAT rock still in the back of the moving limo. The newspaper resting on his lap hid the tension in his tightly clasped hands. Rare November sunshine shone through the back window and reflected off his dark hair, creating a halo above him. The Second sat in the seat across from him, squinting into the glare of sunlight.

"What do you mean, you don't have it?" His voice was cool, not allowing a twitch of his lip or a tic near his eye mar the cool façade hiding the seething rage inside him.

Under Madden's intense stare, The Second cleared his throat and shifted in his seat. "I'm sorry, sir. There were unforeseen circumstances behind our control." He kept his gaze focused on Madden's chest, clearly unwilling to look him in the eye.

At least he recognized the deep shit he was in. The Second only called him "sir" when delivering news he knew could cost him his life.

"Circumstances?" Madden gripped the newspaper and unfurled it with a snap. "Four strangers, dressed in black like a band of cartoon characters, and their little dog, take down an armed drug dealer holding his family hostage— your distraction, I presume—then rush to stop two simultaneous bank robberies." He flung the paper at The Second, sending pages flying in all directions.

The Second caught the front page and smoothed the paper over his leg.

"Superheroes Walk Among Us" screamed the headline, along with a photo of one of the so-called superheroes. Despite the dark glasses worn by the man in the picture, the lower half of his face was an exact replica of Madden's.

"Is it true? Does my son have some special ability to move objects with his mind?" The words came out clipped with an edge. Madden made it a priority to keep up with the exploits of his brilliant and reclusive son. If the story was true, he should have been informed of this phenomenon the moment it was suspected.

The Second neatly folded the paper and set it on the seat next to him. "According to witnesses, yes."

Madden drew a sharp breath through his clenched teeth. "Were you aware?"

"No, sir." Was that a pause before he answered?

"And the others? Who is he working with?"

"We don't know. From what we can tell, they all cohabitate on his mountain. They use code names and are able to maintain anonymity, even with the minimal disguises. No one knows where his hideout is. There are no hidden roads or secret entrances. Infrared picks up nothing. It's as if they vanish into the mist. I don't know how he does it."

"He's a genius, remember? That does not mean his cohorts are. One is bound to make a mistake and reveal their whereabouts."

"But we still need to identify one of them in order to track them."

Madden raised one dark brow. "Make. It. So."

The Second bowed his head. "Yes, sir."

The limo turned into a tunnel that ran under the

sprawling complex of the county jail. A guard stopped them at the gate before conferring with the driver and waving them through.

Sheriff Lancaster waited for them by the back entrance into the jail. The hard chill of his expression matched the seemingly subzero temperature of their surroundings. His frown deepened when Madden's bodyguard climbed out of the front seat to open the back door.

Madden slipped out of the car while The Second remained inside, hidden in the shadows. He resettled his cashmere coat across his shoulders and affixed his best politician smile. "Sheriff Lancaster, thank you for allowing me here today."

Lancaster's lips tightened with a small grunt. "You can thank Senator Cassini. I don't like this, not one bit. If he hadn't gotten the governor involved, I would have told you to kiss off."

The sheriff's less than hospitable manner didn't faze him. "My brother-in-law understands why I need to be here. When thugs attack my business, my customers, I take it personally. I deserve answers straight from the source."

"Just because you have money doesn't make you above the law. You'll get your answers. I'm working with the Canadian government right now to retrieve evidence detailing the exact plans of not only the job at Madden Bank, but also the Bank of America. These men will be put away for a long time."

Exact plans? What did those fools leave to be found? "What evidence? Did you get the leader to talk?"

Lancaster settled back on his heels, his hands resting on his belt. "I have my ways."

Madden didn't like the knowing look in the younger

man's eyes. Did the little worm The Second hired break under the pressure and reveal too much? Or was Max and his band of misfits more involved than he expected? The boy apparently had telekinetic powers. What else was he capable of?

Their gazes remained locked in a silent battle that made Madden want to laugh in the sheriff's face. Did the little pissant think he would look away first? Whatever Lancaster suspected about him would get snuffed out before the idea caught flame. No one got the best of Matthew Maxwell Madden II.

Despite his abundance of confidence, the compulsion to find out exactly what happened the night before stretched his patience thin. His lungs tightened with each measured breath, but he refused to buckle.

That's right, you filthy commoner. Madden let loose with the tiniest of triumphant sighs as Lancaster blinked first and turned to open the door. Patience always prevailed.

The catacombs of the jail were usually reserved for the transportation of criminals to and from the courthouse. It also bypassed prying eyes and the contingent of press waiting outside on the sidewalk. Rumors abounded throughout the city over what had happened at the bank, but those who had been on duty had been ordered to keep their mouths shut. However, there had been hundreds of witnesses in front of Eggers's house, and those lips were flapping to anyone willing to listen. The public wanted answers to the incredible sight they had beheld. So did Madden.

Madden's Ferragamos clicked with a staccato beat in time with Lancaster's heavy step. A deputy stood sentry outside a nondescript door. Beside him, a distinguished-looking gentleman looked up expectantly upon their approach. His Brooks Brothers suit emphasized his fit build and accentuated the aristocratic carriage of his bearing.

"Mr. Madden." Lancaster gestured. "This is Marcus Boudreaux, the court-appointed attorney for Mr. Tseng."

"I'm very honored to meet you, Mr. Madden." His handshake was firm, confident, a gesture of strength.

"Mr. Boudreaux. I realize this is unusual, but I'm sure you can understand why I would want to be present when you talk to your client about last night and his options."

"I have to admit, Mr. Madden, I'm not comfortable having you anywhere near my client. But on Senator Cassini's…request, I will allow you to be present. However, you will not be allowed to ask any questions. You will be there in an observational capacity only."

"Of course. I understand how you wish to not have your client incriminate himself any further. But I also wish to prevent any future attacks on my bank." He smiled and gestured to the door. "Shall we begin?"

A series of beeps emitted from the sheriff's radio. "Lancaster," he barked into the receiver.

"Sheriff, you're needed out front. The press is getting restless, and the street is becoming congested with civilians."

His eyes narrowed at Madden with suspicion. "I'm in the middle of something right now. It will have to wait."

"Sir, they're blocking street traffic. We're bordering on riot-like conditions."

Lancaster spun away with a curse on his lips. He quickly returned and replied, "Give me a minute." He gestured with an agitated hand. "Deputy Arnold, watch them like a hawk. No one goes in, no one comes out, until I get back. Especially him." He pointed at Madden's bodyguard.

Arnold snapped to attention. "Yes, sir."

With a frustrated grunt, he stalked down the hall.

The bodyguard caught Madden's nod and took position to the right of the door as the deputy turned the knob. "This way, gentlemen."

Boudreaux motioned for Madden to precede him into the interrogation room.

"M-Mr. Madden," Big Tim stuttered. He swiped at the sweat that had popped out across his brow the moment Madden walked into the room. "I-I didn't—I thought The Second would be coming."

Big Tim sat alone at the battered card table. Residue of blue paint was caked into the flare of his nostrils and along his hairline. Straight black strands of hair stuck out in all directions from the top of his head.

The grimy beige walls held the stench of cigarettes, piss, and fear, lending a metallic bite to the recycled air. A large rectangular mirror reflected the uncomfortable environment back at them. No doubt Deputy Arnold was taking his place on the other side right now to monitor the proceedings. The Second had made arrangements before their arrival to disable the surveillance equipment. When Madden arched an inquisitive brow, Boudreaux nodded his confirmation that the men were allowed to speak freely.

Madden sat gingerly on the rickety slat-backed chair. "I wanted to be here personally."

"Oh, I—oh—"

"Tell me about these so-called superheroes," he commanded. The last night's events took a backseat to the hunger to learn more about his son.

Big Tim swallowed. "It was like they came out of thin air. One minute it's just Bobby and me ready to blow the safe, the next, these two dudes and a chick are standing there, watching us. One of the guys is huge, and naked, then all a sudden, he changes into a tiger."

"Wait." Madden held up a hand, not recognizing what might have been a slang term. "A tiger? What does that mean?"

"A tiger. Means he turned into a tiger. Like Siegfried and Roy, poof, tiger."

"He turned into a tiger," Madden repeated slowly.

Big Tim threw his hands up. "That's what I said. He turned into a tiger."

Impossible. Madden sat back in disbelief. The concept was completely improbable, but after hearing about Max, he couldn't discount the possibility.

To his right, he noticed that Boudreaux appeared more thoughtful at the revelation than surprised. His dark eyes darted back and forth, his mind working on something.

"Continue," Madden prompted, salivating with the need for more information.

Big Tim leaned forward in his chair, eager to regale them with the tale. "So this tiger jumps at Bobby and rips his fucking arm off. He's screaming and bleeding all over the place when the second guy, the one they call Maestro, comes at me. First, I strike him with a ha—" He mimed throwing his fist in a quick punch. "Then a who-ha. Then I pull my gun. He does this—" he waves—"and the gun goes flying out of my hand. Whoosh. We start to throw punches. I get in more good hits, then he does that hand trick again and I'm out, I cannot move. It was like he put me in invisible ropes or something. And Zero is fighting the girl, and he shoots at her. This Maestro jumps in front of her and caught the bullets. He actually caught them in his hand like they were fucking marbles. That's when the tiger tackled Zero and tore out his throat."

"I knew there was something unnatural about those people," Boudreaux muttered.

Madden turned to him in surprise. "You know of them?"

He shook his head. "We've volunteered for the same search and rescue missions the last few months. Supposedly they're a private security firm. Somehow, some way, they always seem to find the target with uncanny accuracy. The last time out, they conveniently missed being trapped by an avalanche. No one has that kind of luck."

"And you are sure it is these same three people?"

"Maestro and Prism?" Boudreaux replied. "Yes. Although he's also called Garan. But there are more of them. There's a doctor, and a kid. They also have a dog. Perhaps that's the man who can change shape?"

The blood quickened through Madden's veins. *More* of them? A group of mutants. And his son was their leader? "Prism. Is that the woman? What about her?"

Boudreaux shrugged. "She's a luscious piece of ass. Sassy too. Beyond that, I don't know."

Big Tim's sudden silence and intense observation of the cracks in the tile floor drew Madden's attention. "What do you know, Victor?"

"What? Oh. Yeah, what Mr. Boudreaux said. She's hot." His tittering laugh sputtered off under Madden's quelling stare. He swallowed hard, then admitted, "When she touches you, she can read your mind."

"Read—your—mind?" he repeated every syllable.

The little man nodded, a cagey twitch began near his left eye.

"And what did she see in your mind?"

He pulled at the collar of his button-down shirt. "My house in BC where I kept the plans for last night's job."

Madden drew a deep breath through his nose and gritted his teeth before he lost his legendary control. He slowly exhaled and focused on relaxing every muscle that had tightened with alarm. That must be the evidence the sheriff was working on retrieving from the Canadian government.

A tap at the mirror served as a warning. Lancaster was approaching.

"Thank you for the information." He rose to his feet and used his reflection in the two-way mirror to straighten his perfect appearance.

"Hey. When you get me out of here?" Big Tim asked.

"Soon."

The door opened and Lancaster strode in, his sharp gaze searching for anything out of place.

"Ah, good timing, Sheriff." Madden smiled. "We just finished."

Lancaster looked to Boudreaux, who stood to button his own jacket and faced him with a pleasant grin. Big Tim remained seated, looking appropriately put out.

He turned back to Madden, distrust clouding his laser-like stare. "Was it worth your time, Mr. Madden?"

"Yes. It was a very enlightening conversation. Thank you for your indulgence."

He snorted and beckoned Madden to exit the room. "I'll take you back to your car."

Madden turned to Boudreaux and extended his hand. "Thank you, counselor, for allowing me to be present. You have a tough job, but I am positive you have the skill to see it through to the end."

Boudreaux tightened his grasp with understanding before pulling away. "You're welcome."

With a final nod, Madden walked through the doorway, his gaze briefly holding Deputy Arnold's, receiving the two-blink signal. His bodyguard followed with Lancaster close behind.

A handful of steps later, chaos erupted.

"What are you doing?" Boudreaux shouted from the interrogation room. "A knife! He has a knife!" A crash echoed down the cement halls.

"Drop the weapon," Arnold barked. "Drop it."

Lancaster spun on his heel and raced toward the commotion.

"What the fuck?" Big Tim yelled. "No! Don't—"

A single gunshot rang out.

Madden watched with utter calm as Lancaster skidded to a stop at the door. He knew what the sheriff saw: Big Tim dead on the floor with a box cutter near his hand. The deputy seeing to Boudreaux who was probably bleeding from a cut somewhere on his person. An unfortunate end to a beautiful suit.

"Jesus Christ," Lancaster bellowed, his accusatory glare swung to Madden. "Tseng's dead."

He forced his features into a shocked expression. "Why would he do something so stupid?"

"I don't know," the sheriff snarled. "But I'm going to find out." He pulled up his receiver and called into the switchboard. "Jones, I have a 10-36. I need a medic sent to room B immediately. And I want all video from this room for the last twenty-four hours in my office now."

"10-4 on the medic, sir. But room B doesn't have any surveillance. I have it marked as out of order due to electrical problems until tomorrow when maintenance is supposed to come and fix the wiring."

His lips curled over his teeth as he glared at Madden. "Are you shitting me?"

Her surprised gasp squawked over the speaker. "Excuse me, Sheriff?"

"Never mind," he growled.

"How unfortunate." Madden tsked and shook his head. "I can see that you'll have your hands full. I'll let myself out." He didn't wait for a response.

His smooth stride ate up the tile floor. In his stomach, a rising tide of turmoil threatened to overwhelm him. His lungs tightened as sweat broke out over his skin. The news from the afternoon did not bode well. Not well at all.

As if sensing the shift in Madden's world, the body-guard scampered ahead and opened the door to the limo so that Madden could slide onto the creamy leather seat without losing momentum.

The Second watched him with concern. The longer Madden remained silent, the tighter his features pinched.

The unfamiliar sensation of panic rolled through his body in the most unpleasant way. Desperate to break free of the constricting hysteria, he focused on The Second. "Max has gathered together a small band of mutants. There are others who appear to have powers of their own"

"He's what?" The Second blinked with confusion.

"The others who were with him also possess superpow-ers, including a shapeshifter and a woman who can read minds."

"That's impossible. How can that be?"

"It's Max. He's a master of the unexplainable." The starched collar around his throat began to irritate him. "We may have been compromised. The mind reader pulled information from Big Tim's mind. I want his house in BC destroyed. I've taken care of the man myself."

"Yes, sir."

"Just as important, I am still in need of those identities. Our comrades require them to bring their people into our country. Without them, we cannot proceed."

"It will be done. You have my word."

"*Your* word means shit to these people," he spat. The flinch in the other man's eyes appeased him somewhat.

"It will be done."

"If not, it will all come down on you. We are in it too deep to fail on any level now. If it wasn't for all of the ass kissing I have to do in Washington to ensure those imbeciles continue to slit their own throats, I would see to it myself."

"I understand."

"You have until the party, tonight. Our investors will be there waiting. This is the night I have been building toward for years. I expect success and a gesture of good will for last night's fuckup."

"Yes, sir." The bite in The Second's tone had the muscles in Madden's jaw tensing.

Why was his world being threatened? And now? Hadn't he forged through every painful step to fulfill his destiny? Planned down to the most minuscule detail? He would reign supreme. And there was no way in hell he was going to let that be jeopardized by a group of...others. Fate was still his to dictate.

Superheroes.

He leaned his head back against the seat.

What he could do if he had control over their powers? A

shapeshifter. A woman who could read minds. The possibilities were endless. As were the ways they could destroy him.

This anxiety filling his chest was unnatural. His cock swelled, ached with the need to control, to enforce his dominance. He was still Matthew fucking Madden, ruler of the world.

Something out the window caught his eye. "Stop the car. Pull over now."

He turned around to look out the back window to eye a woman sitting at a table at an outdoor café. Her dark hair fell in a thick sheet to frame large breasts created by man, for man.

Yes, he rubbed his erection through his slacks, she would do nicely.

"What do you want me to do about these mutants?" The Second asked. Disapproval compressed his mouth into a tight line.

"Find them. I want them to work for us."

"And if they refuse?"

"They die," he replied without hesitation. "Even Max."

CHAPTER TWENTY-ONE

MAX TOOK HIS place at the front of the great room and looked on with pride as his team settled in for the meeting.

His team. He couldn't have asked them to perform any better than they had the night before. Everything had gone as planned—except for the getting shot at part—and Ripley ripping the throat out of one of the bank robbers. But for their first official time officially out, it wasn't half bad.

The amazing high of being one of the baddest asses out there continued to vibrate along his skin. The fear and awe that had flashed in the eyes of the enemy had been like a drug feeding his power. He had felt invincible. There wasn't anything he couldn't accomplish. The only experience that had been more euphoric had been afterward with Crystal in the workout room.

Crystal. Damn. The complex yet simple puzzle that was Crystal Evans.

God, the way she had clung to him, her taste. The way her cries echoed in the room as he sank inside her had been a symphony for the senses. The memory alone sent a wave of heat from his belly down to his groin.

As if she could hear his thoughts, Crystal turned away from her conversation with Alisia and met his heavy-lidded gaze. A smile brought out the dimple in her cheek before she returned to her discussion.

Was she even aware how well he knew her? The hours of observation he put in studying everything there was about her?

Despite her bright smile he saw brittleness edging her lips and the glint of worry in her now-green eyes. She was afraid. Last night's reality had hit her over the head with the subtlety of a baseball bat, and by her reactions he could tell she was still reeling.

On that, he could totally relate. When it came to Crystal, he was scared shitless.

No doubt about it. She was his weakness, his kryptonite. The absolute terror that had fired through his body when the bullet shot out of that gun toward her had almost crippled him. If he hadn't reacted when he did, the bullet would have hit her right between the eyes.

Funny how one minute he'd felt stronger than Hercules and the next, a helpless plaything to the gods of fate. No way in hell was he ever going to allow her to be that close to danger again. He was cocky, not stupid. Defeat bad guys—no problem. He could do it in his sleep. Protect his woman—he'd do anything and everything. Cautious didn't even begin to describe the care he'd take. Crystal's safety was his priority and he trusted no one or their powers. Not even his own.

When his mother had killed herself, the grief that consumed him had been a combination of immense sadness and the profound loss of what could have been. She could have done so much with her life, but instead had allowed insecurity, jealousy, and deceit to destroy her.

Crystal had such spark, such fire—to see her light extinguished would destroy him. Life without her was unthinkable.

He loved her.

Or at least he thought he did. Never had a woman left him twisted in so many knots. She inspired him with a smile, soothed him with a touch. Inflamed him with a well-placed barb from that wicked tongue, and frightened him with her courage. Surely, that must be love.

And because of that, he had to keep her safe. Of course, he was smart enough to realize that Crystal's independence and determination would make pulling rank and keeping her out of the fray go over as well as a pacifist at an NRA convention.

Sure, she'd scream at him, but it was for her own good. She had her talents, which he would use when needed, but when it came to physical combat, her place was back on the mountain. To have her anywhere near conflict would drive him insane and weaken his focus if he had to be constantly on alert. In time, she'd understand.

"I'm here. I'm here." Ripley strode into the room with a gallon-size jug of sports drink in his hand. "We can begin now."

"Thanks," Max said with a snort. He nodded at the bottle. "Thirsty?"

Disgust scrunched the shapeshifter's features. "I still have the taste of bad guy in my mouth. My animal likes it, but it turns my stomach."

"Did ingesting that blood make you sick?"

"No, just nauseous. Doc did a scan. I'm fine." He turned to take a seat then stopped. He sniffed once, then again in a long deep breath. His gaze flicked back and forth between Max and Crystal as a shit-eating grin split his face. "How you doin'?"

Max stilled. "I'm fine."

The grin stretched wider. "I just bet you are."

Max narrowed his eyes and the bottle in Ripley's hand began to tremble and expand, the pressure inside building.

"Hey, knock that off," Ripley demanded, holding the bottle away from him.

"Take your seat," Max said softly. "Please."

"Sure, sure. Must not have been that good," Ripley mumbled as he walked away.

The top of the bottle popped off like a bottle rocket and red sticky liquid bubbled over his hand. He glared at Max over his shoulder. "Man, not cool."

Max chuckled and clapped his hands together. "Let's begin."

The lights dimmed as Addison downloaded several photos onto the screen behind him.

"We prevented Madden from getting his hands on millions of identities, so now the question becomes why he needed them in the first place," he said.

"Invasion?" Ripley suggested, only half in jest.

"Correct." Max nodded. "I believe he's preparing to bring an army into the country and needed those identities. My theory is that by using his own clients, he'll able to hide any suspicious activity that might arise. If an anomaly in someone's credit does come up, then he could claim the error was fallout from the bank robbery."

"What about the Bank of America clients?" Chase asked.

"He needs to spread the suspicion. It wouldn't look good if Madden clients were the only ones with their identities stolen."

Doc raised her hand. "So now what? Any idea what he's going to do now that his plan was foiled?"

"He's going to make another attempt," Addison answered. "Just not as elaborate as last night." A photo of a handsome man in a tailored three-piece suit appeared on the screen. "James Dittmar, regional manager of Madden Financial. About thirty minutes ago, his computer at work launched a program that is harvesting client information and downloading it onto a flash drive. It's a riskier plan, since it will be easier for law enforcement to track the leak if any of Madden's scheme becomes known, so they must be in desperate need of the information now."

Max stroked his chin with his forefinger. "Was the program loaded remotely?"

"No, he launched it at the terminal. The program is still running."

"So why can't you stop it?" Ripley asked.

"I could, but the Madden Financial network has a genius firewall." The hacker glared pointedly at Max. "It will send a virus to any out-of-network computer and fry it, which I would like to avoid. I can monitor that activity, but that's all. The best and less damaging solution would be to intercept the flash drive."

"How?"

"Take it from him before tonight."

"Why tonight?"

She typed a few more keys. "Madden is throwing a party for his investors. Big affair with CEOs from about every technology company there is, including foreign dignitaries from South America and the Middle East, and suspected members of the Italian and Irish mafia. My guess? This is when he's passing along those identities."

Max's pulse quickened. This party was the perfect opportunity to take out not only Madden, but many of the other players in his organization at the same time.

"Addison, access the blueprints for Madden's house from my files. I have a plan on where we can enter."

"Not so fast," she warned and pulled up an image of the morning newspaper. "Apparently you haven't seen today's news. You wanted attention, you've got it."

"Superheroes Walk Among Us" read the headline, right above a photo of Maestro decked out in his sunglasses and leather coat. If his father paid even the slightest bit of attention to the news, he'd recognize the Madden chin for certain.

Ripley read aloud. "'Are these people friend or foe? Authorities are now scrambling to ascertain not only who these people are, but if they plan to stay altruistic. The fear is these people will demand payment for their "services," and the price will be more than humanity can afford.' What kind of bullshit is that?" he sputtered.

"Expected," Crystal replied and gazed up at Max. "We knew it was a possibility we'd be recognized if we went public."

"You can see the problem," Addison said. "I bet Madden is working on a plan to counter anything you may do right now."

"Okay." Max held up his hand. "If Madden knows about me and my powers, fine, let him come after me. But that's a big *if*. First things first, get that flash drive. The rest we'll plan after we have the drive. Any ideas?"

A collective silence fell upon them.

Crystal burst out with a sharp laugh and doubled over in her chair. While everyone exchanged glances, wondering what the joke was, she wiped the tears from her eyes and leveled a look at Ripley that made Max grateful not to be the recipient.

She caught her breath and sighed. "I have an idea."

CHAPTER TWENTY-TWO

"WHAT A CUTE little dog you have there," commented an elderly woman passing Crystal on the street. "Boy or girl?"

Oh, how Crystal wanted to answer that the little Pomeranian riding shotgun in her Dior canvas tote was a girl, but knowing Ripley, he'd probably retaliate and pee in her bag.

"Cuddles is a boy. And a manly boy at that. Aren't you, sweet baby?" she cooed. Ripley yipped and licked at her lips before she could pull away.

The woman laughed. "And so rambunctious. What a darling."

"Isn't he?" Crystal replied, barely able to keep from gagging. "You have a good day, ma'am."

"You, too."

"I swear to God, I will put a muzzle on you," she muttered as soon as they were out of earshot.

Based on the goofy expression on his face, if dogs could laugh, Ripley would be bent in two and slapping his knee right at that moment.

There was enough about this mission to be nervous about without adding a puppy-sized practical joker to the list. As it was, it took everything within her to keep from fidgeting with the diamond pendant hanging around her neck. Concealed behind the stone was a camera; on her earrings, a microphone. Every sight and sound monitored back at base by Addison.

And Max.

"You can still back out, Prism." His voice came through her earpiece as if he sensed she was thinking of him. "We can still get the data another way."

"No," she replied as best as she could without moving her lips. "I can do this."

Now stop coddling me and let me do my damn job.

It was clear she was the best one to extract the information from Dittmar, but Max had argued she wasn't ready to go alone. Actually, his exact words were, "You're insane if you think I'll let my woman be placed in danger."

Yep. Just like that. In front of the entire team. As if she were a special snowflake and they expendable.

She would have been insulted if she hadn't seen the twitch near his eye, and the way the tight line of his mouth trembled as the team came to her defense.

Max was afraid for her. He knew she was their best bet, yet he refused to put her in danger. A most surprising development in their relationship. Not a few days prior, Max was jumping on any opportunity, ready to risk anything, for the chance to destroy Madden.

Now he wasn't willing to risk her.

Did that mean Max was finding purpose beyond the need for revenge? Was he developing feelings for her, beyond teammate and bed partner? Did she want him to?

That was silly. Of course she did. But at what cost? Her place on the team? If she and Max were going to become "her and Max," then it was imperative she make clear the mission came first. Always.

Which meant on this mission she was going to have to be flawless. At the end of the day, no one, especially Max, would have cause to doubt her abilities.

"You distract me for one second, Maestro," she said loud enough for the mic to pick up her voice. "I'm shoving my heel up your ass. Radio silence now."

She fixed a smile on her lips as she approached the front door of the downtown branch of Madden Financial. A young man held the door open for her, and she felt his gaze linger on her ass as she sashayed across the tiled lobby with her three-inch stilettos clicking like gunfire.

The receptionist glanced up and missed restraining a roll of her eyes as she took in Crystal dressed in all her wanna-be socialite glory.

Yes, she was well aware that November in the Pacific Northwest was an odd time to be wearing a short-sleeved silk sundress that hugged her shape like plastic wrap. At any moment she expected the goose bumps on her skin to start quacking, she was so cold.

However, the heavy layer of makeup covering her skin did keep her face warm, and her carefully coiffed helmet of hair was like a wool cap. If there had been a casting call for a remake of *Steel Magnolias,* she'd be a shoo-in for certain.

"Can I help you?" the receptionist asked when Crystal came to a stop before her desk.

She turned up the wattage on her smile and added a little twang to her accent. "Hi, my name is Crystal Winters. I have an appointment with Mr. Dittmar."

The receptionist squinted at her over her spectacles. Her gaze traveled over Crystal's cleavage and purse puppy, then turned away with a dismissive huff. "Mr. Dittmar has an event this evening and cleared his calendar to depart early."

Crystal picked up the nameplate on the desk and held it at necklace level. "Are you certain—Ms. Samuels, is it? I was told he would be most anxious to see me."

"Dorthea Samuels," Addison replied through the earpiece, reading the name off the plate. "Got it."

"I'm certain," Ms. Samuels reiterated without looking up from her monitor.

"Check again. Please."

The older woman sighed and rolled her eyes again. "What did you say your name was?"

"Winters. Crystal Winters."

That was all the time Addison needed to link into the receptionist's login and add the appointment to Outlook.

Ms. Samuels looked back at the monitor and typed in the information. Her eyes widened. "What? I could have sworn the afternoon was blocked out."

"Well, I was told I'd be the last appointment of the day. Believe me, I am very appreciative."

"I—I'll ring him for you, Ms. Winters." She eyed the monitor with confusion as she reached for the phone.

"Thank you so much." Crystal smiled and took a step back from the desk.

"Yes, I know, Mr. Dittmar," Ms. Samuels said in a hushed tone. "I don't know who took the appointment, but she's here and said you were very interested in meeting with her. I promise, there are no further appointments on your calendar. All right." She hung up and turned back to Crystal with a strained smile. "He'll be right with you, Ms. Winters."

"Thank you."

As she waited, Crystal checked out the layout of the lobby, noting exits and hallway entrances. This wasn't a typical branch of Madden Bank, but rather a division of Madden Financial. An office reserved for financial planning, loans, and for clients with bank accounts big enough to warrant special attention. According to Max, if you wanted your money hidden, these were the people to see.

"Good morning, Mrs. Winters." A smooth, cultured voice spoke from behind her. "I'm James Dittmar."

Even in her high heels, she had to tilt her head way back to maintain eye contact with the handsome bank manager. Hair the color of wheat swept off his face and highlighted his high cheekbones and square jaw. A black silk suit was tailored perfectly to his swimmer's physique, drawing appreciative glances from many women in the lobby. The photo Addison had dredged up did not do him justice.

Dear Lord, she was supposed to flirt with that?

Her confidence took a dive until she noticed the spark of interest in his green eyes as they zeroed in on the swell of her breasts spilling out of her fuchsia sundress.

The pink diamond of her ring sparkled as she reached for his outstretched hand. "It's *Miss* Winters, but please, call me Crystal. Thank you so much for taking time out of your busy day for me."

His white teeth flashed brilliantly against his tan cheeks and his gaze took another journey to cleavage-ville. "Believe me, it's my pleasure."

He clasped her hand with both of his, giving Crystal the added boost to search through his memory and witness him receiving the package that contained the flash drive. Before she could search for more intel, he broke the contact.

"Shall we continue in my office?" He gestured ahead of them with one hand and placed the other low on her back. Really low.

Cuddles growled softly in his throat, expressing his displeasure of Dittmar's proximity.

His smile faltered and he eyed the growly pooch with a

distasteful curl on his lip. "That's uh, that's a tiny dog you have there."

"Isn't he precious? And so loyal, too. He gets a little nervous around new people, but he's very obedient." She patted Ripley's head a bit firmer than necessary. "If he knows what's good for him."

Ripley licked at her fingers as Dittmar escorted her into his office.

"Muzzle. I swear," she hissed under her breath, and took a seat in one of the chairs.

Dittmar stood in front of her and leaned back against his desk. His hands rested not so subtly to frame his groin that was right at her eye level. "To what do I owe the pleasure of this visit, Crystal?"

She batted her lashes and hunched her shoulders together to deepen the vee of her cleavage. "I would like to open an account, but my circumstances are a little unusual. You see, a few weeks ago I was fortunate enough to hit the winning numbers in the lottery. I opted for the lump-sum payment, and I'm now ready to transfer the funds from a trust into my name."

"The lottery? Really?" He snorted with surprised laughter. "How much did you win?"

"Seventy-six million dollars."

His gaze jumped from the leisurely perusal of her body to meet her eyes. "I'm sorry, did you say seventy-six *million* dollars?"

"Yes." She smiled sweetly. "Actually, it was more, but that's what was left after taxes and all of that. Now as you can imagine, I would like to keep this transfer as quiet as possible. That's why I'm not using my regular bank. I already have people I barely know asking for handouts."

"Yes, I can see that being troublesome," he mumbled, suddenly all business, and walked around to sit behind his desk. The prospect of landing a multimillion-dollar client seemed to have cooled his flirtation.

His fingers typed with a spring of excitement. "Have you thought about what type of accounts you wanted to open?"

"Here is a list an accounting friend of mine gave me as a start." She withdrew a piece of paper from her bag and attempted to smooth the wrinkles from the page before sliding it across the desk. "I know I'll want to invest the majority of it. But I'm not sure on what just yet. I guess I'll need to book a financial planner for advice soon."

He looked away from the computer and stared at her as if she had offered him the key to El Dorado. A smile curled his lips as smoothly as a slick of oil over a placid lake. "I'd be happy to assist you with that, Crystal."

"But won't you be busy managing the bank?"

He placed his hand on his chest. "I would be honored to assist you during this time of transition. Here at Madden Financial, we treat our customers like family. It would be like helping one of our own."

She shuddered to think what kind of activities went on at a Dittmar family reunion if he considered her family.

"Are you sure I wouldn't be putting you out? I've been told it can take me forever to reach a decision."

"I insist."

"You are too sweet." She clapped her hands with delight and bounced in her seat to add a little jiggle to her top half. "Thank you, Mr. Dittmar."

"Please, call me James."

"All right. James," she said with a coquettish bat of her

lashes.

Step one: become friendly with the target. Check. Now for the next step of the plan.

According to Addison, they had timed her visit at the bank to coincide with the conclusion of the downloading of the files. Unless Dittmar had a computer that was as fast as Chase, the flash drive still had to be in his office.

She reached into her bag to pull a card from her purse before setting the bag on the floor. Ripley jumped out and immediately began to sniff around the room with his little pudgy nose.

"Here's the information on how to transfer the money." She extended her hand with the card.

His fingers brushed hers, but the contact wasn't long enough to obtain a vision of where he placed the flash drive. Damn it, she needed to get her hands on the man.

While Dittmar called the phony lottery service Addison had created to make it appear as if her story was legit, Crystal kept an eye on Ripley. Every now and again he'd shake his head and continue to another part of the room. After sticking his head underneath the desk, he pulled back and gave an enthusiastic yip.

Dittmar held out the receiver. "They would like to speak with you to confirm your identity."

"Certainly." She crossed to his side and took the phone, making sure to stay within his personal space. "This is Crystal."

It was quite comical to see him try to divide his attention between her cleavage and his computer as he set up her accounts.

"And how are we doing today, Ms. Winters?" Addison asked.

"Fine, thank you. Excited to get this process over with."

"ETA on locating the drive?"

"That would be one, five, zero, zero, M."

"Fifteen minutes is too long," Max's voice could be heard in the background. "Tell her to get out of there now."

"Is there anything else you need?" Crystal asked.

"If you can aim the camera at the monitor, I'd be greatly appreciative."

"No problem."

"Awesome. Now put the hunk back on the phone."

Crystal held the receiver out to Dittmar and leaned over, brushing her breasts against his arm and aiming the pendant to capture a glimpse of the computer monitor. "She wants to talk to you again."

A flush tinged his cheeks as he continued the call. His keystrokes weren't quite as smooth as he finalized the transaction and hit enter. A box appeared on the screen and slowly started to fill with a green bar until it pinged and flashed "Transaction Complete."

He stood and held out his hand again, this time with an anticipatory light in his eyes. "Welcome to Madden Financial, Crystal."

"Thank you." She clasped his hand and held on, desperate to read more information. "Um, there is one more thing. I bought a few baubles for myself to celebrate, but I'm afraid to leave them at my house. I haven't installed any type of security system yet, so I'd like a safe deposit box as well."

"Of course." He dropped her hand. Damn it. "Let's get one for you immediately."

"Excellent." She reached into her purse and withdrew several flat, Tiffany blue boxes. "Is it all right if Cuddles stays here?"

Dittmar's smile widened. "That's probably for the best."

"And we won't be gone long, right?"

"Ten minutes tops."

"Okay. Cuddles, Mommy will be gone for a few minutes. Be a good puppy." Ripley yipped in reply then lifted his leg at the ficus in the corner. "Stop. Don't even think about it," she snapped, dropping the sugar in her tone. She turned back to Dittmar with her sunny smile back in place. "Shall we?"

He closed the door behind them and placed his hand along her back again as he ushered her down the hall. "I bet your family was excited to hear about your good fortune."

"I'm not close to my family. My daddy died when I was little. He got caught in the combine on the farm we lived on. My momma lost herself in booze and men. I've been on my own since I was a teenager." She tilted her head and leveled her most vulnerable, heartbreaking expression at him. "You can see why I'm trying to keep a low profile. I don't want her, or her current scuzzy boyfriend, to find me."

"I completely understand." He lowered his eyelids and puckered his full lips in what she could only guess was his compassionate face. "I hope you're not totally alone and have someone you can rely on. A friend or husband…"

"I'm not married. No boyfriend either."

"That is a shame." His fingers tightened on her hip, caressing her through the silk.

What was it with men and butts? Why couldn't he place his hand on her arm or shoulder where they could be skin to skin? Nope, let's just go right for the booty.

They passed by a series of gates to the area that held the safe deposit boxes. The room was dimly lit and so cold, she got closer to Dittmar just for warmth. A lone chair and a table stood in the middle, topped with a metal lamp that cast a white circle on the wood surface. Definitely not the most hospitable place to linger with your valuable possessions. An awareness of the danger she walked into by stepping in the enclosed space sent another bout of chills down her arms, and for the first time she questioned this part of the mission.

Dittmar handed her a clipboard and pen and instructed her on how to fill out the deposit form while he laid an empty safe box on the table and sorted through keys. There was only so much stalling she could do by fumbling around with the jewelry boxes, and before she was ready, Dittmar slid the safe deposit box into its designated home and locked it in place.

"Your key." He held it close to his chest.

It made her stomach churn to know she was going to have to do more to encourage his flirting, but she needed to make sure Ripley had enough time to find the flash drive and replace it with their dummy version.

Taking the bait, she stepped closer. "Thank you." Brushing his fingers with hers, she took the key and slipped it into the bodice of her dress. She met his gaze through the veil of her lowered lashes.

Hunger and lust tightened his features, narrowing his stare. He ran his fingers across the goose bumps on her arms before gripping her around the bicep. "You're cold. We'll have to do something to warm you up."

Finally, contact. Seizing the moment, she dove into his past, pulling images of him installing the flash drive and downloading the program. There was a letter in the package from The Second. By Dittmar's delighted grin, the news was good. Had he worked with Madden's man before?

"You're a saucy little minx." Dittmar broke her concentration, seizing her around the waist before claiming her lips in a bruising kiss with a technique that was all teeth and tongue.

Too late she realized she should have kept her focus divided between the past and what was going on in the present as he lifted her onto the table and pressed his hips between her thighs.

Focus, focus, focus, she ordered her racing heart. *Do not panic.*

She softened her lips and melted against him, in the hopes that if she slowed, he would follow. The object all along had been contact, not sex. But she should have been prepared for someone who worked with Madden to go from zero to sixty in a nanosecond. Somehow, she was going to have to slow this bullet train down.

Think. What would Scarlett O'Hara do?

She clung to his shoulders as she ripped her lips away and heaved a dramatic sigh. "Oh, James, this is too fast. I can't think when you kiss me this way."

"Then don't think. Just feel. Feel me." He ground his suit-clad erection against her cleft.

She bit back a whimper. "But I can't be with a man who only wants me for my money."

He paused and pulled back. Not as far as she would have liked, but enough for her to breathe a little easier. "Why would you think that?"

"Well, look at you. You're gorgeous and successful. You can have any woman you want. There is no way a man like you could be attracted to me, unless it was for my money." She batted her lashes.

He lapped up her compliments with a snake charmer

grin. "I don't want you for your money. I have plenty of my own." He resumed the grinding of his hips as his head lowered to scrape his teeth along the skin of her neck. "I want you. Just as you are. Except naked and panting for me, like you are now. You're so sexy and taste so good. I want to taste you all over. You'd like that, wouldn't you? I bet your panties are wet right now, wetter than you've been for any man before," he moaned in her ear. The one that held the earring with the microphone that was broadcasting right into the communications center and everyone listening.

Including Max.

Max was going to kill her! Flat out tie her up and never allow her to leave the mountain again.

Her heart threatened to burst out of her chest. "James, I do want you, but I want your respect more."

"I do, I do respect you," he murmured into her skin. "I'm sorry. I can't think straight when I'm faced with these gorgeous tits." He pressed his face between her mounds and wiggled his head back and forth. Charming.

Yep, she was so dead. She needed to escape, now.

"Come back here, you little mutt!"

A dog's high-pitched yelp and rapid footfalls of whom-ever was chasing him made Dittmar jump back as effectively as a jolt of electricity.

The little Pomeranian rounded the corner, his tiny feet slipping on the smooth floor as he raced into the room. A security guard was hot his heels and skidded to a stop when he spotted them.

"Sorry, Mr. Dittmar," he wheezed as he caught his breath. "I spotted him in the hall. That little pooch is fast."

"Cuddles," Crystal exclaimed and picked him up, clutching him to her chest. "Did you miss Mommy? I'm sorry I left you for so long."

"I swear I shut the door when we left," Dittmar said, eyeing Ripley with a frown.

She reached out and smoothed her hand down his tie. "Perhaps you were a little distracted."

"Hmm." He grabbed her hand and placed a kiss on her knuckles, sneaking his tongue out to lick at her flesh. "Perhaps."

She giggled and pulled her hand away. "You're so bad."

If they gave out medals for keeping one's lunch in their stomach when they really wanted to wretch, she'd win gold. Hands down.

"Will you be needing any assistance, Mr. Dittmar?" the guard asked.

"No. We're finished here. Thank you, Stewart. Well, my dear. I guess we should get you back to my office."

"That's right. I should probably check to make sure Cuddles didn't leave you any surprises to find later."

Even in the dim light, she could see the color leach out his tan cheeks at the possibility of puppy poop anywhere on his expensive carpet. He practically ripped her arm out of the socket as he rushed her back to his office.

While he searched for "treasures," she retrieved her bag from the floor and set Ripley inside. "I think your office is safe. If he'd done his business, you would know. For a little guy, he sure creates quite a stink."

"I can imagine," he drolly replied.

"I guess I should be going. I know you had other plans for this afternoon. Thank you for all of your hospitality, James."

"Wait up there." He slipped his arm around her waist. "What are you doing tonight?"

A million-dollar question if she ever heard one. "Nothing. Why?"

"I'm attending an event at Matthew Madden's mansion. Come with me."

A way in to Madden's private residence? This could be the break they needed.

Cool, girlfriend. You have to play this cool.

"Me? You want to take little ole me to meet Matthew Madden? I'm sure there are much more sophisticated women you'd rather go with."

Judging by his conceited smile, she could tell he agreed with her. "I want you. Besides, this could be a golden opportunity for you. There will be lots of major players in the business world. A great way to network and see who you might want to invest your money in."

She couldn't argue with that. Maybe he was sharper than he appeared. "I wouldn't know what to ask, or say."

"Don't worry, baby. I'll be there with you the entire time. Say yes."

In her mind's eye, she imagined Max shouting at the monitor, demanding that she turn down the offer.

But this was the best way to get in to Madden's stronghold without exposing their powers. When would a lucky break like this come again?

"I accept. Pick me up at my hotel at eight? I'm at the Marymount."

"Absolutely." He leaned in for another kiss.

Ripley barked, causing them to both jump back. She smiled sheepishly. "I should take him outside. I'll see you tonight."

She pressed a quick kiss to his cheek and beat a hasty retreat. With every step toward the exit, her pulse pounded and her cheeks grew hot. She was jumping from one danger straight into another.

A bitter laugh stuck in her throat. What was she more afraid of, entering the lion's den at Madden's, or facing Max when she returned to the mountain?

"You're all clear, Prism," Addison said. "Security cameras in the area show no one is following you."

To continue with her country bumpkin appearance, she had driven Ripley's battered truck into town. The instant she jumped behind the wheel, she turned on the ignition and cranked up the heat. Between stress from the mission and Dittmar's advances, a cold had seeped so deeply into her bones, she didn't think she'd ever be warm again.

To ensure that she wasn't followed, she meandered through the city, doubling back on occasion, before merging onto the highway.

"We're clear," she announced when they were officially on the mountain pass.

Ripley scooted under the blanket on the seat and shifted. Once in human form, he leaned close and inhaled. "Davidoff or White Water?"

"Don't," she whispered and pointed a finger in at him in warning. She tugged off her earrings and stashed them deep into her purse.

"He's not going to let you go," Ripley said in a low voice, mindful of the ears that might still be listening.

"Which is why you need to remind him of the importance of why I must."

He sighed and looked out his window. "I'll try, but you have to know that when it comes to you, all his rules get shot to hell."

Her grip tightened on the wheel. That was what she was

afraid of.

"No." She tried to rationalize. "He'll be mad at first, but he wants his father to go down, bad. All we need is a foolproof plan, and he'll see reason."

Ripley snorted. "That might have been true before, but don't fool yourself, darling. Once he sees those hickeys on your neck, he'll be out for blood."

CHAPTER TWENTY-THREE

MAX CUT AN imposing figure as he waited for them at the entrance of the garage. He stood ramrod straight, his arms crossed and his face a stone mask. The glacial blue of his eyes made it feel as if the temperature of the chilly afternoon dropped another ten degrees.

Crystal drew in a steadying breath and took her sweet time turning off the truck and gathering her bag before opening the door.

Of course, his laser-beam glare zeroed right in on the marks on her skin. In response to the anger in his gaze, the hickeys began to ache and her skin grew tight and grungy. When he raised an eyebrow and his lips quirked as if to suggest she had enjoyed herself while she had been undercover, any shame she had felt at her actions gave way and she turned into a pissed-off operative.

What was she supposed to have done? Her talent was touch, and that was what she used. That was the reason why she had been the one to go. She went in, got the information, and got out safely. All of her objectives had been met, and as an added bonus, she had found a way into Madden's mansion. No one could have done the job better. So was she going to let one look from Max diminish what she accomplished?

Hell no.

Lifting her chin, she met his gaze. "Let's get the flash

drive to Addison, then we need to make a plan for tonight."

He grabbed her arm as she brushed past him. "You're not going."

"Why not?"

"Because I said so."

She flicked a glance at Ripley, who just stood there scratching his bare chest. His brow crinkled in confusion before he caught on to her pointed glare. "Ah, yeah, look, boss, we've been brainstorming and we have a few ideas."

"You are not going," Max interrupted, not even sparing a glance toward Ripley. "You are not getting within a hundred yards of Dittmar or Madden. Period."

She jerked her arm away. "I have a job to do." Spinning on her heel, she left Ripley to deal with him.

How dare he! How dare he treat her like a child, like a disappointment. Yes, she expected him to go all alpha-asshole, but part of her had held out hope that he respected her as a teammate and would treat her as such.

As she crossed the threshold to her room, she reached behind her and shoved the door hard, needing to hear that satisfying slam. When it didn't come, she turned to see Max standing in the way.

"We need to talk." He closed the door with much more self-control than she had a moment before. The bastard.

"No, you want to talk *at* me, and that's not going to get us anywhere." She kicked out and settled for the smack of her shoe hitting the wall to express her displeasure.

"There is no way I am letting you walk into that viper's nest alone."

"I won't be alone. Ripley will be with me. And it doesn't matter what you think. We needed a way in, and now we have one."

He loomed over her. "At what cost? If you are found out, they will kill you, or worse."

"I know," she shouted. Did he honestly think that she hadn't gone over the risk a billion times on the ride home? "But you said it yesterday. This is what we are here for, what we've been working toward. I have a shot, and I'm going to take it."

He drove his hands into his hair and pulled at the ends. "Are you insane? Dittmar wants you. How far are you willing to take the deception? Will you let him fuck you?"

Her denial caught in her throat. She wanted to say no. Everything inside her rebelled at the thought. God, she hoped it didn't come to that. But if it meant success or their lives, she knew she'd do whatever was necessary.

When she didn't reply right away, his eyes widened and he emitted a strangled groan. He caught her under the arms and lifted her so they were eye to eye. "No. You—I—Do you know what it did to me, to listen to him touch you? Kiss you? I can't let you do that."

"And I don't want it to come to that. But if it leads to information that will bring down Madden, I might have to."

He shook her as if she were a ragdoll. "That doesn't matter."

"Don't say that." She broke free of his hold and stood on her own feet again. "You know how important this is. It's not just you and me involved."

"What if it was me, Crystal? What if you had to listen to me seduce another woman? Listen to her moan with my hands on her, my tongue in her mouth?"

Her heart fell into her stomach as the tears sprang in her eyes. It would kill her. She would rage and shout out against the unfairness of it all.

And that was the point Max was missing now. She didn't blame him for how he felt. She wasn't telling him he was wrong. Her argument was about his utter refusal to send her in to finish the job. If the roles were reversed, she'd feel exactly as he did now.

Exhaustion swept over her, curling her shoulders down under the weight. "I'm sorry, all right? I didn't mean for it to go so far. It was horrible, and every second I died inside, but there's nothing I can do about it now."

"You will not go." He punctuated his decree with a finger pointing to the ground with each syllable as his nostrils flared. "We'll come up with something else. Send someone else in, like Doc."

"Like that's going to work. And why should she take the risk and not me?"

"Because I don't love her like I do you!" Max shouted, his eyes wet. "I love you and I—" He slid his fingers into her hair to hold her still for his desperate kiss.

Salty, bitter tears burned the back of her throat. He loved her. He really loved her.

Or did he, whispered that little voice of uncertainty buried in her mind.

For months she had watched Max struggle to keep them all at a distance. But there was no hiding the pleasure in his eyes and in his smile about being part of the group. But love? Allowing another into the inner sanctum of his heart? Making himself vulnerable to another, *to her,* was a dream she wished for what had seemed like forever.

And this was the way he chose to tell her? In anger and frustration? No, no, no.

The flutter in her heart at his words died. Did she believe he cared for her? Yes. Love her? Possibly. But even so, the situation they were now in hadn't changed. And if he was using his love to manipulate her, he was a right cold bastard.

Hurt and anger flavored his kiss with a spicy bitterness, while his fear radiated in the tension of his touch.

And then she saw it. A flash of memories slammed into her with the speed and intensity of a hurricane.

The dark-haired woman she recognized. Max's mother. Image after image flittered as if they were pages in a flipbook, showing over time the slow decay of Daria Madden's self-worth as her husband engaged in affair after affair. Max's scream as he tried to stop his mother's suicide echoed in Crystal's mind like an ear-piercing whistle on a train.

Was that what was pushing Max to this frenzy? Did he worry she was going to wither away if she had to engage his father?

Or did he see himself in his mother? Desperate for his father's attention but constantly losing to Madden's thirst for power and control.

The complicated dynamics of the Madden clan were no secret to her, but did she have the power to save Max from the shackles of his past?

"Please, Max. We have no choice," she pleaded against his lips. "The mission is bigger than the two of us."

In response, he picked her up and tossed her onto the bed. His body covered hers before she had a chance to catch her breath. With rough fingers, he yanked at the bodice of her dress, exposing her breasts while an invisible force pulled her arms above her head and pinned them in place. No matter how hard she struggled, she was held tight.

"Max. Let me go."

"Never." His hot breath washed over her nipple. "I'll never let you go."

The calm, in-control man she knew was gone and in his place was a frantic, needy soul. He stroked and kissed, bit and nibbled her skin as if to consume her whole.

Her heart broke under the onslaught of his anxiety. If he would just let her hands free, she could hold him tight. Comfort him, assure him of her love and understanding.

But she doubted that would be enough. Deep inside she sensed he needed this, needed this control over her, over her pleasure, to secure his place in her world.

Max hiked her skirt above her hips with hands harsh with frustration, then slipped her panties down her legs. He spread her thighs wide open to his hungry, feverish gaze. His thumbs parted her swollen, wet flesh as anticipatory chills raced up her torso. A groan broke past his lips as he dipped his head to taste her, his tongue swirling, lapping up her cream.

Her hips jerked, the pleasure too much to take as she writhed in his hold. "Max, please," she begged. For what exactly, she didn't know.

"I am trying to please you." He thrust two fingers deep into her channel as he sucked her clit into his mouth and lashed it with his tongue. "Scream for me, sweetheart. Scream for me."

Her abdomen cramped. It was so good, it was painful. She gave herself over to his keeping and allowed the intense rush to sweep her away. Every nerve ending exploded and burned as she screamed his name over and over. The invisible bonds held her down as the strong contractions fought to lift her off the bed. That wicked mouth of his never let her rest as he dragged her along the course he dictated, working her fevered flesh until she came again, loud and hard.

Max pulled back, his fingers continuing to keep her on edge as he tugged at his zipper until his cock sprang free. Hard and red, it pulsed with the anger that still flashed in his eyes. He stroked his shaft with the wetness from her orgasm and mixed it with the bead of cum dripping from the tip.

"No man makes you as wet as me."

Dittmar's words punched her in the chest. Tears she no longer had the power to hold back fell down her cheeks. "No one but you, Max. Only you."

He worked the blunt head up and down her slit before wedging into her entrance. "Never let you go," he whispered, then plunged all the way into the hilt.

His heat scorched her, his length stole her breath. Bare. He had taken her bare. The importance of the act was not lost on her. This was the last intimacy they could give to another person, and not for a second did she think to argue or try to stop him. She was his. The possessiveness in his gaze and the deep thrust of his hips marked her forever.

"I love you," she panted. "I love you, Max."

At her words, his teeth clenched and his pace quickened.

Ah, if only her hands were free. She needed to touch him, ease him, show him how much she loved him. She wrapped her legs tight around his waist, trying to deepen the connection. Everything she was belonged to him. Didn't he know that by now?

The tension around her wrists fell away as his back bowed and his cock drove deep, pushing her over the edge.

The sensation of his cock spilling inside her sent a shock

wave through her body. Her vision dimmed as she felt her spirit float away. Only her fingernails digging into his shoulders tethered her to the earth.

"Crystal." His voice broke. His arms collapsed, crushing her under his weight.

Against her breast, his heart beat in a frantic rhythm that matched hers. She brushed his bangs off his damp forehead and hugged him tighter. For long minutes they stayed locked in each other's embrace, only the sound of their ragged breathing breaking the silence.

"Don't go," he said in a voice so low, she almost didn't hear it. "Please, don't go."

Everything around her stilled as she lay terrified over how to respond. He might as well have snuffed out all life on earth with his forlorn request for the darkness that instantly plagued her.

The last thing she wanted to do was leave this bed, especially knowing what was most likely to come in a few short hours, but there was more at stake than their love for each other.

When she didn't answer, he propped himself up on one arm and looked down at her. "Crystal?"

She laid her palm along his cheek and prepared for his disappointment. "I have to."

"No." He scrambled off the bed, his glare filled with shards of ice as he straightened his clothing.

"You can't be mad at me about this." She too rose to her feet and smoothed her skirt down her thighs. "I love you, Max. So much so that it feels like my heart will explode. If there was another way, I'd take it, but we both know there isn't. And if Madden gets away because we didn't take this chance, you would never forgive yourself. Or me."

As she spoke, he shook his head harder and harder in denial, but she saw it in the tightening of his lips: he knew she was right.

"Please, Max. I need your support."

The cold mask fell into place as he shook his head one last time, then stalked out of the room.

Damn, damn, damn. She pounded her fist on the dresser, refusing to chase after him.

Okay, he was angry. Understandable. Never mind that *she* was the one taking all the risk, and *she* was the one facing the possibility of whoring herself out to save the world. Which, by the way, was only the slightest, slimmest, teensiest possibility because she was going to do everything in her power to keep her clothes on and men off. But no, apparently the only opinion that mattered was Max's, who believed all she was capable of was using her body to complete the mission.

Sons a bitches. Bumpasses.

Ah! She doubled over, falling against the dresser as lightning struck her brain and a profusion of images assaulted her mind.

A starry night sky blazed overhead. Water bubbled from a fountain. A gunshot. Cold concrete bit into her skin as she lay on her back. Max kneeling by her side. He was crying. He never cried. Blood streaked his cheek. The words pouring from his lips were unintelligible, but he was begging, pleading with her. The images blurred in and out until…

Oh, God no.

Crystal sank to her knees. Agony ripped her chest in two as fear coursed through her veins. Deep, wrenching sobs shook her entire body as her tears soaked the top of her dress.

"No, no, no," she wept, even as she tried to not fall into despair. If she gave in to the terror of the moment, she wouldn't have the strength to stand.

It was only a vision. The future could still be changed. Free will. She still had free will on her side.

If only her heart believed the weak pep talk.

After all, it wasn't every day she envisioned her own death.

CHAPTER TWENTY-FOUR

M AX STRODE STRAIGHT from Crystal's room to the creek that ran a quarter of a mile from their headquarters. The cold November air was a much-needed shock to his system. Anger had him burning so hot, he wouldn't have been surprised if steam rose from his skin.

That woman had him so bent out of shape, he'd be permanently kinked. If he hadn't left when he had, he would have done something foolish, like bind her to the bed forever. Yeah, as if that would woo her to his way of thinking. She was stubborn, determined, and had a Florence Nightingale complex as big as the Grand Canyon.

And she was absolutely right.

"Damn it," he shouted and thrust out both of his hands, focusing his powers on lifting a boulder the size of a sedan. With a guttural cry, he hurled it into the forest. The ground shook and several trees toppled like bowling pins in its wake.

He stumbled to a nearby rock and sat down hard, burying his head in his hands as he struggled for breath and tried to still the wooziness of his mind. His stomach curdled with the realization of what he had to do.

He was going to have to send her in. Send her into the viper pit and hope to God she made it out okay.

It wasn't Crystal's abilities that he doubted. It was the role she would have to play that made the bile rise in his throat. The images wrought from the stories Max had heard about his father and the women he charmed into his bed, and what happened to them, flashed through his mind like an X-rated flipbook.

It might be an antiquated and chauvinistic thought, but in his mind, Crystal was pure with an open heart. She was a woman who made love with her mind, body, and soul. She wasn't the type to use sex for any sort of gain or advantage. Good God. They were practically asking her to whore herself out.

Unfortunately, if they wanted to get inside that house, Crystal was their best and most immediate hope. Even if it made him sick to use her in that capacity.

The hopelessness of the situation surged through him until he tipped back his head and bellowed with rage. The wounded cry echoed through the forest until his vocal chords burned and pressure in his lungs forced him to breathe.

All his life, although he refused to acknowledge it, all he had wanted was to be loved. Loved for him and not the power and wealth his genius could provide. With Crystal he believed he had a chance at that kind of relationship. But to have her beautiful soul tainted by Madden was an injustice that had his hands burning with the need to destroy.

How in the hell did he make this right?

A tingle began at the back of his neck. He lifted eyelids that felt as if they were weighted down with coins and froze when he saw the large brown and white wolf standing in the clearing. His muscles tensed, ready to run, until he noticed the necklace around the animal's neck.

Max relaxed with an embarrassed twitch in his lips. "Hey."

Ripley padded over and looked up at him with his bushy eyebrows lowered in question.

"I'm a little upset." Unwilling to say more, Max turned his gaze to the rushing river.

The wolf snorted and sat by his feet. The warmth of his big, furry body seeped through Max's clothes as they sat in the quiet of the soggy forest for who knew how long.

It was an intuitive reaction for Max to reach out and slide his hand over to the wolf's great head. Over and over he stroked the thick fur. The motion lulled them both as Ripley leaned against Max's leg.

"I'm going to have to let her go," Max murmured so quietly that only the fog from his breath gave any indication that he spoke. "She's our only in. We could wait, but what if more people die because we don't act? If we want to end this now, she'll have to go. God, Rip, what are they going to do to her? Force her to do? Shit, what if she likes it?"

The wolf barked and jumped him, knocking him to the ground. He stood over Max with a snarl in his throat as his lips curled over his fangs.

"I'm sorry," Max shouted and held up a hand. "You don't know. When my father started bringing his women home, I could hear them. I know my mother must have been able to as well. Listening to that today brought that all back. Made me think about how she must have felt. The helplessness. Reminded me of the night she killed herself. Even if you go with Crystal, they'll find a way to separate you. What if she snaps and falls into her role? How can I keep her safe?" He took a breath. "What would you do if it was Alisia going in?"

Ripley backed away with understanding in his blue eyes. The fur along his back rippled, followed by the cracking of bones as he straightened to his full height.

Max nodded at the semi-hard erection bobbing in his face. "Please tell me that's not for me."

"You wish." Ripley snorted and took a seat next to Max on the wet grass, seemingly impervious to the cold. "She loves you. We all can see that. Today was hard on her, but she'll endure whatever she has to if she thinks it will save others. And she'll do it for you. She knows how badly you want Madden."

"Not that badly. I can't sacrifice her like that."

The wide-eyed look Ripley shot him was a mixture of shock and respect. "You *do* love her."

Max nodded, saddened that Ripley would think he would put any of them in harm's way to get to Madden. Did they all think of him as so ruthless?

Ripley sighed. "All right. This is what you do. You tell her that you'll be there for her, no matter what. If she knows that you're behind her, that will be one less thing for her to worry about. Then we'll make a plan for every possible situation. I'll watch your woman for you."

A plan. Max liked plans. Plans were good. Ripley was right. Crystal needed him now more than ever. With his full support, she'd be better prepared and have more confidence than if she was worried about what he would think of her. She said that she loved him. Now was his chance to prove that he deserved that love.

"Okay. Let's do this." Max got to his feet and brushed the dirt off his backside. "Thanks for listening, by the way."

He'd never had a friend whom he trusted enough with his personal feelings. It was...nice.

Ripley shrugged. "Sometimes it's easier to talk if that person can't answer back."

"Right." Max chuckled. "Well, I've never been in love before. This is one area where I have no idea what to do."

Commiseration rang in Ripley's sigh. "I hear you." He flicked a worried glance in Max's direction. "You're not going to hug me, are you?"

"No." Max made a gagging noise. "Seriously, you need to think about packing clothes with you."

"Yeah, because an animal with a backpack is so inconspicuous. Get real. You're just worried that your girl will start liking what she sees." He flexed the muscles of his chest.

"Excuse me?" He lifted Ripley in the air and dangled him over the icy river.

"Put me down. Dude, if you drop me in this water, I'll tear your throat out."

Max laughed and set him back on firm ground. "Wuss."

"Ha! Can you do this? Race you back to the cave." He leapt and shifted into a cheetah, taking off in a blur of yellow and black.

Ooh. A pocket-sized tranquilizer gun. Now that would be a great addition to their uniform. He'd get on that project ASAP as soon as Crystal was safely back at home.

CHAPTER TWENTY-FIVE

"CRYSTAL, YOUR FOOT is going to fall off." Ripley nodded to her rapidly bouncing appendage.

"Oh, right." She placed both feet on the floor and immediately her right knee resumed the frantic cadence.

He leaned forward in his seat on the couch opposite her, his eyes warm with compassion. "You don't have to do this."

"I'm fine, really. Just anxious." She smoothed the silk of her black dress over her thighs, hoping that he didn't catch the tremble in her hands.

The hotel room they were waiting in was luxurious and spacious, holding every amenity a young, multimillion-dollar lottery winner could ever want. A bottle of champagne rested untouched in bucket of melting ice water, and the complimentary cheese and fruit platter looked as though it was straight out of a Martha Stewart magazine, but the choking claustrophobia surrounding her prevented her from indulging in the slightest.

"You know I'll be with you," Ripley assured her. "And so will the rest of the team. Especially Max."

"I know," she responded softly, blinking back tears.

When Max had stormed out of her room, she didn't know what type of reception she'd receive the next time they crossed paths. As the time came to gather to plan their strategy, uncertainty and fear from her vision weighed heavily in her heart. Was he going to prevent her from taking the risk? Did she dare tell him about her vision? Was he still angry at her for allowing another man to touch her?

But Max had greeted her with a soft smile and not a single mention of their argument. He placed a kiss on her cheek and squeezed her hand before calling the meeting to order. That was all.

Their primary objective was to find out who was attending the party. She was to do everything in her power to avoid direct contact with Madden. Objective two was to find out who else might be involved in Madden's plan and what their next step might be. Once they knew exactly who and what they were up against, then they would come back better equipped to put an end to Madden's master plan.

"Crystal's safety is top priority," Max had said in a tone that brooked no argument, even from her. "We'll give you as much leeway as possible to get the intel, but the moment you smell trouble, call in reinforcements. No matter what. Understand?"

"Yes, sir," she replied, barely able to restrain saluting him. Did she wonder what had prompted his change of heart? Hell, yes. But she was too cowardly to ask. With or without his approval, her visions of the evening hadn't changed, so the reason why didn't matter in the end. In fact, it had the potential of adding another level of stress to the situation that could place them more in danger. No, it was best to accept his willingness to allow the mission to continue by doing her best to reassure him that she was committed to the task. "I promise. I won't take unnecessary risks."

"Then let's get to it."

The room cleared and as she was about to leave, Max

grasped her by the elbow and swung her around to face him.

Tenderness warmed his gaze. Tenderness mixed with a heavy dose of fear, but he didn't say a word as he slowly leaned in for a kiss and waited for her to meet him the rest of the way.

She answered his silent request without hesitation. He sighed into her mouth, caressing her with the softness of his lips and the gentle glide of his tongue. While his kiss was gentle, his hands were not, holding her tight as if he would never let her go.

A burst of light had flashed behind her closed eyelids and soon her mind was flooded with his memories. Memories he was projecting into her mind. The way she had looked kneeling at his feet in a puddle of espresso and broken porcelain at the café when they first met. The sunlight catching the red in her hair after he kissed her at the zoo. All the times he made her laugh, even when she didn't want to, and the sight of her lying on the bed beside him as she slept. On and on, he fed her his memories of her and his love.

"I'm sorry," he rasped, pressing his forehead against hers. "I have every faith in your ability, and I know you would not take a risk without thinking it through. It's just that, for the first time in my life, I have someone to live for. You're irreplaceable, Crystal. I don't want to lose you."

She couldn't speak for the lump in her throat. Max with all his wealth had the resources to give her the world, but it was the love and vulnerability in his eyes that was the most precious gift he would ever bestow upon her.

This man before her was so different from the cynical, closed-off person she had first met. That Max would never have admitted to any weakness, while this man lay his heart at her feet.

She placed her hands on either side of his face and ran her thumbs over his dark brows to his cheeks. The liquid blue flames in his eyes heated her, and with the visions of her own death running on repeat in her mind, she pressed her mouth to his to store memories of his texture and flavor. A hint of chocolate burst across her tongue. He did like his chocolate.

"I love you, Max." She stood on tiptoe to press her cheek against his. "No matter what, remember that I love you, always."

She felt his answering smile. "I know. You've always been honest with me. Sometimes to the point of pain." He brushed the hair off her face. "When tonight is over, I'm taking you away for at least a week or two, maybe three. All I want is time to focus on you. On us."

"That sounds nice." Provided she survived the night.

Thanks, conscience. Why don't you just set fire to my soul?

"I don't suppose you've had a vision and know how this plays out?" he asked.

Her heart skipped a beat. To admit the truth burned the tip of her tongue, but to say it out loud had the possibility of changing the future. What if instead of her, one of the others died? What if it was Max? She wouldn't be able to live with the guilt.

She forced a smile. "Nope. I wish."

"Guess that would be too much to expect your powers to suddenly work on demand, huh?"

Crystal tried to hold her smile as she stepped out of his arms. The action was like ripping off a Band-Aid, with a sting that lingered long afterward.

She should receive an Oscar for her cool, calm performance as she had traveled to the hotel and dolled up for the evening. The fact that she hadn't sweated through her cocktail dress was a bloody miracle.

Please let me be wrong. Please, please, please.

Stop it. Stop it! She shook her head and tried to avoid Ripley's worried gaze. Just because she saw her death didn't mean it would come true. How many times had she seen her and Max making wild love in a sea of teal satin and that never happened? So what if she had a 98 percent accuracy rate? That still left a margin for error. A slim margin, but wiggle room all the same.

The shrill ring of the telephone jolted her from her thoughts and she jumped with a squeak.

Ripley shook his head. "You're so not fooling me, doll. We can call it off."

"We're doing this. Are you with me or not?" She nailed him with her fiercest stare, daring him to question her judgment.

He sighed and ran a hand over his whiskered chin. "I'm in."

"Good." She juggled the receiver in her slippery hands and answered with a breathless, "Hello?"

"Hello, beautiful." Dittmar's smooth drawl oozed over the line. "Ready for me?"

"Absolutely," she purred. "I'll be right down." She hung up.

Ripley got to his feet. "Showtime." His Velcro pants split open and an orange ball of fur stood in the puddle of fabric.

She pulled out her cell phone and dialed headquarters. "We're a go."

"Copy," Max answered. "Audio and visual are up and

recording. Good luck, sweetheart. I love you."

She tucked his words in her heart, wishing she could see him one last time. "I love you too."

There was so much more she wanted to say, but she ended the call before she broke into tears and slipped the phone into her clutch. She tucked Ripley into the crook of her arm. "Come on, boy."

Each step toward the elevator made her heart pound faster, and the deep lungsful of air she sucked in did little to help slow her pulse. She adjusted her jewelry to make sure the camera in her necklace was positioned in the exact right spot and the microphone earrings were secured.

Ripley licked her hand with his wet tongue in support. If anything, she had to keep it together for him, since he was going into the fray with her. He was going to need her as much as she needed him.

Dittmar waited for her in the lobby looking tall and handsome, as if he were a model straight from the pages of GQ in his charcoal gray suit and maroon tie. His eyes widened with appreciation when he spotted her and his gaze roved greedily over her exposed flesh. The black silk halter dress fit her to perfection, highlighting all her curves and hinted at the ones still concealed.

He licked his lips as she drew near, then did a double take when he spotted Ripley in her arms. "You're bringing the dog?"

"Of course, silly. I can't leave him locked in the room." She handed him her cloak and spun around. The back of the dress lay open to the curve of her buttocks. Not the most comfortable of gowns, but the warm expanse of skin would hopefully encourage a man to lay his bare palm against her flesh, allowing her to see more of his memories. "Help me with my coat?"

He groaned and pressed his hard body along her back. "Damn shame to cover all of this up."

She glanced over her shoulder and batted her lashes. "You wouldn't want me to freeze from the cold, would you?"

"Of course not." He pressed his lips to her bare shoulder and licked a wet trail to her neck.

The urge to rack him with her stiletto made her toes curl. This seduction bullshit was a lot harder than it appeared in the movies. If she hadn't seen the memories herself, she never would've guessed that this slinky, slithery act of his worked on bagging babes. All it made her do was want to heave.

His smile stretched, revealing his artificially whitened teeth. "I'm going to make tonight one you never forget."

Gag.

"Oh, James," she gushed when he escorted her to the limo waiting outside. "I thought this was a simple cocktail party." She slid across the bench seat and placed Ripley at her feet.

"Baby, nothing Matthew Madden does is simple."

The driver shut the door and the locks clicked into place like a shot from a nail gun.

Yep. There it was. The final nail in the coffin. There was no turning back.

They barely cleared the hotel driveway before Dittmar made his move. He swooped in for a kiss but paused as he eyed the heavy gloss on her lips that shimmered even in the dark. He frowned then shifted his attention to the tender flesh of her neck. He nibbled her skin as he dug his hands under her cloak to curl around the curve of her ass and drag her closer.

"James. James," she panted. Panic bubbled as his fingers skimmed up her side and pulled the bodice down, exposing her nipple, which he hungrily latched onto. She grabbed handfuls of his hair and tugged. "James, please wait."

He let the nub go with a pop. "I want you, Crystal. Right here, right now."

"I want you, too, but not like this."

"Why not? Damn, you're so sexy."

She tugged his hair again when he dipped his head back to her breast. "Please, James. You're making me wonder if you didn't plan to have sex with me in the back of your limo, then leave me on the street somewhere."

"I would never do that." The curve of his smile reminded her of the Grinch that stole Christmas. "I intend to take my sweet time with you over and over again."

It physically hurt to restrain the urge to roll her eyes. "We're meeting with some very important people, and I'm nervous enough as it is. I don't want to walk in looking freshly rolled and smelling like sex. I don't want to embarrass you. Would you want to embarrass me that way?" She pouted.

His lips curled over his teeth for a second before he drew away and slumped against the seat. "I'm sorry, baby. I just want you so damn much." He grabbed her hand and pressed it to his hard cock.

She played along and stroked him through his trousers. "I'll make it up to you later. Promise."

He arched in her grasp. "How about you start now."

Just as he reached for his zipper, Ripley yipped and jumped on his lap. "Fuck. He's getting fur all over me." Dittmar shoved the pup off, sending Ripley flying into the opposite seat.

"Poor thing." Crystal picked Ripley up and set him between them. "Cuddles gets jealous of other men. Especially when they get too close."

"Well, he better get used to it." He eyed the dog as if he were shit stuck to his Ferragamos. "Because I intend to get really close to you."

Again, gag.

Fortunately for her, the limo pulled past the gate and into the drive of Madden's fortress.

Her jaw dropped as she took in the grandeur of the palatial mansion. It looked like a miniature version of the White House, complete with columns standing tall along the front. Anyone who stood before the massive double doors would not doubt that the person who lived there was very powerful indeed.

And to think, this was once Max's home. Well, at least when he hadn't been away at school.

Sadness settled in her heart and made her throat ache as she recalled Max's memories of his mother as she had killed herself in this house. This was where his powers were born.

And the place she was going to die.

Stop it. You're not dead yet.

The car door opened and she took the driver's hand as she stepped onto the cobblestone drive. "Come here, boy." She beckoned to Ripley.

Next to her, Dittmar made a strangled noise. "Baby, Oodles should stay in the car."

"But I can't leave Cuddles out here. That's worse than leaving him in the hotel room."

He leveled his most charming smile at her. "Matthew Madden is not an animal lover. We wouldn't want to insult our host, do we?"

"What if he needs to go potty?"

A tic began in his jaw. "Davidson here will take care of him, right?"

The driver looked less than thrilled. "Right," he repeated tightly.

The team had known there was a good chance she would get separated from Ripley. She just wished it wasn't going to be so soon.

"Well, I guess it will be all right." Not. But better not to protest too much and draw suspicion. "Take good care of my baby." She gave Ripley one quick squeeze and whispered in his ear. "Thank you for earlier. Be careful."

He yipped and licked her face before getting in one last growl at Dittmar.

Dittmar slipped his hand around her waist and escorted her up the walkway. A mantra began in her head in time with the click of her heels on the cobblestones.

You are Mata Hari. You are James Bond. You will succeed. Madden is about. To go. Down.

Just as Dittmar reached for the doorbell a sound like a lion's roar, followed by a cutoff scream, broke the silence of the night.

He looked around. "What was that?"

Well, Ripley wasn't wasting time. "What was what?" She batted her lashes.

"Didn't you hear that? It sounded like a wild animal."

She tittered and playfully slapped at his chest. "Seriously, I can't hear anything over the pounding of my heart. I'm so nervous."

"Don't be. They'll love you."

The door opened, revealing a brick wall of a man wearing a suit and a headset. He nodded at Dittmar before accepting their coats and passing them along to the girl in a French maid's costume standing by his side.

So, the guard was familiar enough with Dittmar that he allowed them in without asking for their names. Apparently, Dittmar was a bigger player then they thought. Interesting.

The inside of the mansion was just as opulent as the outside with marble flooring covering the entire lower level. The black and silver veined rock sucked up all natural light and heat, making it feel as welcoming as the inside of an icebox. Mahogany Chippendale furniture matched the dual curved staircases that dominated the foyer and led up to the second floor.

As Dittmar guided her through the oversized rooms, she noted that while beautiful, the house was as impersonal as a furniture store. Not one photo was displayed. Nothing gave a hint of any character trait of the owner other than wealthy. She might as well have been walking through a design catalog of the rich and famous.

Even Madden's guests reminded her of department store mannequins as they lounged artfully against the leather furniture with their Botoxed faces and artificial tans.

The ballroom ceiling soared so high, she had to crane her neck to look up at the fresco design. Couches and tables formed conversational areas, and the muted lighting resembled nightclubs like the ones in Las Vegas.

Dittmar pressed a kiss to her shoulder and caressed her backside. "I'll get us some drinks. What would you like?"

Fifth of whiskey. "Syrah, if they have it."

He smiled and trailed his finger along her arm before disappearing into the crowd.

Crystal scanned the gatherers, sorting out those who

appeared to be bodyguards from guests. She smirked as she noticed that while the men were dressed in styles ranging from jeans and cowboy boots to three-piece suits, the women were attired in barely there skirts with plunging necklines. They were nothing but eye candy as they stood around, fidgeting with their wine glasses and looking bored to tears while their men ignored them but for the occasional pat on the ass.

No, it did not escape her notice that she too was dressed more for sin than conversation, and it became clear that Dittmar had only brought her to be an accessory for the night and not the potential investor he told her she would be.

"What's a nice girl like you doing in a place like this?"

Enveloped in the lame opening spoken in a sexy rasp was a hint of sarcastic humor.

She glanced over her shoulder to make a smartass comeback of her own and froze, her jaw dropping in shock.

Oh. My. God.

CHAPTER TWENTY-SIX

T HERE WERE TWO of them. They were gorgeous.

And they *glowed.*

Identical in appearance, the men had the dark, swarthy, good looks of Mediterranean playboys. Their black sport coats were tailored perfectly to fit their lean bodies, and the bright white of their shirts deepened the tan of their skin. One wore a tie, his espresso brown hair swept neatly off his face, highlighting the strength in the square cut of his jaw. His twin wore his shirt open at the collar, his hair mussed as if someone else repeatedly ran their fingers through the thick waves. One by himself was heart-stoppingly handsome. The two together were devastating.

And they glowed.

Her brain finally registered that she had yet to respond. She snapped her teeth together and hoped she didn't look like a teenage girl getting her first look at a naked man.

Remembering her undercover hayseed persona, she hoped to God that they weren't like Ripley and could smell her powers, or something similar. She bit her bottom lip and flashed a sheepish grin. "Is it that obvious that I don't belong?"

The tousled one on the right nodded and flashed her a bone-melting smile. "If you mean by not belonging because you appear to have a brain to go with the beauty, then yes."

Was that a pickup line, or was he alluding to knowing

her secret?

"Please ignore my brother," the more straightlaced one said. "He believes he's God's gift to women. I remind him repeatedly that he's not. I'd love for you to back me up on this."

"I do my best to reserve judgment until I get to know a person better." She smiled. *What could their powers be?*

The brothers exchanged a curious glance before Mr. Straightlaced held out his hand. "I'm Ethan Daniels. This cad is Ronan."

Daniels. Daniels Software. She recognized the name from Max, who had done quite a bit of work for their father in the past. Were they involved with Madden too?

"Crystal Winters." She clasped Ethan's offered hand.

Once their palms touched, both gasped in shock and tightened their grip.

Holy shit, they were telepathic. A power both brothers shared, along with the ability to control other people's emotions. The latter she experienced first-hand as her panic escalated, bringing heat to her cheeks even as her heartbeat kept a steady rhythm from the wave of calm Ethan projected at her.

She broke away with a jerk. *Shit, shit, shit.* If they could read her mind, then they knew what she was doing there, what her mission was. They could ruin everything.

"No," Ronan started to speak out loud but instead lifted his glass to his lips. "*Your secret is safe. Just like we know that you will keep ours.*"

Oh, now she could hear his voice in her head. A sensation that was both weird and awesome.

Ethan continued to stare at her in awe. "There are others? We read the story in the paper. About the bank. But wasn't sure if it was true."

"Ah—" What could she say? How much could she trust them?

Dittmar appeared at her side and handed her a glass. "There you are, darling. I should have known you would attract the attention of the Daniels twins."

Ronan laughed. "Well, I am infamous for my exquisite taste in women. And Crystal here is very special indeed."

Dittmar curled her into against his chest and pressed his lips to her ear. "Did you know that they share their women?"

The sip of wine she drank stuck in her throat. Tears sprang in her eyes as her nose burned. "That's not really a topic of conversation that immediately comes up after you say hello," she wheezed.

Dittmar continued on a whisper, "Can you imagine, all of those hands on you? The tongues. Multiple cocks pumping inside of you."

Part of her was horrified that he would speak so crudely to her in front of complete strangers, but as she risked a glance at the bronze gods, the unbidden thought of being the filling in that man sandwich didn't seem as if it would be a hardship at all.

Oh crap, she flushed. *They probably just heard that.*

Ethan had the grace to look the other direction even as the corners of his mouth fought back his grin. Ronan smiled at her from behind his glass and tossed her a saucy wink.

If Max could read her mind right then, he would so kill her.

"Max? As in Madden Jr.?"

Get out of my head! She aimed her shout at both, since she wasn't sure which had spoken.

"I can't help it. I'm curious about you."

Well, you're going to be less curious when I shove my heel up your ass.

Ronan sputtered and coughed on his drink with laughter, drawing Dittmar's curious stare.

"Ladies and gentlemen," a woman's voice announced over a microphone as the lights dimmed. "Your host, Matthew Maxwell Madden II."

Enthusiastic applause broke out as a spotlight turned to the stage at the end of the ballroom. Crystal stood up on tiptoe, curious for her first in-the-flesh glimpse of the man who had fathered Max.

The man who walked across the stage appeared to be much younger than his fifty-plus years of age. Not a streak of gray touched the raven black hair that was swept away from his unlined face. He was a handsome devil indeed, and shared the same pale blue eyes as Max. But in the gaze he swept around the room, she saw avarice and calculation, as if he was judging every person on their value, both monetary and political.

He raised his hands and the applause died down. "Welcome, my friends. Well, isn't this an impressive group of people I stand before. Did you know that the net value of every person in this room combined exceeds the gross national product of most of the countries in the world?" He held up a finger. "Including the good ole U.S. of A. Yes, how the mighty have fallen. That is the beauty of capitalism. Even when your government falls, the strong shall endure. Or do they? Any idiot with an idea believes they have the intelligence and wherewithal to make millions, and when they fail, we all pay the price."

As Madden continued to speak, a screen lowered from

the ceiling to hang behind him. "These are unusual times. The rules of old no longer work, and no one has stepped forward to establish a course for the future. Until now."

"Are you running for President then, Madden?" a voice called out. Several people whistled in approval.

His predatory smile widened. "No, no. That would take four long years and require that I work with the less than intelligent on Capitol Hill to even begin to make progress. No, I have something more immediate in mind. Yes, immediate and direct. Behold, my vision."

On the screen appeared a wide sweeping shot of rolling green hills that led to a valley of cornfields. Beyond the fields, a city sprawled in its cement and glass splendor. Men and women smiled as they walked into office buildings and factories, ready to work. Children in neatly pressed uniforms sat in schoolrooms with brand-new books on the desks. There was no litter in the streets, no graffiti on the buildings, every house freshly painted. It was a modern utopia.

"Several years ago, I began an experiment on an island off the coast of Asia. I opened businesses, built schools. Everyone who worked was paid an equal wage. But those who showed aptitude and dedication were granted bonuses in housing, education, and money. The people take pride and ownership in what they accomplish. I now own six thriving island nations in the Pacific. Crime does not exist there. There is no such thing as drug addiction. Any who dare disrupt the harmony of island life are dealt with swiftly and efficiently."

A group of demonstrators appeared on the screen, all of them dressed in blue or green scrub-like outfits. Crystal didn't recognize the language on their banners, but the fists raised in anger and resentment on their faces as they shouted told her that they were not happy with their totalitarian lifestyle. A dozen men in black body armor and carrying rifles swarmed them like scarab beetles. Those who struggled were beaten, cuffed, then tossed into the back of a truck where they were taken to God only knew where.

"Right now in Washington sits an impotent government. I know, I'm related to some of them," Madden said, chuckling. "They're either so afraid of insulting their constituents, or unwilling to see beyond their own backyard to work in harmony, that the government is at a standstill. That lack of action is hurting the very people who voted them into office in the first place. The time to act is now." He smacked his fist into the palm of his hand. "I plan to take this country back and turn it into a land that *I* can be proud of. *We* can be proud of."

He stood center stage again, his arms out in supplication. "I asked you here because you are the best at what you do. No one understands hard work and sacrifice more than you. Join me in an investment in all our futures. I know, I know." He chuckled. "It is the God-given right of every American to live in squalor if they choose. Well, that's not the America I choose to live in. And if that's your opinion, then get the fuck out of my country. You, my friends, are standing at the threshold of a new era. Just think. Your products, your businesses can be a part of the infrastructure of the country of the future. Join me in building a new America, a stronger America. A country that stands tall and spits in the eye of all who oppose her. To life, liberty, and the pursuit of happiness!"

The room got to its feet in thunderous applause as shouts of "Madden! Madden!" shook the walls. Above

Crystal's head the chandeliers swayed with the tremors.

"Oh my God, they drank the Kool-Aid," Crystal murmured in shock.

Behind her she could hear Ronan ask Ethan, "Can you hear them?"

"Yep. This isn't going to be good," he replied in a grim tone.

The lights came up, and terror made Crystal's skin pebble. All around the perimeter of the room stood men dressed in the black armor similar to the soldiers in the movie. Helmets with dark visors covered their heads and faces. Each one carried an assault rifle at their side and looked prepared to use it. They hadn't made a sound when they entered, but she guessed that the twins heard their thoughts as they took their places.

"That's our software in their helmets," one of the twins murmured.

"Yep."

"And he knows where we live."

"Yep."

"Shit."

"Yep."

Dittmar turned to her with a beaming smile. "Wasn't that fantastic? You are going to be part of a new revolution." He frowned at her when she continued to stare in fear at the soldiers. "Aren't you excited?"

She swallowed and forced her lips into a semblance of a smile. "I guess I'm just a little confused about what's going on. Is he talking about taking over the American government? Isn't that considered treason, or something?"

"I would like to see them try to take *him* down. The man is invincible."

That was what she was afraid of.

"Don't panic," she heard Ethan's voice in her head as Ronan sent another comforting blanket of emotion around her. *"Keep smiling and having a good time. Madden has instructed his men to note any person who might not be enthralled with his plan so he can...persuade them later."*

She took a sip of wine. *We knew he was planning something. We just didn't know how far along in his plan he was.*

"Well, now you do. Might I suggest a change in tactics? I don't think Dittmar is going to let you waltz out of here on your own. Find a way to ditch him, and we'll help you get past these guards."

That's probably for the best. Give me a minute to relay information.

"Get going, then."

She placed a hand on Dittmar's forearm. "I'll be back. I need to use the little girls' room."

"Don't be long."

She placed a brief kiss on his cheek before heading for the door. "Restroom?" she asked one of the soldiers. He gestured down a long hallway. "Thank you."

Her legs urged her to run for the now-guarded front door, but she forced her stride to remain smooth and easy. Once in the bathroom, she braced her hands on the counter and took long, deep breaths. A wicker basket filled with rolled-up cotton hand towels sat in the corner. Wetting one with cold water, she ran the cool cloth over the heated skin of her neck. She had to remain calm.

"I hope you saw all of that," she whispered toward the microphone in her earring. "The Daniels brothers are supers, telepathic. I think I can trust them. They told me that the soldiers in there were ordered to watch for anyone who might not comply with Madden and to deal with them later. I think it's best for me to get out of here now, and we form a new plan. The brothers said they would help me escape. Look for me to be with them. And please, someone, find Ripley."

She dried her hands and smoothed down the skirt of her dress. Pasting her most breezy smile on her face, she opened the door and jumped back with a startled yelp.

"James." She placed a hand over her racing heart. "What are you doing?"

He reached for her wrist and pulled her into the hall. He wrapped his arms around her and swooped in for a kiss.

She wrenched her mouth away and panted, "If I'd known you were going to miss me so much, I would have stayed away longer."

The lust and hunger in his eyes made her take a step back. He didn't say a word as he tugged her farther down the darkened hallway. The noise from the ballroom faded with each step, an eerie metronome marking the time until she'd be alone with a horny Dittmar.

Ethan! Ronan! Dittmar is taking me somewhere. I can't get away, she mentally shouted in the hopes that the twins could find a way for her to break free.

She pulled against his hold, but his grip didn't loosen. "James, where are you taking me? We can't just go traipsing around the house like this. Those guards look mean, and I don't want to get in trouble." When he still didn't respond, she began to struggle in earnest. "James."

They entered a room that appeared to be an office. A large desk with two overstuffed chairs placed before it dominated the space. Heavy velvet drapery covered the windows. The only light came from a small desk lamp that glowed in welcome. It wasn't working. She felt far from welcomed.

The door closed behind her with a decisive click. Dittmar pressed her against the cold wood and devoured her mouth. His hands cupped her buttocks under her skirt and lifted her so her legs went around his waist.

This was it. Her heart pounded a painful rhythm against her ribs as tears filled her eyes. He was going to take her against the door and if she wanted to live, she'd have to play along. *Please forgive me, Max.*

She let a moan well in her throat and ran her fingers through his hair. She rubbed his temples with the pads of her thumbs with the hope to slow his pace. Maybe if she could bide her time, one of the twins would find her.

"Crystal," he groaned against her neck when he broke for air. "I can feel your heat through our clothes. You are going to be so hot when I fuck you."

The sound of a man clearing his throat jolted her as if she'd been electrocuted. Dittmar jerked and turned to face the intruder.

Near the desk stood Mathew Madden with his hands clasped behind his back. Crystal blinked in disbelief. Where the hell had he come from? She was positive the room had been empty when they entered. She slipped from Dittmar's grip and used the doorknob to hold herself upright.

Madden cocked his head. "You weren't thinking about sampling my gift before me, were you, James?"

Gift?

Dittmar's throat worked as he swallowed hard and straightened his jacket and tie. "No, sir. I—" Madden raised a brow. "Well, I—I'm sorry, sir."

If Madden could make James kowtow with just a glance,

she was in deep shit.

"Excuse us, Mr. Madden." She offered a small smile. "We didn't mean to intrude on your privacy. We'll leave immediately."

His eyes flashed with humor as the corner of his lips turned up. "Bring her here, James."

Dittmar gripped her around her biceps and pulled her across the room to where Madden stood, presenting her as if she was a sacrifice on an altar to greatness.

"She's everything you said, James." His nostrils flared slightly, and the skin over his cheeks tightened as his gaze raked over her face and down to her cleavage that spilled over the cups of her dress. "Absolutely lovely."

She took a step back and ran against the human barricade that was James. Her breathing quickened and spots swam in her vision as she rode the line of hyperventilation. She drew a deep breath in through her nose and forced herself to calm down.

"Tell me, Miss Winters, what do you think of my world vision?"

"It's very," *deranged, are you out of your fucking mind,* "ambitious."

His throaty chuckle sent shivers along her scalp. He lifted a hand and, as gentle as a feather, ran the tip of his finger down the length of her nose and lower to caress her lips still tender from Dittmar's bruising kisses. "You have the most delectable mouth."

She jerked her head away. "Look, I know this is your home, and that you are a very powerful man, but I did not give you permission to touch me. I don't know what impression you may have gotten about me, but I did not agree to be tag teamed."

His eyes widened in surprise before he threw his head back and laughed deep and hearty. The delighted sound made the hairs on the back of her neck stand on end.

"Ah, my dear, don't you know that I already own you? Mind, body, and millions." He skimmed his hand along her collarbone before plunging down the bodice of her dress to palm her breast.

The more she struggled between the two of them, the rougher his fingers pinched and played with her flesh. The fact that it was Max's father touching her made her skin crawl.

Wait. He was touching her.

Immediately, her mind dove into his past. Good Lord, there were so many women. How did he ever get anything done?

Plans, plans, plans. Image after image showed Madden strategizing between marathon sex sessions. He was a delegator who never personally got his hands dirty. Those chores were left to The Second to carry out.

Just as an image of the infamous lackey came into focus, Madden spoke, "You are going to be such a delight to tame. Don't you think?" he asked over his shoulder.

"I'm looking forward to watching you work, Matthew."

A third man had entered the room. He stood with his shoulders relaxed and his arms by his side with a confidence that spoke of years of having his will obeyed. It was the same stance Madden had when he addressed his guests. His easy smile belied the ruthlessness held in the hard line of his jaw and the glitter in his blue eyes.

Holy shit. She knew those eyes.

The world around her froze, her hearing dimmed as her gaze zeroed in on the newcomer. That face. She had seen that face before, in the memories of another.

This was bad. Her heart sank to her roiling stomach. This was very, very bad.

Why was she staring at Anthony DeMateo?

CHAPTER TWENTY-SEVEN

A CREASE FORMED in Anthony's brow as Crystal continued to stare at him in shock and horror. The man standing before her was far from dead. In fact, he was the epitome of health with a golden tan and his blond hair trimmed and styled as if he were an advertisement for a high-priced salon. His appearance was a stark contrast to the wounded, bleeding man she had seen in Max's memory. A man who had been attacked by the enemy he now stood beside. What the fuck was going on?

His smile dimmed as he stepped closer. "Is that recognition I see in those eyes?"

Crystal's breath shuttled in and out of her lungs as she tried to stem her panic. This was Max's friend. A friend whose death crushed him and set him on a course of vengeance.

A scream welled in her throat to demand answers for why he would allow Max to be hurt like that by believing he was dead. Was he a double agent, or was he just as duplicitous as Madden?

"Have we met before?" Anthony asked. When she didn't respond, he looked over at Madden. "May I?"

"Be my guest." He gestured magnanimously.

She tensed in anticipation of a blow as Anthony grasped the back of her neck and tilted her chin up with his thumb. But the hit never came. His mouth covered hers in a kiss so gentle she almost burst out laughing.

What was he doing? These men had just been making nonchalant threats about taking her against her will. Did he seriously think a tender kiss would make her more pliable to their dark plans? That she would immediately trust him enough to answer his questions? The only feeling he was evoking within her at that moment was gratitude for allowing him easy access to his memories.

Anthony's memories...

There were not enough curse words in the world to convey the emotions that boiled as she witnessed the extent of Anthony's betrayal. He had set Max up. Anthony had known those men were going to be at his house that night. His death had been faked to allow him the autonomy to go underground and implement Madden's plans.

Where he had been caught unaware and began to form a new strategy was when Max had revealed his telekinetic powers. DeMateo had wanted a witness to his death, and Max saving him had not been part of the plan.

However, the night still worked out in Anthony's favor. He "died" and Max had assisted in killing most of the men that Anthony had been tasked with disposing of once he had been declared dead.

Anger surged through her at the knowledge that Max had been used by someone he loved and trusted. Before she thought better of it, she bit down on Anthony's lip until she tasted blood.

He jerked away with a grunt of pain, his eyes wide with surprise. He put his hand to his mouth, and drew it away to stare incredulously at the blood on his fingers. The narrowing of his eyes was all the warning she received before he backhanded her across the cheek.

She choked on her gasp as stars swam in her vision. There was the slap she'd been expecting. Damn, that hurt.

With Madden's laughter echoing in the background, Anthony grabbed her by the hair. "Who do you think you are?" He sneered in her face. "I know you know who I am. How? How do you know me?"

"I know you, Anthony DeMateo. I know you from the man who used to call you friend, you lying, traitorous bastard!"

Using James as a brace, she lifted both knees high then drove her stilettos into Anthony's chest. He stumbled back against the wall with a satisfying thud.

As her weight came back down, she dropped to the ground and rolled James over her back. Oh, how she wanted to follow up with a few extra kicks to his head, but escaping took priority.

She ran across the marble floor toward the exit. Just as her hand closed around the doorknob, she was tackled from behind and slammed against the door.

Anthony's body pinned her in place as he reached for her flailing fists. One well-placed punch, that was all she needed to break free.

With her front pressed to the wall, he captured both wrists and placed his mouth near her ear. She grimaced and shuddered as he panted hot, moist air against her neck. "You know Max?"

A hysterical giggle bubbled up her throat. "I know Max. *Very* well."

Madden, who had been standing off to the side being entertained by the theatrics, stepped closer. "You know my son?"

"Don't you dare lay claim to him," she spat. "He deserves better than you. Better than either of you."

Anthony shook her. "How do you know him?"

She glanced meaningfully at Madden before returning Anthony's stare. "Do you really want me to tell you that?"

Oh, yes. She had seen many things in his memories. Anthony's plans of betrayal included more than one Madden. A tidbit she hoped to leverage as a means to use Anthony to get out of Madden's lascivious clutches.

"Do you want me to tell you *everything* I know about you, The Second?"

He sucked in a breath then let it out slowly. "Well, this game just got interesting."

A blink later, the hard row of his knuckles zoomed forward to connect with her head, plunging her into darkness.

CHAPTER TWENTY-EIGHT

MAX STARED AT the monitor displaying Crystal's reflection the camera picked up off the bathroom mirror. He folded his arms and dug his fingers deep into his biceps with the effort to keep his panic in check.

"I think it's best for me to get out of here now, and we form a new plan," she was saying. "The brothers said they would help me escape. Look for me to be with them."

Chase and Doc were hunkered with him inside a large van with the name of the caterer working the event displayed on the side. Back at headquarters, Addison and Alisia were ready with technical support. A sideboard in the cargo area of the van held two tablets, scanners, and several computer monitors. Max sat in the lone desk chair while the others sat on the floor.

"Good girl." Max trailed his finger over her image. The fear in her eyes made him anxious to rush in to save her, heedless of the consequences. Patience. He needed to be patient. If she made her own way out, then they wouldn't need to blow their cover. "Just get out."

"Who are the Daniels brothers?" Chase asked.

"Ethan and Ronan own Daniels Software," he replied. "I've worked with them in the past when their father owned the company. Several years ago the entire family was in a plane crash. They were the only survivors. That must have sparked their powers."

"I would love to get my hands on them," Doc drawled in a husky voice that drew curious glances from Max and Chase. "For scientific purposes."

"Liar." Chase coughed.

"Fuck," Max muttered when Dittmar's face filled the screen.

"What?" They both crowded around him.

"Dittmar has her."

A bolt of terror shot through Max at the determined look in Dittmar's eyes as he pulled Crystal down the hall. He dragged her into a room Max recognized as his father's formal office and pushed her against the door. The camera went dark as his suit covered the lens. Each moan over the speakers tightened the tension in Max's body until the wood countertop under his fingers splintered with the force of his grip on the edge.

Bam. And there was the end of his patience.

"We need to get her out of there," he barked. "Where's Ripley?"

Chase pointed to another monitor. "Rip's a little busy right now."

On the screen a panther's paws appeared in the frame as he ran through the grass. Ripley leapt and startled a soldier who gaped in shock. He tried to pull his weapon just as the panther brought him down. Lifeless eyes filled the screen before the cat moved away to silently stalk his next prey.

Max got to his feet, hunching over in the confines of the van. "We need to move out now."

"You weren't thinking about sampling my gift before me, were you, James?" said a voice over the speakers that made Max stop cold.

He whipped his gaze back to the screen displaying the

feed from Crystal's necklace. A haze of red clouded his vision as he sucked in a breath. Madden was in the room.

"Don't you touch her," he muttered between gritted teeth. "Don't you fucking touch her."

"Wouldn't she want him to touch her so that she could read his past?" Chase asked.

Max growled and flicked his hand, shoving Chase against the wall of the van with a thought.

"Oww. Right. Bad idea."

Max's worst fear came to fruition as he watched his father fondle Crystal. An angry wave radiated from his body to rattle the equipment. The sides of the van began to creak and buckle under the force of his restrained rage.

"Max." Doc tried to rein him in with a plea that sounded as if she were calming a rabid beast. "Ripley will get to her. Don't lose it now."

"We go," he said, ignoring the request for calm. He reached for the door handle.

"Wait." Doc stopped him, pointing at the monitor. "There's someone else in the room with them."

"Who?"

"They're out of range. I can't hear what he's saying."

"Addison, turn up her mic," Max instructed.

"Is that recognition I see in your eyes?" the newcomer's voice rumbled.

Max's heart stopped. "What the fuck?" *Impossible.* It was impossible.

Anthony's face came into view and Max's head swam.

"What the fuck?" Blood rushed in his ears. Sweat popped out on his brow as sickening realization dawned. He clenched and unclenched his fingers as he struggled for breath. "What the fuck? *What the fuck!*"

Doc started to reach out then thought better of it. "Max, who is that?"

"Anthony," he choked, still not believing what he was seeing.

She frowned. "Your friend who died?"

"Apparently he didn't die," Chase murmured out the side of his mouth.

Anthony DeMateo, his best friend, was alive and apparently working with Madden. Probably had been the entire time. Bile rose in Max's throat at the thought that he had been played. Anthony was the one person he had trusted above all others. Anthony knew he would go after his father when he died. Why did he set him up?

Mac grabbed the back of the chair when Anthony kissed Crystal, caught up in the shock of the moment. When she bit Anthony and he backhanded her in response, the chair snapped, the plastic crumbling in Max's palms like sand.

"I know you, Anthony DeMateo. I know you from the man who used to call you friend, you lying, traitorous bastard!" Crystal shouted in outrage.

"No!" Max braced his hands on the sideboard, his nose inches from the screen. "What are you doing? You're going to get yourself killed."

"Holy shit," Chase breathed as they watched in horror.

The smack of Crystal's body hitting the wall made them all flinch. Max was going to kill Anthony himself and make sure he damn well stayed dead.

Crystal's low sultry chuckle made his throat tighten in dread and kept his feet rooted to where he stood, helpless to do nothing but watch. What was she thinking? "Do you really want me to tell you that? Do you want me to tell you *everything* I know about you, The Second?"

Max fell back against the side of the van.

Anthony? Anthony was the one they had been working against all this time? Nausea swirled in his belly. Fuck, he'd been such a fool.

Anthony's fist pulled back then swung at Crystal. The view blurred as she fell to the floor before the image refocused on his shoes.

Max froze, his brain overloaded and incapable of processing the fact that his woman had been knocked cold by his friend.

Chase bolted up. "Why did he punch her?"

"Maybe she saw something in his past when he touched her," Doc answered. "Something he didn't want let out, so he silenced her before she could blab."

Chase shot a nervous glance at Max. "He's going to explode, isn't he?"

Max blinked once. His eyes narrowed with diamond-hard focus as every muscle in his body tensed. There was no need to blow up at that moment. All of his energy was required for the field.

"We go in now." His voice was low and as smooth as shards of glass. "DeMateo is mine."

A knock on the back of the van snapped their gazes toward the double doors. One of the monitors showed Ronan Daniels standing just outside.

"Open up, Max. I know you're there," the twin called out to him telepathically.

The back doors flung open and the metal smashed into the sides with a loud clang. Max jumped to the ground. "How did you find us?"

Ronan raised an incredulous brow. "Are you kidding? You're broadcasting so loudly, even a non-telepath could hear you." His expression sobered. "Your girl's in trouble."

"No shit," he barked then sucked in a breath.

He needed to keep his cool and his priorities in check. DeMateo would get what was coming to him, but Crystal came first.

Ronan glanced into the van and his mouth fell open. "Impressive. Hello." He nodded to the others. "Ronan Daniels, but we'll get to that later." He turned back to Max. "Was Crystal on her own in there?"

"Sort of. One of our teammates, Ripley, was supposed to be with her, but they were separated. He was taking out guards so we could go in."

"Ripley is the shifter?" Max nodded and Ronan placed his hands on his hips. "That's a start. I'm not sure what you know so far, but that place is teaming with soldiers, and they're not just there for show. I was able to sneak out, but Ethan stayed behind to keep an eye, or his mind, if you will, on Crystal."

Max snorted. "He sucks at it. Madden has her. They knocked her out."

The playboy's expression softened. "I know. There were guards posted at the door. He couldn't get in. But he's tracking her progress, and between the two of us, we can keep her in the loop when she comes to."

"They're moving her," Doc called out.

Crystal was lifted, the camera swinging wildly on its chain. Max couldn't tell who was carrying her to one of the floor-to-ceiling bookcases. The case opened, revealing a tunnel.

"Where does that lead?" Chase asked.

"I don't know." Max narrowed his eyes. "I didn't know it existed."

Ronan held up a hand. His head cocked as if he were listening to the wind. "Ethan's tracking them. They're taking her to an underground room. Some kind of…" he paused to flick a glance at Max, "playroom. We need to move."

"Right." Max stalked back to the van and opened a metal locker. Rifles and hand guns glinted in the moonlight. "Load up and let's roll."

CHAPTER TWENTY-NINE

MAX LED THE others through the woods back to Madden's mansion. The faint sound of laughter and music drifted on the air from the ballroom. One would think the presence of armed soldiers in full body armor would put a damper on the festivities, but apparently not. The frivolity only went to show what kind of sick fucks Madden hung out with.

They approached a gate built into the high rock wall that bordered the property. One of the armed guards lay on the ground. His eyes shined like glass and were just as vacant as they stared up at the moon with his throat ripped out.

"Anyone near?" Max asked Ronan.

He paused for a moment to listen. "No. It's quiet."

Max lifted his hand. The metal gate screeched as he tore it off its hinges and tossed it to the side.

Ronan let loose with a very unmanly giggle. "That was sweet."

Normally, Max would be just as impressed with himself, but at the moment the only thing that mattered was getting to Crystal.

To his right, Doc and Chase were in full combat gear, ready to follow his lead. He knew they would do anything to save one of their own. But the Daniels brothers were wild cards with no vested interest in the team's cause. Crystal was too important to put his trust in them so quickly. And if they were hurt or killed in the upcoming confirmation, the guilt would be a burden he didn't want to bear.

"Look, Ronan, if you go in there, you'll be tying yourself to us and probably expose your powers. If you want to back out, say so now."

Max appreciated the fact that the man took a moment to think before he answered. Ronan's eyes unfocused, as if he was having an internal conversation, before his gaze sharpened and looked back to him. "I talked it over with Ethan. We're in. And we do have a vested interest in this. Madden dragged us in when he used our software to build his army. Speaking of which." He pulled the headset and goggles off the body at their feet and looped them around his neck. "It'll be nice to know exactly what he's done with our product."

"Thank you," Max replied.

Huh. Who would've thought he'd be grateful for the extra hands on his team. But with the brothers on their side, that increased their odds and he could end this fight with his father, once and for all.

A snarl in the dark preceded a shadowy black panther looping across the lawn. The fur morphed into skin with a crack of bones. Ripley appeared before them, sweaty, out of breath, and nude. "What have I missed?"

Max kept it short and sweet. "Madden has Crystal, and Anthony DeMateo is alive. He's The Second."

"Your friend, Anthony?"

Max nodded once.

Ripley cursed then did a double take when he noticed Ronan standing with them. "Who are you?"

"Ronan Daniels. Telepath. My twin is inside keeping

track of Crystal. Try not to eat him."

"I'll do my best."

"What's going on inside?" Max asked.

"Madden disappeared for a while, but is now back in the ballroom schmoozing the lemmings. There's a guard posted at every door, except for the few I removed."

Max crossed his arms. "If he's in the ballroom, who's with Crystal?"

"Ethan said DeMateo is alone with her," Ronan answered.

A twitch started near his eye. "All right, here's the plan. We're keeping it simple. We'll enter through the garage and head straight for the office. Only kill if necessary. I'm hoping that once we start causing trouble, the guards will come after us without alerting the guests. Madden is not going to want to show any weakness in front of the very people he is asking to back him. Ronan, you and Ethan come up with a reason to get everyone out of the house as quickly as possible. We'll sort out who the so-called lemmings are from the innocent later. Ripley, you take Madden." He tossed him an earpiece.

Ripley's eyes sparked in surprise. "You want *me* to take out your father? Are you sure?"

Never had he been more certain in his life.

As long as his father was brought down, Max didn't give a shit as to who actually did the deed. His sole purpose now was getting to his woman. "Yes. I'll get Crystal and take care of DeMateo. Chase, you and Doc cover them."

"We'll get her back, Max." Doc set her jaw.

Max nodded. "Follow me."

The team dashed across the lawn to the side entrance of the garage. Ripley took the unconventional route and shifted into a bat. His furry mammal flew off into the night sky and down a chimney.

With a wave of his hand, Max opened the side door. Spotlights illuminated the interior of the cavernous room, highlighting dozens of luxury vehicles. Each car was more ostentatious than the next.

"Whoa," Chase exclaimed. "Nice wheels."

"Who's there?" a voice asked from the shadows.

"Oops. Sorry." He shrugged in apology.

Max sighed with restrained impatience. "Take care of it."

"Right, boss."

In a blur of motion, Chase raced toward the direction of the voices. The sound of jaws breaking and bones snapping preceded the thud of two bodies hitting the floor.

Doc took off after Chase, her favorite Glock in hand, with Max and Ronan hot on her heels. They burst into the hallway to see several guards trying to take aim at Chase working his way through the gauntlet of men and Madden's antiques. Doc took position behind a seven-foot-tall marble statue of Zeus and laid down a layer of cover fire.

"Go," Ronan shouted at Max and shot off two rounds of his own. "We've got this."

Max pulled the priceless oil paintings off the wall and hurled them at the sea of soldiers streaming their way.

"Take care," he said, taking off down the hall, the sounds of shouting and gunfire echoed behind him.

Each long-legged stride took him away from one nightmare and closer to another. He had to reach her. He had to save her. Anything less was not an option.

Blood pounded in his head and raced through his veins to settle in his gut as image after horrible image of possibilities filled his mind.

Please, dear God, let me find her in time.

CHAPTER THIRTY

CRYSTAL'S EYES FLEW open as the acrid stench of smelling salts hit her nose. She instantly regretted the slight movement as her head swam and her stomach roiled. The painful throbbing and swelling in her cheek reduced the visibility in her left eye to crap and her right eye wasn't able to focus any better. The last thing she remembered was learning Anthony's secrets, but who had hit her? And more important, had she been drugged and if so, for how long?

Wait. The scent of the smelling salts faded to an after-shave that was familiar. Recently familiar.

Her vision focused and she realized the support holding her upright was Anthony DeMateo. Noticing that she was gaining consciousness, he released her to stand on her own feet. Her knees buckled and a cry broke past her dry lips despite the determination to not show any weakness.

A hook in the ceiling held a chain that connected to the bands securing her wrists above her head, keeping her on her feet. The muscles along her shoulders burned under the strain of her weight.

With her one good eye, she searched the room for a possible means of escape.

Where in the hell was she?

Soft, almost romantic lighting glowed from sconces from the four corners of the room, bathing the brown suede–covered the walls. An oversized bed covered in sumptuous pillows of cinnamon and tan lay to her left. Tied to each of the hooks drilled into the corners of the four-poster frame was a rope that ended in fur-lined handcuffs. A shelving unit stood next to the bed stocked with bottles of lubricant and an assortment of dildos and whips displayed in neat rows.

On her right sat the heavy equipment. A St. Andrew's cross and two other tables made to separate and fold into any desired position lined up like soldiers ready for duty. What was this place? BDSM Depot?

She wanted to snort at the clichéd setting, but her face hurt too much to even grimace.

"Crystal?" A deep voice penetrated the haze of her brain. *"It's Ethan. Are you awake?"*

A relieved breath escaped before she could school her features. *Yes. I'm tied up somewhere. Anthony is with me. I think he's alone.*

"I know, honey. Just sit tight, the cavalry is coming. I'll stay with you and keep you updated on their progress."

Thank you.

She was not alone. Even though he stopped communicating, she felt Ethan hovering in her mind like a soft hum along her consciousness. Embracing that small comfort, she warily lifted her head to search for Max's true enemy.

Anthony sat across from her in a straight-back chair near the only exit to the room that she could see. He watched her with assessing, questioning eyes, his legs casually crossed. His suit jacket was draped off the back of the chair, his cuffs rolled over his forearms, and a snifter of brandy rested loosely in his grip. As she continued to stare at him, he relaxed further in his seat and met her gaze.

A full minute passed in silence before she wiggled her

arms. The chains clanged, dispelling the silence. "Bondage? How unexpected," she drawled. "Were your friends too tired to play?"

He blinked once and a small smile flirted with the corner of his mouth. "They had some business to take care of. They'll be along shortly. Believe me, it wasn't a hardship to hold you in my arms. I am going to guess you're the clairvoyant. The one they call Prism." He lifted the snifter to his lips and took a drink. "So. What does the future hold for me?"

This time she let her grin bunch her cheeks despite the pain. "Certain death."

He gave a short bark of laughter, then tipped his head back to chuckle longer and heartier. He composed himself with a sigh and winked at her. "I see why Max likes you. But that was perfectly trite. Everyone will face death. I want to know more specifics."

"I want to know why you betrayed Max. He would have fought to the death for you."

"Lucky him, he still might get his chance." He placed the snifter on a low table next to the chair and stood. "I know it may appear as if I've betrayed him, but in actuality I was protecting him, protecting everyone. Matthew is a visionary. His ideas are genius, and he has the power and ambition to make them a reality. But his attention span is shit. All it takes is a pair of tits and a tight ass to make him lose focus. He's a sex addict, and that type of man is not what the world needs as a leader."

"And you think you are."

"I know I am." He stepped closer, his alcohol-scented breath aggravating her stomach. He brought his finger up to trail a scrolling pattern along her battered cheek. "If I went after Madden myself, it would show a weakness in our organization that would lead the cause to certain failure. But Max... Ah, now Matthew burned that bridge himself years ago. I knew all I had to do was point Max in the right direction and he'd take out his father as I continued my work. But I thought he would accomplish that the old-fashioned way, with computers and information. Place Matthew in jail forever. If only I had known about Max's power. I would have definitely tried a different tactic to achieve my plans. Where did his powers come from? How did you get yours?"

His fingers stroked along her neck and shoulders with reverence, and he gazed at her as if she were a rare treasure he couldn't wait to plunder. Her skin crawled under his touch, and she wished she felt sick enough to vomit all over him, just to get him to back away.

"Max would never have helped you. You said it yourself, he's the smartest man on the planet. He would've seen through you in an instant."

"You're right. Max is smart. But he'll see reason when I explain what it is I am trying to accomplish. After you're dead, he'll believe me when I tell him that Madden was the one who killed you. Max will seek his revenge for certain."

She laughed in his face despite his threat. She had seen her death, and it wasn't in this S&M den.

Anger, on behalf of herself and Max, gave her the courage to hold her ground. "Max knows all about you, about how you're The Second. He will never join you."

Anthony stilled and his smug grin faltered. "That's impossible. No one but Madden knows my true identity."

"Uh, duh. Superhumans here." She smirked.

He gripped her hair at the back of her neck and pulled

hard, tilting her head back. "How?" he growled.

Tears welled in her eyes as she spat through gritted teeth, "Doesn't matter. He knows all about you, and he's going to rip out your heart and piss in the hole. Just give up now, and take it like a man."

A flash of fear made his pupils widen, before his brow furrowed while he formulated a plan. The look reminded her so much of Max it broke her heart.

He released her hair and slid his palm down her neck to rest over her thudding heart. His thumb brushed the stone in her necklace once, then twice, before he stopped and scooped it up in his palm. His knowing laughter made the hair on her arms stand up with dread.

"Ingenious. You can barely see it." He unlatched the heavy chain and turned the stone over and over. "Has he been watching the entire time?" He flicked the matching earrings. "What are these? Microphones? Can he hear us right now? Well, let's give him something worth watching."

He walked across the room and hung the necklace off a hook attached to the back of the door. He stalked back to her with the hungry look of a predator about to enjoy his meal.

"Yes. This will do nicely," he murmured and picked up a flogger with a two-feet-long suede tails. He brushed his fingers over her lips. "Let's show Max just how well I can treat his girl."

The silk of her dress bunched and rippled as he ran the flogger in teasing glances over her body. The gentle smack of suede on skin made her flinch more than the contact, but she knew that at any moment the gentle brushes could turn violent.

Ethan. Please. Where is everyone? Silence. *Ethan? Ro-*

nan? Someone please hurry.

Nothing, not a glimmer of response. Oh God, something must have happened. They would not leave her on her own without good cause. Plan, a plan. She needed a plan.

"Come on, Max. Come out, come out from wherever you are," Anthony taunted as he used the end of the flogger to lift the hem of her skirt.

Fuck a plan. She needed to act now.

Taking a deep breath, she allowed her body to sag. Her hands crept up the chains binding her wrists and tightened into fists around the cold metal.

With a grin, Anthony shifted his stance in preparation of swinging the flogger, giving her just enough room to drive her knee up into his groin, bending him double. His grunt of agony was oh so satisfying, but not nearly enough punishment.

She took several steps back, then ran forward to swing from the hook like Tarzan. The bottom of her pointy Louboutins punched into his chest and sent him soaring. The table and chair crashed under the weight of his falling body.

Crystal eyed his limp form, each of her panting breaths matching his groans as he rolled on the floor.

Working past the pain in her shoulders, she grabbed hold of the chain with both hands again and jumped. Up and around, she tried to dislodge it from the hook until third time was the charm. She ducked to avoid the fall of heavy links before kicking off her heels and making a run for the door. Thankfully, the door was unlocked and flew open at first try.

As much as she would have loved to stay and kick his ass some more, she raced down the darkened hallway.

Hallway? It was more like a tunnel without a single window to give her any indication about where she was or how to get out.

Right or left? Right or left?

Instinct drew her to the right and she ran as best as she could while juggling the chain still attached to her wrists with each step.

Ethan, Ronan! Where are you guys?

"Crystal?"

Relief at hearing Ethan's voice made her stumble. *I'm running down a hall. I don't know where I'm going.*

"Max is right behind you, but he has company. Find a place to hide."

Okay.

Her lungs burned with every breath, but she kept running, determined to find safety. Hope spurred her faster as the floor began to rise at an incline. A door with a steel bar across it stood at the end of the hall. She paused just long enough to release the handle and throw it open. Damp grass met her bare feet, making her toes curl with the cold.

The chain smacked against her shins as she ran across the open lawn in search of shelter. Goose bumps broke out over her flesh in the chilly night air even as her silk dress clung to her sweat-dampened skin. At least it wasn't raining.

As she approached a row of hedges, she could make out light coming from the main building. If she could reach the ballroom, hopefully she could become lost in the crowd or find Max.

She dashed through a break in the shrubbery and entered a courtyard, complete with stone pavers and wood benches. A cute little fountain burbled in the center that she would have stopped to admire if she wasn't running for her life.

Madden burst into the courtyard, running in her direction from the other side. They both pulled up short when they spotted each other. Blood oozed from a cut across his cheek. His expensive suit hung off him in shredded ribbons.

He must have run into Ripley, she thought with a smirk. Was it a good or bad thing she still found humor in the midst of her fear? Perhaps she was closer to losing her ever-loving mind than she thought. Of course, crazy could also work in her favor.

Madden's chest rose with a deep breath, and he straightened. Even dressed in his shredded suit, he exuded power and authority. "Well, isn't this fortuitous."

Crystal gathered the length of chain and let it swing from her hand. The clink of metal on metal sent a warning. "Excuse me. I would like to pass."

He smiled at her. "Such backbone, such courage. It's exquisite. My son couldn't have picked a finer woman."

"I'm so glad I have parental approval. Now get out of my way," she snarled.

He hedged closer and reached for her. "I can't do that. I seem to be without protection, and you're my ticket out of here."

"Guess again."

She swung the metal chain like a whip, striking him in the arm. Madden grunted and backed away, then approached her from the right. She countered and swung again. This time he wrapped the chain around his arm and pulled. Instead of resisting, she allowed him to tug and used her momentum to plow into him.

Her forehead connected with his nose with a loud crack that made them both stagger back with a moan as stars swam in her vision. One Madden turned into two images before her. With all the hits to the head she was taking, if she wasn't careful, she was going to suffer permanent brain damage.

"All right. I'm done playing." Madden pulled a gun from what was left of his suit and leveled it right at her.

She stopped short as familiarity triggered her memory. Suddenly, she realized exactly where she stood. The foliage, the fountain, the gun. This was her vision. This was where she died.

All the fight went out of her in one deflated gasp of air. Fear crept into her mind in a dank mist bleeding her of hope.

Was this really her end? Would she never see Max again, hold him, love him?

Madden had played a part in the death of Max's mother. That grief triggered his superpowers. What would Max do if his father killed her too? Would his powers grow to the level where he could destroy the planet with a single thought?

In her heart, she knew he would never let her death go unavenged. Dittmar had touched her and Max had been ready to fight to the death. Madden might as well turn the gun on himself afterward, because that would be a much less painful ending than what Max would inflict.

But what about afterward? Would he return to that dark, solitary existence where he trusted no one? Would he allow the others to fight without him? The thought of Max alone and bitter weakened her knees.

Tears filled her eyes, and she angrily blinked them away. No. No. *No!* If she expected Max to choose to live without her, then she had to fight to live now.

Ethan said that Max was right behind her. She couldn't

give up yet.

She lifted her chin and held out her arms to show her acquiescence. The chain clanked softly between her spread hands. "So what's your plan?"

Madden blinked at her as if he was surprised by her change of compliance. "We walk out of here. There is a break in the fence through the woods. Once we're on the road, we can go our separate ways."

She snorted at that. "Yeah, right. Like you'll just let me go. My team will be on us before we get ten feet." She hoped.

"Which is why you are going to guarantee my protection."

"Of course," she replied with a touch of sarcasm. Her smile turned sickly sweet. "And who will protect you from the threat within your own organization?"

A curl of satisfaction warmed her insides as she saw his confidence falter. His stance wavered a little as his brow furrowed. "What are you talking about? I'm in complete control of my people."

Her deep throaty laugh echoed in the night. "That's a crock. How do you think Max knew about your plans? He was at Anthony's the night he supposedly died. Max was the one who killed most of the men there. Anthony told him all of your secrets with the hope that Max would take you down. Apparently your love of sex has made you an unfit leader in Anthony's eyes." She smirked.

The muscles of his jaw flexed and his nostrils flared. His furious gaze moved to a point over her shoulder. "Is that true?"

"Yes," a voice behind her answered.

Her heart sank further. Well, shit, just who she wanted

to see.

Anthony appeared to her right with his own gun drawn and aimed at Madden. The tip of Madden's gun wavered back and forth between the two of them. Hmm. Perhaps she could turn him into a temporary ally.

She slid a sideways glance at Anthony. "So, how's your nut sack?"

He glared at her with murderous intent. How unexpected. Not. "Don't. Start."

She laughed and winked at Madden. "Well, you'll have one less man to compete for the ladies with. His equipment won't be functioning properly for a while."

"He hasn't felt pain yet," Madden sneered. "You think you can overthrow me? How dare you. I made you."

"Yes, you did. So it should be no surprise that it took very little effort to undermine you. Everyone knows I am the one makes things happen. You're just the poster boy. The pretty bait to lure in the public. But you've dropped the ball there, Mattie. You lose focus too easily. That's why you'll have to go."

The nose of Madden's gun rose higher. "I'll see you in hell first."

Anthony grabbed her arm and dragged her in front of him. "That's the point."

Madden's laugh made her stomach twist. "You think hiding behind a woman will save you? Think again."

The blast of the gun echoed into the night.

CHAPTER THIRTY-ONE

MAX RAN TOWARD the beacon of light in the dark hallway with his heart in his throat. Considering what his father had exposed him to as a teenager, Max grew more fearful over what Crystal might be forced to endure. Why didn't he know about this part of the house? Was it a recent addition, or had his father engaged in more illicit dealings than Max had been aware of while growing up in the mansion?

He burst through the open door with hands raised in defense. Harsh disappointment slammed into him when he found the room empty.

Terror twisted his gut as he took in the padded tables and S&M equipment decorating the space. This was a room designed for pleasures of the flesh. And Crystal had been held here. Good God, what did they do to her?

As he took a step forward, he stumbled on an object, drawing his attention to the floor. A black stiletto. Its mate lay near an overturned table. An empty snifter rested on its side in a wet puddle.

Hope sprung in his chest. Whatever happened, she didn't go down without a fight.

"*Max,*" one of the twins called to him. "*Crystal escaped. She's on the run.*"

I'm in the room now. Which way did she go?

"*To the right. Hurry. She thinks—*" The sudden pause

made Max's heart skip.

What? She thinks what?

"She had a vision. She believes she's going to die."

What! When? How? He ran for the hall.

"I don't know. I was only able to catch a fleeting image."

"Stop right there," a male voice ordered.

Max ducked back into the room, narrowly missing a barrage of bullets.

Motherfucker. A couple of bullets he could deflect, but a hailstorm of lead was something he didn't want to test his powers on, especially with his energy waning.

He pulled his .45 from his belt and slid home his magazine. With a kiss on the barrel for extra luck, he took aim around the doorframe and pulled the trigger.

"Fuck, fuck, fuck," he muttered with each pull of the trigger until the gun emptied.

In a last-ditch effort, he held out his palms. The broken chair and table sailed through the air as piss-poor excuses for missiles.

"Come on. Come on," he muttered, trying to peer around the doorjamb into the hall. If he could just focus for a few seconds on one of the shooters' guns, he might have a chance to snatch it for himself.

But the constant barrage of bullets prevented him from leaving himself exposed for more than a heartbeat.

A weapon. Where the hell was he going to find a weapon?

A wicked smile twisted his mouth as he snatched a whip from a shelf.

"Thank you, Dad," he said aloud.

Heavy footsteps approached the door. Quickly, he took a stance to the side and held his breath in anticipation.

The end of a rifle appeared first. The tip of the whip cracked as Max looped it around the barrel, jerking it free and tossing it toward the bed, where it landed with a gentle thump.

Not so gentle was the technique Max used to break the soldier's arm and slam his forehead into soft cartilage. As the man crumbled to his knees, a second guard opened fire, spraying the room haphazardly. A bullet grazed Max in the arm, cutting a swath through the leather and taking a chunk of skin with it.

Max's bicep burned as he slung the whip out to encircle the gunman's neck. The solider dropped the rifle to grasp the strip of hide. His eyes started to bulge behind his visor when Max yanked back and snapped his neck.

In through the mouth, out through the mouth. He tried to ignore the coppery scent of the blood seeping into his jacket. This was not the time to get sick.

After ensuring the hall was clear, Max raced in the direction Crystal had taken. A door at the end stood ajar. He eased it open and peered out.

"Which way, which way," he murmured.

The vast expanse of lawn stretched out before him. Dew was already forming and clung to each blade of grass, except for where a darker trail snaked off to the left. The courtyard.

"Whoever's available, come to the courtyard," Max directed to his earpiece. "It's the hedged-off area near the ballroom. Crystal's there and she's in trouble."

"On it," Doc answered.

His breath puffed out in swirling clouds as he raced toward the courtyard. During the spring, his mother had loved to sit under the cherry blossoms and read to him when he was a child. Within the confines of the hedges, he had been allowed to play, to imagine, to be a little boy when his father had wanted him to be a man. The courtyard was a haven.

If Crystal made it there, then one of the others could catch up with her. She'd be safe.

In the distance, he spotted the break in the hedge. A man stood at the opening. The back of his white shirt appeared to glow in the moonlight. Anthony.

Max's legs pumped harder as anger surged through him, coating the back of his throat with the bitter taste of vengeance.

As he approached the entrance, his view of the interior widened and he saw his father standing to his right, a gun drawn. The faint light glinted on the weapons both men held pointed at each other with Crystal caught in between.

Suddenly, Anthony hauled Crystal in front of him as if she were a shield. Madden's laughter reached Max's ears a second before he squeezed the trigger.

"No!" Max reached out into the air, throwing his energy in an effort to deflect the trajectory of the bullet. Blades of grass bowed out in a ripple, and the leaves swirled as the surge of energy rolled in a wave toward Crystal.

No, no, no. He was too far away. He wouldn't make it.

Crystal jerked and slumped in Anthony's hold as he fired back twice in quick succession.

Madden stumbled backward. The bullets added more holes and splotches of blood to his shredded shirt. Shock slackened his face before he fell back into the fountain with a heavy splash.

Anthony set Crystal's limp form on the stone pavers and straightened a second before Max tackled him from behind. Over and over they tumbled across the hard surface.

DeMateo rolled on top of Max and blocked the right hook aimed at his face. He answered back with a punch that connected with Max's jaw, snapping his head to the side and dislodging his sunglasses.

Murderous rage took over Max's mind, numbing him to everything else. Stiff armed, he grappled with DeMateo, who had his hands wrapped around Max's neck, while digging his knee into his gut.

"I'm sorry, Max," DeMateo panted. "I'm sorry your father hurt your girl." His fingers tightened. "We can make this right. Work with me. Together we can save the world."

"Crystal *is* my world, you son of a bitch," Max rasped.

He narrowed his eyes, concentrating on DeMateo's beating heart. Molecule by molecule, Max manipulated the blood racing through Anthony's veins.

Anthony gasped and keeled over, writhing and clutching at his chest. The whites of his eyes turned pink with breaking blood vessels.

Max staggered to his feet and stared down at the man he once loved like a brother. There wasn't enough pain he could inflict to ever make up for what the bastard had done.

"Please." DeMateo reached out. His breath rattled in his faltering lungs.

"Payback's a bitch, huh?"

With one last wheezing breath, Anthony's head lolled to the side. His empty gaze stared in the direction of Madden's loafers that hung over the side of the fountain. Neither man was getting up again.

He rushed to Crystal's side. Blood seeped from a hole above her heart and trickled down onto the stone beneath her. In the shadows, her pale skin glowed ghostly white, the dark crescent of her lashes laid like half-moons on her cheeks.

"Crystal," his voice cracked. He ripped a section of her flimsy skirt off and pressed it to the wound. For once, it was his utter helplessness that weakened his stomach and not the stench of blood. "Sweetheart, baby, please open your eyes."

Her lids fluttered ever so gently. "Max," she mouthed.

"Doc's coming, sweetie. Doc!" he shouted. "Just stay with me."

Her mouth trembled in a weak smile. Her face was pinched tight in pain. "Love you." The barely whispered words speared through him.

"I love you, too. Stay with me, baby. Stay with me," he ordered, then begged. Her eyes drifted closed and her body wilted. "Stay! Stay!"

Under his palm her pulse slowed, then stopped altogether.

"Crystal. Crystal!"

"Max, I'm here. Move." Doc shoved against his hunched form. "Dammit, Max, move!"

When he didn't budge she jumped to the other side and shoved his blood-covered hands out of her way. She placed her bare palms over the hole in Crystal's chest and closed her eyes.

Max gritted his teeth, every muscle in his body tensed as if to feed her his strength. He took Crystal's icy hand between both of his and bent to whisper encouragements in her ear. Failure burned like acid in his gut when he saw her face. Bruises marred her cheeks, the entire left side swollen and red. Heat scorched down his cheek as his first tear fell.

Losing her now was not an option. Without her, his world was as dark and empty as his mountain had been before he met her. She was his light, his warmth, his reason for believing in the good of man.

Please, baby, please, please, please.

Continuing his prayers, he lifted his gaze to the clear night sky, then over to where Anthony's body lay. A bolt of fury shot from Max's core and raised the body in the air and slammed it back to the ground. Over and over he bashed the corpse against the earth until the last of his energy gave out and Anthony was nothing more than a bloody pulp. He sagged with exhaustion, yet the rage still roiled inside him.

"Holy shit."

Max whipped his head around to see Sheriff Lancaster and Deputy Davis running into the courtyard with weapons drawn.

"Sheriff?" Max blinked in confusion.

"Gunfire was reported to be coming from Madden's mansion. We sent in the SWAT team and found your friends." His sharp gaze took in the scene. "Holy shit," he repeated and reached for his radio. "Send me a medic around back. Now. We're near the cherry blossoms."

"No," Doc gasped. "Don't."

"Your medics can't help," Max added. "Please."

Lancaster's mouth pinched as if he wanted to argue, but he nodded and placed a hand on Davis's shoulder. "Get blankets, first-aid kit, whatever. Keep the EMTs on standby." He dropped to his knees next to Doc. "What do we have?"

"Gunshot. She—" Max broke off, unable to say anymore.

"Shock," Doc panted. Her arms shook from trying to keep her weight off Crystal. Deep lines bracketed her mouth and sweat beaded on her brow.

Lancaster placed his arm around Doc's shoulders to keep her upright. Uncertainty creased his forehead, but he held his tongue. Collectively, they focused their energy as if by will alone they could somehow help revive Crystal's heart.

This could not be happening. He had *superpowers*, for fuck's sake. He could manipulate molecules. There had to be something he could do.

Wait. He could manipulate molecules.

"Doc, hold on. I'm going in."

Her eyes widened with alarm and the line of her lips tightened, but she didn't say a word, continuing to concentrate.

Max placed his palm on Crystal's chest, careful not to block Doc's efforts. He imagined Crystal's heart, struggling, broken, and used his power to keep the muscle beating as Doc worked her magic on repairing the damage.

Long seconds dragged, with only Doc's labored breathing and his own breaking the silence. With his free hand, Max lifted Crystal's limp hand and pressed his lips to her cold fingers and resumed his prayers while more tears fell from his tightly shut lids.

He meant what he said to DeMateo. Crystal was his world, and the thought of not having her in it was beyond torture.

An icy touch brushed his cheek, tickling his evening stubble. He pulled back and stared at Crystal's fingers. They were twitching.

They were twitching.

Crystal hitched a short breath, then a longer one. Her eyelids fluttered open just as Doc collapsed against Lancaster.

"Doc," the sheriff gasped.

"I'll be okay." She smiled and sank deeper into Lancaster's hold. "Tired. That was close."

"Max?" Crystal whispered.

"Hey, sweetheart." Euphoria crashed over him, and he collapsed over her prone form, hugging her head with his arm. "You're gonna be okay."

Underneath him, her little body began to shudder. Damn, he should have known she was freezing. He pulled his duster off and draped it over her before gathering her back in his arms.

She blinked as if waking from a dream. "I died."

"Doc saved you. You can't leave us that easily."

"Doc." She turned her head.

"I'm here, sweetie." Doc reached out and brushed the coat with her trembling fingers. "Don't die on me again."

"I'll try not to." She glanced over and did a double take. "Sheriff?"

"Prism." He nodded. "You're looking a lot better than you did two minutes ago."

"Thanks." Her weak chuckle sounded more like a wheeze that died as she caught sight of the bloody cut in Max's arm. "You're bleeding. Do you need a medic?"

His bark of laughter caught him by surprise. Even at death's door, she still wanted to fuss over him. "I'm fine." He pressed his forehead to hers and gazed into the brown depths of her eyes. "I can't lose you, don't you know that? You make me whole."

"I'm sorry." Her lips quivered. "I'm sorry about everything."

He feathered his lips against her. "I'm sorry, too. You do realize that I am never letting you out of my sight again."

"We'll discuss that later. Just hold me for now."

"Done."

He gathered her closer and pressed his nose into her hair. Through the fabric of his shirt, her warm breath seeped into the cotton and heated him to his soul. She was alive. He inhaled her scent again. She was alive.

Lancaster cleared his throat, drawing their attention. When he lifted his brow, Max realized that he had lost his glasses and was facing the sheriff unmasked.

"You're the son. Max Madden." It wasn't a question.

Max swallowed and clutched Crystal tighter. "Yes."

Lancaster tipped his head toward the pair of feet hanging out of the fountain. "Who is that?"

"My father." Max jerked his head toward what was remaining of the other body. "He fired a shot at Anthony, who was using Prism as a shield. That's how she was injured. DeMateo fired back and killed him."

"Anthony DeMateo? I thought he died in an explosion a few months ago."

Max shook his head and swallowed down bitterness that lingered with that lie. "That's what I thought, too. It was a coverup."

"So if DeMateo killed your father, who killed De-Mateo?"

Max met his gaze without flinching. "I did."

Lancaster stared at him hard then nodded. "Inside the house is a hell of a shit show. Rich people being chased by a panther and men decked out with machine guns. Care to explain?"

"I'll tell you everything, but first I'd like to get my girl someplace she can rest. It's been a long night."

"We'll see." He glanced back and forth between Crystal

and Doc, who still lay limp in his arms. "This feels wrong. Shouldn't we get a doctor?"

"I *am* a doctor," Doc answered without opening her eyes. "Give me a minute to recharge, and I'll be fine." She cracked one eye open to look at Max. "We'll both live."

"Thank you."

She closed her eyes again. "I know. We all need her, Max. Take care of her. Or I'll rip you apart." The threat would have been more menacing if she hadn't been interrupted by a jaw-popping yawn.

"Hey, bossman?" Chase asked in his earpiece. "We're contained in the house. Do you have Prism?"

"I've got her." He gazed down at the sleeping woman in his arms. More hot tears filled his eyes and he wished his power included the ability to transport them to the comfort of his bed. Until then, he'd make do with sheltering her with his body and his love. "I've got her."

CHAPTER THIRTY-TWO

CRYSTAL GAZED OUT the window of the fast-moving Jeep and tried to separate all the shades of green from the jungle's canopy. The flight to the private island in the Bahamas had been long, but joining the mile-high club with Max had made the time pass in the most delightful way.

A soft smile touched her lips as her fingers twirled the emerald band around her ring finger. Inscribed in the silver were six words. *My heart. My soul. My love.* Such simple words, yet nothing else in the world gave her such joy.

A warm hand slid across her bare knee and smoothed up the inside of her thigh. She turned to see her husband gazing at her with a heat in his smoky eyes that made her toes curl in her sandals.

Her husband.

She licked her lips and placed her hand over his. They hadn't wasted any time in making their union official, heading straight to the courthouse at the first opportunity. Life was too short to wait for the "right" time.

It still amazed her that this was the same troubled man who had walked into her coffeehouse on that hot August day. Now a smile always hovered on his firm lips, the light in his eyes sparkled, and the world no longer appeared to weigh on his shoulders. For now.

Those first few weeks after the incident at Madden's had been insane. She slept for two days solid while Max worked on the cleanup of the mess left behind. All the evidence they collected was handed over to Sheriff Lancaster, who took over the responsibility of working with the CIA and FBI in arresting those who had broken the law.

The truth about the events that had occurred that night had been mitigated to avoid causing a worldwide panic. Anthony had been correct on one thing when he had approached Max all those months ago. If word of Madden's plans and subsequent failure had hit the web, confidence in the financial system would have been weakened to the point of a global economic breakdown. Tiny bits of the truth had been fed to the media, and Max, as Madden's heir, temporarily took the reins as CEO of Madden Financial until a suitable replacement could be found.

Of course it was easy to bury Madden's indiscretions when the world was abuzz with the discovery of superhumans in the general population. The press dubbed their team the Evolutioneers, and now they had every newshound, government agency, and glory seeker combing the state looking for them. Lancaster promised to keep their identities a secret, and with the help of the Daniels brothers and their software, Addison managed to sidetrack anyone who came close to discovering their hideout.

They were wanted people. Glorified and vilified by a society who wanted their help and feared their power at the same time.

Yes, life had taken a monumental turn, which made these few stolen days all the more precious.

The road broke through the tree line and ended in a small pullout in front of a tiny cabin. Before them, the bluff rolled down to the white sandy beach a few yards below.

They hopped out of the car and took a moment to stop

and stare at the cozy hut that would be home for the next week. The ocean pounded the surf with a rhythmic cadence that matched the gentle beating of her heart as the sun warmed her bare shoulders. She glanced over at Max and found him lost in his own observation of their retreat.

Effervescent laughter burst out of her and set a flock of birds fleeing from the trees.

"What's so funny?" he asked.

"Are we really alone? All alone? Not a soul nearby?"

He cocked his head to the side and listened to the wind. He turned toward the trees and parted the forest as if it were the Red Sea. His smile grew wicked. "Yes, we are."

She laughed again and dashed into the hut with him hot on her heels. Their bags trailed behind them as if they were being carried by invisible bellboys and clattered in the entrance before the door shut behind them with a bang. He caught her around the waist and carried her into the bedroom. They could check out the rest of the cabin later.

He set her on her feet as his lips nuzzled, sipped, and drugged her to a state of bliss that made her melt against his body. He brushed aside the straps of her sundress and followed the fabric down with wet, open-mouthed kisses that turned her insides molten. With the tip of his tongue, he traced the pink pucker of scarred skin above her heart. She raked her nails across the cotton of his shirt, loving the flex of muscles underneath.

He buried his face in the crook of her neck and inhaled. "God, you smell so good. Like woman and fresh air. Sweet and sultry." His nimble fingers found the tab of the zipper on her dress and tugged it down. "It's been far too long since I've been inside you."

"It's only been a few hours." She giggled.

"Like I said, far too long."

The dress caught on her curves, rasping over her skin on its way to pool at her feet. His hot hands followed, cupping and molding her breasts and hips to his liking. He hooked an arm under her legs and carried her to the bed. The comforter floated to the floor as he set her on the cool satin sheets before he stepped back to remove his clothes.

Each inch he revealed to her hungry gaze made her mouth water in anticipation of running her tongue in every dip and hollow. Her hands itched to reach out and touch, but instead, she crushed the teal-colored satin in her fists to draw out the delicious torture.

Her eyes widened in surprise and she sat up and stared in disbelief at where she lay.

Teal satin sheets.

"Sweetheart, what's wrong?"

"Nothing," she croaked, then laughed self-consciously. "It's just," she laughed again, "I used to have visions of us on a bed with teal satin sheets."

"Used to?"

"I haven't had that vision in a while."

He crawled across the mattress and draped a muscular leg over hers, his forearms coming to rest on either side of her head. "When did you start having these visions?"

She bit her lip and focused on his chin. "In the parking lot at the zoo, the day we met Ripley."

His brows shot up. "That was the day after we met."

"I know." She couldn't stop grinning.

He narrowed his eyes. "What were we doing in this vision?"

She ran her fingers down his spine and around to cup his hard buttocks. "I can tell you, or you can guess and I'll let you know if you're right."

Nudging apart her legs, he settled into the vee of her thighs. The hard length of his cock rubbed along the slick folds of her sex. "Is this close?"

"Spot on."

She arched her neck in pleasure as he palmed her breast. The flick of his tongue on the hard peak bathed her in want, stoking the embers that always burned for him. His teeth barely sank into the tip when he jerked up. "Wait. You had a vision of us having sex the day after we met? Why didn't you tell me?"

She placed her hands on each side of his beloved face. "You weren't ready. Now make love to me, or do I have to find someone who will?"

A rumble worked up his chest. He curled his fingers over the edge of the mattress above her head. In one hard thrust he seated his cock fully in her sheath and robbed her of breath. "Is this what you want, Mrs. Madden?"

"Uh-huh," she panted, unable to speak anything more coherent.

He lowered his head and took her mouth while he claimed her body. At the moment it was just Max and her in the universe. Her entire being was centered on his heat and the strength he used to move inside her.

The creak of the bed competed with her cries. Torn between laughter and tears, she rode the current of passion, rising and falling with the need to mark him as hers. She scored her nails across his shoulders while her teeth nipped the muscles of his chest. She planted her feet on the mattress to push her hips harder against him, silently begging for more.

In the fury of the storm they created, she was a tree

bending in the wind. Any second she would snap under the pressure and splinter in a thousand directions. The line of tension ran from her core to her heart, tightening with each deep plunge.

Max planted his hand near her head and reared up to grasp her hip with the other, stilling her to drill deeper. Sweat dripped in his eyes as he gazed at her with love and desire sculpting the hard planes of his face.

"Love you," he groaned, then his spine bowed back. Warmth filled her as he released deep in her channel.

Her scream echoed in the cabin, joining him in the fall into darkness. Her inner muscles locked down, squeezing every bit of life from the both of them.

Her pupils widened then narrowed as her powers once more threw her into the future. More challenges, more enemies would rise to stop their call to protect the innocent. Heated disagreements, long nights spent in each other's arms. Friends would come and go. Children. Fear and courage, tears and laughter.

And through it all, they would be side by side. Together. Always.

"Crystal?" He brushed the tears from her cheeks with a shaky hand. "Sweetheart? Come back to me."

It took several long blinks for her eyes to focus. "I love you," she whispered, homing in on his blurry image. The strong embrace of his arms never failed to bring her back to the present.

Tender fingers swept aside the hair clinging to her damp cheeks. "Where did you go?"

"Our future. It's going to be quite an adventure." She hugged him close.

His chuckle vibrated under her ear. "Should I be worried?"

"Nope, because I'm going to be with you, forever."

He kissed the corner of her mouth. "Forever. I like that word. Especially if it involves you."

"Always, Max. I love you."

"I love you, too." He slapped her on the ass. "Now go make me a sandwich. Loving you burns a lot of calories."

She blinked at him. "You want a sandwich?"

He relaxed deeper into the mattress and closed his eyes. "Mm-hmm."

She brushed his oblique with the tip of a finger and smiled when he flinched. The second brush opened his eyes. "What are you doing?" He scowled.

"I see in your future an ass kicking," she crowed before she jumped on top of him, her hands a flurry of movement as she hit every ticklish spot she knew.

He bucked underneath her and grabbed her wrists. "You're going to pay for that."

"I hope so, Mr. Madden," she drawled and pressed her breasts against his chest. "Now do your worst."

He didn't disappoint.

EPILOGUE

THE GIRL WAS just asking to get her ass paddled.

Lack of moonlight and the impenetrable darkness of the forest hid the black panther prowling over pine needles and damp leaves. His ears flicked in displeasure, his muzzle twisted into the feline version of pissed-off alpha male.

How long did Alisia think she could continue sneaking around without him finding out? He was a freaking shapeshifter. With his acute hearing and overdeveloped sense of smell, of course he'd learn about her late-night escapades.

His nose twitched, sorting through the assortment of odors that assaulted his senses. Diesel fuel and truck exhaust mixed with rich earth and dying vegetation. Underneath it all was the subtle scent of citrus and the musk of woman. His woman.

Through the shadows, Ripley made out the shape of a large bush growing against the base of a giant pine tree. Upon closer inspection, the black gleam of a Honda CB 919 motorcycle was barely visible between the dense leaves. Thirty yards away, the rumble of logging trucks rolled down the dirt road, hauling the last loads of the night.

So that was how the little minx was getting down the mountain. She was good, he'd give her that. Stashing bits of clothing around the forest to throw him off her scent. His little nurse should've remembered that when she was ovulating, her scent changed. The aroma was like catnip, enticing him with the promise of hot, nasty, body-draining sex. Just how he liked it.

Anger and fear for her well-being cut through his lust. Why would she risk going out alone?

Yes, life in their mountain home required some getting used to. As much as Max and Crystal worked at making it feel like a home, they were still cohabitating under layers of volcanic rock with very little sunlight and forced ventilation.

But much to his surprise, Ripley discovered he loved living underground. He was surrounded by nature, nestled deep within her bosom, and there was plenty of room for his animal to take whatever form it wanted.

But where he had the luxury of stretching out his legs and running in the fresh air, his two-legged companions were required to take more caution. A human suddenly appearing from between two boulders would draw much more attention than Ripley in one of his animal forms. The constant vigilance of their privacy would drive him stir crazy, too. Still, jeopardizing her safety, as well as that of the rest of the team by sneaking out, was just plain foolish.

Was she meeting another man?

A snarl broke free with the thought as the fur rippled along his body. No, the cat shook his head, that wasn't it. He would smell it if she was. Alisia belonged to him. She just had yet to acknowledge it. The woman was being stubborn which, under different circumstances, he usually admired.

He followed her trail back to headquarters. Slipping through a fissure in the rock in the guise of a ferret, he made his way to the secret entrance to his room to change into some clothes. It wasn't the first place he wanted to stop, but the others appreciated it when he didn't walk around naked.

The ferret dropped to the floor and stood on his hind legs. His bones snapped like firecrackers, growing into a large, brawny, giant of a man.

Knowing Alisia was at home released the worry in his mind but did nothing to ease the fury bubbling under the surface. His fangs, still extended over his lips, throbbed in his gums as they receded and changed. His claws curled into his palms as they shaped back into fingers.

Yet his muscles quivered, urging him to follow his instinct and claim his mate. Command her to put her in his care and keep her safe. The swollen length of his cock agreed wholeheartedly as pre-cum dripped from the dark crimson head in a steady stream.

Oh God, not again.

"No. No!" he shouted. He would not come at her like an animal.

He stumbled into the bathroom and turned the shower on full force. Icy water cooled the heat of his skin, but the fire of lust continued to flow in his veins. This was the third such attack in the past two months, and by far the strongest.

"Motherfucker," he groaned, curling into the tile. His long nails tapped a staccato rhythm on the porcelain as he continued to shake.

Sex and fighting. That was all that seemed to dominate his thoughts lately. Sex and fighting, fighting and sex. A vicious cycle that worked him up to the point of explosion. The only time he found any sort of peace was when he took animal shape. But he couldn't live like that forever. He was still a man, dammit.

Calm down, calm down, calm down.

In through the nose, out through the mouth.

He blindly reached out to adjust the spray of the water and knocked a bottle of shampoo to the floor. The cap popped open and the smell of sandalwood drifted from the puddle of soap mixing with the flow of water.

He snatched the bottle up and held it to his nose, huffing like a junkie.

"Seahawks are 30-1 odds of making it to the Super Bowl. Chargers 15-1, Pats 3-1. Hernandez finished seven for sixteen with seventy-nine strikeouts." In through the nose, out through the mouth.

Between the deep breathing and random sports statistics, his fangs receded and his fingers returned to normal. When his extremities grew numb from the cold, he shut off the water and staggered out of the bathroom dripping wet. The fight with his instinct left him as weak as a kitten.

A smart man would have fallen on the bed and let sleep take him away, but Ripley couldn't rest until he was certain that Alisia was safe and confined. He wouldn't survive if she snuck out again.

He dragged a pair of sweats and a cotton T-shirt over his damp body then padded barefoot down the hall.

The cave was quiet, with everyone already settled in for the night. Again, it made him wonder what Alisia was doing out so late on her own. Her supportive position on the mountain kept her out of the public eye and completely anonymous, but the Evolutioneers were wanted people. It would only take one observant person to follow the beautiful blonde on the motorcycle and give away their position.

His pretty bird wasn't going to like it, but he was going to have to clip her wings. Or at least Max would, he thought with a rusty chuckle. Make the boss man put his foot down, and then Ripley could console her with a comforting hug followed by heated kisses.

In through the nose, out through the mouth. *Don't go there, or you'll end up back in that icebox of a shower.*

He crept to the door of her room. Laying his ear against the panel, he strained to hear what was happening on the other side. Water ran in the bathroom sink and shut off with a squeak of the knob followed by the soft scrub of bristles against teeth. Safe, homey sounds of Alisia getting ready for bed.

Ripley sighed and rested his head against the wood. Unbidden images of what she might wear to bed drifted through his mind. A lacey, stretchy camisole and short set? T-shirt and panties? Nothing at all?

In through the nose, out through the mouth. In through the nose, out through the mouth.

The scent of apples and hand sanitizer brought his head up in time to see Doc Kelly coming around the corner.

"How did I know I would find you here?" she asked in a hushed voice.

He snorted. "Because I'm a glutton for punishment?" he answered just as softly.

She nodded and smiled with a touch of compassion in her eyes. Then she jerked her head pointedly behind her and headed back down the hall.

Ripley followed her along the twisting walkway to her laboratory/medical center. Once he was inside, she shut the door behind him. The click of the lock sounded much too loud in his ears, like the banging of a gavel, sentencing his fate.

Bracing his feet apart, he folded his arms across his chest. "Well. Did you find anything?"

Doc leaned back against the counter and brushed a lock of hair behind her ears. That sharp gaze of hers looked him over from the top of his head to his bare feet and back up again. Her chest rose on a breath, her mouth fell open to speak, before she deflated like a balloon. "No. Not a thing."

He bit back a snarl of frustration. "Nothing whatsoever?"

She shook her head. "Physically, you're normal. Well, normal for you, anyway." She smirked. "I checked your current blood samples with older ones. There is a higher level of testosterone than before, but nothing to be concerned about. The mood swings you told me about, the aggressive urges, the higher body temperature all fit with the raised testosterone levels. But again, you appear normal." She paused. "For a human."

For a human.

His fingers tightened around his biceps at her words. A growl rumbled in his chest as he wrestled with the need to punch his fist against the rock wall. Broken fingers weren't going to help.

Doc bit her lip and glanced at the ground before meeting his gaze. "Rip, sweetie, I can't ignore the fact that you're not entirely all human." As if he needed her to remind him. "Have you ever seen anything like this in your vet practice?"

He closed his eyes and sank back, letting the wall support his weight. "Yeah, I have."

Long, tense seconds passed while Ripley contemplated the uncertainty of his future. The problem with being a rarity was that the unknown brought both exhilaration and utter terror. Unfortunately, he had a bad idea of what was in store for him.

Doc's brow furrowed, worry darkening her eyes as she

waited for him to elaborate. "Ripley?"

He sighed and scrubbed a hand over his face. "I've seen this type of behavior in animals who were feral."

"Feral?" she gaped in horror. "As in deranged?"

A humorless grin twisted his lips. "Not deranged. What it means is, I'm turning wild."

Also by Anna Alexander

The Evolutioneers Series

Genesis

Instinct

Men of the Sprawling A Ranch Series

The Cowboy Way

The Marlboro Man

To Have Faith

Sweetest Kisses

Eight Seconds to Forever

Heroes of Saturn Series

Hero Revealed

Hero Unleashed

Hero Unmasked

Hero Rising

Cavern Series

A Night at The Cavern

Only at The Cavern

Elite Metal Series

Bound by Steele

Adamantium's Roar

Thallium's Submission

Vibranium's Truth

About Anna Alexander

Award winning author Anna Alexander is the author of the Heroes of Saturn and the Sprawling A Ranch series. With Hugh Jackman's abs and Christopher Reeve's blue eyes as inspiration, she loves spinning tales of superheroes finding love. Anna also loves to give back and has served on the board for the Greater Seattle Romance Writers of America as chapter president and on the committee for the Emerald City Writers Conference.

Sign up to receive news about Anna's latest releases at
http://eepurl.com/Q0tsz

Anna welcomes comments from readers.

Website

annaalexander.net

Facebook

facebook.com/pages/Anna-Alexander/282170065189471

Twitter

twitter.com/AnnaWriter

Newsletter

http://eepurl.com/Q0tsz

www.ingramcontent.com/pod-product-compliance
Lightning Source LLC
Chambersburg PA
CBHW050910250626
47155CB00001B/170